LIABLE

GOLD AND COURAGE SERIES

KAREN S. GORDON

PRAISE FOR KAREN S. GORDON

"Smart, quick, and wildly entertaining, LIABLE is Gordon at her very best. If you aren't reading this series . . . start!" — **Ryan Steck, The Real Book Spy**

Dedicated the millions of young people struggling under student debt.

1

DADE-HOMESTEAD GENERAL AVIATION
HOMESTEAD, FLORIDA, 30 MILES SOUTH OF MIAMI

Vance Courage gazed out the hazy picture window at the chain link fence and the endless grassy wetlands surrounding the small regional airport. The local weather forecast was hot and humid with a 30 percent chance of rain. Typical for the month of May. He checked the time on his phone. 3:10 in the afternoon, plenty of time to get to Nassau, Bahamas before nightfall.

When they'd arrived at precisely 2:30 p.m. as instructed, they'd checked in with the woman at the desk who'd told him and Lauren Gold to take a seat and wait. It was now going on an hour.

"I'm going to go see what's going on," he said to Lauren.

He walked to the counter and waited five minutes but there was no sign of the woman. He headed back to the waiting area and took his seat next to her.

"What did you find out?" she asked, riffling through her purse.

"Nothing." He stared at the action outside the west-facing window. A pack of skydivers leaped from the gaping door of a dull gray transport plane, their tiny black stick figures free falling against a pale blue sky. He winced as they pulled the rip cords, their bodies jerking upward as their chutes unfurled with a final jolt as if being saved by an invisible hand.

"Do you have anything for a headache."

"That's too bad," he said, lifting his duffle from the floor and setting it on the open seat next to him. He hand-searched the side pockets before digging through his clothes, feeling his 9-millimeter Glock wrapped inside a pair of jeans at the bottom of his bag. He had nothing for pain. "I don't have anything."

She let out an audible sigh. "You brought a gun but no aspirin."

He lowered his voice. "Our Cayman bank set up a line of credit to the casino."

"For how much?"

"A hundred thousand each."

"A hundred thousand dollars?" she whispered.

"That's not enough?"

"Of course, it's enough. It's enough to put someone's kid through four years of college. Maybe not an Ivy League school, but you know what I mean. Besides, I don't care about the money. All I want is to chill for a few days."

A crusty guy with a five-day beard and slicked-back salt and pepper hair approached.

The old guy cleared his throat. "You the two heading to Nassau?"

"We are," he said, standing.

The man rested an old wooden clipboard against the middle buttons of his black and blue plaid shirt. "Names?"

"Vance Courage and Lauren Gold," he said.

"Passports?"

Lauren reached into her purse and handed hers to Vance, and he passed both passports to the man and watched him flip them open and scan the first pages. When the man was finished, he handed Lauren's back to her. He closed Vance's passport, turned it upside down and slid his thumbnail under one corner and plucked it like a guitar pick.

"I'm Blade, your pilot. I got a full load this afternoon and we got more coming. They just informed me they're running a little late."

Lauren fanned her face with her passport. "That's your policy? People call in late and you hold the plane?"

Blade ran his tongue over his front teeth and polished his canines, then smacked his lips. "Yep, that's my policy. Do you have a problem with it, 'cause if you do, there's the door. And I don't give refunds. That's my policy."

Lauren stood. Vance held his arm out in front of her like a crossing guard. She sat down.

"May I have my passport back?" he asked.

The pilot slapped Vance's passport against his open palm before handing it back to him.

"Wait here," Blade said, slinging the wraparounds hanging around his neck, over the back of his shirt. He tucked the clipboard under his arm, turned and duckwalked away, sunglasses swaying between his shoulder blades. He turned the corner and disappeared down a dimly lit hallway.

"I don't have a good feeling about this," Lauren said.

He didn't like him either, but not enough to blow up the

trip. He placed his hand on her knee. "We might be a little late getting there, but so what," he said, "right?"

She shrugged, then grimaced. "If you hadn't insisted on bringing *it*, we could've flown commercially."

She was referring to the gun. It was a non-negotiable issue: he wasn't traveling without it which is why Lauren found Blade on the 'Net. He ran daily flights between Miami and Nassau, reselling seats on his old Beechcraft Baron 58 for a few bucks more than what the airlines charged for economy fare. The biggest drawback, the one she'd complained about, was the luggage policy: one carry-on per person, sized to the same specs as the commercial carriers. The upsides were worth it. No lines, no TSA fondling and no customs agents riffling through his duffle bag at the private runway a few miles outside the city of Nassau. He checked the time, 4:13 p.m. Seventy-three minutes behind schedule. He began to have second thoughts.

A beat-up black Toyota RAV4 with missing hubcaps pulled up and parked illegally in the fire lane. The driver, a young woman, got out, ran around the front bumper, and argued with one of the passengers.

"What do you think that's all about?" Lauren asked.

"Who knows?" he said, watching.

The glass door flung open and the three twenty-some-things who'd gotten out of the Toyota headed for the desk.

"Oh God, say that's not them," Lauren said, reaching into the side pocket of her roller bag.

"Nah," Vance said, "they're here for skydiving. Look at her. She's dressed to jump."

"I'll be right back," Lauren said.

"Where are you going?"

"I think I left my book in the car. Will you watch my stuff?"

Lauren passed the young woman accompanying the two men. The girl carried a royal blue backpack twice as wide and two-thirds as tall as a golf bag on her back. She tipped forward at the waist while walking as if fighting a headwind. She and her companions stopped at the desk. She unbuckled the padded strap securing the backpack around her waist and squatted like a dead-lifter. The backpack slid onto the scuffed linoleum. The girl propped the bag against the wood-paneled counter.

Lauren returned from her car with a small hardcover book in her hand. "Thank God," she said, sitting next to him. "You're right. They can't be flying with us. That bag's too big for the trip."

A moment later Blade returned. Vance watched as he huddled with the threesome, looking over their paperwork and passports. The tall guy handed the pilot an envelope. Blade opened it, thumbed through the contents, folded it in half and shoved it in his pants pocket. Blade waved his hand motioning to them to join the group.

"Jesus," Lauren said. "You have to be kidding."

"We could bail out now if you want," he said, half hoping she would say yes.

She hesitated. "At least it's a short trip. It could be worse. How would you like to be that guy?"

He watched her eyes shift to one of the young men.

"How tall do you think he is?" she asked.

"I don't know. Six-eight, maybe more. How about that head of hair? It probably adds another three inches."

"You're just jealous."

Blade stuck two fingers in his mouth and let out a high-pitched whistle that tickled his eardrum.

Lauren stuck her finger in her ear and twisted it. "What an asshole. Whistling like we're dogs."

"Come on," Blade hollered across the empty room. "Let's get going."

Vance grabbed his duffle, slung it over his shoulder and grabbed her carry-on.

"Is it too late to back out?" she asked.

"Yeah. Let's go." He motioned her ahead.

"They're traveling with us," Lauren complained, glaring at the three late arrivers.

"Yep," Blade said.

Lauren clamped her hands on her narrow hips. "What about her bag?"

"What about it?" Blade asked.

"On your website—"

"I already told you what my policy is. There's the door. One way leads to an airplane heading to The Bahamas, the other doesn't."

The pilot pushed the clunky metal bar on the glass door open with his hip and let the other passengers out ahead of him.

"Come on," Vance whispered into her ear.

Blade jaunted to the front of the pack, leading them to a dull, white twin engine airplane with faded orange stripes parked on an angle alongside the chain link fence near the grass. Blade stepped up on the wing and opened the cockpit door then dropped down onto the pavement.

"Leave that big bag out here," Blade said to the girl, bending over and removing the heavy yellow plastic wheel chocks beneath the airplane's tires and tossing them in a pile.

Lauren opened her mouth but before she could speak, Vance wrapped his arm around her waist. "Let it go," he said. "We're on vacation."

The shorter of the two male passengers approached, adjusting an olive green knapsack over his shoulder.

"I hate man buns," Lauren said under her breath. "Especially greasy ones."

He wasn't a fan either. The guy was pudgy, especially around the middle with a weak chin and skinny mustache that gave him a sinister smirk. He wore black polyester bike shorts a size too small and a neon green muscle shirt that accented his man boobs and gibbous belly button. He wondered if consuming too much soy or not enough beef was a chicken-and-egg argument. Evidence he was a man came in two forms. Wiry black hair on his limbs and a *Get Shorty* tattoo taking up most of his right forearm.

"Best movie ever made," Vance said, gazing at the ink.

"Best script ever written. I'm Tonk."

"Vance Courage."

"You guys hear that? Guy's name is Courage. Can't lose with a last name like that," Tonk said.

"You'd be surprised," Vance said.

Tonk grinned. "This is my friend, California Jack."

Vance held out his hand. "Nice to meet you."

"Call me C.J."

"Are you vacationing together?" Vance asked.

"I guess you could say that," Tonk said.

"You must like movies," Vance said.

"He studied screenwriting," C.J. said.

"I used to write fiction," Vance said.

Tonk's eyes widened. "Really?"

"Yeah, I used to be a plaintiff's attorney. After you bend the facts far enough, it turns into fiction."

Everyone laughed, including Blade.

The girl asked, "Where're you headed?"

A small single-engine airplane flew low overhead.

After the plane passed, Lauren said, "We're heading to Paradise Island. I'm Lauren."

"We're sharing a dump conveniently located near a bus stop in Nassau. I'm Chantico but everyone calls me Chan."

Though she wasn't his type there was an agreeableness about Chan that reminded him of his sister Kathy. She had coarse straw-colored hair that brushed the tops of her shoulders, maple syrup eyes and a smattering of freckles evenly distributed across the bridge of her nose. Medium height with broad shoulders and sinewy calves almost as muscled as a man's, she wore tan hiking boots with thick white socks folded at the ankle. He wondered what she did to build that much leg brawn. Other than hauling a giant backpack around.

Blade strolled past. "A lawyer, huh." He stepped up on the wing. "Ladies first." He skipped over Chan and offered his hand to Lauren. "Why don't you ride up front with me."

Lauren turned to Vance, eyebrows raised, as if asking him for permission.

He faked a smile then climbed onto the wing and ducked beneath the low cabin doorway, squeezing Lauren's shoulder as he passed. He dropped his duffle bag on the floorboard and used the toe of his shoe to kick it halfway beneath the seat in front of his—Blade's—then squeezed into the old leather seat. The space was cramped, and the interior of the airplane was a hothouse of sticky, stale air with an odd musky smell. Sliding his hand between the seats, he grabbed the seatbelt straps, untangled them, then pulled the belt tight around his waist.

Tonk climbed aboard next and removed his smartphone from the thigh pocket of his tight black shorts and holding it close to his chest, tilted his torso away as if hiding something. The phone case was unusual, thicker than normal, by as much as an inch with a dark gray and black herringbone pattern. Tonk leaned forward and waved the phone around then put it in his backpack. If he was making a video, Vance couldn't imagine why or what.

C.J. boarded next, shoehorning his body into the third-row seat directly behind Vance. Chan climbed in next, ducking her head, taking the last seat next to C.J.

Lauren turned around and spoke to Tonk. "Would you mind changing places with me?"

Blade appeared in the open doorway. Sweat dripped from his brow. Gripping the cockpit doorway, he swayed in and out doing air pushups before swinging one leg over Lauren as if mounting a horse. Blade straddled her as he faced the passengers. "Looks like you're all set back there."

Who did this guy think he was?

"Wait," Lauren said, "I changed my mind. I want to trade places."

"You sure you don't want to ride up front with me? The view's better."

"I'm sure," she said.

"Then hurry it up," Blade said.

Tonk switched places with her, pulled the cabin door shut and buckled into the co-pilot's seat.

Once the cabin door closed, the odd smell blossomed: secondhand marijuana smoke. Lauren fish-eyed him and grimaced.

Blade slapped a ball cap on his head, clamped a dull green headset over his ears, adjusted the mic close to his mouth and started the engines. The small plane jumped in place as the props spun, vibrations growing more intense as he turned the dials on the dash bringing the packed airplane fully to life. He chatted on his radio but mostly listened before turning toward the runway. He pulled the throttle and the plane sped down the tarmac and lifted off in a lurch, the overhead wing jolting erratically as the old Beechcraft Baron gained altitude.

He closed his eyes and when he opened them, saw that the plane was flying low, a couple of thousand feet, over an archipelago of small islands surrounded by pale blue water so clear he could see white sand at the bottom.

He shut his eyes and dozed off, unaware that a nightmare was about to unfold.

2

Vance awoke to Blade's booming voice.

"YOU FOLKS BUCKLED UP BACK THERE? WE'RE COMING UP ON SOME ROUGH STUFF."

"WHAT'S GOING ON?" Vance yelled.

"WE GOT WEATHER UP AHEAD. IT'S GONNA GET ROUGH."

So much for sleeping through the short hop from Miami to Nassau, Bahamas. He pressed his cheek against the port-hole and looked out at something new and ominous: a wall of charcoal clouds on the horizon. Deep into the fore-ground, the storm had turned the turquoise waters into a grayish blue obscuring the dozens of small islands below.

He wasn't a pilot, but it was common knowledge the weather in this part of the world could flip in an instant. He grabbed onto the back of Blade's seat and yelled over the cockpit noise. "WHY DON'T YOU GO AROUND THE STORM?"

Blade twisted his head and lifted one earmuff. "WHAT?"

"CAN'T YOU GO AROUND IT?"

"NO. IT'S TOO HIGH TO FLY OVER AND I DON'T HAVE ENOUGH FUEL TO GO AROUND IT."

Vance turned in his seat and yelled to C.J. and Chan, "DID YOU GUYS HEAR THAT?"

C.J. funneled his hands over his mouth. "YEAH. IT DOESN'T LOOK GOOD."

C.J. was crammed into his seat with his knees up his nose, eyes glued to the window.

A series of jagged white bolts lit the barrier of dark clouds. As they approached the storm, the plane began to shake.

"THAT LOOKS BAD," Vance yelled to the cockpit.

Blade didn't answer, his focus was ahead, white knuckling the control wheel, head bobbing, shoulders jerking.

"YOU SHOULD TURN AROUND," Vance said.

"SHUT UP!" Blade yelled. The plane dropped like a carnival ride, pitching hard on the starboard side. Lauren gripped the arm rests. The Baron groaned and creaked, wings dipping in jagged thrusts. It went dark in the cabin, the only light emanating from the bank of ancient gauges on the instrument panel.

Vance been a passenger in rough weather before, on commercial jets with flight attendants serving booze. This was different. A layer of sweat beaded on the back the pilot's neck wetting the short gray hairs along the edge of his ball cap. With no points of reference, they may as well have been flying inside a black hole.

Blade reached for the cockpit controls but was unable to steady one arm.

Hot dogs like this asshole got people killed.

A lightning bolt struck the tip of the starboard wing, lighting the cabin with a green tint, blinding everyone for a moment.

"SHIT!" Tonk yelled.

Sheets of rainwater spewed sideways on the windows. The plane plummeted. His stomach did a somersault.

Blade gripped the yoke, arms shaking.

He felt for Lauren's hand and squeezed it so hard he felt it go limp.

"What's he doing?" she asked, voice quivering.

"We're going to be fine," he said.

"I love you," she said. "I want you to know that."

The aircraft yawed violently to the right, then to the left. Up. Down. Sideways. How much could the old Beechcraft take before it broke apart midair? He craned his neck to check the back row. C.J.'s eyes were closed, head tilted back, with hands clasped on his lap. Where was Chan? He let go of Lauren's hand for a second to take a quick look. She was balled up with her head planted on her knees. What a way to go. With strangers in a flying shit tube with a two-bit washed-up pilot at the helm.

He clamped his left hand on the armrest with the airplane pitching and shuddering and groaning in darkness. Good God. They weren't going to make it. He closed his eyes and counted his breaths waiting for the movie in his head to start, the one about his life passing by, but all his mind saw was darkness while his gut fought the urge to vomit. If any one of them puked, it would start a chain reaction. He squinted out the window, one eye half-open, fixed on the red light blinking on the tip of the starboard wing. He breathed deeply through his nose, exhaling slowly. If death was coming, it might as well hurry up.

The plane convulsed. Vision blurry, he cupped his chin in the palm of his hand, but it didn't do shit to steady his focus. Suddenly the plane plummeted downward, forcing the contents of his stomach up his esophagus. He swallowed hard three times. Lauren's head bobbed erratically.

He squeezed his eyes shut and gulped more air, and when his lungs were full, he inhaled some more. He looked out the window and gazed at blackness. The turbulence worsened, pitching him forward. A vein of lightning struck close enough to spotlight Blade for an instant, hunched forward in the pilot's seat clutching and fighting the yoke. The windshield, a travel brochure a few minutes ago, was nothing but a black hole.

Lauren looked at him, batting away tears.

"It's going to be fine," he lied.

She tightened her hand around his wrist, digging her fingers into his flesh.

He shut his eyes. If this was how it was going to end, there wasn't a damn thing he could do about it.

3

Vance sensed flashes of light through his eyelids, the way the sun woke him on the mornings he'd overslept. He squinted out the airplane window, then blinked, pupils adjusting to the shades of gray mixed with the flickering of white light, like the last images at the end of an old film reel. The ride steadied, and as the sky dissolved to solid white, visibility still sucked, just differently. There were no points of reference: no water, no land, no horizon. Just the back of Blade's head and his sweaty wrinkled neck. What sort of faulty brain circuitry made flying into a violent thunderstorm seem like a good idea?

"Jesus," Lauren said, dabbing her brow with a tissue. "Do you think that's the worst of it?"

He nodded. He wanted Blade to put this puppy down on solid ground. He leaned forward and looked out the cockpit window, trying to get a fix on their location. Visibility had improved, but not enough to see water or land.

As the clouds thinned, the nose of the plane broke through into pale blue air, so bright it stung his eyes. Leaning over her and looking out her window to the west he expected to see Andros Island, or maybe the northern tip of Spanish Wells to the east, but he saw neither. He pulled his cell from his pocket and checked the time. They'd been airborne for just under an hour. Where was New Providence? Or Paradise Island?

He tapped the navigation app and waited for the page to load. They were on a north-northwest heading. They should've been on a south-southwest heading. What was going on?

Blade banked the plane hard left, tipping the wings at an almost 45-degree angle.

"WHAT ARE YOU DOING?" he yelled over the rumble of the engines.

Blade pulled the mic from his mouth and turned his head sideways. "CAN'T LAND IN NASSAU. THE WEATHER'S BAD AND EVERYTHING'S CLOSED."

Lauren looked at Vance, the expression on her face was one of fear and confusion.

"WHERE ARE WE?" he yelled.

Blade ignored him.

He looked out the plane's starboard window at dozens of cays — smaller land masses not big enough to be called islands. He'd done homework before the trip. The Bahamian archipelago was made up of more than 700 islands and most were cays, too small for human habitation.

Where was Blade planning to land the plane? He looked out the window to the south, the route they should've been traveling. The wall of storm clouds to the south had turned black as night, but the view up ahead where they were now heading was clear as a robin's egg. The shades of ocean water directly beneath them ranged from aquamarine to sapphire to dark green. "WHERE ARE WE?" he asked a second time.

"WE'RE ALMOST OVER THE TROPIC OF CANCER." Blade pointed out the window. "SEE THAT DARK BLUE LINE? THAT'S THE TONGUE OF THE OCEAN, IT GOES DOWN TO A DEPTH OF OVER SIX THOUSAND FEET."

"He can play tour guide," Lauren grumbled, "but he can't tell us where he's going to land."

They continued north heading back toward Miami, but the ride got rougher and the fixed wing plane hit what felt like deep invisible potholes and speed bumps. His stomach did another backflip as Blade put the Beechcraft into a steep decline, gradually leveling off at what Vance guessed to be an altitude of about 500 feet. He observed a graveyard of fuselages scattered on the shallow seabed like fallen trees. How long had the wreckage been submerged? Maybe these were skeletons from the Cuban and Colombian cartel days when drug runners used the out-islands to stage loads of cocaine bound for the U.S. mainland. He'd heard plenty of stories of aborted missions with millions of dollars of product on board, dumped by smugglers tipped off by scout pilots

Blade buzzed the shoreline of a small island. Turquoise water surrounded the ivory sand dotted with skinny palm trees. The island couldn't have been more than a thousand acres and appeared to be a fully developed community. A large kidney-shaped swimming pool had been built on the beachfront side. A sprawling three-story white building was surrounded by swathes of bright green grass, and gardens, and circular hedges with matching inlaid concrete walkways. On the back side he saw the aerial view of an expansive marina with floating docks jutting perpendicular from a manmade U-shaped bulkhead. He counted around 75 yachts and space for at least 50 more. A three-story mega-yacht was docked parallel to the bulkhead at the ocean end of the marina.

Blade continued his low altitude flight giving them a bird's-eye view of the less habitable parts of the island. Rocky cliffs and coves with twisted mangroves and dense vegetation. Blade turned the Beechcraft to the west and flew for five minutes over open water. Vance checked Lauren who sat motionless in her seat, arms folded tightly across her chest, eyes closed unsure if she was stewing or chilling. Blade made another turn, this time banking hard to the east. It was beginning to make sense. He leaned his face close to the glass and spotted what appeared to be an airstrip on a jagged piece of land that stuck out from the mainland like a giant witch's finger.

He pushed his luck a fourth time. "Where are we?"

Blade pulled the headset off and threw it down. "What are you? A four-year-old? This isn't the back seat of the family minivan. I need you to shut up. I gotta put this thing down on the ground, and to do that, I need you to close your pie hole and keep it shut."

Blade's shoulders rocked as he held the yoke, visually lining the Beechcraft up with a strip of asphalt running the length of the witch's finger. Gripping the armrests during the final approach, the landing was rough. The plane bounced three times before sticking to the ground. Blade brought the plane to a hard stop, then steered left and taxied slowly with the underside of the starboard wing skimming the top of thick jungle overgrowth.

He stopped the plane, killed the engine, then instructed Tonk to open the cabin door and ordered the boy out.

Vance's stomach lurched at the smell of fuel and sweat. He unlatched the jettison window and pushed it wide open. It created enough cross ventilation to clear out the stench of weed and fear. The sweet aroma of salt water wafted into the cabin along with a heavy dose of humidity and a handful of mosquitos.

Tonk climbed out and stood on the wing. Blade slid across the seat Tonk vacated and offered Lauren his hand. She accepted, and with his assistance, she crawled out.

"Come on," Blade said to Vance, "let's get going."

"Where are we?"

"Chub Cay," Blade said.

"Where?"

"Think of it as a nice place to regroup," Blade said.

"What's the plan?" Vance asked getting out.

"I'm working on that. Why don't y'all go over to the marina and have a bite to eat while I keep an eye on the weather reports. Or you can wait here with me. In the heat. Your choice."

He grabbed his duffle and jumped down.

"I need the rest of you to take your stuff with you. I don't want to be responsible for it," Blade said.

"Come on," Chan said. "Are you serious?"

"You can leave it here if you want. But not on my airplane." He unlatched the cargo door and pulled Chan's backpack out and laid it on the ground. He removed Lauren's roller bag and dumped it on its side.

"That goes for you, too," he said to Tonk.

Vance got in Blade's face. "What were you thinking? Didn't you check the weather report?"

"Yeah, I checked it. If I turned back every time a raindrop smacked the windshield, I'd be out of business."

"A RAINDROP?"

Blade pinched the brim on his ball cap, adjusting it while licking his front teeth. "You're standing here talking to me, aren't you?"

"Didn't you see it on radar? Why didn't you turn around?"

"I did turn around."

Lauren approached, pulling him aside. "Come on, let it go."

He shrugged her off and faced the pilot. "You had plenty of time to turn around before you flew into that storm. You could've got us all killed."

"Listen to me, hero, I did three tours in the sandbox. I flew choppers in white out blizzards and sandstorms—"

"People going on vacation aren't signing up for combat duty."

"Good point." Blade grinned.

Vance rushed him, delivering a mean upper cut to the jaw. Blade fell backwards on his ass, then hit the back of his head on the front tire of the plane. Vance looked down at him, then turned away from the fight he'd started. But Blade wasn't finished. He scrambled forward on all fours grabbing Vance's ankles from behind, trying to pull him down. Vance spun and kicked him in the ribcage, but the old guy was tougher than he looked, the vice grip he held around his left leg was good enough to unbalance him. With nothing to break his fall, Vance toppled forward, landing on top of Blade. The two rolled on the ground, grappling.

"Stop it!" Lauren yelled.

"HEY," Tonk hollered, jumping onto Vance's back, riding him, restraining him with a chokehold.

He wrenched Tonk's arm away from his neck, then twisted his arm at the elbow 'til the kid's eyes welled.

Vance scrambled to his feet. "Keep your hands off me you little piece of shit or next time I'll tear your arm off. Got it?"

Tonk sat on the ground, nodding and rubbing his shoulder.

Blade stood, dusted himself off, then picked up his wraparound sunglasses and ball cap. He slapped the hat against his pant leg and hung his shades around his neck. "Fair enough," he said. "It was a bad call. There's cold beer and fat hamburgers at the marina. Why don't you go cool off. I'll text you when the weather clears and they open the airstrip in Nassau. I got some business to take care of."

"What kind of business?" Vance asked.

Blade checked his watch. "Let me worry about that." Blade rubbed his jaw and used his tongue to check the underside of his lip. "You got a decent right hook, I'll give you that." He spit blood on the tarmac.

The sun painted swathes of pinks against a gradient blue canvas.

"Come on," Lauren said, slapping at a cloud of mosquitos and no-see-ums. "Unless you have a better idea."

Vance rubbed his hands together, cleaning his palms before wiping them on his pant legs. He picked up both their bags, slinging his duffle over his shoulder. "How do we get there?"

"On foot," Blade said, pointing to an opening leading to a narrow gravel path lined with shoulder high, thick vegetation.

"How far is it?" Chan asked.

Blade massaged his chin then wiped the sweat from the back of his neck and licked his teeth. "Runway's five thousand feet so I'm guessing the marina's about the same distance from here."

"That's five city blocks," Vance said, "through a freaking jungle." He couldn't see through the thick overgrowth, but he could make out the tip of the gray A-shaped rooftop he'd seen from the air.

"Five blocks. Sounds about right," Blade said. "The sooner you guys get moving, the sooner you'll be feeding yourselves instead of the bugs. Unless you want to go with me to pay Customs a visit. Most folks would rather not."

"Customs?" Vance asked.

"The island has a part-timer. I don't know if he's on duty today, but you're welcome to find out. You're also welcome to join me for a meditation session in the cockpit because that's where I'll be waiting for the weather to clear."

"A beer sounds better," Vance said.

From the size of the yachts he'd seen from the air and the newness of the tarmac where they stood, guests jetting in weren't schlepping their luggage on foot for five blocks.

Chan balanced her bag upright, then squatted, and slipped one arm through a shoulder strap. The bag tipped over. "Shit," she said, breaking her fall with her hands.

"Gimme that," C.J. said. He picked up Chan's big backpack and slung it over his back. "Carry mine," he said.

"I'd rather stay with you," Tonk said to Blade.

"No. Go with the others. I'll let y'all know when the weather clears. Go on. Get out of here before someone from Customs and Immigration shows up. That'll mean a whole lot of paperwork."

Blade's phone pinged. "Well how about that," Blade announced, "they may be part-timers, but these customs agents have a way of staying on top of things."

What did 'staying on top of things' mean? They'd been forced to make an emergency landing and the whole point of flying with Blade was to avoid Customs. If they searched his bag, they'd find the gun. But what happened next wasn't even on his radar screen.

4

L auren shaded her eyes from shards of afternoon sun cutting through the dense vegetation. She stopped to shake sharp limestone pebbles from her flats. She wasn't sure which was worse, the burn of emerging blisters or the sting of biting insects. She felt a zing on her back. As she stretched her arm to scratch the itch, she torqued a muscle, wincing in pain. "Jesus," she said unable to reach the spot.

Vance slowed and waited for her to catch up. "You're limping."

"I didn't think to pack my hiking gear on a gambling trip."

The others were so far ahead, she figured they were probably at the bar by now. She grabbed his shoulder to balance, alternating on one leg at a time like a flamingo and removed each shoe, flattening the heels, converting them into slippers.

They may as well have been in the Amazon jungle. The vegetation on either side of the path was so dense it created a tunnel effect. She tried picking up the pace but with the heels flattened on the back of her shoes, she had trouble keeping them on her feet. She'd have gone barefoot, but the chipped limestone path felt like broken glass.

"You don't have any other shoes?" he asked.

"What do you think?"

By now she should have been checked into the luxury suite she'd booked at the resort on Paradise Island. Freshly showered, sprawled on a memory foam mattress and leafing through the room service menu. She mopped the sweat from the back of her neck and wiped her hand on her slacks, then pushed her hair behind one ear.

"I'd loan you a pair of mine," Vance said, "if I thought it would help."

"So far," she said, "this trip sucks. I wish we would've flown commercially."

"Where's your sense of adventure?"

She gritted her teeth and pressed on smacking mosquitos and no-see-ums along the way.

The path opened to a view of a modern marina filled with eye-candy yachts and a smattering of Key West style buildings. A tiered flower bed near the bulkhead was topped with an enormous bronze statue of a billfish. She gazed up at the yellow brick road, an intricate walkway of inlaid pavers at least a block long, splitting velvety green grass into two halves. The walkway led to a white three-story mansion built on higher ground. She soldiered on, dragging one foot and when they reached the base of the path to the clubhouse, she removed her shoes.

"Who do you think that belongs to?" Vance asked, pointing to the bow of a mega yacht docked at the opposite end of the marina.

It was so sleek and futuristic it looked more like a stealth bomber than a boat. And if her feet weren't killing her, she'd have liked to have seen it up close.

"Who knows," she said, debating whether to walk barefoot on the grass. Deciding not to, she walked the paved path.

The gardens surrounding the main house reminded her of the English countryside with boxy hedges and semicircular mazes of grass puzzled together with arch-shaped concrete poured flush with the billiard green grass. Closer to the clubhouse, the walkway split in two directions making a complete circle around another triple-tiered bed of flowers and hedges at least eight feet in diameter. As they walked around it, it opened to an unobstructed view of the Colonial-style structure with expansive wrap-around porches, and second and third story balconies lined with Greek columns reminiscent of pre-Civil war southern plantations. The construction was not original, rather it had been recently built with modern materials: cement-board siding, composite columns, metal roofing and hardwood decking.

"There they are," Vance said, spotting C.J., Chan and Tonk.

"Yeah, well they were dressed for the occasion."

When the trio saw them, they cut across the grass and met them at the entrance to the main building. C.J. jerked his shoulders and slipped his thumbs beneath the padded belt of Chan's backpack, adjusting it again by twisting at the waist.

She slipped her shoes on and followed as Vance led the way into the resort clubhouse. It was light and airy with tile floors and lots of windows and soaring white ceilings and dark wooden tables and chairs. They waited at the hostess stand but no one greeted them. Vance headed to the bar to chat with the bartender. How did a place like this survive with no customers? On the other hand, it was an off-hour: too late for lunch and too early for dinner for most people. She took a menu from a box attached to the side of the hostess stand and opened it. Chan followed suit.

The prices were eye-popping. She watched as Chan stepped away to huddle with Tonk and C.J. They pointed at the menu and chatted in low voices, but were too far away for her to listen in.

Vance approached. "Come on," he said.

She and Chan returned the menus to the side slot of the hostess stand and followed him to a round table for eight in the middle of the empty restaurant.

"This place is fancy," Chan said.

Vance set Lauren's bag down between them, slid his duffle under the table, then pulled her chair for her. She sat, removed her shoes, and put her bare feet on the bottom railing of her wooden chair.

A waiter wearing a black vest over a crisp white shirt brought five menus and passed them around. "What can I get you to drink?" he asked in a mild British accent.

"She'll have a club soda and I'll have a beer," Vance said.

The other three ordered water.

She scanned the menu, then checked her phone. A message inviting her to join the resort's wireless network popped up. She dismissed it. "Does anyone know what they're ordering?" she asked.

"Not yet," Vance said.

The others didn't answer.

"I'm definitely getting the conch fritters," she said.

"What's that?" Chan asked.

"It's a giant sea snail," she said.

Chan contorted her face. "Ewww."

"They're delicious. You should try them. Will you order for me?" she asked Vance. "I'll be right back."

"Where're you going?" he asked, without looking up from the menu.

"To find the gift shop and see if they have a pair of flip flops for sale. My feet are killing me. There's no way I'll make it back to the plane unless you give me a piggyback ride."

"I'll do it," C.J. said.

"You're just trying to get out of backpack duty," Lauren said.

C.J. tilted his head toward Tonk. "He can carry it."

"That's not happening," Tonk said.

Vance looked up. "How many fritters do you want?"

"A dozen," she said, sliding her chair out. "Thanks for the offer C.J., but I don't want to get a nosebleed." She slipped her shoes on, pushed the chair forward and hobbled toward the doorway leading to the beach side of the island. She leaned against one of the exterior columns, removed her shoes then scratched the red bug bites on her ankles. The pool and tiki bar, surrounded by chaise lounges and chairs with navy blue umbrellas, overlooked the white sand, swaying palms and turquoise water. But there were no signs of people.

THE YOUNG GUY running the gift shop greeted her, then steered her to a pegboard at the back of the store displaying the usual resort fare: frisbees, snorkels, miniature footballs, dive masks, straw hats, ball caps and a half dozen kinds of bug repellent in spray, gel and cream forms. She chose the cheapest pair of flip flops hanging near the hats, surprised at the thirty-dollar price tag. She added a travel-sized bottle of bug repellant, and after paying cash, she slipped them on, spritzed her body, then took the original route back. She walked along the floating dock admiring the yachts, many longer than 50 feet. She stopped and knelt to get a closer look at the kaleidoscope of reef fish darting around the pylons submerged in the shallow water. Beautiful big pink and white shells dotted the sandy bottom: conch in their natural habitat.

What if she and Vance bought a yacht and lived off the grid, sailing from island to island? They had the time and money to do it and could afford a crew to run it. She took a deep breath and watched a school of parrot fish nibbling at the feathered algae. Vance would never agree to it. He'd already owned a sailing yacht—a byproduct of the drug money salvage—and showed no disappointment when the million-dollar boat was destroyed during Hurricane Irma. With millions hidden in offshore accounts in Grand Cayman, they'd been very careful, keeping low profiles. A yacht big enough to live on would be conspicuous. Whoever owned the super yacht docked at the resort didn't have the same concerns. He—or she—was someone who flaunted their money.

She knew a little Bahamian history, that pirates—most notably Blackbeard—ruled the islands until the early 17th century when the British invaded and he was killed in battle. After the Brits were defeated during the Revolutionary War, many Loyalists left America and settled in New Providence making Nassau the capital of the Commonwealth. It was strange to think the island nation declared its independence from Great Britain in 1974, not all that long ago.

Strolling up the walkway leading back to the clubhouse, from higher ground she had a view of the tarmac and

Blade's plane still parked on the same spot where he'd dumped them.

Returning to her place at the table, she hung the shopping bag over the back of her chair. The four of them ignored her, staring at their phone screens. "What did I miss?"

"Nothing," Chan said.

"Did you hear from Blade yet?"

"No," Vance said getting up from the table. "I'll be right back. I'm going to go clean up."

"What did you guys' order?" she asked the others.

"Nothing," Tonk said, downing the rest of the ice water in his glass. "I'm gonna go for a walk."

"You guys aren't hungry?" she asked.

"Nah," Chan said, "I'm going with Tonk."

"Me too," C.J. said, getting up to join them, hoisting Chan's bag up onto his shoulders.

"You can leave it here," she said.

"We should be ready to go when we hear from Blade," C.J. said.

"Will you come get us if you hear from him first?" she said.

"Gimme your phone," C.J. said.

He typed his number in her CONTACTS list and pinged her phone.

"I'll message you when we hear something."

"Ditto," she said.

Vance returned to the table just as the trio was leaving.

"Where're they going?" he asked.

"For a walk. They didn't order anything. Maybe we should've offered to buy."

"Why? They're able bodied young people. If they could afford to go on a vacation, then they can feed themselves."

Her cell chimed with a voice message, but her phone hadn't rung. She looked at the screen. Two MISSED CALLs from the same wireless number popped up. Probably spammers. They often called twice to leave a message on the second go around.

The waiter dressed in penguin colors appeared carrying a silver basket lined with white paper and set it down in front of her. The sizzling fritters were served with lemon and cocktail sauce and pencil-thin fries, all air fried to perfection, crispy not greasy, the conch meat tender not chewy like the ones served at most places back home. Her nose guided her eyes to his plate. It looked terrific and smelled even better. "What did you get?"

"The bourbon-bacon ribeye," he said, cutting into it, clear pink juice swirling on the white plate.

"A little fancy for a Neanderthal."

"What's that supposed to mean?"

This was the first time they'd been alone since they'd left the flight base operation in Homestead. "I can't believe you punched the pilot."

"He had it coming."

"Maybe so, but do you think it was a good idea to hit him? What if he sues you?"

"He's not stupid, he's not going to sue me. He knows I'm a lawyer. Does he look like a guy with a lot of expendable income? Not to mention it's an international incident. Literally."

"I know, but what good does it do to piss him off," she said, popping a crunchy fritter into her mouth.

He cut a hunk of bacon-flavored meat from the ribeye. "It felt good to me," he said before proceeding to wolf down the meal, chasing the food with beer. "When the waiter comes back, will you order me another?" He held up the empty bottle of Kalik, a local brand.

"Sure. Where're you going?"

"To the men's room."

"Again?"

"Yeah. I'll be right back."

"I'll hold the fort down," she said, unaware of the disaster about to unfold.

5

The beer and water mainlined to Vance's bladder. He stood in front of the shiny white urinal and relieved himself, then headed to the sink to wash his hands. The faucet in the men's room was elaborate, a round green tinted glass bowl set on an angle above a copper counter. He pumped liquid from a silver bottle and lathered the spice-scented soap in his hands, then looked for the faucet handle but didn't see one. What was the point of complicating this? He waved his hands beneath it trying different angles, but nothing happened. He tried the sink next to it, but got the same result. No water.

Jesus.

"Piece of shit," he said, hammering a chrome button on the middle of the green wash bowl. Water flowed. So did the pain.

He rubbed his right knuckles, sore from the upper cut he'd delivered to Blade's jaw, then turned the dial clockwise until the water ran hot. He rinsed the soap, then turned the dial the opposite direction and let the water run cold, splaying his fingers, holding them close to the faucet, moving his hand around, and letting the jets of cool water massage his aching knuckles.

What the hell was Blade doing flying that old Beechcraft into a storm? He'd lied when he'd told Lauren everything would be alright; he'd worried the plane was going down. He leaned forward and cupped both hands in the sink, collecting enough water to splash his face.

Back when he was practicing law, a woman had come to him after her husband—the family patriarch, a doctor— died in a plane crash. She wanted to file a wrongful death suit against the airplane manufacturer. At first the case seemed promising. Then he did his homework. The 50 year safety record of the Beechcraft Baron was impeccable, and according to the N.T.S.B., nearly a 100 percent of crashes had been caused by pilot error. So much so, the plane was dubbed *The Doctor Killer*.

He wet his hands again and ran his fingers along the sides of his scalp, then smoothed his hair.

Blade might've been a very experienced pilot flying a plane with an excellent safety record but reviewing the course of events made him angry all over again. He plucked a fancy paper napkin from the countertop dispenser and looked in the mirror as he blotted his face and hair.

The bathroom door flung open.

"Jesus, what are you doing in here?"

"He's leaving," Lauren said, breathless.

"What are you talking about?"

"Blade. He's leaving without us."

He pushed her aside and punched the bathroom door open. He raced down the hall and flung the front doors wide open. Together they stood on the grassy knoll watching the Beechcraft, airborne, heading south-southeast in the dimming sky. "No one told you?"

"No."

He stood silently and watched until the plane disappeared.

Vance stared at the rosy sunset, then clenched his fist and punched the sky. "I should've known. I should've duct taped that fucking prick to a palm tree. Come on," he said.

Lauren followed him back inside the mostly empty restaurant. Instead of returning to the table, he pulled a barstool for her and one for himself.

"What can I get you to drink?" the bartender asked.

"What kind of whiskey do you have?"

The man reached under the counter and handed him a drink menu bound in leather and opened it to the page with bourbons and whiskies. He pointed at the menu. "Gimme a double."

"On the rocks?"

"Is it safe to drink the water?"

"We purify it."

"Rocks," he said.

"And for the lady?"

"She'll have a club soda."

"With lemon?"

"Sure," she said, eyes darting around the room.

When the bartender was out of earshot, she asked, "What are we going to do?"

He barely shrugged. "I don't know."

A trophy billfish was mounted high on the wood paneled wall above the bar. An old guy with a few strands of greasy gray hair and a naturally occurring clown nose sat alone at one end, in the corner watching a soccer game on the flat screen hanging overhead.

The bartender returned, placed two monogrammed

cocktail napkins in front of them, then set the drinks down. "Would you like to run a tab?"

He nodded.

"Do you want to charge it your room or dock number?"

"No." He reached into his pocket and handed him his credit card, the Visa drawn on his Cayman account.

The waiter came up from behind. "Here's your tab." He presented a black vinyl folder, setting it on the bar next to the whiskey. "Also," he said, "I think you left this at the table."

He turned to see. It was Lauren's navy-blue carry-on bag.

"That's mine," she said. "Can you leave it here?"

"Sure." The waiter rolled it next to her chair, then hovered.

"The bartender has my credit card," Vance said. "Get it from him and add a twenty-five percent tip."

"Thanks."

Vance left the bar and walked toward the round top table where they'd first gathered. Their table had already been cleared and reset with fresh settings. He looked for his duffle, but it wasn't there. He checked around the chairs, then searched under the table. Not there either. He walked a lap around the open-air dining room, peering under each table, then strolled to the service area near the kitchen where their server was running his credit card. "Did you see another bag?" he asked him.

"What?"

"I left my duffle bag at the table. Did you see it?"

"No, sir."

That was weird. The only place it could've been was at the table where he'd left it when he'd gone to the men's room. Aside from the salty barstool sailor watching the game, the only other patrons were the senior couple sitting nearest the east-facing picture window overlooking the water.

"Do you mind asking around to see if anyone found it? Maybe the busboy picked it up."

"Me and Skip are the only ones working the room tonight."

"You're sure about that?" he asked.

"Yeah. We had a lot of last-minute dinner cancellations due to the bad weather. A lot of our guests went to Nassau for the day and now they're all stuck there overnight. All the commuter flights between the islands are delayed 'til tomorrow. The boatsmen who sailed to New Providence aren't coming back tonight either. There're reports of ten-foot swells."

"Commuter flights?"

"Yeah. A few different local airlines have daily service between the islands."

"Did you see where the guys who were with us earlier went?" he asked.

"You mean Tonk and his friends?"

Vance cocked his head. "You know them?" he asked, noticing Jimmy's name tag.

"I know who Tonk is, but I never saw the other two before."

"How do you know him?"

Jimmy didn't answer. He handed Vance his credit card and receipt. He looked at it. The waiter had added the twenty-five percent.

"You need to sign it."

"How do you know Tonk?" he asked again, scribbling his name on the receipt, removing his credit card, and snapping the folder shut.

Jimmy held his hand out.

Vance tapped the credit card folder on his open palm. "Is Tonk still here?"

Jimmy fixed his eyes on the folder, hand still open. "I haven't seen him or his friends since they left the table."

Lauren approached.

"Did you find your bag?" she asked.

"No." He continued tapping the black folder on his palm.

"Did you fly in with Blade?" Jimmy asked.

"What if we did?" Vance asked.

"I thought I recognized his plane."

"Blade's a regular?" Lauren asked.

"A regular rogue," Jimmy said. "I'm surprised he had the stones to land here."

"It was an emergency landing," Vance said.

"Last time he was here he bought fuel and his credit card was declined. He promised to make good on the account, but he didn't. The boss let him go based on his word. He promised to come back and pay but he hasn't. Lucky him."

"Lucky how?" Lauren asked.

"No one's working Customs today. The boss man is old-fashioned, and he told the agents if they ever caught him here, to hold him. He thinks a man's word is all he's got, and Blade lied."

"You have a full-time customs office?"

"No. When we have international arrivals on the schedule, we make a request to have an agent on-site to clear them. But with the bad weather, everyone's grounded. I assume you're Americans."

Vance narrowed his eyes and swatted the credit card folder against his pant leg.

"It was an emergency," Lauren said.

"An emergency landing doesn't excuse him from his

obligations," Jimmy said. "Maybe you left your bag on the plane."

"No," Vance said.

"You're sure about that?"

"He's sure," Lauren said. "Blade insisted we take all our belongings with us. We hand carried our stuff."

Jimmy raised his eyebrows.

Vance handed him the folder with the signed receipt.

"You walked here from the airstrip?"

He felt the muscles in his neck twitch. "That's right."

Jimmy handed him his copy of the receipt.

Vance turned and headed back to the bar. Lauren followed, taking the same seat on the stool next to her blue bag.

"You must've done something to piss Blade off," Skip the bartender said, polishing the bottle of whiskey with dried red candle wax dripping down the neck. "That's the only time he dumps passengers."

"He's done this before?" Lauren asked, eyebrows arched.

Skip set the bottle on the bar. "Once or twice, maybe more. Some say they're glad it happened. There's a lot worse places to get marooned."

"What about people who can't afford it?" Vance asked.

Skip didn't have an answer for that. Neither did Jimmy who'd returned and leaned against the mahogany bar, listening in.

Vance downed the whiskey, set the glass on the bar and turned toward Jimmy. "How do you know Tonk?"

Skip stepped into answer. "It's not a secret. He's Blade's son. He's been flying with his dad since he was a little kid. I haven't seen him around for a few years. Rumor has it he moved to L.A. to go to film school or something." Skip wiped his hands on a towel, turned his back to them and started the water. He dropped a white tablet in the sink and swung the faucet head to fill one side of the stainless sink with water.

"What about the other two?" he asked.

"You mean the tall guy and Bridezilla?" Skip said.

"Bridezilla?" Lauren asked.

"I guess didn't you see her tattoo," Jimmy the waiter said.

Vance had. "You mean the garter belt."

Lauren glared at him.

"Her shorts covered it up 'til she sat down at the table," Jimmy said.

"Who is she?" Lauren asked.

"I don't know," Jimmy said, "I've never seen either one of them before."

"Do you know where they are now?" he asked.

"Paddle boarding," Skip said with his back to them, dipping glasses into the water and setting them on a rack to dry.

"You're kidding," Lauren said.

"Yeah," Jimmy said, "he's joking. We don't rent paddle boards after four in the afternoon. They must've left with Blade and Tonk."

The only restaurant customers were an elderly couple seated in the dining room. The old man held his hand up. "I gotta go," Jimmy said.

"Can I get another?" he asked.

Skip wiped his hands on the bar towel, picked up Vance's empty glass, dunked it in the water and put it on the rack to air dry with the others. He got a fresh glass, added ice, then free poured from the bottle.

"I have an app on my phone that I listen to," Skip said. "It has all the weather reports. There'd been warnings of squall conditions in Nassau since early yesterday."

He swigged the whiskey, swallowing each gulp slowly, letting the booze burn his throat. He ran his finger around the rim of the short glass. "Are you sure they all left with Blade?"

Skip shrugged. "No, I'm not sure, but I haven't seen them since they left your table."

The old guy in the corner watching the game raised his empty glass.

"Captain Morgan's calling," Skip said. "I'll be back."

"What are we going to do now?" Lauren asked.

"I don't know. Wait here," he said.

"Where are you going?"

"To go look around."

"For what?"

"I don't know, for the others, for my bag. Rest your feet. I won't be gone long."

"Here." Lauren handed him the bottle of mosquito repellent.

Jimmy stood at the bar waiting to put in a drink order.

"Be careful," Jimmy said.

Being careful would have nothing to do to with lessening the shock of what he was about to discover.

Vance jogged out the marina-side door, down the hand-lain stone path, around the circular raised flower beds and stopped where it came to a T at the concrete bulkhead. He covered his eyes and spritzed his body with insect repellant, then shoved the bottle in his pants pocket. He surveyed the perimeter, his eyes tracking the floating docks jutting out a thousand feet from the bulkhead into the harbor. It had been designed with plenty of space between the docks and slips making it convenient for boaters to navigate out the manmade jetty to open water.

He retraced his steps, hurrying toward the path leading to the airstrip, the limestone gravel crunching under the weight of his shoes. Soon there wouldn't be enough daylight to find his way back without a flashlight. The dense vegetation lining both sides of the trail reminded him of midwestern corn crops in late summer, and the path was eight, maybe ten feet at its widest. He stopped to look over his shoulder, back at the marina, then ahead, studying the footpath shaded by the tall overgrowth. He took his cell from his pocket, activated the flashlight and pointed it at the ground, waving it slowly, noticing the areas where the gravel had been pressed into the sandy soil. Several sets of tire tracks and footprints going both directions were clearly visible. He took a knee to look closely.

The footprints were new and likely belonged to their group after Blade had sent the five passengers to the restaurant, but the tire tread marks could've been there for days. How long ago had it been since it rained? He didn't know. The weather app on his phone only showed the future. Not the past. He walked purposely, scanning the ground with his cell phone flashlight. Halfway to the airstrip, he stopped. His heart pounded under his shirt. A trail of stuff he would've noticed if it had been there during their trek to the restaurant was strewn on the ground, in the middle of the path.

"Damn it."

He recognized the stuff as the personal items he'd packed for the trip. He collected his belongings one by one, balancing them on the crook of his left elbow: a stick of deodorant, phone charger, toothbrush, toothpaste, a comb, clean socks, and several pairs of underwear, still folded. He spotlighted a larger pile of clothes—two button-down shirts, a T-shirt, and a pair of slacks with the price tags still attached—that had been dumped near the shoulder of the path where the vegetation grew densest. He collected the clothes and continued the search. He saw something else, his black duffle turned inside out. They had to be kidding. He took a knee and searched the bottom and side pockets then walked the perimeter, stopping every few feet, using his cell light to scour the ground.

"Fuck, fuck, FUCK."

The waning rim of sun would soon dip below the horizon, leaving the half-moon overhead as the only natural light.

He wadded his empty duffle and kicked hard enough to send it through a set of imaginary goal posts.

His Glock and passport were gone.

Maybe Blade's story about Customs and Immigration was a ruse to buy time. Maybe Lauren was right. He should've kept his temper in check. Or at the very least, kept his fists in the pocket of his pants. If the situation had been reversed and someone sucker punched him—if he'd been Blade, or Tonk—he'd have done the exact same thing and left their sorry asses behind as payback. He gathered the rest of his belongings and shoved them inside the bag, then headed back to the resort. The moon lit the rooftop of the main building and cast eerie silhouettes of crooked palm trees.

Blade was going to pay for this. One way or another.

7

T onk had flown the route from Miami to Nassau hundreds of times with his dad but only a handful of times from Chub Cay and rarely at nightfall and never after ditching passengers. Most of his father's business was with billionaires and celebrities who owned private islands, and with various companies on New Providence and Paradise Island. Once he'd helped his father transport a body bag for a Bahamian politician whose young daughter had died of a drug overdose in Miami. They'd been met at the airport in Nassau by a convoy of hardened vehicles. It had been both a somber and surreal experience.

He glanced across at his dad behind the controls noticing for the first time the outline of the fat lip Courage had given him. It'd been a devastating blow, an uppercut to the jaw and lip. He'd fantasized about the day something like this happened. He imagined he would relish the moment someone finally took a swing at the old man. Maybe he'd join in and give him a kick to the ribs for good measure. But that's not what happened. He'd intervened. *He'd helped.* It'd been an involuntary response.

He watched as his dad's tongue slithered out of his mouth and licked the swollen skin, running the tip back and forth across his upper lip. The old man crunched one side of his face like Popeye lifting the corner of his injured lip and polishing a tooth with his tongue.

Keeping focus on the windshield, his dad turned his head left and right three times before tilting his chin to his chest, moves he recognized his father used to stretch the muscles that knotted from hours sitting behind the controls. His dad wasn't a young man and the kind of weather he'd battled earlier had taken a physical toll. The old man pushed the headset off his head and the earmuffs dropped and hugged the sides of his wrinkled neck.

He took it as a sign that his old man wanted to talk. A question followed.

"Where's that scanner?" the old man snapped.

He had to almost yell to be heard over the engine noise. "It's in my bag. Where did you get it?"

"From a friend."

"From the same guy who sold you the tracking device?"

"Yeah," his dad said, "but the scanner is a loaner. Same guy owns the company that designed it and he's talking to some folks who're talking to Homeland Security. He asked me if I wanted to test it and I said yes. If you ask me it's gonna be a game changer, especially for the schools. I'd like to see what you saw."

Tonk released his seatbelt, twisted around and grabbed his backpack from the empty row where Courage and his lady friend had sat. He placed it on his lap, unzipped the side pocket and removed the device with the gray and black herringbone case that could pass as a clunky smart phone. "The thing works. It's awesome."

His father leaned forward in the pilot's seat holding the throttle steady, squinting through the dirty windshield, scanning the gauges on the dash. The sun was coming down and dusk was the most dangerous time to fly. Colors morphed into shades of gray making it featureless and difficult to distinguish between land and sea. At night the city lights helped but at dusk only a smattering were visible.

During preflight leaving Miami, his dad had asked him to scan all the passenger bags with the device. The lawyer had kept his duffle slung over his shoulder and he'd had to wait until they were on the plane to scan it. When his dad invited Lauren to sit up front, it gave him a chance to scan Courage's carry-on. He'd been excited when he'd detected a concealed weapon in the duffle.

He powered on the device and tapped the screen searching the menu for captured images. Locating the shot he'd recorded of the gun, he held it up for his dad to see. "Check it out."

"I can't look at it now. Describe it to me."

"It's an almost perfect outline of a handgun."

"Gimme that."

Blade snatched the device from him and studied the image but said nothing. He lifted a hip and stuffed the scanner into his front pants pocket.

A moment passed before his father said, "I knew it."

"How did you know he was carrying?"

"It's not rocket science, son. I did a background check on both like I always do with new clients. It's not her that caught my attention. It was him. He's an ex-cop."

"I thought he said he's an ex-lawyer."

"Did they strike you as discount shoppers? Did you see

how bent out of shape his lady friend was over the size of your gal-pal's bag? You don't know much about women, son. For a woman like the one with Courage, packing lightly for vacation is a concession. For your friends the park rangers, packing light is no big deal."

"They're not park rangers. C.J. has a big job with the State of California."

Blade stared straight ahead. "I wish I could say the same about my son. The only thing big about my kid is his student loan."

Tonk felt his fists tighten.

"Either way, Courage and his lady friend had other options. Better ones to get to Nassau. The way I see it, he had a good reason to smuggle a firearm into the Bahamas and he was using me to get it past Customs which he might've. Besides, you asked me to get you a gun and now you have one."

The last time Tonk was in Nassau on Spring Break he'd been mugged and punched in the head. But that's not why he wanted the gun.

"I thought you wanted me to take it as payback for him punching you. Maybe he'll report it stolen. He might even be stupid enough to come after us."

Blade faced him. "I'll tell you who's stupid."

Tonk saw movement but it was too late. "WHAT THE FUCK?" he yelled. "AWWW." The back of his dad's hand landed on the left side of his head. It popped his eardrum with the sound of a cannon. The hearing on that side of his head faded. He kneaded his fists. One of these days he was going to fight back. But not now. As the pain faded and his hearing returned the humiliation inside him grew.

"Do me a favor. Next time you fly with me dress like a man. And get a haircut. When I sent you off to that school you left looking like a man and came back as . . . I don't know what. Like a latte-drinking garden fairy." His dad hesitated. "If it wasn't for you and your poor decision making, we wouldn't even be in this position."

He rubbed his ear trying to stop the buzzing in his brain over the drone of the engines. He stuck his finger in his left earhole and turned toward his dad. "You dumped them. Do you think it was a good idea?"

"We could debate that. But yeah, knowing what I know now I'd say yes it was a good idea. It wasn't the plan but the fucker sucker-punched me and that created a few opportunities. Sending him off with you to cool down at the bar gave me time to plant the tracker on the yacht and the chance for you to steal his weapon. No one gets on this plane with a gun without telling me. Not heading to The Bahamas. And no one punches me and gets away with it."

Tonk tried to swallow but his throat froze.

"Do you know what happens if I get caught with an illegal gun on my airplane? I'd lose everything. My pilot's license. They'd seize my plane, not to mention being sent to the Fox Hill prison," he added. "Do you know that jail has the highest mortality rate in the world? Maybe these are things you didn't know. But I bet that fucker Courage knew."

Tonk screwed his finger deeper into his thrumming earhole and changed the subject. "No one saw you near the yacht?"

"I don't think so. It must be off season or something. The place was practically a ghost town. Was the restaurant busy?"

He shook his head.

Over the last three decades his father had built up a list of wealthy clients that trusted him, keeping him busy moving valuable freight between South Florida and The

Bahamas. The old plane had a limited cargo hold beneath the nose and when he needed more space, he removed the rear seats. When it came to payload his dad was strict. Nothing illegal. All cargo had to be inspected first and manifest documents delivered in advance, fully disclosing the contents of the shipment. He'd accompanied his dad on trips transporting everything from human organs to relief aid and life-saving drugs, to gold bars, jewelry, pets and cash. Blade kept a low profile flying an older plane and selling seats to the public when it suited him.

He calmed down enough to be civil. "Why did you fly into that storm? Why didn't you stick to the plan? Land at Chub, plant the device on the yacht, wait for the storm to pass and continue."

"I wanted to knock Courage off his game, scare him because he's not some yahoo with a bottle of coconut rum in his bag I coulda told to hang out while I took care of some business. And she's no dummy. If I hadn't flown into the storm, what do you think the chances are that I'd've been able to land at Chub without an explanation? Those kids wouldn't have questioned it. I thought if I rattled the lawyer and his lady friend with a rough enough ride, they'd be glad to be alive. But I misread him. When you get settled in Nassau call your park ranger friends. Blame it on me. Tell them I'm an asshole."

It wouldn't be a stretch. He reached into his backpack and held up Courage's passport. "You don't have to worry about the lawyer. He'll be stuck where he's at for a while."

Blade squinted at the small blue folder. His face glowed purple like he was about to explode. "Are you out of your fucking mind? Put that back in your bag." He grabbed the brim of his ball cap and jerked it side to side. He watched his dad stare out the cockpit window at the last streaks of a magenta sunset floating above the horizon. A protracted silence ensued.

He didn't expect his dad to react this way. His head throbbed from the blunt force of a fist to the ear and he worried he might puke.

As they approached the city, the lights over Nassau twinkled. But the mood in the cabin was tense.

Blade finally spoke. "What were you thinking?"

Tonk stuffed the passport back into the side pocket of his bag and zipped it shut. The truth was that he hadn't had time to think. His father didn't afford him that, changing the plan last minute when he'd mentioned the gun, texting him, telling him to hurry. How was he supposed to know flying into a storm was a strategy to keep a couple of passengers off balance? He wasn't a mind reader.

"I didn't tell you to take his passport. Reporting a stolen passport is a lot different than reporting a missing illegal firearm."

"I'll get rid of it," Tonk said, reaching into the bottom of his backpack, fondling the solid polymer grip of the Glock.

"How is it that I send you off to college and you come home dumber than before you left. If he hasn't already, he's going to figure out his passport is missing. How many suspects will he consider?"

He placed his finger gently on the trigger inside the bag where his dad couldn't see what he was doing. "Four. Not counting his lady friend."

"Two, you idiot. One of 'em is me."

Tonk shuddered at what his dad didn't know. It was stupid to toss the duffle bag and leave a trail of evidence that would leave no doubt about who ripped him off.

"I see the runway," Tonk said, pointing at three o'clock through the hazy windshield. "See those headlights?"

"I see 'em," Blade yelled. "Back me up."

Tonk took his smartphone from his backpack and woke it up. A barrage of messages bubbled up, at least a dozen texts and voicemails from Chan and C.J. He ignored them, promising himself he'd deal with them later. He tapped the yellow icon for the aviation app. A little airplane appeared on screen showing their mileage to the airstrip from information he'd saved with a pin from a previous flight. Flying at an altitude of 450-feet made it difficult if not impossible for air traffic controllers at the nearby busy Lynden Pindling International Airport to distinguish between a small aircraft and what the tower called ground clutter.

The wings of the Baron yawed gently as they came in low. Tonk saw the vehicle headlights flash in the distance and braced himself as the plane touched down on the dirt, coming to a stop a hundred feet from the end of the runway.

The driver killed the high beams and drove to meet the airplane.

Tonk unbuckled his lap belt and unlatched the cabin door.

"Did you download the app, son?"

"What?"

"For the tracking device."

"Yeah."

"Check your phone and let me see it."

He closed the airplane navigation app and opened the one he'd downloaded yesterday. He showed the flashing yellow dot to his father. The yacht hadn't moved.

"Okay," his dad said reaching under the pilot's seat. "Here, take this with you."

He opened the small white plastic bag and saw the items he'd asked for: a burner phone still in the box and two thumb drives.

"There's a prepaid phone card still in the box. We'll meet back here. Don't call me 'til you're ready to come home. Use your gambling skills and win some money off those tourists. One more thing," his dad said, "don't do anything I wouldn't do."

Too late for that.

He opened the bag and removed the thumb drives. They had logos on them from a timeshare outfit. "Where did you get these?"

"I don't know," his old man said, "can't remember."

He felt a cold sweat soaking the back of his neon green tank top. What if Vance Courage made finding his gun his life's mission? It'd take days, maybe longer to get a new passport and that would buy time. There was another wild card, and one just as unpredictable: C.J.

He needed his friend's computer skills to download the information he planned to steal. He smiled to himself. His dad finally did right by him.

These thumb drives will never be traced back to me.

8

Vance hung his dirty duffle over the back of the barstool and sat next to Lauren.

She eyed the bag. "That was lucky. Where did you find it?"

"On the footpath back to the runway."

She looked confused, snapping her neck back slightly. "They must have accidentally picked it up and dropped it when they realized their mistake."

"I highly doubt that."

"Why?"

"My stuff was dumped out."

She crinkled her brow enough to create three parallel lines across her forehead. "What?"

"They emptied my things out and tossed the bag." He lifted the duffle from the chair back, unzipped it and held up a white T-shirt shaded with dirt, then loosely folded it and stuffed it back in the bag.

"That sucks," she said.

Skip leaned forward with his elbows on the bar. "How about one on the house?"

"Sure. I'll have a shot of the twenty-five-year-old stuff."

"I can't do that." Skip said, eyeing his duffle. "At least you found it. That's more than the last group can say." He picked up the same bottle of whiskey with hardened red wax dripping from the neck. "How about a compromise, I'll pour you a double."

"Sure."

Lauren fish eyed him. When Skip turned away, she raised her brow and mouthed 'the last group.'

He shrugged, also confused.

Skip towel-dried a freshly washed glass, added a half scoop of ice and poured for a three count and set it down in front of Vance.

He picked up the glass and swirled the ice. "What did you mean when you said, 'the last group?'"

Skip ignored the question and walked to the end of the bar to check on the old guy nursing his drink.

Lauren threaded her silky blond hair behind one ear. "What are we going to do now?"

"I don't know," he said. "I was going to defer to you. We're in a foreign country and I don't have a passport."

"What are you talking about?"

"My passport's gone." He wadded a used cocktail napkin into the size of a golf ball and lobbed it toward the tall garbage can behind the bar, missing the shot. "Remind me, how did you find Blade?"

"On the 'Net. You're the one who didn't want to fly commercial because you said something always goes wrong with the airlines. I sent you the link to Blade's charter service and you said it looked fine. How was I supposed to know he'd do something like this?"

Skip returned. "If you plan on staying the night, you should make arrangements at the desk." He gestured to the clock on the wall, next to the trophy blue marlin mounted above the bottles of booze. "They're going to close-up in less than an hour. You could stay the night and go online and try to book a flight to Nassau in the morning. We have cell service and there's wireless in the rooms. Most of our guests book their flights online. The local carriers have automated reservations like the big airlines."

"Can you recommend one?" Lauren asked.

"Island Hopper is good. They don't have regular service here, but they have several flights a day from Nassau. You can make arrangements to have them stop and pick you up. If not, there're others. There's more information in the rooms. We have golf cart service that'll take you out to the runway to meet the plane, but I suggest you get a room now before they close."

"How about a golf cart ride to the desk?" Vance asked.

"Sorry," Skip said, "but no one's available."

"You don't think Blade's coming back?" Lauren asked.

Skip took the red apron hanging around his neck and untied it from around his waist. "If he does, it'll be a first. He's not a bad guy, he's just got a bad habit of screwing tourists he doesn't like. From what I hear, he only sells seats when he needs the money."

"How can he make a living without passengers?" she asked.

"He flies cargo."

"What kind of cargo?" Vance asked.

"I don't know. Special delivery stuff," Skip said.

"Like what?" Vance asked.

"A while back one of our best clients was having a yacht party and when they ran out of champagne, I told them to call Blade and he had a couple of cases here in ninety minutes."

"Who owns this place?" Vance asked.

"A guy who'd rather not have us talking about him."

"An American?" he asked.

"Listen. This place went bankrupt in 2007 and the previous owner defaulted on millions of dollars of bank loans. The Bahamian government guaranteed some of that debt. When a new buyer with real money appeared and the deal went through, he re-hired all of us, paid the back taxes and created a lot of construction jobs. Have you looked around? Over forty people work here full time. The only thing he's asked is that we keep his identity private."

"I could find out. It has to be public record," she said.

"I can't stop you from doing that," Skip said. "But I don't know why it matters."

"Why would you refer your clients to Blade if you know he's half-rogue and he owes money to the resort?" Lauren asked.

"They needed champagne. Plus, this was before he skipped out on the bill. You must've done something to piss him off because you're the first adults he's ditched. He has a problem with the college kids, he doesn't like them, the rich ones. A lot of them go to Paradise Island on spring break instead of Daytona Beach or Lauderdale. You should've seen what he did to a group of snotty-nosed preppies last week. He was flying them home and told them he had engine trouble. He made an emergency landing here and did the same thing to them he did to you, told them to go get a drink and wait. By the time they made it to the bar, he'd already taken off with their bags."

"It's not funny," Lauren said.

"I know, but you should've heard them on their phones calling their daddies and threatening to hire lawyers. They got so drunk I had to call the police."

"The police?" she asked.

"We have our own. It's only a few guys but they're highly trained. All the private resorts need their own security. Our clients are targets, and one breach is all it takes to put a place like this out of business." He paused, adjusted the red apron around his waist and raised his eyebrows. "A couple of hundred years ago the Jack Sparrows oversaw the deep waters east of here where the big merchant ships once sailed. You know what they say, the more things change, the more they stay the same."

"Amen," Vance said, downing the liquor, savoring the burn as it coated his throat. "Ahhhhh," he said, contorting his face. He smacked his lips and set the empty glass on the bar. "I'm going to go see about a room for tonight." He placed his hand on Lauren's shoulder. "I'll be right back."

"Do you want me to go with you?"

"No. Stay here and keep an eye on your bag."

She swiveled the bar stool. "Do you have your phone?"

"I do. I'll be right back."

"Thank God," she said. "Losing your phone would be worse than losing your passport."

"We'll see about that."

HE TAPPED the bell at the reservation desk, then waited, looking around at the amenities. The lighting was dimmer than the bar. Banker style table lamps with green glass shades. A tall wooden hutch neatly lined with paperbacks and classic hardcover books with gold leaf on the spines. Framed watercolors of seascapes, and clocks on the wall showing four different time zones. Orchids blooming white and pink, their long spindly stems sprouting from shallow ceramic dishes. He grabbed a lime-flavored mint from a crystal dish, ripped the cellophane and popped it in his mouth. A minute later a middle age Black woman in a bright orange sundress and dangling silver earrings appeared. Her eyes were big and shiny and her smile so infectious for a moment he forgot how pissed off he was. Or maybe it was the bourbon still kicking in.

"May I 'elp you?" she asked in an island accent.

"I'd like to get a room for the night."

"Las' name?"

"I don't have a reservation."

"De charter service usually notifies us when someone is coming in."

"It's an impromptu visit."

"I see," she said studying him. "De marina usually text me when dey need land accommodation."

"I didn't arrive by boat."

She put her hands on her wide hips, raising one of them the way his mother used to when he was about to get a scolding. "You fly in with Blade?"

"You know him?"

"More or less. He stopped in to use de bathroom, but he was in such a hurry, he dint even say goo'-bye."

Vance took another green mint and opened it. "He left us behind. That's how I ended up without a reservation."

"Dat rascal. Da weather was real bad to de south. Dat musta been why I saw de plane, an' den I seen 'im. Lord Almighty, I couldn't believe my own eyes."

"Was Tonk with him?"

"His boy was wit him? I'll be. I 'aven't seen him in," she gazed past him and shrugged, "I don't know how long." She laughed and shook her head. "I wish I hadda, see if he looks any smarter 'den de last time I saw 'im. Let me see what we 'ave to get you fixed up for de night." She tapped her keyboard and looked at the flat screen monitor. "How many guests?"

"Two."

"A king, queen, double or a suite?"

"Sounds like a poker hand."

She grinned. "I 'ave a one-bedroom villa on de beach with ocean view an' a fire pit." She handed him the rate card.

Four-hundred and twenty-five a night seemed fair.

"There's a refrigerator wit snacks. And don't you worry, we get our liquor from a reputable source. Those mini bar deaths a while back kilt our bar business."

Interesting choice of words. "I'll take the villa."

She handed him a detailed paper map of the island, then used a yellow highlighter to show the way to the bungalow. "You go out of de main building an' turn right, then it's de last yellow one on de left. Here's de key."

"Thanks."

"One of dese days someone going to punch Blade right in de nose."

"Or the mouth," he said.

"Either way, sorry for de way you arrived, but I 'ope you enjoy your stay. If you need any-ting from 'ousekeeping or room service, de information is in de room. I need an I.D. an' a credit card."

"Will a Florida license do?"

She nodded.

HE JOGGED to the room to check it out, surprising a flock of birds nesting for the night. They mewled as they took flight, then flew back to claim their perches on the wooden pilings.

A short set of wide, weathered stairs led to the cozy

yellow cabana built beachfront on higher ground. He used the key to open the door. Gauzy white curtains let in moonlight. He used his phone flashlight to find the wall switch and turned on the overheads. The living room was decorated with dark wicker furniture, a matching sofa, love seat and chairs with plump navy-blue cushions with thin white piping along the seams. The living room furniture was arranged around a brass and glass coffee table with a colorful tropical floral centerpiece made of silk birds of paradise and palm fronds arranged in a dull green vase.

The room was outfitted with a mini bar stocked with airplane bottles of booze, a microwave, a full-sized fridge and a stainless stove. The cabinetry above and below the gray quartz kitchen counters was filled with shiny pots and pans, and glass and dishware. The door to the bedroom was halfway open. The queen bed—size being something he didn't recall having been discussed after agreeing to the suite—had a navy-blue bedspread with a repeating pattern of small white boat anchors. The bed was flanked by a pair of natural pine nightstands set against a darker wood paneled wall. If he'd seen it first, he might've chosen different accommodations, one with a king bed, without a sailfish mounted on the wall above the headboard. Otherwise, it was perfect.

He sat on the edge of the mattress, then laid down, resting his head on the crisp pillowcase. He closed his eyes for a moment, too tired to think, maybe too pissed to think straight, the booze wearing off and a mild headache setting in.

He lifted the binder from the nightstand, sat up and leafed through it. If they hadn't stolen his gun and passport, the trip might've ended right here. On a high note. The resort offered sailing lessons. Daily snorkeling trips to a nearby coral reef. Paddle boarding. Sport fishing and lobster dives. Even a daily round trip charter from Nassau to Paradise Island, though the thought of gambling had lost its appeal. His mouth watered when he got to the room service menu.

Even if he could get home without his passport, the Glock was registered to him, and he had to get it back. If it fell into the wrong hands, which it already had, the serial number could easily be traced back to him and that was not an option. Although it was by accident, he was guilty of bringing a firearm into the country illegally. He wasn't the first ex-cop who'd forgotten to unpack a firearm before flying. He knew another guy who'd done it and he'd given him some serious shit. Blade and his kid were up to something. Why else rip off his gun and passport and ditch the bag?

He headed back to the bar, taking his time, stopping for a moment to inhale the sweet and salty ocean air until the bugs discovered him. As he hurried along the lit footpath back to the main building, he saw Lauren through the picture window seated alone at the bar with her phone to her ear. Who was she talking to? The old Santa Claus soccer fan who'd been sitting in the corner nursing a drink since their arrival hadn't moved. He wondered what his story was: some sad sack glued to a barstool, staring at a TV screen, his faculties dulled to the natural beauty, maybe wishing for a change of scenery. Like the bustle and noise of big city life.

He walked up behind her.

She must've sensed him coming, holding her phone close to her side, slyly dropping it into her purse.

"Did you find a room?" she asked.

"I did. Who were you talking to?"

"I was listening to a voice message."

He waited for her to say from who, but she didn't, and he was too tired to press the issue. "Are you ready?"

"I am."

He grabbed his duffle from the chair back and slung it over his shoulder.

"Do you want one for the road?" Skip asked.

"Sure. Charge it to the room." He reached into his pocket and laid the key on the bar for Skip to see.

The bartender filled a fresh glass with ice and free-poured whiskey to the brim, then handed it to him.

He set the glass down and removed his wallet from his back pocket. He folded a fifty and placed it under the cocktail napkin.

Skip fish-eyed it.

"It's for the extra trouble."

"Thanks."

He grabbed Lauren's bag and picked up the whiskey. "You ready?"

"Beyond ready," she said.

They had everything they needed. Food. Water. Shelter. Wireless internet and cell service. Little did he know the last item on the list was the thing that was about to fuck things up.

9

V ance escorted Lauren out the lobby door leading to the marina, holding the door open, noticing for the first time the elaborate nautical compass three times the size of an extra-large pizza inlaid on the tile floor beneath his feet. With sharp points marking north, south, east and west, he admired the intricate craftsmanship of the design. Surrounded by an endless black horizon of water and no visible landmarks beyond the resort, the mosaic was a nice touch.

The walk from the pool to the villa was shorter but it was dark out and the lighting was better on the marina side of the resort.

"Can we take a detour?" Lauren asked. "I want to check out that mega yacht."

"Sure," he said, leading the way down the brick path. LEDs set atop tall poles planted into the concrete along the bulkhead cast enough light to spotlight the harbor.

The air was still, and it was eerily quiet but for the rhythmic sounds of the sea water softly breaking against the bulkhead and the occasional gust of wind rocking the boats in their slips. The halyard lines hanging loosely from the masts of the luxury sailboats played a melody of metal clinking against metal like wind chimes in the breeze. The waxing half-moon cast a wavy reflection of itself on the glassy dark water, like a fun house mirror. As they approached the bow of the super yacht, Lauren backed up a few steps to take a wider look at it.

"Wow. I could live on that," she said.

It was massive, probably a hundred feet long, maybe more. He watched Lauren march alongside it, high stepping like a North Korean soldier. He strolled behind wondering what she was doing. He counted the daisy chain of rubber bumpers the size of punching bags draping from the gunwales protecting the fiberglass hull from the concrete dock. The ship's continuous curved wraparound windows were tinted almost black. When they reached the stern, he tilted his head back and looked up, impressed as much by the height as the length. Three stories tall.

He'd counted thirty bumpers hanging from the gunwales. "I wonder how big it is?" he asked.

"It's a hundred and twenty feet long."

"Where did you come up with that?"

"It's not exact. I walked it the same way I walk the jumping courses at the horse show. You learn how to take three-foot steps to calculate how many strides the horse will travel between jumps. It's forty steps from bow to stern, roughly a hundred and twenty feet, give or take."

They stood on the bulkhead looking at the futuristic sloped stern with him wondering who owned it and whether anyone was on board watching them snooping around. The yacht was dark but for the exterior security lighting coming from the decks. Small green and red lights on the bow cast a Christmassy tint against the white fiberglass. At the stern where they now stood, a larger, brighter white light attached to a metal flagpole worked like a spotlight highlighting the transom and swim deck. The name of the ship was stenciled or maybe hand-painted in cursive in gold metallic paint. '*The Parent Minus.*' There had to be a story behind that. He gazed up at the two different flags drooping from the flag poles. One was American but he couldn't see enough of the other to identify it other than it was turquoise along the seams.

"What a weird name," Lauren said. "The Parent Minus. It sounds depressing like maybe whoever bought it used life insurance or something."

"That's an uplifting thought," he said.

She strolled toward the bow of the boat, and he followed watching her gazing up and admiring it.

"You have to wonder who could afford something like this," he said.

"We could," she said, taking her phone from her purse and unlocking the screen. "Here," she handed it to him. "Take a picture of me." She held her hand up. "Wait a sec." She walked toward the bow and looked up at it.

He knew she was setting up the shot.

She smoothed her hair, then said to him, "Squat so the picture will show the height."

He obliged, taking a knee and snapping four pictures from slightly different angles.

She took her phone back and said, "If we hang around here for a couple of days, we can see how we like island life."

"We might not have a choice," he said.

"You sound disappointed."

"It's not that. It's that this isn't the plan."

"Maybe if you hadn't punched the pilot, we'd be on Paradise Island by now."

He raised his left shoulder to adjust the strap of the duffle. "You might not want to go there."

"What's that supposed to mean?"

"You let someone steal my bag."

She turned and faced him, glaring, eyes throwing sparks at him. "Really, you think this is *my* fault?"

He stared back at her, gripping the whisky glass. "Don't raise your voice."

"Don't raise my voice? Did you notice they took your bag and not mine?"

"Hey, hey," he said, tossing the booze into the water and setting the empty glass on the top of her roller bag. "Look, I'm sorry. I'm tired and I'm half drunk and it's not your fault. Come here." He dropped the duffle from his shoulder and pulled her close, hugging her. A gentle breeze kicked up. He held her by the shoulders and pushed her back gently, brushing the hair from her face, then looked into her eyes. "How are your feet?"

"They hurt and you smell like you should be living under a bridge."

He heard a bell ringing. Something dropped from the second story of the yacht and landed near his feet. Lauren turned to run. He grabbed her arm, stopping her. The white cat rubbed against his pant leg, eyes glowing orange in the darkness, the animal unbothered by their reaction.

"Jesus," she said, clutching her hand over her heart. She knelt and massaged the cat's neck. "You scared the heck out of me. Come here." The cat purred loudly and arched its back, a silver bell jingling around its neck. "Do you live here?"

"If it does, it's pretty fancy digs," he said.

The cat strolled away from them with its tail erect and leapt onto the swim deck of the yacht and disappeared.

A mosquito screamed in his ear. He slapped at it.

She waved her hands in front of her face.

"Come on, let's hurry," he said. He grabbed their belongings and led the way, jogging toward the sandy path leading to the yellow villa.

He'd left the outside light on and ran the weathered wooden porch stairs two at a time and opened the door, ushering her in quickly, and closing it ahead of the bugs. He set their bags down and watched her reaction.

"Wow," she said.

"You like it?"

"It's perfect."

"Does that mean you forgive me?"

"I wouldn't go that far."

He carried their bags into the bedroom and set hers upright next to the pine dresser and his on a dark wooden bench at the foot of the bed. He stuck his head out into the living room. "There's water and stuff in the fridge. I'm gonna take a shower," he said, "unless you want to go first."

"No. You go ahead."

"I'll be quick. Why don't you see about getting a flight to Nassau tomorrow?" He picked up the guest information binder and the tabletop placard with the wireless information from the nightstand. "Here," he said, handing it to her through the open door. "See what I need for I.D. Who knows? Since I'm already here maybe I can fly between the islands without a passport."

"Do you mind if I do it first thing in the morning? It's been a long day."

"Yeah, sure, of course. Relax. You deserve it."

. . .

HE GRABBED the chrome handle on the glass surround shower door, opened it, reached inside, and turned the biggest knob to start the water, then undressed waiting for it to warm. The shower stall was modern with seamless glass and light gray tile planks extending up to the ceiling. A rectangular metal fixture three feet high and a foot across was attached to the wall. It had a series of knobs with an array of levers and nozzles. While he preferred simplicity, rich people seemed to prefer complicated things. He pressed a small red button on the side of the fixture. Dozens of blue pin lights beamed from the underside of the shower head. Tinted mood lighting. It was a nice touch.

He left the blue lights on as he stepped into the steaming hot shower and twisted knobs until he activated the half dozen jets that pummeled his torso. He turned slowly letting the jets of water pound the tension from his muscles. Just what his body would've ordered had it'd known it was on the menu.

He heard a noise. He opened the fogged glass door and stuck his head out. A noise, a human voice. He turned the water off and listened. He heard Lauren yelling his name. Grabbing a towel from the rack, he wrapped it around his waist and sprinted toward the living room. She stood barefoot on the sofa staring at the kitchen.

His heart pounded. "What's wrong?"

"There's something in here."

"What?"

"I don't know. It ran into the kitchen."

"What do you mean *it*?"

"I don't know. An animal of some kind."

He entered the small kitchen and scanned the room. He heard a strange noise, a clattering, and looking in that direction saw an ugly land crab sidling along the baseboards.

When it ran into a dead end near the fridge it stood upright and faced him, flinging a set of snapping claws at him. He'd never seen one like it before, reddish and slightly translucent, more like a scorpion than a crab.

Searching for something to trap it, he fetched the tall plastic garbage can next to the sink and approached the crab. It performed a pirouette, then tried to squeeze into the narrow gap between the wall and the refrigerator. But the space was too small. He opened the kitchen drawers looking for tools and grabbed a long-handled grill spatula and used it to prod the crab away from the wall. He dropped the trash can over the top of the crab, corralling it.

Lauren watched from her perch on the sofa. "Now what?"

He tightened the towel around his waist. "It's not going anywhere. I'll figure it out in the morning."

It rattled inside the plastic container trying to escape.

"No. You have to get it out of here."

He sighed, then knelt and tilted the bottom edge of the garbage can far enough to slide a flat edge of the spatula under one of its claws. When it reared up, he batted it into the container, then flipped it upright, closing the lid.

"It's not going anywhere," he said.

"It's not spending the night with us," she said.

"Fine."

"Eww," she said, as he passed by carrying the container.

Holding the towel in place with one hand, he opened the door and set the trash can on the stoop. "I'll be right back."

He trotted down the grayed splintered stairs toward their private beach, listening to the salt water gently rolling on the shore, the crab clattering inside the container. As he stepped from dry to wet sand, he wished there was light to better see. Pin lights twinkled from two sailboats moored in the anchorage in the distance.

He tilted the plastic trash can near the sea to free the crab.

"Ouch, you little shit." The crab clamped one pincher on his thumb. He batted it off with his free hand and when it fell on the sand, watched it make a beeline back toward the house.

"Crap," he said, picking up the trash while sucking a drop of blood from his thumb. A light flickered in the distance, from land to the north on the wild side of the island where he'd remembered seeing rocky inlets. He shrugged it off. He'd seen the terrain from the air when Blade buzzed low over the island thinking how inhospitable it was and how much money and manpower it must have taken to build this paradise.

The light probably came from a firefly or from a ship passing in the distance.

He was wrong.

10

V ance restarted the shower, stepped in, and let the hot water pound his neck and shoulders. He stretched his arms over his head and leaned forward, placing his hands on his knees. Man were his muscles tight. He tilted his neck side to side then grabbed his left elbow and pulled his arm across his chest, straightening it then repeating the motion with the opposite arm. What a day it'd been. He looked at the cut on his thumb and the bruise on his right knuckles, the looks of the latter not doing justice to the soreness that had set in. He made a fist, then squeezed and released, splaying his fingers like a cat showing its claws.

Which one of them stole his stuff and why? He'd put his money on Blade or his kid, but it could've been the other two.

While Lauren had been reading her book at the airport while they waited for the late passengers to arrive, he'd surreptitiously looked up Bahamian gun statutes published on the government website.

The laws made it next to impossible for law-abiding

Americans to bring legal guns into the country. There was one exception: The Bahamas Defence Department urged boaters to arm themselves. The rules were strict. Firearms and munitions had to be declared before entering Bahamian waters—including reporting serial numbers, manufacturer names and exact ammo counts for every gun and rifle.

There was a bigger catch: Guns had to be stored on the vessel in government-approved containers or surrendered to local authorities. After reading about mandatory jail sentencing for violations—including a maximum term of seven years in prison—he'd considered cancelling the trip after discovering he'd accidentally forgotten to take his Glock out of his bag. Now he wished he had.

He pressed the shampoo button on the wall dispenser and massaged his scalp with his fingertips, whiffing the coconut-scented lather mixing with steam. He showered until the hot water ran cool, then dried himself and dressed in the resort bathrobe he'd found in the bedroom closet. After combing his hair and brushing his teeth he rejoined Lauren in the living room.

"How was your shower?"

"Invigorating."

She held up a deck of cards. "Care to play a little poker?"

"You don't want to shower first?"

"You were in there for a long time. Is there any hot water left?"

"Good point," he said. "I didn't know you brought a deck of cards."

"I didn't."

"Huh. I guess it makes sense to keep a deck in the rooms," he said, grabbing a cold bottle of water from the fridge. He held it up. "Do you want one?"

"No thanks." She held up the unopened box. "They weren't in the room. I found them on the plane. Finders keepers."

"What are you talking about?"

"Someone left them on Blade's plane." She picked at the cellophane wrapper with her fingernail.

"Maybe they belong to one of the other passengers," he said, grabbing a serrated steak knife from the kitchen drawer and sitting next to her on the wicker sofa. "Allow me." He slit the protective plastic and tore off the cellophane. It wasn't the usual set of playing cards, the ubiquitous Bicycle brand with blue or red spades on the cover. Instead, there was an illustration, the fat face of a pink cartoon pig wearing a mortarboard. He turned it over. The same strange image was repeated on the back side. He opened one end of the box and tapped it with two fingers. When enough of the deck poked out, he removed the cards. He set the empty box on the glass table next to the knife. "What do you want to play?"

"How about Blackjack?"

"What do you want to play for?" He tapped the cards on the glass tabletop, cut and shuffled the deck.

"I don't want to bet anything. I want to practice."

"Not sure what there is to practice, but okay." He dealt each of them two cards then picked up his hand.

She lifted hers and turned away from him, holding them close to her shirt. "I know what happened to your fist, but what happened to your thumb?"

He'd cleaned the cut in the shower, but it oozed blood. "The crab pinched me."

"Ouch."

He stared at his hand. The cards were weird, too, with human faces in the white spaces where the hearts, clubs, diamonds and spades were printed on normal decks. "You found these on the plane?"

"Uh-huh. I'll take another," she said.

He set a third card face down and slid it across to her. She picked it up and inserted it between the two in her hand, then studied it for a half minute.

"I'm gonna hold," he said, staring at the faces of the middle-aged strangers printed on the 6 of hearts and 9 of spades. The photographs were low quality. Who were these people?

She lowered her hand, shielding her cards from him. "I'll take one more."

He cocked his head. "Are you sure?"

"I'm sure."

He took another from the top of the deck, placed it face down and using his fingertip, pushed it slowly toward her.

She lifted a corner with her thumbnail and peeked. "Crap," she said, flipping it over and tossing the other three cards face up.

She had a 3, a 5, a 7 and a jack of clubs. 25.

"I'm bust."

"Let me see that."

"See what?"

"Your jack."

She handed it to him. A photo of a human face had been digitally superimposed onto the two heads of the jack, the same one facing up and facing down. He set the card down, then fanned the deck, pulling the four kings, four queens and three remaining jacks from the stack. Every one of them had been altered with faces of what appeared to be actual people. The queens had faces of women and the jacks and kings, of men. "Which one was your fourth card?"

"The jack," she said.

"You should've held."

"Duh."

He turned his cards over. He had a 6 and a 9. "If you'd held with fifteen, you would've beat me. Where did you find these on the plane?"

"Under the seat in front of me."

"When?"

"After we landed."

He examined the box again. The plastic wrap was in good shape when he'd opened it. Given the low level of hygiene on Blade's airplane, they couldn't have been there long.

She picked up a random card and looked at it. "My guess is they're probably swag from some corporate event."

"What makes you think that?"

"The quality of the pictures isn't very good. Look."

She held up the 9 of clubs so he could see it.

"This one's black and white. It looks like they cobbled up the pictures from different sources. Blade's route is a popular destination for convention organizers. They might be freebies from a timeshare pitch. Have you ever been to one of those? They're the Olympic Games of salesmanship."

"So, I've heard."

"Someone might've left them on the plane to get rid of them. People give this stuff away."

"Or toss it in the trash," he said. "I don't see why a timeshare would put a graduation cap on a pig."

"So maybe they're vanity cards for some other event, like a junket with an education theme. It's easy to get almost anything customized these days."

He thumbed through the deck, chose the four aces, and placed them face up.

"What are you doing?"

"I'm studying them."

"For what?"

"Why would someone make a custom deck of cards with pigs wearing graduation caps with the headshots of a bunch of seniors and middle-aged people whose photos look like business profile pictures? No names or anything. Aren't you curious?"

She held up a card and snapped a picture with her phone.

He slipped the ace of spades under his thigh without letting her see him doing it. "What are you doing?"

"A reverse search."

"How?"

"Facial recognition." A moment later she turned her phone screen around so he could see it. "The Queen of Diamonds is the provost of a state university in Wisconsin."

"Here, try this one." He held up the 9 of spades.

She took another picture and showed him the results.

"He's the president of a private college in Rhode Island."

"What about this one?"

"Okay, but my guess is it's going to be another college administrator."

He flicked his thumbnail on the corner of the ace of hearts. "If they were athletes or famous alumni," he said, "it would make sense. But the upper management of colleges around the country? Who'd want to make a deck of those?"

"Maybe a corporation hosted a seminar. Or the schools hosted some sort of seminar. What better way to suck up to people than putting their faces on something?" she said. "I've worked enough business events to know that the organizers understand the way to make people feel part of something is to find a way to create a personal connection to it. I had a client who hired me to put together a slide show that ran on a continuous loop at the company Christmas party. He insisted that each image stay up on the screen for exactly eight seconds. I used to watch the people. As soon as they saw themselves or anyone they recognized on the big screen, they got excited. I could tell after that they were distracted, waiting to see themselves again."

"Same theory as the high school yearbook," he said, "with a twenty-first century twist. Ever notice there really aren't any new ideas?"

"The trick was finding flattering pictures," Lauren said, "especially of the women."

He glanced up at her. "I bet you were good at that."

"It's what I got paid to do, make things look better than they actually are."

"Who called you earlier?"

"What?"

"While I was getting the room, you said you were listening to a voice message from someone."

"Oh." She hesitated. "My stepmother."

"You have a stepmother?"

"Technically speaking I have two. Don't say it."

"Say what?"

"You know. Runs in the family."

He'd obviously hit a nerve. They were both over forty and while she was three-times divorced, he'd never been married. He hadn't decided which paradigm was weirder. "That's not what I was going to say. I was going to ask why she called you?"

"I called her to see if she might be able to help."

"With what?"

"Your passport."

"How?"

"She's a Bahamian citizen."

"You never told me that."

"You never asked."

"Don't you think it might've been nice to mention it when we decided to come here?"

"I don't know. I guess."

"How can she help?"

"She comes from a prominent family, she has connections. Her brother is the Registrar General, at least he was the last time I heard."

"When did you talk to her last?"

"I don't know. A while."

"What's the Registrar General?"

"It's a political position. That's all I know."

"Do you think she'd be willing to help?"

"I have no idea. I told you. I haven't talked to her in a while."

"Why not?"

"My dad. He screwed it up, like he screwed everything up."

"How did he screw it up?"

"The usual way men do. He had an affair. My step-mother, wife number three if you're keeping count, worked for The Ministry of Tourism and traveled a lot. I guess my dad couldn't let the opportunity go to waste. Deal another hand. I need more practice."

"What do you mean by opportunity?"

"Use your imagination."

He cut the cards and shuffled the deck. He felt bad for them both. What would that have been like, having a father who was a cheater? "Does she have a name?"

"Vivian."

"How long were they married?"

She kept her eyes cast down on the coffee table. "I don't know. What does it matter?"

"How did they meet?"

"Why are you interrogating me?"

"I'm not interrogating you. I'm trying to learn some background in case I need her help."

"My dad decided to take sailing lessons and they met at a yacht club in Miami. They dated for a while and got married quickly. It was the only time I'd ever seen him happy."

"What about when he was married to your mom?"

"I don't remember, I was too young. But when he was married to Vivian, he was fun to be around." Lauren shrugged. "At least he didn't meet her at work."

"What are you talking about?"

"My dad was a shrink."

"You never told me that."

"Yes, I did."

"No, you didn't."

"I'm sure I did. You probably forgot. Anyway, he bought a sailboat and moored it at Sailboat Bay."

"Across from the Hotel Mutiny?"

"That's right."

"He helped you get the job there."

"You remember. I'm waiting."

"I remember everything you've told me." He dealt them each two cards. "Where's the boat now?"

"Who knows. I think he sold it." She picked up her hand and looked at it. "Did you know the M.D. psychoanalysts have more education than any other profession? Four years of undergrad, two years of grad school, residency, internship, then eight years of psychoanalysis. My dad could've been any kind of doctor. He interned in an emergency room."

A head-shrinker had more education than a heart surgeon? He didn't know that—and while it seemed like a waste of time and money—he was sure she'd never told him her dad was a shrink; he'd have remembered it. His father and grandfather were both medical doctors, though in his mind shrinks weren't on the same level. He remembered that she'd told him her father wasn't the protective type. But she never told him he was a psychiatrist. How odd. On the other hand, psychoanalysts were the cosmetic surgeons of mental health. They didn't deal with psychos. Cops, homicide detectives and staff psychiatrists at the nut-huts were the ones who dealt with the crazies.

Either way, what would that have been like—not to be safeguarded by her own father? His own father was very protective of his younger sister, Kathy.

"The day he cheated on Vivian, he may as well have cheated on me. I never spoke to him after that. She was such a kind-hearted person, and she didn't deserve to be kicked to the curb, the same way he did to my mom. Or so goes the family folklore."

"You're estranged from your dad?"

"Isn't that what 'never spoke to him after that' means?"

Whoa. This was new territory, and it was wired with emotional land mines. He treaded lightly. "Is that why you didn't tell Vivian you were coming?"

"I didn't know what to say to her. May I have another card?"

"You're not the one who had the affair and caused the split."

"I know, but I still feel like shit about it. Please, deal me another card.

"You shouldn't, you didn't do anything wrong," he said, sliding a third card toward her.

"You don't understand."

He didn't. There was a lull in the conversation. He changed the subject. "Poker doesn't take practice. It takes strategy."

"Strategy, huh. What's yours?"

"I figure out what my bottom line is before I start playing."

"What's your bottom line?" she asked.

"It depends. If there're four players, and no one's out, I'll hold if I have fifteen or higher. Sometimes I deviate from the plan."

"When?"

"It depends."

"On what?"

"On a million things."

"So, you don't actually have a strategy."

"I guess not." He reached under his right thigh and handed her the ace of spades. "Who's this?"

"You cheater." She threw down a pair of kings and a two of hearts.

He repeated the question. "Who is it?"

"Show me your hand first."

He laid down two jacks then held up the ace of spades again.

"Shit," she said, looking at his winning hand, then turning her attention to the ace of spades. "It doesn't have a photo," she said.

"It has a name. Look it up."

"Give me the card."

It had one of those generic black and while silhouettes often used as a placeholder when a photo wasn't available.

He handed the ace of spades to her and watched her type with her thumbs, then swiped the screen several times. She narrowed her eyes at the phone which he took to mean that something didn't add up.

"This is weird," she said. "I thought maybe a picture of him might come up on the Web, but I don't see anyone named Harold Fuchs that fits the profile."

She turned the screen around so he could see it.

"You look disappointed," she said. "Who were you expecting, the Secretary of Education?" She turned her phone around and continued browsing.

He'd seen decks of cards like this before. They weren't swag. They were called *Kill Cards*. When he was an active-duty detective, he'd seen the decks the Bureau of Prisons handed out to inmates with pictures and details about cold case homicides. Dozens of cases had been solved with the help of inmates. In 2003 the U.S. military passed out decks with pictures of the 52-most wanted in Saddam Hussein's government to troops deploying in Iraq. Saddam was pictured on the ace of spades. He'd heard stories about similar decks given to troops deployed in Afghanistan. The G.I. cards included a tip line where reports could be called in anonymously from anywhere in the world. Osama Bin Laden made the ace of spades on the post-9/11 deck. Harold Fuchs was the highest value target on this deck.

"All I see is a bunch of obituaries for people named Harold Fuchs."

"Are they all the same guy?"

"No. They're different."

"Any recent ones?"

"What are you getting at?"

"Just check."

"One's fairly recent. A month ago."

"What does his obit say?"

He watched her swipe using the tip of her finger.

"The usual," she said. "He was a loving father and husband, he's survived by three children, and two grandchildren."

"How old?"

"Fifty-two."

"Does it say where he went to school?"

"He didn't. He was a successful plumber who loved his work."

"That's not who we're looking for."

"Now we're looking for someone?"

He picked up all the cards and tapped the deck into a neat rectangle, then slid them back into the box and closed it. He patted his knee with his hand. "Put your feet up here."

"Why?"

"Just do it."

"They're dirty."

"I don't care. Put 'em up here."

She placed both ankles on his thigh. He twisted them gently looking at the matching blisters on her heels and toes, then rolled the cuffs of her pants halfway up her calves. He accidentally touched a sore spot.

She flinched. "Ouch."

The skin on the backs of her feet were a bright yellowish red and had bubbled. He lifted her legs and swung them onto the sofa cushion. "Wait here."

"What are you doing?"

"I'm going to give you a foot massage. No arguing. I'll be gentle." He went to the bedroom and riffled through his bag, then returned with a first aid kit, a handful of shampoo, an oversized bath towel draped over his shoulder and a miniature bottle of lavender lotion he'd put in the pocket of his bathrobe. He set the stuff on the kitchen counter and pulled a large lobster pot from under the sink and started the water. He held his right wrist under the flow and when it ran warm, added the shampoo cupped in his left palm, swirling both hands in the pot. The steamy coconut shampoo turned sudsy, and when the pot was half full, he dried his hands on the towel, removed it from the sink and carried it to the living room, setting it down on the floor at the base of the sofa. He sat next to her. "Put one of your paws in and give me the other one."

"What about your thumb?"

"It's nothing."

She dipped her toe in, then lowered one foot up to her ankle.

He took the lotion from the pocket of his robe, squeezed a dollop in his left palm and massaged the ball of her other foot with his good thumb while he used his forefinger to work carefully around the blisters.

"Ooh, that feels good." She tilted her head back and closed her eyes. "I was curious, so I looked up the meaning of Chantico while you were in the shower. It's Aztec for the goddess of fire."

He chuckled. "Makes you wonder what kind of temperament Chan had as a baby."

"I'm sorry about what happened to your bag," she said, "maybe I should've paid more attention to Blade's bad reviews."

"He had bad reviews?"

"He had a few complaints, but most people were happy with his service. There's always someone who'll find something to bitch about because they worry that they might be doing the world a disservice if they fail to report the slightest thing that went wrong."

"Some people like to bitch."

"True," she said.

"What did they complain about?"

A phone rattled on the coffee table. "I think that's mine." She pointed at her foot soaking in the scented water. "Will you grab it for me?"

He held her free ankle on his knees, leaned forward, picked up the phone and answered it. "Hello."

She shot him a stern look, narrowing her eyes, holding her hand out, jabbing at the air. He turned away from her.

A woman with a husky voice came on. "Is this the right number for Lauren Gold?"

"It is. May I tell her who's calling?"

"My name is Jennifer Watkins."

"Hold on a sec." He rolled up the left sleeve of his bathrobe and pressed the phone against his chest. "Do you know someone named Jennifer Watkins?"

She shook her head.

"May I tell her where you're calling from?"

"I'm from Mother of Mercy Hospital in Miami. Is she available?"

He looked at the time. It was almost nine o'clock at night and they were in the same time zone as Florida. "Hang on." He put his thumb on the mic. "It's someone calling from a hospital in Miami."

She stuck her hand out. He passed the phone to her, and he listened to her side of the convo thinking he should've put it on speaker.

"Hello? . . . Uh huh . . . Yes, that's right . . . When? . . . What? . . . Why? . . . No, I can't do that right now . . . No, no, I'm out of the country . . . The Bahamas . . . A week . . . I don't know . . . Maybe sooner if it's an emergency."

She cradled the phone on her shoulder and mimed a

pen and paper. He walked to the bedroom and returned with a notepad and pen, then continued to listen to one side of the conversation.

"Is he going to be alright? . . . How did it happen? . . . I'm ready," she said, balancing the pad of paper on her thigh, neck cranked over to one side as she wrote down the number. When finished, she put the phone to her ear. "Yes, I'll call in the morning . . . I understand . . . I can't promise anything, but I'll do my best . . . No, no I get it . . . Alright . . . Okay . . . Thank you . . . No, no, I understand you're just doing your job."

She set the phone face down on the sofa cushion.

The blood had drained from her face, and from her expression, looked like she'd just seen a ghost. "What was that about?"

She leaned forward and pulled the bath towel from his shoulder, then took her foot out of the water and blotted the sole. "My ex-husband was in an accident."

"Peter?"

She nodded.

"Why is the hospital calling you?"

"He has a head injury. He's in a coma."

"I still don't know why they called you?"

"Because I'm still his designated D.N.R."

He knew what that was. *Do Not Resuscitate.*

"He must not have updated the paperwork," she said. "His family is at the hospital and apparently, they're very upset. The hospital told them they can't make any decisions on his behalf. When we were married we had mutual Powers of Attorney and Durable Medical Powers. I'm the only person who can make medical decisions if he's inca-pacitated."

"Jesus," he said.

"You're the lawyer. Is there a way I can change it?"

"Not that I know of, and not from here, and certainly not without his permission. Maybe he'll wake up in the morning."

"It doesn't sound like that's going to happen."

He felt for her hand and squeezed it. "What are you going to do?"

"I think I have to go to Miami."

"Did they say what happened?"

"No, just that he was in an accident."

She put her face in her hands, and when she looked up at him, he saw tears welling.

"When he asked for a divorce, I thought I was going to die. He went around telling people that I wasn't in love with him anymore. He's the one who had a fling with someone at work. My therapist said that's what the guilty party does, they go around blaming the innocent person." She dabbed her eyes with a dry corner of the towel and sat cross-legged with her pant legs still rolled halfway up her calves. "When you accuse someone of doing what you're doing it's called projection. Not that hearing a logical explanation for it made me feel any better. How am I supposed to face his family?"

"Look at the upside."

"The upside?"

"You can't fuck it up."

She yanked the towel from him and balled it up on her lap.

"Ah, come on. You'll handle it. Come here."

She scooted away from him.

There was a knock on the door.

"Are you expecting someone?" she asked.

"No." He walked to the kitchen, leaned over the sink,

and lifted the curtains enough to peer out sideways toward the porch, still lit. "Wait here."

"Where are you going?"

"To put some pants on."

"Who is it?"

"Don't answer it."

Man, this had been a long day and it was about to get a whole lot longer.

11

THREE HOURS EARLIER

Chan closed her eyes and listened to the sounds of water breaking gently against the limestone sea wall. It had been almost three hours since she and C.J. had taken shelter outdoors and she couldn't sleep, sweating under two layers of clothing. A shrill sound whizzed past her ear.

Freaking mosquitos.

Using one hand, she grabbed the collar on her sweatshirt and twisted it, tightening the cloth over her nose and mouth. She peered up at the fuzzy half-moon casting an eerie glow on C.J.'s beige hoodie pulled over the top of his head. His eyes were closed, and he looked peaceful leaning against the hull of the dilapidated boat. When she felt the sting on her hand, she shook it, then lowered the collar covering her mouth and whispered loudly, "Are you sleeping?"

C.J. took the orange foam plugs from his ears. "I'm trying to."

"I don't see how. I can't stand this." She waved her hand in front of her face. "How much money do you have?"

"Not enough," he said, moving to a more upright position where he'd been sitting on a mostly flat boulder. He lifted one hip and removed his wallet. He cupped his billfold in his hand, trying his best to keep his sleeves pulled over his hands and activated his cell light to count the cash in the darkness. "About two hundred dollars. I have a stack of plastic, but we can't rent a room with a dozen different gift cards without looking suspicious. Besides, the desk's closed now."

"Maybe we should call it off and go home tomorrow. What if Tonk is playing us?"

"That doesn't make sense. He can't pull it off without us."

"Then why is he ghosting us?"

"I don't know. Maybe there's a good reason. Maybe his phone's dead. Maybe he tried to text us, and the message didn't get delivered. I'm exhausted. Let's get some sleep and talk about it in the morning. Maybe then we'll call it off."

"Okay," she said.

She and C.J. had left the table at the restaurant earlier because they didn't have enough money to pay for the restaurant meal at the resort. They'd walked the island with Tonk, killing time, waiting for the weather to clear in Nassau. When Tonk got a text message from his father, he'd told them to wait, that he'd walk to the plane and check in with his dad, then update them with the departure information. But he didn't come back. By the time they'd heard the old Beechcraft taxiing down the runway, it was too late to catch up or stop him. They'd taken turns texting and calling but he'd been ghosting them.

After they'd been stranded, they steered clear of the marina and resort so as not to arouse suspicion. It was a private island and camping without permission was trespassing, but they didn't have any other options. While it was still light out, she and C.J. had explored the uninhabited parts of the island, hunting for a place to camp for the night. They'd stumbled onto a rocky cove on a limestone cliff four feet above the water's edge where an abandoned sailing trimaran had gone aground up on the rocks, probably during a storm. From the condition of the boat, it'd been there a long time. The white paint was as dull as chalk and a variety of sea grasses and other vegetation had grown all around it, and a tree—now almost as tall as she—had taken root between the hull and one of the outrigger floats. The ground was covered in sand mixed with a layer of pink and white shell fragments: the remnants of conch shells that had been crushed.

The cove was set back about 20 feet from the shore and camouflaged by wild hedges and natural ground cover with green leaves the size of silver dollars. It provided shelter and had been easy to climb with a view from the top that had a partial line of sight to the marina clubhouse and the beachfront villas. The resort was nearly empty and there were so many vacant units, it seemed unfair that they were sleeping outside in the elements. She adjusted her big blue backpack on the ground and using it as a headrest, stretched out on the sandy surface with an angle on the misty sky.

She could make out Venus—the LED bulb of planets—but where were the stars? Sleeping under them was something she'd done as long as she could remember. Growing up, family vacations were spent at public campgrounds where her father had taught her to appreciate the outdoors: how to pitch a tent, build a campfire and cook on a propane stove. The everyday conveniences that she'd taken for granted at home became coveted tasks.

There was nothing better than fresh brewed cowboy coffee on a cold morning. Grinding whole beans by hand, setting the dented tin percolator atop the red coals, waiting until just before it reached the boiling point, then pouring hot coffee into cobalt blue and white speckled metal cups, watching the steam rise, the aroma of fresh brew filling the air. Memories like that one, and of toasting marshmallows on sticks until they turned a bubbly caramel brown, and of picking wild mushrooms and bird watching—those were the ones she had about the outdoors.

But that place was thousands of miles away in the mountains of California where she'd been mindful of rattlesnakes and coyotes, not mosquitos or sharks or what-ever else she should worry about on a remote island. She'd had a bad feeling about the trip but C.J. convinced her to come along. He said they needed her. She should have spent the little bit of money she'd been setting aside for this trip to visit her mom instead. Something rustled in the ground cover.

She poked C.J. "Did you hear that?"

He unplugged his ears. "Hear what?"

"I heard something moving in the brush."

"It's not brush. It's mangrove trees and sea oats. And no, I didn't hear it." He opened his eyes. "Be thankful it's not rain-ing." He pushed the orange foam buds back in his ears and closed his eyes.

She'd have offered to go halves on a room for the night, or even ponied up the entire amount but all her credit cards were a combination of past due and maxed-out and after paying her student loan, the cash balance in her bank account was barely enough to cover this month's insurance on her old pickup truck. The state of California paid C.J. 20 percent more than it paid her and gave him a vehicle and gas card. She'd made the mistake of telling her mother about it, who was prompted to deliver a diatribe about gender inequality.

The disparity in compensation had nothing to do with sex. C.J. was a math whiz who could write software algorithms; she was the weather girl who, like him, had minored in forestry. He could've made a lot more money working for a tech company in Silicon Valley. God knows plenty of them had courted him before he'd graduated. But not her. The market for meteorologists—for on-camera talent for TV and streaming platforms—was saturated with pretty girls in short skirts. She hated the ones that used sex to get ahead and would've rather flip burgers at a fast-food joint than undress for success. She'd sent her resume to the handful of media outlets that sent reporters into treacherous conditions, but she didn't have a demo reel, and had barely set foot outside California. When C.J. told her there was an opening for a meteorologist with the California state fire division, she applied for the job and was hired. She suspected that it was him that tipped the scale in her favor.

She sat up, took her phone out of her pants pocket and checked for messages. Still nothing from Tonk although all the messages she'd bombed him with had a DELIVERED notice. Raising the collar of her sweatshirt higher on her face to just beneath her eyes, she spoke again through two layers of fabric. "I feel like I'm going to suffocate."

"Or have a heat stroke," C.J. muttered. "How are we doing on drinking water?"

She unhooked the silver thermos attached to her backpack and shook it. "I have enough to get us through the night but we're going to have to ration it."

He held his hand out. She passed the water to him. He popped the cap and gulped.

"I said to go easy."

The biting insects were so aggressive they'd both dressed in double layers of clothing to try to stop them, long pants over shorts and sweatshirts over their T shirts. Unlike the mountains at home, there was no diurnal temperature drop at night and the moist heat was unbearable. The scream of bugs searching for their next meal was about to make her do something crazy, like strip naked and do a cannonball off the ledge, into the ocean.

C.J. sat up. "I read somewhere the American Indians used to smear alligator grease on their bodies to repel the mosquitos."

"Thanks for the tip. I should've sprung for a jar at the gift shop." She opened the weather app on her phone and looked at current conditions. Eighty-two degrees with 91 percent humidity, wind five miles per hour from the west, and 90 percent chance of thundershowers. She checked the weather at home. Fifty-seven degrees, 31 percent humidity with a 10-mile visibility, and no rain in the forecast for the next 10 days.

C.J. put his fingers to his lips.

She heard the engine sounds coming their way, too. An all-terrain vehicle traveling the gravel road along the embankment above the cove where they'd hunkered down for the night.

"Hide your phone and don't move," C.J. whispered.

She stuffed her glowing cell phone under her sweatshirt. The men on patrol on the road above where they were hidden swept the perimeter with a high lumen LED flashlight. This was the third time the watchmen had passed; why were they on active duty when the resort was practically a ghost town? She huddled closer to C.J. waiting for the vehicle to pass.

A moment later they were gone. She scratched her neck until her fingertips were sticky with blood. "I can't stay out here. I can't sleep in this shit with these bugs eating me alive."

"You're going to have to," C.J. said, pulling the collar of his undershirt up over the shaved sides of his head. He'd lowered the hoodie and threaded his fingers through his hair, puffing up the bushy top of his thick hair that had been flattened with sweat. He covered it back up. "It's just for the night. We'll figure it out in the morning," he said.

"We should've sprung for bug spray at the gift shop," she said.

C.J. shook his head and spoke through the fabric covering his mouth. "It wouldn't do shit to stop them. Trust me."

"Do you think someone knows we're here and they're looking for us?"

"I don't know. Maybe if they find us, they'll give us a place to sleep tonight."

She laid down on her side, rolled into the fetal position and adjusted the backpack horizontally against the hull of the abandoned sailboat like a makeshift headboard. She scooted on the sand as if hog-tied and nestled close to the backpack using it as extra protection from the elements.

At home she and C.J. shared a cramped two-bedroom work trailer paid for by the California forestry division. The last week in May fell between the end of Spring Break and the beginning of fire season and they'd been able to coordinate their vacation schedules. As fire-behavior analysts, the job required living remotely in a confined workspace outfitted with sophisticated computer programs where they spent most of their time staring at topography and weather screens. Living conditions were rustic: mountain snow, smokey air, snakes, and brownouts. But at least it wasn't city life.

She rolled over and scooted out from her roost. "Bitch."

"Shhh," C.J. warned.

"One of those suckers landed on my eyeball." She rubbed her eyelid. "I say we go knock on their door. Their lights are still on. What's the worst that can happen?"

"He could beat the crap out of me. You saw what he did to Blade. I think it's his fault they ditched us."

"All the more reason we should drop in on them, even though I think Tonk's dad had it coming," she said. "That was completely insane trying to fly through that storm. He could've gotten us all killed and if I was your size, I'd've punched him myself. Come on. Either that or you stay here by yourself because I can't stand it." She slapped her cheek and felt a dot of sticky blood on her palm. She pulled her backpack out and leaned it upright against the dried barnacles on the outrigger float, then squatted to pick it up.

C.J. jumped to his feet. "Gimme that." He brushed the sand from his clothes and hoisted her backpack onto the bow of the deserted sailboat.

Chan watched as he grabbed ahold of the pitted metal railing and climbed the hull, rising slowly to peer over the ledge like a human periscope. "Hand me my backpack."

She did as he asked.

He tossed it up onto the ledge above near the road where the ATV had passed, then offered his hand. "Climb up," he said.

She grabbed his hand and stepped onto a rock. Even on

tiptoes, she couldn't see over the ledge. But at over a foot taller than her, he could. "What do you see?"

"Nothing," he said.

A bolt of lightning flashed over water in the far-off distance. A moment later it crackled then finished with a soft boom. Her heart raced. At home there was a risk that lightning would start a fire. Unlike this part of the world, it rarely rained and when it did, the thunderstorm was the lede story. News choppers were dispatched to cover multi-car pileups and landslides. Million-dollar homes sliding off their foundations drew big TV ratings and millions of clicks.

Another bolt struck, this time on land. She looked up at the mast of the trimaran. "If lightning hits this thing, we'll fry."

"Alright," C.J. said. "But you're going to have to do the talking."

"Deal."

He laced his fingers together turning his palms into a stirrup. "You first," he said.

She placed her left hiking boot in his hand and took a step up, digging the toe of her other boot into the ledge. She tried pulling herself up with her forearms but wobbled, lacking the upper body strength. C.J. grabbed her ankles and pushed her up like a wheelbarrow. She slid the rest of the way on her belly. He passed his backpack up to her. It took both to get her pack up the ledge with him pushing overhead and her lifting. C.J. used his arms and elbows to pull himself up and landed on his chest. He took a knee next to her as they scanned the horizon, listening for the ATV.

Earlier they'd shadowed Vance and Lauren and watched from a distance, wishing they'd had the money for an oceanfront villa.

Now, with cloud cover thickening and beginning to blanket the sky they had to hurry. C.J. led the way trudging in the sand along the beachfront. They stopped before they reached the pool area and checked for witnesses. The clubhouse was dark and the pool area quiet. Dim landscape lights marked the paths between the buildings. C.J. looked exhausted, dropping the backpack from his shoulders and leaning forward, grabbing his knees. They were both out of breath, unable to outrun the mosquitos. They rested a minute then continued toward the villa.

As they approached the side of the guest house, C.J. motioned her to take a position next to him where they crouched below a window behind the hedge.

"The lights are still on," she whispered, heart pounding.

"Remember," C.J. said, "you're the one who's doing the talking."

"I know. Let's go," she said, apprehensive about how Vance Courage was going to react to a surprise nighttime visit. Not well, she guessed since he'd been screwed, too. Maybe he and Lauren would be sympathetic when they found out she and C.J. had been left behind.

If she'd known what else Tonk had done, she'd have opted to spend the night outside, feeding the mosquitos.

12

Vance untied the white terry cloth robe from around his waist and tossed it on the bed. He grabbed his jeans foregoing underwear in the rush. Using the doorknob for support, he hopped on one foot, sliding one leg into his pants, then the other. He zipped his pants, grabbed his shirt and pulled it over his head. He rushed out of the bedroom, past Lauren still sitting in the same spot on the sofa. He cracked the door open a couple of inches, just enough to talk. "What are you guys doing here?" he asked.

"Can we please come in?" Chan asked. "It's unbearable. The heat and bugs are killing us."

He watched C.J. lower Chan's backpack onto the wooden porch. Their faces dripped with sweat. C.J. danced in place stamping his feet and brushing sand from his pants.

"Take your shoes off and wait here." He pulled the door shut. "It's Bridezilla and company."

"Who?" Lauren asked.

"Chan and C.J."

"What?" She unrolled the cuffs of her pants and stepped into her flip flops. "They're still here? What do they want?"

"They want to come in. May I?"

"You can't very well leave them out there."

"Yes, I could," he said.

She lifted the pot of cooling coconut-scented water from the foot of the couch and headed for the kitchen. "What are you waiting for?" she asked.

He opened the door, "Come on. Hurry up."

"We're sorry to bother you," Chan said. "We tried to camp but the heat and mosquitos were killing us."

"Where's Tonk?" Vance asked.

C.J. and Chan exchanged glances, then C.J. said, "We don't know. I'm guessing he left with the plane. We've been texting and calling but he's not answering his phone."

"Why did he leave without you?" he asked.

"I don't know," Chan said.

"Which one of you stole my bag?"

"What?" C.J. asked. "Someone stole your bag?"

"We didn't do it," Chan said, pulling her sweatshirt over her head, her thick hair falling over her eyes.

"Someone took my bag and stole my passport."

"Tonk must've taken it," C.J. said, unbuttoning his trousers and lowering his pants to his ankles. He sat on one of the wicker chairs revealing hiking shorts underneath. "Search our stuff if you don't believe me." He gestured to their backpacks near the front door, then leaned over and pulled his long pants off by the cuffs. He tossed his pants on the floor. "Go ahead and search my pockets." He stood and held his hands over his head. "Go ahead."

"He's telling the truth," Chan said, sitting on the floor taking her long pants off. "Why would we steal it?"

"The three of you were together when you left the restaurant."

"So?" C.J. said.

"So, you would've noticed if he took my duffle."

Lauren glared at him. "You both look exhausted. Do either of you want some water?" She held up two cold bottles.

"Yes please," Chan said.

"I'm not going to lie," C.J. said to him, "we left because we couldn't afford to eat in the restaurant."

"Why should I believe you didn't take my bag? People who steal need money."

"What would we do with your passport?" C.J. said. "Do you think we'd show up at your door if we stole from you?"

Chan folded her long pants in half and looked around the villa. "This place is nice."

Vance picked up the white bath towel Lauren had left wadded up on the sofa.

Chan reached down and scratched her ankles. "I know," she said, "I look like I have the measles. They itch like a mother."

"Where were you 'til now?" Lauren asked.

"We found a place to camp for the night," C.J. said.

"It was miserable," Chan said. "I'm the one who couldn't stand it. I still can't believe Tonk left without us."

"How do you know him?" Vance asked.

"We go way back," C.J. said. "We're old friends."

"At least I thought we were," Chan said.

"Why did he leave you behind?" Lauren asked.

"I have no idea," Chan said.

"I thought the three of you were staying together in Nassau," Lauren said.

"We were," C.J. said.

"How well do you know him?" Vance asked.

"We're old college buddies," C.J. said.

"Why would the three of you vacation together?" Vance asked, watching their reactions. Chan and C.J. hesitated, then shifted their eyes making unspoken contact with each other.

C.J. answered, "We thought it would be fun. Chan found a cheap Airbnb in Nassau and we were splitting it three ways."

"Do you think Tonk would steal from me?"

They laughed.

"Yeah," Chan said, "Tonk would rob his mother's grave."

He noticed something caught Chan's eye and he zeroed in on it. The deck of cards on the coffee table.

"Are those yours?" he asked her.

"Are what mine?"

"The deck of cards."

Chan narrowed her eyes and shook her head. "No."

"Why would you think that?" C.J. asked.

"I found them on the plane," Lauren said.

"I didn't drop them if that's what you're getting at," Chan said. She stood and carried the clothes she'd removed and set them on top of her backpack near the front door next to C.J.'s.

"You can stay here tonight," Lauren said. "The place is only one bedroom, so you'll have to sleep in the living room."

C.J. ran his hand through his bushy hair. "I can pay you something."

"Nah," Vance said. "But if you want to shower you better get moving. It's getting late."

"I'll go first," Chan said.

"You could conserve water and shower together," Vance said.

"We're not a couple," Chan said. "We're friends, we work together."

"Hurry up," C.J. said.

Chan returned to her backpack, unzipped one half and reached inside. She removed a clean set of clothes and a quart-sized baggie filled with toiletries and headed for the bedroom.

Vance stopped her. "Don't go through the bedroom. Use that one. It opens to the master bathroom." He gestured to the door that led directly from the living room to a water closet with a toilet and sink. Beyond it, a second door led to the shower. A moment later, he heard the low hum of running water.

Vance asked C.J., "What do you do that you work together?"

"We work for the state of California."

"Doing what?"

"We work in forestry and fire protection," C.J. said.

"You're firefighters?" Lauren asked, sitting next to Vance on the longer of the two sofas.

"No. I'm a fire behaviorist and she's a fire meteorologist. When fire season rolls around, which'll be next month, I'll start building computer models. I try to predict which direction the fire will travel and Chan inputs weather data to see how it'll affect my models."

"Does Tonk work with you?" Vance asked.

C.J. shook his head.

"What does he do?" Lauren asked.

"He's mostly unemployed. He's an aspiring screenwriter. He went to film school and got a four-year degree, and he gets some work here and there as a production assistant on

TV shows and film sets, making a couple of hundred dollars a day. He worked part time as a barista at a coffee shop in L.A. He couch-surfs and plays video games until it comes time to help pay the rent."

"How did you meet?" Lauren asked.

"At school," C.J. said. "The three of us went to the same college our freshman year. We met at an intercollegiate poker tournament."

"You play competitively?" Vance asked.

"I wish. We weren't good enough."

"Did Tonk change schools?" Vance asked.

"No. Chan and I transferred to a state school up north."

"Why?" Vance asked.

"It's complicated."

How complicated could it be? "You've piqued my curiosity," Vance said.

"There wasn't a master plan," C.J. said. "Chan didn't like L.A. It's more of a coincidence that she and I ended up at the same school. Chan is the one who was interested in forestry, and I minored in it with no intention of doing what I'm doing. The job I have didn't exist at the time. I was a math student. Plus, the whole thing is kind of a scam."

"What's a scam?" Lauren asked.

"In the real world they don't practice the stuff they taught us in school. You can't even talk about it without risking getting fired from your job."

"What?" Vance asked. "What can't you talk about?"

"I guess you're not going to record our conversation and turn me in to my bosses," C.J. said. "It's frustrating. They teach forest management in school and then we don't practice it. They let the kindling build up until it's a powder keg and they don't do anything to clean it up. They stopped doing controlled burns decades ago. It's weird because controlled burns are what's in the textbooks but when the fires start, they blame it on everything but poor forest management."

"Welcome to the real world," Vance said, steering the conversation back to the topic at hand. "You remained friends with Tonk?"

"I thought we did," C.J. said.

"When's the last time the three of you got together?" Lauren asked.

C.J. hesitated and furrowed his brow as if searching his memory bank. "You know, I can't remember."

Vance wasn't buying it.

"Hey." Chan stood in the doorway with her hair twisted in a towel like the top of a soft ice cream cone.

"That was quick," Lauren said.

"I feel a million times better," Chan said, dressed in beige shorts and a light green sleeveless top. "It took a while to figure out how that shower worked, but once I did it was the highlight of the day." She carried her dirty clothes and baggie, setting it on the floor near her backpack. She tilted her head forward letting the towel unravel from her head. She folded it in half, tilted her head to the side and blotted hunks of hair. "What did I miss?"

"Not much," C.J. said getting up from the sofa. "Gimme that." He snatched the damp towel from her. "I'll be quick," he said, grabbing his backpack from near the front door and closing the bathroom door behind him.

Chan took a seat in one of the wicker chairs next to where C.J. had been sitting.

"C.J. says you're a fire meteorologist," Lauren said.

"It sounds more exciting than it is," Chan said, combing the knots from her hair with her fingers. "We live in a trailer staring at computer monitors twenty-four/seven. You have hurricanes and we have fires. They've been getting worse and the state has been focusing on finding creative ways to fight them by predicting when and where they'll happen.

"They started getting a lot more serious about it last year after a fire jumped a granite ridge and threatened a resort town, one where a lot of rich people live. No fire had ever breached that area before and C.J. and I predicted it would, but no one took us seriously. I saw unusual weather patterns and when C.J. input the data, the computer model predicted the winds would create hotspots that would cross the ridge and start fires that would threaten homes."

"Is that the one that threatened Lake Tahoe?" he asked.

"That's right," Chan said.

"I read about it," Vance said.

"Everyone did. It was national news," Chan said, leaning over and scratching the small welts on her shins. "We're the reason they were able to contain it. That and the fact that a lot of influential people own homes there. It's not like the rural areas where they shut down the power grid when the wind blows. You know how it goes."

"The poor always bear the brunt," Lauren said.

"Speaking of poor," Vance said, "if Tonk can't afford to pitch in for rent, what's he doing going on a vacation?"

Chan folded her arms across her chest. "Just because he can't find a decent paying job doesn't mean he shouldn't enjoy life."

Vance glanced at Lauren, then asked Chan, "What did the three of you plan to do in Nassau?"

"Hang out on the beach," Chan said.

"There're nice beaches in California," Vance said. "Why fly to the other side of the world to soak up sun when you could do it at home?"

"We like adventures. Have you ever swum the Pacific?"

"No," he said.

"The water's deep and it's always cold and I don't like deep cold water. I read on the 'Net there's an island in The Bahamas where you can walk out into the water for a half mile and the water is only knee high. And there's another one where you can swim with wild pigs. I saw a picture of the pigs dog-paddling in the most beautiful clear light blue water. What about you?" Chan asked, tilting her head to the side and running her fingers through her damp hair. "What are you planning to do when you get to Nassau?"

"I'm not sure I can get there without a passport," Vance said.

Chan made a sad face. "That's right. That sucks. What are you going to do?"

"He hasn't figured it out yet," Lauren said. "We have to wait until tomorrow to talk to someone. What about you? How are you getting to Nassau?"

"We haven't figured it out either. C.J.'s going to try to track down Tonk tomorrow to see if they're coming back for us." Chan got up and walked to the front door and returned with her phone.

"Do you think he will?" Lauren asked.

"I guess we'll find out," she said.

"Check this out."

Chan held her phone up and Lauren leaned forward to look at the screen. It was a news story. Lauren read the headline.

'CALIFORNIA HAS AN ALGORITHM FOR FIGHTING WILDFIRES'

"C.J. was written up in a national news story after he predicted what the Tahoe fire was going to do," Chan said. "It's pretty exciting. His algorithms are going to revolutionize forest management. That's what some people think."

"What about you?" Lauren asked.

"What about me?"

"Did you get any credit?" she asked.

"No, and I didn't deserve to. I'm just the weather girl and there are a lot of people that could do my job. C.J.'s the one who wrote the code."

"Doesn't it just mean they'll be able to make better predictions?" Vance said.

"What do you mean?" Chan asked.

"Meteorologists have taken hurricane predictions to an art form but that doesn't mitigate the damage they do."

"You're right," Chan said. "C.J. keeps reminding me it's a paycheck. We have to pay our bills. It's hard enough staying ahead of student debt."

"Why are you vacationing together if you're not a couple?" Lauren asked.

Vance wanted to know the same thing and had been running ideas in his head about how to pose the question. Lauren did the dirty work.

Chan shrugged. "I don't know. Maybe it's because we don't know very many people. We live and work in a remote area where the nearest grocery store is forty miles away. We have no social life. C.J.'s my best friend."

"He told us you're the one who was interested in forestry," Vance said.

"I was. My dad was a Hot Shot."

"Sorry," Lauren said, "but what's a Hot Shot?"

"They're an elite group of firefighters."

"That's impressive," Vance said, nodding.

"My dad was an impressive person."

"Why did C.J. change schools?" Vance asked.

"Default, I guess. He had a full ride on a volleyball scholarship at a school in Southern California. It's where I met him and where we met Tonk."

C.J. ducked under the doorway and leaned against the threshold. "I was pretty good at math," C.J. said. "Not as good as I was at volleyball, but I was in the top ten percent of my class."

"A volleyball scholarship," Vance said, genuinely impressed, "What position did you play?"

"I was an outside hitter, until I lost my scholarship."

"Did you get hurt?" Lauren asked.

"No. It's a long story," C.J. said, looking refreshed. He took a seat in the wicker chair across from Chan.

"He's being modest. It was a Division One university, and the team won the NCAA Championship his freshman year." Chan pressed her fingers on the insect bites on her forearms. "How long are these going to itch? I thought a hot shower would help but I think it made it worse." She leaned over and scratched the backs of her calves, grimacing.

"If you didn't get hurt, why did you quit the team?" Vance asked.

"He didn't quit," Chan said. "He got kicked off."

"Why?" Vance asked.

"Tell them," Chan said to C.J.

"I didn't get kicked off the team," C.J. said. "They never gave me an official reason. When the new semester rolled around, they didn't extend my scholarship."

"You're a smart guy," Vance said. "You must have an idea about why they cut you. Chan showed us the article about the algorithms you wrote for fire prevention. You were more than an athlete."

C.J. shrugged. "I started out majoring in statistics, studying probability and control theory. I didn't invent computer modeling for firefighting. There've been enthusiasts that've been doing fire forecasting for decades."

"I think it had something to do with a paper he wrote for his statistics class," Chan said.

C.J. turned his head and glared at Chan.

"What was the premise?" Vance asked.

Chan ignored C.J.'s warning. "It was a paper on how grant money is divvied out to university research departments. I read it. It was based on data."

"Did the university think he got it wrong?" Lauren asked.

"No," Chan said. "He got it right. He was right over the target, and they didn't like that."

"What was your theory?" Vance asked.

"Shut up Chan," C.J. said.

She kept on. "He showed statistical data that over ninety percent of grant money is divvied out to researchers that come up with conclusions that fit the results that the university prefers."

"And what conclusions were those?" Vance asked.

"What does it matter," C.J. said. "I lost my scholarship over it. I learned my lesson."

He no longer believed they were just three old friends who'd gotten together for a little sand and surf.

They were up to something, and it was becoming clear what he was going to have to do.

13

L   auren stood, opened the mini-bar and removed an airplane bottle of vodka. "Here," she said, cracking the cap and handing it to Chan. "Put some of this on the those."

"Who knew?" Chan placed an ankle on one knee and used the tip of her forefinger to dab the clear liquid on the red spots.

Lauren had been trying to get a better look at the garter belt tattooed on Chan's upper thigh. Was it barbed wire? A forest? What were the yellow and red accents?

Chan caught her staring at it. "It's in memory of my dad. The day I get married he won't be there to give me away."

"Why not?" she asked.

"My dad died in a fire trying to rescue an elderly woman and her dog from her mobile home."

"I'm so sorry," she said.

"It's worse," C.J. said. "He's a missing person."

"How can he be a missing person if he died in the fire?" Lauren asked.

Chan tilted the bottle of clear alcohol onto the tip of her finger and swabbed more on the red welts on her wrist. "He's not technically dead."

"I don't understand," Vance said.

Chan put the cap on the bottle and twisted it. "There were eyewitness accounts of him running into the mobile home and he never came out, but the state of California won't declare him dead without proof."

"Proof of what?" Vance asked.

"My mom's lawyer has been working on it for almost two years," Chan said.

"Working how?" Lauren asked.

"My mom's attorney subpoenaed the state for DNA evidence but they've been stonewalling."

"Why do you need DNA evidence?" Vance asked.

"Because it's the only way to identify the remains. All the bodies were charred. My dad is a hero. He ran toward the fire. The conditions were right for a fire tornado. It tore through the mobile home park in less than five minutes. There were no survivors."

C.J. said, "If it happened in Palo Alto or Brentwood or Beverly Hills, the state would have directed a lot of resources to the recovery effort. Her dad would have been a hero and his body would've lay in state in the Capitol rotunda. The residents of the city of Paradise were working class people. The folks in Sacramento didn't give a shit about them and would rather sweep it under the rug and forget it ever happened."

Lauren folded her hands across her chest. "Jesus. That's awful." Worse than awful. It was a nightmare.

"Chan's dad was part of an elite unit," C.J. said, "and certain politicians didn't want the media to get wind that a

Hot Shot died in the fire. It would've attracted media attention."

"I used to be a cop," Vance said. "Firefighters are a band of brothers, like cops. They stick together and watch each other's backs. What about them? Why aren't they demanding justice?"

"The union bosses don't want to piss anyone off," C.J. said. "They've been deadlocked in a collective bargaining agreement that ran out last year and it puts the firefighters and the union in a tough position."

She watched Vance shake his head in disgust.

"So, no funeral or memorial service?" Lauren asked.

"No," Chan said. "My mom has to wait until he's declared legally dead before she can mark his grave or collect his benefits."

"I thought the power company was found negligent and settled for a shitload of money," Vance said.

"Over thirteen billion dollars," Chan said.

"That's more than a shitload," Lauren said.

"They never disclosed where the money went," C.J. said. "I tried to find out and there's no public record of it. The whole thing is a big cover up and you know what they say about cover ups."

Chan said, "Missing persons aren't entitled to settlement money. Without physical evidence, my mom has to wait for five years. Then my mom's lawyer can file a petition with the court asking the judge to 'presume' he's dead. Who knows how long that'll take or if there'll be anything to collect by then. Or if the judge will even agree to do it."

"Does your mom have a good lawyer?" Vance asked.

"I don't know. She liked his name. Harry Valiant. I tried to talk to her about it, but she'd already made up her mind."

"How's she doing?" Lauren asked.

Chan narrowed her eyes. "Is that a serious question?"

C.J. got up from his chair, walked around the sofa and knelt next to Chan, putting his arm around her shoulder. Chan rebuffed his attempt to comfort her.

Chan got up from the chair and launched into a diatribe. "My mom's fighting the state of California and a powerful corporation. She lost the house, has no health insurance, and used up all their savings on a lawyer with a promising name that hasn't done jack shit to help her. How do you think she's doing?"

"I'm going to shower and call it a night," Lauren said, the self-inflicted humiliation radiating from her cheeks. How could she have been so insensitive?

"Alright," Vance said. "I'll see you in a few."

"Hey," Chan walked in front of her, blocking the door to the bedroom. "I'm really sorry for going off on you like that. That wasn't fair. It's been a really long day and I just took it out on you. Thanks for letting us stay the night. We both really appreciate this."

"I'm sorry your family had to go through something like that," Lauren said. "I'll see you in the morning."

She sat on the edge of the bed with her head in her hands running the conversation through her head. C.J. had made a valid point. It was always the cover up.

She googled 'wildfire Paradise California' and clicked the top link.

The Camp Fire was the most expensive insured natural disaster in recorded history. The firestorm tore through the towns of Paradise and Concow wiping out 95 percent of the homes and businesses, killing 85 people. Twelve more residents were injured along with 6 firefighters. She looked at the horrific pictures of the fire and the aftermath of destruction.

Her heart stopped. The news article reported a missing person. But there was nothing about a missing firefighter.

Paradise?

More like hell.

Chan was employed by the same people who wrecked her family. How did that work?

14

NASSAU, BAHAMAS
OVER-THE-HILL DISTRICT

Tonk rolled onto his back on the lumpy thin twin mattress and laced his fingers behind his neck. The air inside the dark cramped room was hot and sticky. He opened his eyes and stared at the blades of a wobbly ceiling fan creaking slowly overhead. He'd dozed off once for a few minutes but awoke to calypso music and the smell of marijuana wafting in through the open window. He wiped the sweat from his brow and dried his palms on the edge of the mattress. He'd left the door to his room ajar for cross ventilation but twice he'd seen shadows loitering in the dark hallway. He got up and looked out the window. Across the street the skeleton of a burned-out vehicle, its hood missing and charred engine exposed, listed in the tall grass. The A-frame roof of the house was completely gone and so were the windows.

He'd caught a cab and ridden alone to the Airbnb rental house located off busy East Bay Street bordering the Over-the-Hill district in downtown Nassau. The single public streetlamp out front flickered, emitting a continuous buzzing sound. This was no place for tourists. It was more like the bowels of the city, indistinguishable from the poorest neighborhoods in Miami. On the ride over, the taxicab headlights lit the skinny roads lined with matchbox houses, many built on blocks surrounded by rickety chain link fences and wrought iron gates with knife sharp tips. Others were partially hidden behind crumbling concrete and cinderblock walls. It was nighttime when he'd been dropped off and he'd been on high alert ever since. The locals loitering and partying in the street had clustered in a half circle around the cab when he'd arrived. The driver blared his horn and yelled to get them to disperse.

He'd hurried up the poorly lit concrete stairs and found the key hidden beneath a slimy black rubber mat on the second story concrete landing. Before they'd agreed to split the cost three ways, Chan had sent him a link to the website advertising the two-story pink stucco building. It was now apparent the boxy fixer-upper had been haphazardly subdivided to accommodate multiple small groups when he had to go down the hall to use the common bathroom to take a leak.

The harrowing Mister Toad's Wild Ride he'd been subjected to must've been a shock to tourists expecting to start their island vacation with a leisurely trip from the airport to their local destination. The cabbie spent most of the time hanging halfway out the car window cussing at motorists and pedestrians. The driver steered with one hand and used the other to shake his fist and shoot his middle finger. He blew through red lights and stop signs, driving on the sidewalk more than once scaring the bejesus out of people out for evening strolls. A group of diners sitting at an outdoor café fled their sidewalk table turning the chairs over as they ran for safety.

"Mudda Sick," the driver yelled at them, whatever that meant.

The mattress springs creaked as he sat up and pulled his backpack from under the bed. He fished for his phone and checked for messages. There was nothing new: just the barrage of unanswered texts and calls from Chan and C.J. and a couple of phone messages he missed earlier from Savient, the student debt collection agency. They called him as many as eight times daily every day but Sunday. They could call him a hundred times a day and it wouldn't make a difference. He didn't answer them anymore and he didn't listen to the voice messages. Why bother? He couldn't make the payments on his student loan.

He selected all the messages from Chan and C.J. and tapped the digital garbage can icon. What good would it do to try to explain it to them now? Sure, he'd put up a minor fight on their behalf but what choice did he have when his father threatened to leave him behind? Wasn't it better for someone to check-in to the rental house?

After his dad landed the plane, Tonk followed orders helping transfer dozens of large cardboard boxes stacked in the cargo hold of the Beechcraft into an awaiting minivan. The driver who'd come to collect his merchandise opened a box to inventory the contents. Tonk spied over his shoulder. The boxes were packed with cartons of cigarettes. He'd seen the American brands selling for ten bucks a pack at convenience stores in Nassau and the shipment filled the cargo area of the buyer's beater minivan. The man paid cash to his dad then offered him a carton of smokes and a lift to a local night spot as a tip, he guessed. He'd turned down the cigarettes but accepted a ride, then caught a cab from a busy watering hole where the man had dropped him off.

Jesus. It was too hot to sleep. He got out of bed, fumbled for the wall switch and turned on the overhead light. He opened the text app on his phone and pulled up C.J.'s cell number. He padded the keys with his thumbs: made it to Nassau will call tomorrow and explain everything.

He held his index finger over the green SEND button, then backspaced and deleted the message. He set the phone on the shaky wooden crate next to the bed, turned off the overhead light, walked to the doorway and poked his head out into the dark hall. Hearing the voices outside growing louder, he left the room and headed toward the dark stairwell. When he reached the bottom, he stood in the shadows and watched people mingling inside the chain link fence surrounding two houses. From their accents he guessed they were locals.

A man spotted him and approached.

"Hey mon," the Black man with the Bahamian accent said. "Why you look so sad? 'Dis is party time."

"Long day."

"Maybe a nice girl to cheer you up? Or some-ting else?"

"Nah. I'm waiting for some friends."

" 'ave it your way den," he said. "What ah 'bout some 'omemade Goombay Smash on the 'ouse?"

"Sure," he said, getting up and following the man, catching the people milling about casting sly glances at him. He walked past the musicians. Two men sat in folding chairs flanking a fellow standing in the middle banging on an animal skin drum with his open palm. The drum—the diameter of a bicycle tire and as deep as a lobster pot—was slung over his shoulder, fitted with a wide rainbow strap.

The man to the left of the drummer sat with his eyes closed squeezing an ancient brown accordion.

The man who'd invited him to join the party led him to a rickety card table set up on a patch of brown grass behind the chain link fence in the area between the two houses. A slender young woman in a strapless lime green dress ladled liquid from a clear plastic punch bowl into a triangular paper cup.

"What kind of music is this?" he asked her.

" 'tis called rake 'n' scrape. You come from 'Merica?"

"Yes," he said, sipping from the cup. The fruity coconut rum drink tasted sweet and strong. He left the table and headed to where the alluring scent of marijuana wafted. He was jonesing for a hit, but his dad warned him the local laws were so tough if he were caught, he wouldn't pass Go. The aroma led back to the three old musicians set up in a semi-circle beneath a weak, wide funnel of light emanating from the streetlamp overhead. The trio donned matching white pants and blue and white shirts with a pattern of repeating waves and seagulls. The older man playing the accordion acknowledged him, smiling and nodding as he squeezed and tapped out a melody on the keyboards on opposite ends of the instrument.

What instrument made the scratching sound that reminded him of fingernails on a chalkboard? Or a cat in the middle of a night fight? His brain sucked up the booze like a dry sponge and feeling tipsy he walked closer and took a knee in front of the guy playing the strange instru-ment. With the man hunched over it he couldn't tell what it was, but it was nothing he'd ever heard before. Noticing his curiosity, the man stopped playing and held up both parts of his instrument. Tonk's eyes had adjusted to the low light enough to see one part was an old carpenters saw with a wide, rusty metal blade and the other, a butter knife.

"Please," Tonk said, "keep playing."

He watched as the man clamped the base of the saw between his brown leather shoes making an arc between his knees. He ran the knife along the teeth of the saw and flexed the blade to make different sounds. *Blade 'n' Scrape.* The music was a lot like his old man.

He gulped the rest of the fruity rum drink and returned to the punch bowl. "Do you mind?" He held out the empty paper cup. The woman smiled as she refilled it, the half-moon and fuzzy streetlight overhead highlighting a wide gap between her two upper front teeth. He downed it and asked for more. The man who'd introduced him to the free booze approached.

"I'm Moo. I own de house."

"Tonk," he said.

"I don't remember you an' I would remember dat name."

"My friend Chan booked it."

"Ah, you mean Chantico?"

"That's right."

"Don't take dis de wrong way, but I figured you would be Black."

"And I figured the place would have air conditioning. Go figure," he said, wadding the paper cup in his hand and turning toward the stairs, noticing for the first time the mounds of dead cockroaches piled up like mole hills in the corners beneath the dark stairwell. Moo followed him.

"Where is Chantico? I dint see her."

"Her plane was delayed."

"Too bad 'bout that. Enjoy your stay."

Halfway up the stairs he tossed the paper cup into a dark corner knocking over a hill of dried roach husks. He went inside and closed and locked the bedroom door. Man, the air was stuffy. Even by his standards this shithole was roughing it. He turned on the overhead light, lifted the mattress and removed the 9-millimeter and passport. Holding the gun with two hands, he aimed it at a spot where the bright blue paint had peeled from the wall. The thick polymer grip felt good in his hands. Lightweight yet stout. He set it down then opened the passport and stared at the small picture of Vance Courage. The lousy photo was over-exposed and didn't do him justice. He flipped the page. The most recent stamp was two years old from Cancun, Mexico. He looked at the headshot again, closed the passport and slid it into the pocket of his tight black shorts. He set his backpack on the bed and removed the two spare clips he'd stolen and hid them in the side pocket of his bag. He checked the safety on the Glock then stashed it beneath the mattress.

He checked the time. It was after midnight. He raised his arms and pulled the lime green tank top he'd been wearing since yesterday over his head and threw it at the foot of the bed. He slid the pink scrunchie holding his man bun in place and shook his shoulder length curly hair, now damp from humidity and sweat. He sniffed his armpits and grimaced.

He punched the stinky pillow trying not to think of all who'd slept on it before shoving it behind his neck hoping the place didn't have bedbugs or lice. He'd gotten a case of STD crabs at a drunken frat party-turned-orgy his sopho-more year of college. They were a bitch to get rid of. He shuddered at the feeling of something crawling in his underwear and the bitter smell of the bottled lice killer he'd bought from the drug store. And the look of disgust on the face of the young woman at the cash register who'd sold it to him. It came with a tiny comb he used to rake the dead bugs and eggs from his thick black pubic hair. The memory made him mad. Those were some of the fringe benefits of a useless diploma and a mountain of debt.

It'd help if he could find something to cover the pillowcase. But what? He looked around the room, and not seeing anything fished the clear plastic baggie from his knapsack. He activated the flashlight on his cell phone and took a left out of the bedroom and walked the dark hall to the communal bathroom. He waved his hand in the darkness feeling for the metal chain and pulled it. The bare yellow bulb overhead cast a sickly glow. When the floor came to life his heart dropped into his gut. A mosaic of cockroaches scattered, disappearing down the drains and behind the loose baseboards. He tiptoed toward the sink, started the water and splashed his face.

Towels? There wasn't even a roll of toilet paper on the empty holder. He removed a travel sized bottle of mouthwash from the baggie, rinsed and spit into the rusty porcelain sink. Then he looked at himself in the mirror, turning his neck side to side. He reached into his back pocket and removed the stolen passport. Leaning against the sink he held the passport in the mirror and looked at his own reflection next to the small photo of Vance Courage. Holding his hair behind his head with his free hand and covering his pencil thin mustache with his fingers, he imagined what he'd look like clean-shaven with shorter hair. He tucked the passport back into his pocket and walked to his room. He put the baggie of toiletries in his backpack and tossed the bag on the lower mattress of the metal framed bunk bed located on the opposite side of the cramped room—where Chan and C.J. should've been.

He heard a knock on the bedroom door. " 'ello." A woman's voice came from the hallway.

"Wait a minute," he yelled, pulling the green muscle shirt over the top of his head. He opened the door an inch and peeked out. The same woman with the gap in her teeth who'd served him the rum drink stood in the dark hallway.

"I 'ate to bother you, but I forgot to give you dis."

She carried something in her arms as if cradling a baby. He opened the door farther. She held out two mismatched beach towels with a single roll of thin ply toilet paper on top. Like a cherry.

"Thank you," he said.

"Is there any-ting else you need?"

"No." He closed the door, then changed his mind. She was ten feet down the hall. "I have a question."

She returned.

"Is there a barbershop near here?"

"Dere's one a couple of blocks away on Hay Street."

"Can I walk there?"

She nodded.

"Does it have a name?"

"Prince and Princesses. I don't tink it is right one for you. It's for . . . umm . . . locals. Oh, da sip sip if you go dere. I hear it now." She rolled her eyes.

"Sip sip?"

She held out her hand and tapped her thumb and forefinger, together over and over like a crab claw. "Dey talk, talk, talk."

"Ah," he said, "the gos-sip."

"Sip sip," she said.

"You know what my grandmother used to say?" he asked.

"Come now," she said, raising her eyebrows anticipating his answer.

"That when they're talking about me they're giving someone else a rest."

"Dat is a good one."

"I'm Tonk," he said.

Before she could tell him her name she flinched at three loud popping sounds. "Oh Lordy," she said.

"Fireworks?"

"No. Dem is gunshots."

"I thought drugs and guns were illegal and there's a zero-tolerance policy. Like mandatory jail time."

She put her hands on her hips and shook her head. "You sure yinner 'Merican?"

He heard sirens in the distance.

"If you go to da barber, be careful. Oh, the sip sip," she said, "I swear I kin hear it now." She headed toward the stairwell then hesitated. "Da crime. Da ladies can't walk da streets. How da world is goin' da wrong way."

"I guess," he said. "You better be careful."

He suppressed the urge to follow her, watching until she disappeared down the dark stairwell. He locked the door, pushing the metal hook into the eyelet screwed into the door frame. He dragged a pitted metal folding chair and jammed it under the doorknob. It wouldn't stop anyone, but it'd make enough noise to give him a warning if he needed to react.

He pulled the thin curtain away from the screened open window and saw red and blue lights spinning in the distance. He pulled his tank top off, used it to wipe his brow then tossed it on the lower bunk.

He plugged his cell phone into the wall socket and watched the tiny lightning bolt appear next to the two service bars on the upper corner of the screen. New texts bubbled up. Both were from C.J. and the last one said, Thanks a lot dude.

What could he say? He deleted the new messages from C.J. then set his phone to AIRPLANE mode, spread the beach towels over the sheets and pillow and turned off the overhead light.

He laid on his back watching the silhouette of the fan rotating above. He got out of bed, turned on the light and grabbed the strap of his backpack from the lower bunk on the opposite side of the room. He removed the burner still in the box. He set the prepaid phone card still wrapped in the receipt on the edge of the crate doubling as a nightstand. He opened the phone, inserted the SIM card and battery, unwound the charger and plugged the burner into the outlet below his personal phone. He copied the phone numbers he'd need onto the contacts list of the burner and removed the SIM card from his personal phone then downloaded the tracking app onto the burner.

Was it fair to be angry with his father? Sure, his father made a bad decision flying into the storm and stranding his friends. But he was also risking a lot to help him. It was his own poor decision making that had gotten him into this mess. He'd run the plan by his dad and asked him for help flying him and his friends to Nassau. His father had gone beyond the request and called around, discovering the yacht *The Parent Minus* had sailed last week from Miami and was docked at Chub Cay. Before he'd hatched the plan his father had already sold two seats on the plane.

It was his dad's idea to plant the tracking device on the yacht. In order to do that they had to reroute the plane. The two paying passengers on board complicated the mission. Flying into the storm was a diversionary tactic. It'd scared the shit out of Courage and his friend making it easier to distract them when his dad ordered them off the plane to wait for the weather to clear. Chan and C.J. were collateral damage. They were pissed off but he'd smooth things over later. After Courage decked his dad, he assumed wrongly that his father would appreciate that he'd tried to even the score by taking his passport.

Tonk launched the tracking app on the burner. The flashing yellow dot on the screen showed *The Parent Minus* hadn't moved. He scrolled through the menu options and activated the alert system setting the app to ping if the target moved. Then he opened the weather app to check marine conditions. There was a small craft advisory in effect until tomorrow morning. Although the conditions were forecast to steadily improve throughout the day, conditions in this part of the world were notoriously changeable. He took his personal phone off charge, moved his backpack from the lower bunk to his bed and dropped his personal phone in the bottom.

He got out of bed and removed his shorts. The passport fell out of the back pocket. He turned on the overhead light and looked for it but didn't see where it had landed. Squatting, he looked under the bed and saw the leather folder. Holding onto the lumpy mattress he reached under the bed and retrieved the document. The front cover of the passport slipped out of the black leather sleeve, and something fell to the floor. Sitting on the edge of the bed in his underwear, he leaned down and picked up the green credit card. It belonged to Vance Courage. He checked the expiration. Good for two more years. He slipped the credit card inside the black leather passport holder, put the SIM card for his personal phone behind it and tucked the passport cover back into one of the bifold slots.

Talk about luck. He had a gun. Spare ammo. And a credit card with no limit.

He'd deal with Chan and C.J. first thing in the morning. He'd call them from the burner, patch things up, explain that it wasn't his idea to leave them behind, maybe lie and claim he lost his phone, that it was all his dad's fault. He twisted the corners of his thin mustache and stroked his goatee, smiling at the next thought.

Harold Fuchs didn't know what was coming.

But he did, and he could hardly wait. Good thing he'd downed enough rum to numb his brain, or the excitement would've kept him up all night.

15

L auren stepped to the side and shut off the water. The long, hot shower she'd been looking forward to lasted less than five minutes when the water suddenly ran cool. She opened the thick glass door wishing she knew which towel Vance had used. Grabbing a damp one hanging from a hook on the back of the bathroom door she dried quickly, pulled a loose lavender T-shirt over her head and tiptoed into the bedroom. She pulled the navy-blue bedspread back and climbed under the blanket and sheets warming her body. She'd brought something sexier to wear, a soft, lacy apricot-colored camisole but left it wrapped in pastel floral tissue in her carry-on bag.

She'd been nervous about the trip. While Vance had never pressured her for sex, she wondered what would happen if they did it. How would it affect their relationship? Would he try to keep it casual? Wasn't that something men could do? Her ex told her men showed love through sex. If that was true, how did the one-night stand fit in? She'd asked her ex, Peter, about it and was still waiting for the answer. She'd stayed up late one night googling 'how do men show love.' The answer was 'lovemaking' and 'physical intimacy' —code for sex. While it didn't explain the casual hookup, she was still getting spam from love coaches and dating sites.

She'd planned to talk to Vance about it before the trip but every time the opportunity presented itself, she lost her nerve. How would he answer? He'd never been married or even lived with a woman or had anyone special that he'd ever mentioned. They had a bond that was hard to describe. She was attracted to him but if she slept with him, what were the rules? A pit formed in her stomach.

She wasn't naïve. Some men were into the chase and once they got what they wanted—sex—they moved on. She'd slept with Peter on the third date and look how that worked out. They'd moved in together the first month, and a year later were married at the courthouse. If there was anything she'd learned, it was that things ended the way they began. In with a bang. Out with a poof. She squeezed her temples with her thumbs until her head hurt then heard voices and laughter coming from the living room. It sounded like Chan and C.J. would be entertaining Vance tonight.

She got out of bed, unzipped the side pocket of her roller bag at the foot of the bed and removed her tablet and the book she'd bought for the trip. Climbing back into the toasty bed she switched on the bedside lamp, set the tablet and book on the nightstand, plumped the king bed pillows behind her back and opened the small hardcover book to the Table of Contents.

Who knew there were so many card games? The book began with an *Introduction and History to Card Games* and was divided into four subheadings by genre: *Trick-Takers*, *Rummies*, *Classics* and the one she'd been most interested in:

Casino and Gambling Games. She'd started to read the introduction at the airport while they'd waited for Blade but hadn't gotten further than a brief overview of the modern deck: 52 cards, 4 suits, 1 Joker and two colors—red and black.

She raised her knees and balanced the book on her stomach and thighs picking up where she'd left off with the history. Playing cards dated back to Far East Asia but no one knew for certain who, when or where they'd been invented. How strange. Geologists used core samples and carbon dating to prove that the earth was four and a half *billion* years old but the origin of the deck of cards remained a mystery. According to the author some scholars speculated the first playing cards could be traced to the Tang Dynasty sometime between 600 and 1000 CE.

What was CE? She took her tablet from the nightstand and searched it. CE was Common Era, the non-religious version of AD, *Anno Domini,* Latin for the Year of our Lord. She entered 'Tang Dynasty' into the browser and pressed RETURN. The Tang Dynasty was China's golden age, a time when China basked in the glow as the world's epicenter for art and culture.

Cards had survived thousands of years and had spread to every continent. Today most households have a deck of cards. People played solitaire on their tablets and phones. Online gambling was growing. The city of Las Vegas had literally been built on a house of cards.

Mystics who believed the deck of cards had special power practiced *cardology*—not to be confused with cardiology. They interpreted the deck in much the same way palm readers used human hands and fortune tellers used tarot cards and crystal balls. The 52 cards represented the 52 weeks of the year, 4 suits for 4 seasons, 13 cards in each suit, 13 weeks in each season and 13 lunar cycles in each year.

Twelve court cards—the face cards of Jacks, Queens and Kings represented the 12 solar months. The colors of black and red represented day/night, male/female, yin/yang.

She whispered it aloud.

"Fifty-two weeks. Four suits for four seasons. Thirteen weeks in a season. Thirteen lunar cycles. Twelve face cards for twelve solar months."

She closed her eyes and slid down in bed repeating the numbers in her head. She opened her eyes, sat up, picked up her tablet and typed 'who invented the calendar.'

The information was inconsistent. But the consensus was that Julius Caesar developed the modern calendar in around 45 or 46 BC. It sounded like ancient folklore. There was agreement on one thing: that Julius was off by 11 minutes which was fixed by adding a Leap Year. 11 minutes? How many times had she been on hold more than that waiting for an agent in a call center to pick up?

The modern deck of playing cards had been invented using the solar calendar aligning it with the heavens and earth. How many people knew this?

Holding her place in the book with her left thumb she studied the odd size and good quality printing. She didn't travel with hardcover books—especially on a trip with stringent baggage rules but when she'd searched the 'Net for a book about poker this was the one she'd wanted. And it only came in hardback. It was smallish, slightly wider and taller than a paperback but much thinner. The front cover was red with black lettering and had a large white club that took up a third of the space. Using her thumb to open it she continued to read.

More than 100 million decks of cards were sold every year. Five times more than the number of Bibles. The small icons on the faces of the cards—the little spades, aces, clubs, and diamonds—were called pips. Each suit had a total of 91 pips per deck. There were 91 days in a season. There were 365 pips in an entire deck. The Joker was the offset for Leap Year.

There was nothing random about a deck of cards.

Why had she never heard any of this before?

She wanted to look at the strange deck she'd found on the plane. Hold it in her hands. Study it from a new perspective. But she'd left it in the living room. She felt a prickle travel down her vertebrae. Could defacing the deck bring bad luck? Whoever printed the faces of strangers on the pig deck had mutilated it. *Mutilated.* Her stomach did a backflip.

She laid the open book face down on her stomach and closed her eyes. Scientists had decoded most of the human DNA. NASA—along with three international partners—had launched the James Webb Space Telescope that would orbit the earth from a million miles away. Astronomers claimed it would peer back in time more than 13 billion years ago to see what happened after the Big Bang. What happened when the universe cooled?

Scientists could look 13 billion years into the past but the origins of a deck of playing cards remained a mystery.

She opened the book. Sometime around the 13th century a Swiss-German monk wrote the first historical reference to the deck of cards. By the 14th century cards and dice games were used for gambling. Religious leaders across Europe denounced the practice and those who produced cards as heretics.

Despite warnings from the church, by the 14th century cards had spread across Europe. Historians believed they were imported from Asia by fur traders and merchants. The invention of the printing press made playing cards available to the masses. And while different European countries tinkered with the pips, the French design was the one that spread across Europe and eventually to the New World.

The voices coming from the living room had been getting louder and louder making it harder to concentrate. She got out of bed and peeked out the bedroom door. When Vance saw her the noise abruptly stopped.

"Oh, sorry," he said, looking between Chan and C.J. sitting opposite him with their backs to her. "I guess we're being too loud."

Chan and C.J. turned around in the wicker chairs and grimaced an apology.

"It's getting late. What are you guys doing?" she asked.

"We're taking his money," C.J. said.

"He's a card shark," Vance said.

"You're gambling?"

"We are," Chan said, "and C.J. is kicking his butt."

"Sorry about the noise," C.J. said, "we'll try to keep it down."

"I'd appreciate it." She stood in the doorway for a few seconds looking at the pink pigs on the back of Vance's hand of cards, then closed the door and climbed back under the covers. She laid on her back with her head on the pillow staring at the six-foot-long blue marlin mounted to the wall above the headboard. What was it about fish with sharp bills that inspired men to keep them as trophies? Maybe that's what one-night stands were. Trophies.

She opened the book again to the *Table of Contents* and looked over the lists of games divided into the four categories. Her eyes stopped on a game called *California Jack*.

Hold on. C.J. had been introduced as California Jack. She flipped to page 71 and read. '*California Jack is a trick-taking game with Aces high and Twos low.*' She paged back to the *Table*. There were almost two dozen games in the trick-taking category. She'd heard of a few of them: *Bridge, Hearts, Pinochle* and *Euchre*. She'd played *Euchre* with her grandfather. But she'd never heard of *California Jack*.

She turned back to the *Table of Contents* and scanned *Classic Games. Bingo* was listed first. She'd never considered *Bingo* a card game. Bingo was a place—a brightly lit hall with folding tables and cheap chairs that smelled like mashed potatoes and split pea soup. Where women with blue hair and men in wheelchairs gathered at long tables staring at sheets of paper waiting for their lucky numbers to be called out. Or to keel over and die.

Fifty-two cards. Fifty-two weeks. Four suits. Four seasons. Thirteen lunar cycles. Three-hundred and sixty-five pips. One Joker.

She thumbed back to the index and scanned *Rummy Games*. It was the shortest list with just six. And they were complicated. *Canasta* was seven pages of complex diagrams and mind-numbing rules and intricate scoring. Visual examples of game play were laid out in rows using mini cards. She turned back to the part that interested her more: the history. *Rummy* did not disappoint. The modern game could be traced to Mexico circa 1800 though like the origin of cards themselves, there was debate.

How much money had Vance lost to C.J? Did Chan gamble too, and if so, was she any good at it? Had she taken money from Vance too? What game were they playing?

She turned the page. Whoever named this one hadn't done it any favors. *Hand and Foot*. It sounded like a deadly disease or poor etiquette. She looked but there was no explanation for the name. She flipped past the game play and when she got to the next one, felt her heart skip. She stared at the word, but her brain froze. The letters on the page looked like Russian or Arabic but it was English. Her eyes played tricks.

A rummy game called *Tonk*?

How was this possible?

She took a deep breath trying to stop her heart from pounding. A zinging sound skimmed past her ear. *Damn*. A mosquito must've gotten into the room when she'd opened the door to the living room. And it was hungry for new blood. She chased it with her hand smacking the comforter when it landed but missed. It buzzed past her eyes. Then waved her hands in front of her face like a madwoman.

The door leading from the living room to the bathroom opened. She heard someone urinating. From the long splash it had to be either Vance or C.J. She slipped out of bed and locked the door joining the bedroom to the bathroom. She heard the toilet flushing then water running in the sink. She put the spare pillow over her head and pressed the two sides over her ears like muffs.

What were the chances that *Tonk* and *California Jack* had the same names as card games in the book? What did she know about the two young men? She played back the little she did know in her head. The three of them had met their first year at a college in southern California. Chan and C.J. switched schools after their freshman year transferring to a state university up north. Tonk stayed at the school in L.A.

Tonk was currently an underemployed film school graduate. C.J. and Chan worked for the state of California.

She reopened the book to the game of *Tonk*. Kings were high, Twos were low, and the winner was the player with the least amount of points at the end of the game. She paged back to *California Jack* and looked for clues. Aces were high and Twos were low and the first player to score 10 points won the game. What was she hoping to find?

The bedroom door opened. She slapped the book shut and pulled the covers up to her neck.

"Sorry," Vance said, closing the bedroom door behind him. "I thought you might be sleeping."

"I was reading. Jesus, you smell like booze."

"We hit the mini-bar pretty hard." He sat at the foot of the bed, pulled his shirt over his head and tossed it on the club chair near the window. "How'd you like the shower?"

"It was like cold leftovers."

"Uh oh. I guess that means you ran out of hot water."

"Yep."

"I'm sorry. I know how much you like hot showers."

She could tell he was being sincere by the two little teepees that formed over his eyebrows.

"I'll be right back," he said.

He took his backpack into the bathroom and when he returned wore a pair of long light gray swim trunks. He sat on top of the bedspread on his side of the queen bed. "This must be what it feels like to vacation with your kids," he said.

She chuckled. "I guess."

"May I?" He gestured to the book laying on her lap.

She nodded.

"Is this what you were reading?"

"Yes."

He flipped through the pages. "Did you learn anything new?"

"I did."

"What?"

"That California Jack and Tonk are card games." She took the book from him, opened it to the *Table of Contents* and pointed it out. "What do you think the chances of that are?"

"Low," he said. "But it might explain how I just got beat in thirteen straight games."

"Why did you quit at thirteen?"

"I didn't. They did."

She watched him toss his wallet on the nightstand on his side of the bed.

"Were you playing poker?"

"Yep. Are you going to Miami tomorrow?"

"Don't you think that's weird?"

"What?"

"The names of the games."

"I do. I think the whole day's been a cluster of fucking weirdness. We're stranded on a private island with strangers sleeping on the other side of the door. My brain can't process anything else, or my head might explode. Are you going to go?" he asked again.

"I think I have to."

He sprawled on top of the bedspread, put his hands behind his head and stared at the ceiling as if in deep contemplation.

"What?" she asked.

"There's something I haven't told you."

She flipped on her side and propped herself on her elbow cupping her cheek in her hand facing him. The moonlight seeping through the gap in the curtains cast a glow that highlighted the outline of his aquiline nose and chiseled chin.

"My gun was missing from my bag."

She sprang into a sitting position pulling the covers to her chest. "What are you talking about?"

"Whoever took my duffle stole my passport AND my gun."

"Jesus." She slunk down onto her back and covered her eyes with her hands. "What are you going to do?"

"I have to get it back."

"What? How?"

"I'm working on that. Whoever took my passport, took my gun."

"Obviously," she said, sitting up and stuffing a pillow behind her back. "Is it possible it was someone other than Tonk and his dad?"

"I'm not following you."

"What if it was someone who works here, and they tossed it on the footpath to make it look like Blade and his kid stole it?"

"That crossed my mind but the people who work here are happy. You heard them. The place was bankrupt for years and when a new buyer came along, he rehired the entire staff. That's how the owner created loyalty. Why would anyone risk stealing from me when they have easy access to things a lot more valuable than my gun and passport? Plus, the guy who owns this place has a reputation for not putting up with crap."

"How do you know that?"

"While we were playing cards, C.J. showed me a news story on his phone. A few months back the owner kicked a customs agent off the island because he wouldn't let one of his friends dock his yacht because he didn't have the right paperwork. It created a big stink and The Ministry got involved. The locals got mad posting all kinds of stuff on social media claiming the owner was getting special treatment."

"Same shit, different country."

"Look who's getting cynical," he said, laughing.

"Whose side did The Ministry take?"

"Take a guess."

"Who owns this place?"

"I didn't recognize his name. Some oil tycoon from Texas."

"I could see how he'd get mad," she said. "If we bought an island for millions of dollars of our own money and some low-level government official wouldn't let our friends visit I can imagine how you'd react."

"Would you tangle with the owner if you worked here?"

"No. I wouldn't tangle with him as a paying guest."

"I'm going to report my passport stolen first thing in the morning."

She looked at the white cube clock on the nightstand. It was after 11 o'clock at night. Someone could've already sold his identity for big bucks on the dark web.

"Tonk took my passport to fuck with me knowing we'd be stuck here. The gun was a bonus. If it was just my passport, I'd figure out how to go home with you."

"You're staying?"

"I doubt I have a choice."

"You don't know that, at least not yet."

"The gun's registered in my name."

"So? Report it stolen."

"And admit I brought an illegal firearm into a foreign country?"

"Lie about it. Tell them someone stole it in Miami."

"I already ran those scenarios. I can't lie. And I can't tell the truth."

"What are you going to do?"

"I'm going to Nassau to get my gun."

She inhaled and filled her cheeks with air knowing full well she couldn't change his mind. He'd lied to her. A lie of omission was a lie. He'd known for hours that his gun had been stolen. "How do you plan to get to Nassau without a passport?"

"I don't know yet."

He reached over her and turned off the bedside lamp on her side.

"Assuming you think of a way how do you plan to find Tonk?"

"By following Chan and C.J. They're still planning to meet up with him."

"They told you that?"

"Yep."

"How're they getting to Nassau? They didn't even have lunch money. Oh, I forgot. They beat you thirteen games in a row."

"They're talking about hitching a ride."

"With who?"

"I don't know."

"Vivian can probably help you with your passport but you're on your own with the gun. If I were you, I wouldn't mention it."

"Of course not," he said.

Her eyes had adjusted to the near darkness. She watched the outline of his bare chest rise and fall as he breathed deeply. When he exhaled an invisible cloud of secondhand booze hovered over the bed.

"I'll figure it out in the morning," he said. "I need sleep."

"Me too." She felt for the book atop the bedspread and set it on the nightstand next to her phone.

"This isn't the romantic getaway I was hoping for," he said softly.

"Is that what you were hoping for?"

He tilted his head in her direction and without answering, half-smiled.

"There's something I need to tell you," she said.

"Can it wait 'til morning?"

"No."

He sighed. "Okay."

She reached over, turned on the bedside lamp.

He shaded his eyes. "Can't you just tell me?"

"No. I want to show you something." She sat up and pulled the covers down to her stomach then raised her T-shirt up and exposed half of one breast.

"What are you doing?" he asked, narrowing his eyes.

"I want you to look at me."

He sat up. "What is that?"

"They're scars."

"From a surgery?"

"No."

"From what then?"

"A razor blade."

"Jesus." He swung his legs over his side of the bed. "Who did that to you?"

He stood and walked over to her side where he could get a closer look. Sitting close to her on her edge of the bed he leaned over to look at the dozens of crude little X's carved into her skin.

He repeated the question. "Who did this to you?"

She hesitated.

His reaction was making this more difficult. She looked at his face. His lower jaw jutted.

"I'd like to strangle him with my bare hands."

"I did it to myself."

"What?" He leaned away from her as if she were a leper.

"I was afraid this was how you'd react." She yanked her shirt down and pulled the covers up.

He stood and pushed two fingers deeply into his forehead and rubbed his brow leaving red marks. He took a deep breath and exhaled a soft whistling sound.

"I want to understand," he said. "But I don't. I'll be right back. I need a moment."

She watched him unlock the bathroom door, go inside and turn on the light. He closed the door. She heard water running in the sink. What had she been thinking? She'd completely miscalculated the timing. He was tired and half drunk and what did she do? She dropped a bomb.

The door opened. He stood with a towel draped around his neck blotting his face. "I'm sorry." He hung the towel over the back of the bathroom door, took an empty glass from the dresser and filled it with water, gulped it down, refilled it, turned off the bathroom light and sat next to her. He handed the glass of water to her.

She took it and sipped, then set it next to the book.

"I don't blame you for judging me," she said.

"How can I judge you when I don't understand what happened."

"I don't remember doing it. But it was me."

"You blacked out?"

She nodded.

Then she relived it, shuddering at the memory of awakening with blood on her hands and pools of red streaks of dried blood on her sheets. She'd found a single edge razor blade in the bedding. She checked the house, but all the doors and windows were locked. A small green plastic toolbox she kept in a cabinet in the laundry room atop the washing machine was open, and the black plastic tray had been removed. It's where she'd kept a box of single edge blades she'd bought to scrape paint. The box was open and the thin strip of cardboard protecting the sharp edge had been removed and dropped on the floor.

She cringed inside, remembering when she'd lifted her T-shirt, and seen the self-mutilation for the first time in the mirror. How was it possible? She'd wanted to call Peter and ask for help but when she unlocked her phone, she saw a series of bizarre texts she'd sent him. The messages were time-stamped at 3 o'clock in the morning and they were gibberish. If she didn't live alone, she'd have blamed it on someone else. But she was the only suspect. "Don't look at me that way."

"I'm sorry," he said.

"It was during a very difficult time. It was during the month after Peter moved out. Have you ever been so sleep deprived it made you crazy?"

"I have," he said. "The Geneva Convention considers sleep deprivation torture."

"I'd been having trouble sleeping for weeks and I couldn't think straight. I started seeing a therapist who sent me to a doctor who prescribed sleeping meds. The meds helped a lot, and I was starting to sleep much better. A few weeks later a process server showed up at my door and served me with divorce papers. I was so distraught I didn't know what to do. When I read the papers, I had a panic attack. I couldn't breathe. I felt like I was having a heart attack. I opened a bottle of wine and started drinking and I don't know what happened after that. The next morning, I found the medicine bottle open on the bathroom counter. I don't know how many pills I'd taken."

She stopped talking for a minute hoping he would say something, but he didn't. Lifting her shirt, she showed him part of her other breast covered with the same little white scars. They were fine lines now that had healed a shade lighter than her skin color.

"You mixed sleeping pills with wine?"

"It wasn't like I was suicidal or anything. It was an accident."

"Was that the first time you cut yourself?"

"Yes."

"You never did it when you were younger?"

"No, of course not."

"That must have been frightening."

"It was terrifying."

"That's why you don't drink?"

She nodded. "I can't take the chance of that happening again. Do you know what it feels like to lose control?"

He looked away for a moment, then said, "I woke up once in all my clothes after pulling an all-nighter. What did your therapist say?"

"She said she's had other patients that had the same thing happen."

"They cut themselves?"

"No. One of her patients woke up with a bunch of empty ice cream containers in the bed with no memory of eating it."

"Wow," Vance said, getting up and walking to his side of the bed. He laid down next to her. "I don't want you going to Miami tomorrow," he said.

"I shouldn't have told you."

"No. I'm glad you did."

"Why?"

"Seeing Peter might be a trigger."

"Sometimes I wonder what's wrong with me?"

"I don't think there's anything wrong with you." He lifted the bottom of her T shirt. "May I?"

She nodded.

He ran his index finger over the x-patterns on her breasts slowly retracing each scar. "People go under anesthesia while surgeons cut away with power tools. There's nothing wrong with you. It was the drugs."

She raised her arms and he gently removed her shirt, tossing it at the foot of the bedspread then kissed her breasts softly. Then suddenly he stopped and rolled onto his back. She waited but he laid there silently.

Covering her breasts with her arms, she scrambled to the foot of the bed feeling for her T-shirt. "I don't blame you," she said, pulling her shirt over her head. "I desperately wanted Peter to be someone he's not. People can't be who you want them to be. They just can't," she said. She rolled onto her side with her back to him, hugging a pillow.

"That's not it," he said.

He was lying. She should've kept her secret. She'd taken a risk sharing it with him and couldn't take it back. "I was afraid you might react like this."

He got out of bed, walked to her side, and took a knee. "You're reading this wrong," he said. "On the contrary. I'm not used to this . . . whatever you call it. Intimacy? Honesty? I don't know. I'm confused about how I feel. Maybe I'm in love with you. How crazy is that?"

She rolled onto her back and stared at the ceiling. "You don't have to say anything to try to make me feel better."

Still kneeling he brushed her cheek with his hand then held her chin in his palm. "Look at me," he said, "don't you know me well enough to know I'm not capable of that? The only women I've ever told I love are you, my sister and my mother. I want to wait. I want to do this the right way." He shook his head. "The timing doesn't feel right. Scoot over."

She backed away from the edge toward the middle of the bed.

"Come closer," he said turning to face her and lifting his arm.

She inched toward him.

"I'm glad you told me," he said.

She noticed the sliver of light bleeding under the door from the living room went dark.

He noticed it, too. "I guess the kids are turning in for the night," he said. "I've been thinking about it, and I think they know something more about that deck of cards you found on the plane."

"I agree."

"Take your shirt off," he said.

"I don't want to."

He slid his hand around her waist and pulled her body against his, the skin-to-skin contact releasing a flood of soothing natural hormones. Her shoulder muscles slackened. He stroked her hair then lowered his hand and tenderly massaged the back of her neck. A moment later his breathing slowed, and deep breaths turned into the rhythmical sounds of soft snoring. She began to drift off, but the dark recesses of her mind began to awaken. What did she look like during her zombie apocalypse? Was it just the drugs that caused her to maim her own body or was there a deeper meaning to the actions?

Before tonight it had been a long time since she'd thought about that night. Her thoughts turned to Peter. What happened to him? My God. Would Peter wake up?

There'd be no tossing and turning tonight. She lay motionless in Vance's arms as if bound in an invisible strait jacket but her mind raced.

16

L auren awoke in the fetal position trying to remember where she was. The room was dim and quiet. She rolled over and rubbed her eyes gazing at the empty side of the bed. She squinted at the bedroom window facing the footpath leading to the main building. Although the gray blackout drapes were drawn, a streak of sun leaked through a vertical gap in the curtains. She buried her face in Vance's pillow and inhaled, then rolled onto her back and stretched. She smelled the scent of fresh brewed coffee. She got out of bed, grabbed the robe laying on his side of the bed, threw it on, cracked the bedroom door open and peered into the living room. Where was Vance? Where was everyone?

She followed her nose to the kitchen and opened the white cabinets, grabbed a black porcelain mug and poured coffee from what was left in the pot. Climbing back into bed, she took her tablet off charge and typed 'Island Hopper' into the browser, then waited for the search page to populate. She saw an available seat, called the airline and booked a ticket on a flight that would stop at Chub Cay at ten this morning to pick her up, and arrive at the regional Opa-Locka Airport at eleven-thirty. Next she called Vivian. Her stepmother answered on the third ring.

"Hello."

"Vivian?"

"This is she."

"It's Lauren. I hope I didn't wake you."

"Lauren." Vivian paused. "No, you didn't wake me. I listened to your message, but it was too late last night to call you. I was just about to return your phone call. What a pleasant surprise. How have you been?"

"Good. And you?"

"I've been very well. It's been a long time and I'm glad to hear from you. I imagine there's a reason for the call."

She held the phone away from her face, winced, then said, "I'm in The Bahamas."

"Oh?" Vivian said, obviously surprised. "Are you on holiday?"

"Sort of. We were on our way to Paradise Island yesterday when our plane had to make an emergency landing on Chub Cay."

"Oh, my goodness. That must've been frightening. The weather yesterday was horrendous. Did you overnight at the resort?"

"We did. But something came up and I have to go back home."

"Oh?"

"It's personal business. I was wondering if you could help me with something."

"I'll certainly try."

"My friend, the one I'm traveling with, he lost his passport. I thought maybe you could help him."

An awkward silence ensued. "I'm not sure what I can do. Is he trying to return to the States?"

"No. He's trying to get to Nassau."

There was another lull in the conversation.

"If he can get to the American Embassy in Nassau, they can issue a temporary visa."

"That's the problem. Does he need a passport to get to Nassau?"

"I suppose that depends on how he gets here. How did he lose it, if you don't mind my asking?"

"I don't know. I think it might've fallen out of his carry-on bag."

"I see," Vivian said. "If he can get here have him call me. I'm retired from The Ministry, but I'll see what I can do to help expedite the process. It can be maddeningly slow."

"Thanks. I really appreciate it."

"I'm happy to help. What's your friend's name?"

"Vance Courage."

"That's a fine name. Next time you come for a visit give me more notice. I'd love to see you."

"I might be back in a couple of days."

"You said you're returning to Miami for personal business? Is everything alright?"

"Yes."

"Will your friend be staying in Nassau?"

"That was the plan. We booked a suite at the Poseidon Club."

"That's a nice place. It would be wonderful to see you and catch up. I can't make any promises, but I'll see what I can do to help your friend. By the way, how's your father?"

Uh oh. That was the topic she'd hoped to avoid. "He's fine, I guess. Anyway, thanks for taking my call. I really appreciate it."

"Of course," Vivian said. "Give your friend my number and have him call me. Safe travels back to Miami."

"Thanks, and I'll be in touch."

She held the phone in her hand for a moment, then set it on the nightstand. Vivian was as charming, and cheerful, and lovely, and well-spoken, and kind as Lauren had remembered her.

She headed back to the kitchen, refilled her coffee and turned off the pot. Clutching the mug, she peeked out the curtains squinting at the rising sun glinting off the sparkling teal blue water. A lip of white foam lapped at the white sand. She opened the front door and stepped onto the weathered wooden porch with a view to the gravel footpath leading to the clubhouse. She tightened the sash on her robe and sat on the top step, tilted her head back, closed her eyes and basked in the warm sun. If Peter had updated his paperwork, she wouldn't have had to leave. She could go back to bed. She finished her coffee and went inside to pack.

The spare blankets and pillows Vance had found for their guests had been folded neatly and stacked on the couch. C.J. and Chan's backpacks were at the foot of the sofa, packed and zipped. She set her coffee cup on the glass coffee table, sat, then peeked into the side pocket of C.J.'s backpack. She removed a wad of credit cards held together with a rubber band. The stack of Visas and Mastercards was almost three inches thick. She removed the elastic band and thumbed through them. Some had his name on them. They were drawn on a bunch of obscure banks. Second Redwood Guarantee, California First Federal, Fidelity Group Alliance. Others looked like gift cards. *Couldn't afford lunch?*

She set C.J.'s maroon backpack on her lap and unzipped the main compartment. Setting a wad of clothes on the coffee table she took out the shaving kit at the bottom and snooped inside. Seeing nothing unusual she put his stuff back in, placed the gift cards back into the side pocket and zipped it shut.

She stared at Chan's enormous backpack. Unable to resist, she peeked into the outer pockets. A Fodor's travel book for The Bahamas, sunscreen, a phone charger. A set of keys. Sunglasses in a hard case. Contact lens solution. Eyeglasses in a separate case. Chapstick. A hairbrush. Travel sized tissues. A hat with the California state flag and bear stitched on the brim. When she heard voices, she looked out the window. A young couple attempting to paddle board near the shore laughed loudly at their inability to balance for more than a few seconds before falling into the water.

Heading toward the bedroom, she turned around and knelt next to Chan's oversized blue bag. The metal zippers were sturdy with pink satin strings neatly threaded through the metal pulls. A silver thermos hung from a clip. She shook it, then opened the cap and sniffed. Water. As she unzipped one side, the giant bag tipped over and a pile of Chan's clothes and belongings spilled out onto the floor.

She gathered what she could and stuffed the clothing rolled up like miniature sleeping bags back into the knapsack. One unraveled revealing a pink stiletto pump with a sharp heel. The other shoe was wrapped in a soft black leather miniskirt with a thick gold zipper running from top to bottom. The beige soles of the pink stilettos had no signs of wear. She twisted the skirt around the pink heels and tucked it in the bag.

Maybe Chan and C.J. had lied to them. Maybe they were more than friends. Or maybe their definition of friendship was different than hers. Or maybe Chan had a plan that C.J. didn't know about. She heard another noise, a vehicle. She set the backpack upright and walked to the side window and looked out. A golf cart was heading from the main building along the path next to the villa. She dragged Chan's backpack and set it next to C.J.'s where she'd found it then double checked the lock on the front door. Watching from the window, the cart passed and continued along the gravel road toward the shoreline. When the vehicle stopped, two workers got out carrying long handled tools. She slipped out onto the porch to see what they were doing. They were raking the sand.

She went back inside and dragged Chan's backpack closer to the sofa and reopened it, removing a shiny white plastic tote that had caught her eye. The drawstring was pulled tight and tied into a loose bow. Whatever was inside was the shape of a bowling ball but it weighed practically nothing. She set it on the glass coffee table and removed a clear plastic bag that was packed near the tote. Holding it up, she turned it over looking at the contents: a bottle of beige face make-up, a gold compact with blush and a tube of bright red lipstick with a clear plastic cap. She set the baggie on the table.

Loosening the drawstring on the white tote, she removed a red bundle, unrolled it and held up the strapless cocktail dress Chan used to protect a black wig atop a Styrofoam head. She lifted the wig stand and held it by the throat. The long locks of shiny black hair unfurled and draped over her hand. She wound the hair around the base, covered it with the dress and put it back in the white bag. She riffled deeper into Chan's bag, seeing what she'd expected to see: T shirts, cargo pants, jeans, a sweatshirt, shorts, socks and a pair of worn flip-flops.

She repacked the bag and dragged it back to where she'd found it. Eyeing a bulging side pocket, she knelt, and using one knee to balance the bag, pulled the Velcro tab. She looked inside and saw a wad of credit cards like the stack she'd discovered in C.J.s. bag. She removed the stack of plastic to see them more closely. Her throat constricted when she saw a deck of cards with a pink pig on the cover hidden beneath the credit cards.

What was Chan up to? The make-up and sexy clothing seemed out of character. Where did they get all the different credit cards? Was the story about work a big lie to misdirect them? Did Chan steal her deck of cards, or had Chan packed them by accident? Maybe Vance gave them to her. But they weren't his to give away. She dropped the deck in the pocket of her robe and zipped the backpack shut.

She walked into the kitchen and set her empty coffee mug in the sink. Where was Vance and where had Chan and C.J. gone? Were they together? Her stomach growled. She had to eat something before catching the commuter back to Miami. She sat on the sofa and reached across the glass table for the blue binder with the resort information. She opened it to the white menu tab and checked the time on her phone. If she hurried, she'd have enough time to get room service delivered before she had to leave.

Setting the binder down on the sofa cushion she moved the tropical floral arrangement on the coffee table to the end table, lifted the landline handset and was about to dial room service when she saw something out of the corner of her eye. Was that a deck of cards? Slipping her hand into the pocket of her robe she removed the deck of cards with the pink pig in the graduation cap she'd found in Chan's bag and set it down next to the deck on the coffee table. They were the same.

Heart pounding under the robe, she tightened the belt around her waist and hurried to the bedroom to take her cell phone off charge. Looking out the bedroom window to see if anyone was coming, she hurried back to the living room. Working quickly, she removed C.J.'s wad of credit cards and snapped a picture then did the same with Chan's, removing and taking pictures of the credit cards, mini skirt, make-up, pink heels and wig. She set the two decks of playing cards side by side on the glass coffee table and took a snapshot of them, too.

She heard voices. Scrambling, she swept up the stuff and shoved it back in the bags. After unlocking the deadbolt on the front door, she rushed to the bedroom and closed the door between the rooms and climbed under the covers. A moment later she heard the front door open, then voices filled the living room. Someone tapped on the bedroom door. Vance peeked his head inside. He entered and closed the door behind him.

"You're awake. You looked so peaceful, I didn't want to wake you," he said.

"Where were you?"

"I went foraging for food. Here," he set a plate covered with a cloth napkin on the nightstand.

She peeked underneath. A white ramekin filled with cubed cantaloupe and an English muffin with soft pats of butter and a tiny jar of jam arranged artfully on a white paper doily on a white porcelain plate. "Fancy," she said. "I was going to order room service."

"Did you find the coffee?"

"I did. That was nice."

He looked at her tablet on the nightstand.

"Did you have a chance to check flights?"

"I did and I booked one to Miami."

"What time do you leave?"

"At ten. I also talked to Vivian. She said you should go to the American Embassy in Nassau to get a temporary visa.

She said to call her if you need help. Here's her cell number." She unlocked her phone, looked up the number, scribbled it on the resort notepad and handed it to him.

"No hard feelings?" he said, taking the piece of paper from her.

"What do you mean?"

"About your dad."

"Oh." She shook her head. "No. She was very pleasant. She's very proper so that's what I expected. I always liked her. Have you thought about how you plan on getting to Nassau?"

"I'm working on that."

"Are you going with Chan and C.J.?"

"Maybe."

"Are they still planning to meet up with Tonk?"

"As far as I know."

"What do you think they're up to?"

"I don't know."

She unrolled a fork and knife from a cloth napkin next to the plate of food.

"When you said Vivian comes from a prominent family what did you mean?"

"Just what my father told me." She stabbed a cube of cantaloupe with the tines of the fork and put it in her mouth. It was perfectly ripened. "When my father was married to her, they'd travel to Nassau regularly to visit her mother. He was impressed by the family home which is saying something because not much impressed him. He told me it was a sprawling colonial mansion built on a hilltop of land that was given to her family as compensation."

"Compensation for what?" he asked.

"For fighting on the side of the British during the Revolutionary War. Her family's been in The Bahamas for generations. My dad liked to tell people the license plate on her mother's car had the number one on it because they had the first car on the island. Vivian's father was a barrister who started a prestigious firm. Apparently, she comes from a long line of barristers."

"Then we have something in common."

"Hardly. They're upper crust."

He laughed. "We have time for a walk on the beach before you take off."

"I wish I could, but I have to pack. How about a rain check?"

He walked to the window and pulled back the curtain enough to look out. "I hope you didn't just jinx the weather."

"I need to get ready. Will you see if someone can give me a lift to the plane? And I'd love another cup of coffee."

"Anything else?"

"Yeah. When you meet Vivian, don't mention the gun."

"Do I look like an idiot?"

"No, you look very handsome. I think island life suits you."

He laughed at her joke and sat down on the bed next to her. "About last night—"

"We don't need to talk about that." She paused for a moment. "Go get that coffee. When you get back, I have something I want to show you."

She quickly dressed and finished packing.

"I had to brew a fresh pot," he said. "I talked to Jimmy. He's going to send someone to drive you over to the airstrip. What did you want to show me?"

She lifted the pillow on her side of the unmade bed and handed him two identical sets of the playing cards.

"Where did you get this?" he asked, holding up the unopened box.

"While you were gone, I snooped through their stuff," she said.

"What? Why did you do that?"

"I had a feeling. That's not all I found." She unlocked her phone and held it up.

"What is that?"

"A wig."

He cocked his head. "I don't understand."

"It was in Chan's bag with the deck."

"Let me see that."

She handed him her phone and watched as he scrolled through the pictures. When he got to the credit cards, he used his thumb and forefinger to enlarge them.

"They are definitely up to something," she said. "I thought you'd want to know."

17

A white twin engine Piper Chieftain with shiny royal blue stripes touched down at the end of the airstrip. Vance pressed his hands over his ears to dull the noise as the plane taxied toward them. As a light drizzle began to fall, he dropped his windbreaker from his shoulders and held it over Lauren's head. When the plane stopped, the pilot opened the cabin door and hopped down from the wing holding a blue and white umbrella.

"Miss Gold?" the man said.

"That's me."

"I'm Ryan, your pilot. May I see your passport and ticket?"

Lauren moved closer and stood beneath his umbrella. She removed her passport from her purse and handed him the document.

He scanned it and returned it to her.

"You'll clear customs in Miami," he said.

"Here's my ticket." She held her phone up and turned it toward him.

Ryan checked the screen. "Are you ready to go?"

"Yes," she said, turning to Vance.

"I don't have a full load," the pilot said, handing her his umbrella. He lifted her carry-on. "I'll put your bag in the cabin."

Ryan stepped up onto the wing carrying her bag, ducked, and disappeared inside.

Vance approached and stood next to her under the loaned umbrella. "I wish you could stay."

"Me too," she said.

From the ground Vance could see in through the cabin doorway. Four plush tan leather seats arranged in pairs faced each other. "It looks nicer than Blade's plane."

"That's not saying much," she said, stepping up on the treaded surface on the wing.

He saw a man was seated in one of the passenger chairs facing the cockpit. That's the seat he would've chosen if he were able to leave. Sitting backwards on anything that moved made him motion sick. He handed the umbrella up to her.

She squatted. "I hope you get a visa or whatever you need and come home."

"Me too. Call me when you land."

"I will," she said.

"Let's go." Ryan took the umbrella from her, shook the water then closed the umbrella.

He felt a pit in his stomach as he watched her duck and disappear inside without looking back. The pilot closed the cockpit door and a moment later the engines fired. Lauren peered out the window and waved to him as he watched the plane make a lazy turn then speed down the short runway, lift off and head south before making a sharp turn to the northwest before vanishing into the overcast sky.

He should've been on the flight with her.

The guy in the golf cart drove up. Miguel's voice snapped him back into reality.

"If she'd waited any longer, she wouldn't have made it out of 'ere today," the driver said.

Vance gazed up at the graying sky amazed how the water surrounding the skinny, jagged peninsula remained the color of topaz. He shielded his eyes from a lone streak of mid-morning sun that had found a crack in the darkening blanket of clouds swirling up from the south. If weather was a mental illness, South Florida was bipolar and The Bahamas was what you'd get if she went off her meds.

The drizzle morphed into a light rain. Farther south, charcoal clouds were rapidly accumulating and something menacing was brewing.

"You ready to 'ead back?" Miguel asked.

"Yeah. Thanks for waiting."

"That's my job," he said, turning the cart around and heading for the gravel road cut like a tunnel through the leafy tropical jungle leading to the resort.

"How long have you worked here?"

"Twelve years total. The place went bankrupt for four years right in de middle."

"What did you do then?"

"Went 'ome."

"Where's home?"

"Andros Island. I worked for a company dat barges fresh water daily to Nassau," Miguel said navigating the cart around potholes. "I was 'appy the day I was rehired. Dis place is my 'ome."

"Are you married?"

"Nah," he said.

"Ever been?"

"Nah."

"Why not?"

"I don't know."

"Do you ever wish you were?"

"All de time. But life is what it is. Right?"

"Right."

"The weather's clear 'eading north," Miguel said, "but it's turning bad in de south. De *sip sip* is that you're sailing with Captain Morgan dis morning."

"*Sip sip?*"

"Gossip," he said.

He laughed. Word sure traveled fast, but then again, it didn't have far to go. He'd asked Chan and C.J. to set it up for him and he hadn't yet formally met the captain though he'd seen him at the bar yesterday. Sitting in the corner watching a ballgame. "That's his real name? Captain Morgan?"

"Yep," the driver said. "Captain Boogie Morgan's a local legend. Been sailing de islands since he was twelve years old. Even made some appearances in a Hollywood pirate movie dat was shot 'ere years ago."

"I thought you called him that because that's what he drank."

"Captain Boogie Morgan's not a rum drinker. He's a whiskey man. You sure you want to make dis trip with 'im?"

Vance shrugged. Want wasn't the word he'd have chosen.

"Can't say a guest ever hitched a ride on de mailboat before," Miguel said. "Even de customs agents and day workers avoid it, mostly 'cause it's so damn slow. You de first," he said, turning the wheel hard left to avoid a puddle. "It's none my business, but why did your friend go?"

"She had some personal business to take care of."

"De women are de smart ones. She flies and you go on a freighter. She won't be missing much. De weather's going to be bad all week. 'ang on," Miguel said, stomping the pedal as the sky opened and fat raindrops fell. Pea-sized gravel mixed with mud pinged and slopped against the underbelly of the cart as Miguel raced toward the bungalow.

Vance gripped the side handle holding his green windbreaker over his head. He stopped the cart at the T in the path a hundred feet from the yellow cabana.

"You mind walking de rest of the way? I gotta get back to work."

"No," he said climbing out of the cart. He handed him a folded twenty-dollar bill and slapped his shoulder. "Thanks for the ride. If the kids can handle an adventure, then so can I."

"If you say so," Miguel said, reaching under the dash and putting a ball cap on. "You better hurry it. Boogie's got a schedule to keep and he was bitching to whoever'll listen 'bout 'aving to wait. Meet me back at de bar and I'll get de guy from maintenance give you a lift to de freight dock to speed things up."

Miguel turned the golf cart around and sped toward the main building, kicking up hunks of caked sand and gravel the size of clumps from a litter box.

Vance jogged the rest of the way to the guesthouse where he'd left Chan and C.J. waiting inside. He hustled up the weathered stairs. The pair sat side by side staring at their phones. "Grab your stuff," he said. "Rumor has it the captain doesn't like waiting."

"We're waiting on you," C.J. said.

"I don't want to get stranded twice in twenty-four hours," Chan said.

"Neither do I," he said, slinging his duffle over his shoulder.

C.J. hoisted Chan's bag over his back while she hung C.J.'s small maroon knapsack over her shoulder.

"I was checking the room and noticed this on the nightstand."

Chan handed him Lauren's book. He unzipped his duffle and slid it into the empty inside pocket where he'd packed passport.

C.J. led the way ducking under the front door, holding the sides of Chan's backpack as he trotted down the wooden stairs toward the private beach a stone's throw from the bungalow. The men who'd been raking the beachfront sand when he'd returned to the room from breakfast were gone and the rain had turned the white sand a tan color. Bands of clouds to the south had moved over Chub Cay casting a shadow over the water turning it a bluish green. He paused for a moment to take a long last look, then jogged to catch up to Chan and C.J. walking briskly toward the main building.

Now he was nervous. Miguel seemed qualified to opine the trip with Captain Morgan as a bad idea.

But he had to get to Nassau and without a passport, there was no other way.

18

Vance waited near the front door of the restaurant while Chan and C.J. made pit stops in the restroom. When they returned, Jimmy the waiter came out from behind the empty bar and escorted them through the back entrance of the clubhouse past a pair of rusted blue dumpsters. He followed as they walked beneath a torn corrugated awning to where a guy with curly gray hair waited behind the wheel of an old white Toyota pickup truck. Skipping any introductions, the driver motioned Chan to sit up front.

It'd stopped raining but a thin layer of moisture clung to everything like wet paint. He tossed his duffle over the tailgate onto the driest spot atop the wheel well and climbed into the bed of the truck. C.J. followed suit, first slinging Chan's ball-and-chain bag over. It was a four, maybe five-minute ride from hell along a bumpy narrow dirt road. While he and C.J. ducked to avoid the low hanging palm fronds smacking the roof of the truck, the jungle overgrowth brushed the sides of the truck. At the end of the road, he saw the bow of a freighter docked on the rocky side of the island, the full view of the ship obstructed by a canopy of black mangroves growing in the salt water.

The driver stopped. Vance jumped down from the tailgate and walked toward the wooden dock feeling the softness of the rotting lumber under his shoes. He had a clear view of a workboat with a gantry crane jutting from the deck. Stacks of cargo piled on pallets rose above the dull orange hull. In her day she must've been a beauty. He pictured her new in her original red paint as shiny and bold as a big city fire truck. Streaks of rust dripped over the faded white trim. The name of the ship—the *Mis Mama*—had been neatly stenciled in Old English lettering near the tip of the bow. As the wind turned direction a blast of black diesel smoke billowed through the copse of mangroves. A sailor's trick to keep the mosquitos at bay.

Boogie Morgan waved them aboard. "Let's get a move on," the bar stool sailor said, dropping a pitted aluminum ladder over the side.

C.J. held the legs steady as Chan went first. Dressed in her park ranger shorts and hiking boots she mounted the gunwale from the top stair like a horse, swinging with one leg over before sitting on the ledge then hopping down onto the deck.

"I don't have a month of Tuesdays," Morgan yelled.

Vance held the ladder while C.J. went next wrangling Chan's bag.

He slung his duffle over his shoulder and climbed aboard.

The captain pulled the ladder and tossed it on the deck. "It'll be forty-five dollars apiece."

While C.J. counted money Vance studied the man. Specks of thick yellow skin on the whites of his eyes and the webbing of red veins fanning from his pupils to his eyelids said he'd led a hard life. His face was unshaven and his eyelashes gray and crusty. Morgan had changed into chest-high boot waders held with suspenders over a long-sleeved plaid shirt and a ratty Panama hat. Up close he smelled of oranges and whiskey.

C.J. and Chan paid their combined $90 dollar fare in small bills. Vance paid with three twenties.

"I don't make change and I don't want to hear no moaning," Morgan said, stuffing the cash inside the chest pocket of his waders. "Perfectly happy if you change your mind and want a refund. You still got time before we shove off."

"I'm good," Vance said, slowly nodding his head.

Morgan gave no instructions before disappearing into the wheelhouse. A moment later the engines churned in reverse. The clarity of the water turned into a milkshake. Helped by the wind and current, the *Mis Mama* rotated 45 degrees on her bow like a slow-motion cutting horse on its back hooves and plowed from the dock on a south-southwest heading. Toward a foreboding horizon.

Surrounded by pallets of bricks and piles of lumber wrapped in heavy plastic stacked four feet high on the bow, he saw Boogie Morgan standing above in front of the salt-crusted window of the pilot house. As the captain peered through a set of binoculars he heard the clunk and felt the massive boat shimmy as the transmission dropped into a low, forward gear. The *Mis Mama* groaned, and the cargo vibrated as she picked up speed. Balancing on a metal rail attached to the side of the pilot house he stepped up atop a pallet of cinder blocks to watch as the ship cast a wake of two-foot waves that disappeared into the gnarled trunks of the thicket of mangroves lining the shore.

From his perch atop pallets of cargo, he looked over the bow. Ahead the water turned darker shades of blue to

almost black as the ship sailed toward the deep channel
he'd seen from the air. He hopped down and snaked his way
between the pallets. Leaning his right hip against the
gunwale he turned and watched the island slowly shrinking
away. He scanned the deck and saw Chan standing on a
pallet of red bricks on the opposite side of the wheelhouse.
He headed her way.

She rolled her hands over her mouth and yelled over the
splashing water and the droning diesels. "Did you know
mailboats have been used for inter-island travel and cargo
transport for over a century?"

"Who knew?" he hollered.

A hundred years ago the bare legs of a woman would've
been an unspeakable scandal. Not to mention the tattoo on
her thigh. He imagined if Chan had been born during the
bygone era of pirates, she might have been the type of
woman who'd have passed herself off as a man.

"We have a couple of hours to kill," C.J. said. "Do you
want to go inside and play cards?"

"I already have plans," he said.

A puzzled look crossed Chan's face. "To do what?" she
asked.

19

His plan was to keep breakfast down and to succeed he intended to stay outside where he could breathe fresh air and focus on the horizon. As Chan and C.J. navigated between a maze of pallets stacked on the deck he stopped at a row of golf carts chained together and loosely covered with opaque plastic wrap. He lifted the cover brittle from age and sat behind the wheel of one the new carts.

Removing his windbreaker, he pulled his shirt over his head and stretched out on his back across two carts. Squinting up at the mottled gray clouds he covered his face with his shirt and stuffed the wadded-up windbreaker under his neck for support. The sweet saltwater air cleared his nostrils. Black bands formed in the sky to the south. In a pleasure boat he'd have been sick by now in the four-foot swells, but they weren't big enough to rock the freighter. He closed his eyes thinking about what might happen when the mailboat landed in New Providence.

Suddenly the bow of the boat dipped like an elevator car dropping in a shaft. He levitated momentarily as a tsunami of cold water splashed over the deck splattering his bare chest. He sat up as the second wave crashed over the deck soaking his pants. Ocean spray sloshed the pallets of cargo pitching gallons of chilly water onto him. The sky had turned solid black, and the waves had grown to ten, maybe twelve feet but it was only a guess with the white caps at the tops of the waves as his only points of reference. These weren't rolling swells. These were steep mountain peaks, the kind that jerked the bow of the *Mis Mama* as her gunwales slammed sideways into walls of water before her bow dropped again. And again.

What the fuck?

Didn't people come to this part of the world for the weather?

He rolled onto his left hip and reached for his duffle bag, losing his balance, hitting his head on the golf cart steering wheel. He rubbed his head then clamped one hand on the edge of the wet vinyl seat and reached down and felt for the bag. He placed the duffle on the seat and used the golf cart wheel to pull himself to a sitting position. He fished his phone from the side pocket of his bag and closed one eye trying to read the screen, hoping to get a weather report or a GPS location. He couldn't steady his hand enough to focus. Another wave smashed over the bow bringing a tidal wave of rushing water that flooded the deck. He wrapped his phone in his shirt and waited for the water to recede. He blotted the screen dry then shoved the phone in his pants pocket.

The bow dipped sharply and another massive wave smashed over the deck. *Mis Mama*'s pallets of cargo slid forward and back testing the chains and stretching the thick nylon straps holding the load in place.

Bare chested and now cold, he grabbed his wet clothes

and slung his duffle over his shoulder. Standing in the narrow space between the tethered carts hoping not to be crushed, he grasped at anything he could as he inched his way toward the pilot house.

Staggering, he took a wide stance and pawed at the knob of the door to the old pilot house. Another wave slopped over the deck soaking his shoes to the ankles. As the water receded, he pushed his face against the salt-frosted glass and saw C.J. and Chan huddled together on a wooden bench inside the tiny room.

He flung the door open and swaying like a drunk, wobbled into the cramped wood paneled room. He clutched a handrail as he pulled the door shut. "You two doing alright?" he yelled.

They nodded, then looked up wide-eyed, heads bobbing uncontrollably.

The engines roared and the smell of burning diesel permeated the pilot house as the sea pummeled the freighter. He reached into his pants pocket and checked the time on his phone. It was just past noon, but the sky was dark as midnight. Leaning against the splintered window frame he looked out the window at the white topped waves, trying but unable to get a fix on the horizon.

The bow of the boat rose and plunged into an endless sea of blackness up ahead.

Was Mother Nature telegraphing him a message?

No.

This wasn't a hint.

This was a full-on ass kicking that was about to get worse.

20

L auren gazed out the port window of the small commuter plane as the pilot hugged the shoreline flying low over Biscayne Bay. She'd never seen the city from this vantage point above a dense forest of high-rise condominiums and Olympic-sized swimming pools and heliports atop some of the priciest real estate in Florida. The plane turned slightly left at the tip of downtown Miami revealing the wide inlets cut inland like Venetian canals lined with glass skyscrapers and palm trees. A tropical version of the Manhattan skyline. She peered below at power boats cutting white lines into the greenish water and the orangish silhouettes of coral reefs in the shallow waters and the shadow of the plane and lazy sailboats and concrete bridges built over the bay linking the mainland to Virginia Key and Key Biscayne. And Miami Beach to South Beach.

A pit formed in her stomach as the Piper Chieftain with two other passengers on board turned sharply to the west. Not from airsickness. Not from fear of facing Peter's family. Rather from the sordid memories of the past.

Decades ago, Pablo Escobar conducted his first reconnaissance run flying a hundred kilos of cocaine into Opa-Locka inducting it into the international cocaine traffickers' hall of fame.

Before that, it'd served as a listening post during the Cuban Missile Crisis. If that weren't enough it was the same airport where the 911 hijackers trained. Where Vance's fugitive kingpin uncle Tony and his imprisoned drug lord partner smuggled tons of white powder. The source of millions of dollars she and Vance now possessed, held in secret offshore accounts.

She searched the seat pocket of the armrest and removed the white waterproof sack. The passenger facing her shot a warning look. She swallowed hard, tucked the vomit bag back in the elastic seat pouch and took the customs documents she'd filled out during the 90-minute flight from her purse.

Looking out the window, she saw the Opa-Locka airport control tower sprouting from the earth like a chess game rook topped with thick planks of smoky glass. Ryan flew above fields of green grass and two-lane roads and further out, over a landscape of flat-roofed bungalows and trailer parks.

As the pilot buzzed City Hall, she wished she had binoculars to see the Moorish architecture of rundown pink domes and white watch towers up close. Florida was a weird place full of failed real estate ventures like this one. What inspired an eccentric millionaire to attempt to recreate the Arabian Nights here, in the middle of a swamp? What would he think of his failed vision now? Opa-Locka was one of the poorest and most corrupt communities in Miami: a no-man's land of crime that locals knew to avoid.

The pilot turned 180-degrees back to the east and lined the plane up with the runway. The airport perimeter was greened-up from the recent rains. The spread below housed the usual unspectacular general aviation buildings and cargo hangars surrounded by jumbo jets from UPS, Amazon Prime and FedEx.

A moment later the Piper touched down. As Ryan taxied toward the terminal, he stopped to let a skinny, futuristic tube touch down and cross the runway. The needle-nosed plane looked like the billfish mounted over the bed at the villa. Did Vance make it off the island? She took her phone from her purse and turned it on. No messages. She texted him: Arrived. She stared at the screen waiting for an answer and when none came, she dropped her phone back in her purse.

Ryan parked the Piper walking distance to the terminal and cut the engines. Lauren released the seat belt and waited for the cockpit door to open. A moment later he stood in the aisle hunched over and facing them.

"Welcome to Miami-Opa-Locka Executive Airport. For those of you who need help with your luggage, go ahead and deplane. After I unload your bags, I'll walk you to the terminal. There's a customs agent inside. Make sure you've filled out your forms. And thank you for flying with Island Hopper."

He'd stowed her bag in the cabin where she'd have to climb between the seats to get it.

"Go ahead," Ryan said to her. "I'll bring yours out."

He popped open the cabin door. The heat and humidity seeped inside causing the windows to fog. Two men in florescent yellow vests carrying wooden blocks and orange cones walked toward the Piper. She deplaned first, stepping onto the wing then down to the asphalt where she waited for the others. Ryan exited last carrying her bag. He set it down. She released and extended the handle, then followed as he led the way stepping around the pools of rainwater that'd settled in the low spots.

This place was a four-star resort compared to the F.B.O. in Homestead where they'd departed yesterday. Manicured boxwood hedges lined a white concrete walkway leading to the terminal. The tall glass wall facing the tarmac was accented with big squares of aluminum like a two-story game of tic-tac-toe. When Ryan opened the door to the terminal for her, she felt the blast of arctic air conditioning. The interior looked newly remodeled with soaring ceilings and gleaming concrete floors. She paused to admire the metal art installation inside next to the entrance. The smooth silver surface reflected a fun house mirror image of herself.

"It's an airplane propeller," Ryan said, holding the glass door open. He addressed the small group. "See that room over there?"

He pointed to an INTERNATIONAL ARRIVALS placard affixed to the top half of Dutch Door at the far end inside the building.

They nodded.

"Wait there and someone'll be right with you."

She looked around and didn't see anyone working behind the long dark wood counter. Off to the right where Ryan had told them to go, she saw a large open area with a half dozen squat, mid-century chairs with skinny metal legs. The faux-wood seats were set in a circle along the edges of a large, round navy-blue rug. A scale model of an airplane was mounted to the wall like a hunting trophy. A long bench carved from the trunk of an ancient cypress tree was pushed up against the glass wall near the entrance. Her tailbone ached looking at it.

She walked toward the waiting area and sat in one of the

low, hard chairs. The other two passengers leaned against the wall near the room marked INTERNATIONAL ARRIVALS.

A moment later a man in a brown uniform opened the top half of the Dutch door. She was last in line. After he checked her documents and stamped her passport, she walked to the reception area.

Leaning against the counter she peered around the corner looking for help. A young Hispanic woman arrived in a high-tech motorized wheelchair. She raised it with a lever. "May I help you?"

"Do you have a designated Uber pickup area?"

"They'll meet you at the curb. You can wait here until they arrive."

"Thanks."

"There's free coffee and bottled water while you wait."

"Thanks."

She returned to the waiting area and sat in the same low, backbreaking chair and opened the rideshare app on her phone, confirming the location. It was a 45.5-mile drive south to Homestead where she'd left her vehicle at the airport. The estimated drive time was one hour. The tiny car icon showed the closest driver was 15-minutes away on the Florida Turnpike heading north. She confirmed the ride then set her phone to SILENT MODE and placed it on her knee. With time to kill she unzipped the side pocket of her carry-on and felt for the book she'd brought on the trip. It wasn't there.

Crap. She didn't remember packing it and must've left it on the nightstand at the resort.

She checked her phone again. Still nothing from Vance. She drummed the tips of her fingers on the phone screen then opened the browser and searched '*cardology.*' Tapping the link to the most popular website she watched a short promotional video posted on the HOME PAGE. It was slickly produced with flashy mystical images of the universe and stars and the sun and the moon. Like all good teasers it had a closing graphic tempting her to become a subscriber to learn more. She declined the offer then navigated to the ABOUT PAGE and scanned the text. In a nutshell cardology was described on the website as 'the intersection of astrology, numerology and tarot cards.'

The people she knew who were interested in the metaphysical world always seemed to be the ones who smoked dope and ate magic mushrooms.

At the bottom of the page, she saw a button titled YOUR SOLAR CARD.

Who could resist? Cross referencing the day and month of her birthday from a chart on the page she discovered she was a Six of Clubs. There was another button linking to YOUR PERSONALITY. She turned her phone upside down on her knee and looked out the window as a Boeing 767-300 plane touched down. She watched the light blue and white cargo jet lumber toward the hangar.

She picked up her phone, woke up the screen and tapped the YOUR PERSONALITY button. Links to all 52 cards came up on the page divided by suit and number. She scrolled down to the Six of Clubs, clicked on the link and began to read.

'*The Six of Clubs is always on a path seeking the truth. They are connectors and being dishonest always leads to a loss of focus and direction.*'

Good to know. She changed screens and checked the rideshare app. The tiny black car was 6 minutes away.

She hesitated, then reopened the YOUR SOLAR CARD tab and looked up Vance's birthday. He was A King of Clubs.

She hesitated, then tapped the YOUR PERSONALITY tab and changed screens to see what it had to say about him. *'The challenge for the King of Clubs is balancing leisure with work.'*

Wasn't that true for everyone?

She checked the rideshare app. The rideshare driver was one minute away. She grabbed the handle of her bag and exited the terminal, feeling the sucker punch of hot humid air as she opened the door. She stood at the curb waiting as a thin layer of sweat beaded on her brow. A silver SUV approached. She checked the license plate against the one on the app. The driver, a middle-aged woman, stopped in front of the terminal, released the latch from inside, jumped out and lifted the hatchback door. "Are you Lauren?"

"I am."

"I'm Bonnie. How was your trip?" She took Lauren's bag and hoisted it into the vehicle, then reached up and closed the hatch door.

"Uneventful."

She tilted her head slightly and raised an eyebrow. "Those can be the best kind."

"True." Lauren climbed into the backseat on the passenger's side and pulled the car door shut.

Bonnie pulled from the curb. "Are you in the business?"

"What business?"

"Aviation."

"No. Why?"

"You're Ubering between two airports. I wondered if you're a cargo pilot or something."

"No."

"I shuttle a lot of them from here. The neighborhood is hinky, so you have to know which way to go to avoid getting into trouble. It's gotten a lot worse lately. All those morons on TV and the internet squawk about it but they never do anything."

It was true. She'd stopped watching the news. The murder rate had doubled since last year and she didn't want to see the face of another dead child or an interview with another grieving mother.

"I was on vacation. I flew out of Homestead yesterday then something came up and I had to cut my trip short. The only option to get home was to fly here."

Bonnie made eye contact in the rearview. "That's too bad about your vacay. Where were you, if you don't mind me asking?"

"The Bahamas."

"That really sucks," Bonnie said. "We had a hell of a storm yesterday afternoon. Travel was a complete mess."

She watched Bonnie take her eyes off the road long enough to adjust the smartphone connected to a swivel arm attached to the cup holder on the center console.

"If I take the Turnpike, I can get you to Homestead in just over an hour. It's not the scenic route, but it's faster. Provided there aren't any surprises."

"It's Miami," Lauren said, "there're always surprises."

"I hear that," Bonnie said. "But we're lucky it's a Sunday."

"Yeah, lucky us."

Workweek traffic could easily be a two-hour trip.

She typed another message to Vance: Promised to text when I landed. Smooth flight. On my way to get my car. Where are you?

Lauren stared at the screen waiting for a green text bubble to appear. Still nothing from Vance. That was weird. Why wasn't he answering?

·   ·   ·

LAUREN LOOKED over Bonnie's left shoulder at the tall green and white sign for Miami Homestead General Aviation. Bonnie slowed, activated the left-hand turn indicator and hugged the painted yellow road lines opposite the airport entrance. The grass along the front was flooded with standing water. Bonnie stopped and waited for a break in traffic.

The airport looked different today. Lauren didn't remember the giant F.B.O. letters crudely painted in blood red on the side of the ugly white two-story building. She hadn't noticed the row of juvenile queen palm trees planted out front, supported by wooden stakes and pink plastic ties. Maybe because yesterday, she was wearing her vacation goggles.

While Bonnie waited for a break in traffic, a flatbed semi-tractor trailer approached from the opposite direction. It swung wide to make a right-hand turn into the airport entrance, so wide it almost skimmed Bonnie's front bumper.

"Fucker," Bonnie said, immediately apologizing for the slip of the tongue.

An orange helicopter was anchored to the flatbed with straps and chains. Although it was three-quarters covered with a heavy canvas tarp, it was obviously a Coast Guard asset.

Bonnie turned left and stopped the SUV behind the semi blocking the driveway. A yellow taco truck was parked on the inside of the chain link fence parallel to the shoulder of the road. A Hispanic woman with two small children sat on a picnic bench under the open-air *palapa* facing the street.

"Where do you want me to drop you?" Bonnie asked.

Lauren leaned against the passenger's side door and pressed her cheek close to the window. "I parked up ahead on the right. I think there's enough room for you to go around."

Bonnie backed up and approached the narrow gap between the tractor trailer and the parked cars.

"Mine's the black Audi next to that red pickup."

Bonnie eyes flicked left and right watching the side mirrors as she squeezed her vehicle between the tractor-trailer and the parked cars.

Lauren checked her phone again. God, she hated it when Vance ignored her.

Bonnie stopped adjacent to the tailgate of the red pickup and popped the hatchback from the cockpit. "In order to leave enough room for you to get out on your side, I don't have enough on my side to open my door and help you with your bag."

"I got it from here," Lauren said, opening the car door, careful not to hit the bumper of the pickup. She walked around the back of the SUV and grabbed her bag.

Bonnie turned around behind the wheel and yelled from the driver's seat. "Do you mind closing the hatch?"

"Sure," Lauren set her roller bag down behind the bumper of the red pickup. She stuck her head inside the back of Bonnie's car. "Five stars and a twenty percent tip," she said, then reached up and pulled the hatchback shut.

Bonnie then backed up and rolled down the passenger window. "Be safe."

"You too," Lauren said, riffling through her purse for her car key. She noticed the back taillight of the Audi was broken out. Pieces of red and clear plastic lay on the ground near the rear tire on the driver's side.

Dammit. A hit and run.

Dragging her roller bag, she marched around the tractor trailer blocking the driveway, grabbed the front door handle and strode to the reception desk. The truck driver, an athletic man with red sideburns wearing khakis and a white polo, stood in front of her at the counter waiting for the receptionist. The clerk sat in her chair with her back to him, the receiver of the landline resting on her shoulder. Lauren paced back and forth the length of the counter. The truck driver looked up at the security monitor on the wall. Noticing her on the screen he turned around.

"Sorry, ma'am. Am I blocking you?" he asked in a slight drawl.

"Yeah, you're blocking me."

The receptionist hung up the phone. "Head on back," she said to the truck driver. "A guy named Bill will meet you and show you where to park."

As the truck driver headed for the exit, Lauren approached the counter. She was same woman who'd been manning the desk yesterday. The woman got up from her chair holding the same big fingernail file she'd seen her using yesterday and drummed it against her left knuckles. "May I help you?"

"We flew out yesterday and—"

"I remember you—"

She pointed out the window toward the tractor-trailer blocking the view to the parked cars. "Someone hit my car in the parking lot, and I wondered if you might have a video of it." She gestured up to the flat screen monitor on the wall.

"We do, but you don't need it," she said, turning her back, walking to her desk, sitting and thumbing through piles of paper. She pulled a sticky note from a stack of pink, yellow and white papers. "Here." She got up from her desk and handed her a lime green Post-It note. "The lady who hit you asked me to give this to you. She said she left a note on the car, but it was raining, and she was worried you wouldn't get it."

"When did it happen?"

"Um," she squinted with one eye and tapped an emery board the size of a tongue depressor on the chipped Formica counter. "I don't know." She raised one shoulder, then dropped it. "Sometime after you left, I guess."

"Do you know her?"

"The woman who hit your car?"

"Yes."

"No. I've never seen her before."

"What was she doing here?"

"How should I know? Maybe she was taking a skydiving lesson, or dropping someone off, or picking someone up. Perhaps she was hungry and stopped for a *chimichanga*. If I were you, I'd be happy she left her phone number."

"Do you remember what she looked like or what she was driving?"

"You have the number. Find out for yourself."

"Fine." Lauren took her phone from her purse, dialed the number on the sticky note then put it on speaker. It rang six times, then went to voicemail.

She didn't bother to listen to it. Rather Lauren stabbed the red dot and ended the call, folded the green paper into fours and slid it beneath the driver's license in her wallet.

"That was a short trip," the clerk said.

"Something came up."

"Nice car," the woman said.

"Past tense. Don't even bother trying to have anything nice."

"I never had to worry about that."

"Has Blade been back?"

"If he has, I haven't seen him," the receptionist said, returning to her desk.

Lauren reached inside her purse for her key and not finding it in the usual inside pocket of her leather bag, sat in a chair and dug but it wasn't in her bag. She grabbed her rolling suitcase and headed for the exit, shouldering the door to open it.

The freaking flatbed tractor trailer was still blocking her car.

She pushed the button on the trunk of her car with her finger. That was weird. It didn't open. The car electronically sensed the fob. She tried the driver's side door. Same result. Where was the key? She recalled running to her car just before the flight left for The Bahamas to get the book about card games she'd left on the back seat.

"Can I give you a hand with anything?" the truck driver asked.

He'd startled her. "I doubt it." She leaned against the driver's side door and folded her arms across her chest.

"What's the problem?"

"I can't find my key."

"Did you lose it?"

"What if I did?"

"I could help with that."

"How?"

"Wait here."

He returned with his phone in his hand and pointed it at the locked car door. The blinking red lock light visible through the car window stopped.

"Try the door," the truck driver said.

It opened. She leaned over and popped the trunk. The truck driver loaded her bag and shut the lid.

"How did you do that?"

"I can help you start it, but I can only do it once. Do you have another key?"

"I have one at home."

"Once I get you going, don't stop until you get home. Or you won't be able to restart the car."

"I don't understand how you did that?"

"Push the ignition button."

She hopped behind the wheel, pressed the start button on the center console and the engine turned over. She closed the car door and powered down the window. "How did you do that?"

He shrugged. "I move Coast Guard helicopters for a living. Appreciate it if you didn't mention this to anyone. I'll move my rig so you can get going."

A few minutes later she was driving north on the Florida Turnpike.

A LOW FUEL light flashed on the dash. She didn't have enough gas to get home.

Crap. How would she make it home if she couldn't restart her car?

21

POTTERS CAY, NASSAU, BAHAMAS
THE ISLAND PORT SITUATED BETWEEN NEW
PROVIDENCE AND PARADISE ISLAND

Vance watched from the bow as Captain Boogie Morgan piloted the *Mis Mama* into the blue mouth of Nassau Harbour. The sun pushed through the clouds like a searchlight spraying a cone of light on the docks ahead in the distance. A jetty built from huge boulders stacked in the shallows of a sandbar served as the channel marker on the port side of the inlet. Up ahead on the same side, a 60-foot-tall white lighthouse sprang from the westernmost tip of Paradise Island.

As the freighter slowed, he saw the lighthouse up close, the decaying white brick base topped with a red lantern in the late stages of disrepair. Beyond the lighthouse a dense thicket of bright green vegetation grew wild along the skinny peninsula reminding him of a tropical Central Park.

Low tide exposed a vertical limestone cliff along the rocky shoreline and beyond the old lighthouse he saw the resorts and casinos rising from the teal water like the eponymous mythological city, Atlantis.

Vance stood leaning against the bow of the freighter scanning the hazy white horizon. He took deep breaths, letting each one out slowly. His plan to keep breakfast down only held because his stomach was empty. When the storm had calmed enough to walk the deck, he'd left C.J. and Chan in the pilot house and snaked his way between the pallets of cargo packed on the weathered deck.

Morgan slowed the 70-foot freighter to a crawl as he came upon an enormous 6-story cruise ship creeping toward port. Passengers on the lido and promenade decks looked down and waved to Vance on the old mailboat and to folks on luxury pleasure vessels and to the local journeymen on the aluminum jon boats hauling the day's catch. As they sailed past downtown Nassau, he caught a strong whiff of fried fish coming from the waterfront cafes.

Flocks of mewling gulls dive bombed a shrimp trawler anchored in the channel with its spidery outrigger nets pulled up for the day. Pelicans perched on the rocks and begged tourists for food. The wake of the cruise ship rocked the bow of the mailboat, but it was nothing compared to the beating Mother Nature had dispensed earlier during the storm. It'd been a miracle he hadn't puked or been washed out to sea by waves crashing over the deck in a squall that had brought darkness and blinding bolts of lightning strikes in the middle of the day.

The side of the dock where they'd landed at Potters Cay acted as the exhaust pipe for boat traffic, sparing the tourists. Overhead, gigantic cement pylons rose from the dirty blue waters supporting a massive concrete bridge connecting the capitol city of Nassau to touristy Paradise Island. Built to accommodate the mighty cruises ships, the floating hotel they'd followed into the channel sailed beneath it and onward toward the terminals located on the cleaner side of Potters Cay. Morgan slowed the freighter, reversed the engines, and steered toward the freight dock. Workers lined up along the bulkhead ready to lend a hand.

As the captain landed the *Mis Mama* men scurried alongside catching the bowlines as Boogie tossed them from the deck like lassoes. Sea water sloshed between the hull and the bulkhead; worn car tires on ropes strung from the gunwales served as bumpers. A flock of seagulls passed overhead checking for scraps, their spray of watery droppings barely missing Vance. He ran his hand over his head, making sure. The scene along the dock suddenly sprang to life as if a director had yelled action on a movie set. Men barked at each other in their slightly British island accents. He watched as the dock workers hand carried a portable gangplank like a gurney and connected the freighter to land. An old forklift rumbled toward the ship puffing gray exhaust.

Chan and C.J. emerged from the pilot house.

"We've reached," Morgan yelled down from the poop deck. "You three wait."

A minute later the captain joined them. He removed a pint of whiskey from the front hip pocket of his waders. He gulped, stuffed the bottle back in his pocket, then climbed atop a pallet of bricks to supervise. Waving his hands and hollering he conducted the workers as they offloaded the freight.

"You three gonna be all day? Move it," Boogie barked from his perch. "Off my boat." He waved his arms as if chasing flies.

Vance slung his duffle bag over his shoulder and led the way toward the gangplank waiting for a break in foot traffic.

"That trip sucked," C.J. said, catapulting Chan's bag onto the gunwale.

"Yeah," Vance said, waiting for the gangplank to clear then leading the way with Chan and C.J. following, relieved to set foot on dry land. When he spotted a big block of concrete holding a light on a pole, he dropped his duffle at the base and sat on the edge, his brain swaying inside his skull.

C.J. leaned Chan's backpack against one side of the concrete block. "Scoot over."

He made room for C.J. who sat next to him. C.J. motioned to Chan to join them but she waved him off and stood with her back to them watching another behemoth cruise ship filled with passengers crawl past. Waves rippled from the wake, rocking the work boats tied to the dock.

He tilted his head and eyed Chan's backpack. "You must be tired of hauling that thing around."

"It wasn't the plan," C.J. said.

True. None of what happened so far was part of the plan. He shaded his eyes and gazed across the harbor waters at the fantasy hotel and casino rising from the sea where Lauren had booked a room for them. An enormous façade in the shape of an arch linked a pair of coral-pink towers topped with medieval turrets and sharp spires. He would go there, but first he had to find out where Chan and C.J. were staying.

A stranger carrying boxes stacked three high headed toward them balancing the load with his chin.

"Excuse me," C.J. said, "do you know how we can get to Nassau?"

The man ignored them, hurrying his step, flip-flops smacking the bottoms of his feet.

"Look." Vance pointed to Boogie waddling along the gangplank like a feral hog on two back legs. He'd taken off his waders and changed into a pair of baggie jeans and a dry plaid shirt.

Boogie saw them sitting and strolled over. "Why you boys still here?"

"How can we get an Uber from here to Nassau?" C.J. asked.

Boogie guffawed, like he'd heard that question before. He looked skyward. "You could walk the bridge."

"I don't want to walk," Vance said. "I want a lift."

Boogie pointed to the main street running down the centerline of Potters Cay Island. "Go to the corner and turn right. Look for a blue and white building 'bout the size of a phone booth."

"What are we going to find?" C.J. asked.

The captain slid his thumbs through the belt loops of his jeans and cleared his throat. "You'll find a way to get a ride to the mainland."

"How far from here?" Vance asked.

"A block, maybe two," Boogie said.

Vance looked in that direction and saw thick vehicle traffic traveling slowly in both directions.

"If you's goin' to Nassau," Boogie said, "you can go by bus or water taxi."

"Come on," Vance said to C.J, "get Chan and let's go."

He led the way taking a right-hand turn at the corner, walking past cardboard boxes and crates of fruit and vegetables stacked ten high along the dock. There was a sense of organized chaos as workers stood guard over their goods. He choked on the smell of burning hydrocarbons coming from the delivery trucks and dented mini vans staged on the street still wet from a recent rain, engines idling. Delivery drivers waited their turn then exchanged handfuls of cash through open windows while workers loaded fresh seafood and produce into the backs of their vehicles.

The ocean water around the docks was a murky gray blue, dulled by boat traffic and propellers. Bile bubbled up his throat at the sight of a bloated, rotten fish bobbing in the water surrounded by empty plastic soda bottles floating in rainbow sheen of motor oil. A fishmonger wearing a blood-stained leather apron gutted a red snapper on a rusty metal table tossing slabs of skin into a rubber tub. His ab muscles clenched, fighting to keep the contents of his stomach down while his brain reminded him there was nothing left to puke.

He trudged past a commercial trawler tied to heavy duty metal cleats embedded in the concrete. Gleaming private cruisers passed through the channel dwarfing the small panga fishing boats, the fishermen fighting the waves and wakes with their tiny handheld outboard motors.

He looked around for the blue shack but didn't see it. They came upon food stalls jam-packed on both sides of the street, many filled with tourists sitting on barstools and weathered benches. Most of the shanties had been cobbled together from corrugated metal and planks of brightly painted plywood with crude signs affixed to the kind of flimsy latticework he'd seen around trailer parks back home. The five-star entrepreneurs operated out of portable storage sheds, the sort for sale in the parking lots of the big box hardware stores.

Chan and C.J. stopped to read the Bahamian pea and rice special handwritten on the chalkboard. The chef-owner hawked fritters and chowders and salads and fried fish. The couple huddled, to discuss prices he suspected.

"Can we stop and eat something?" C.J. asked.

"We need to check the ferry schedule first," he said.

`They continued their trek until C.J. and Chan stopped again at the rolling carts big enough to move hospital laundry loaded to the gills with produce and shellfish. He read the names hand painted on the sides. *Foxey's, Twilight Grocers*, and *Boners*. One cart overflowed with shiny pink and white conch shells that would've been a prized possession had one washed ashore on a Florida beach. They continued their walk, passing a yellow and turquoise food stall selling fresh barracuda with a warning written in cursive on a white board: '*Barrcuda, eat at ur risk, 5 dollars per peace.*'

A woman with opaque eyes sat on a rusted metal rocking chair strumming a guitar, a tune faintly familiar, though he couldn't place it. Two locals sat at a picnic table playing checkers on a baby blue and beige board. He turned back and dropped a five spot in the woman's straw hat laying on the ground. Another pair of men stared intently at rows of Dominoes—a game he should've understood but didn't—the ivory and black polka-dotted game pieces laid in lines atop a weathered wooden table.

He needed this walk and all the sights and sounds to clear his head from the nightmare aboard the *Mis Mama*. He wanted the wobble in his knees to go away.

He stopped when he lost sight of C.J. and Chan behind him. He backtracked through the crowd and saw them standing next to a wheel barrel loaded with green fishnet bags packed full of small red chili peppers.

"What are you doing?" he asked them.

"We're enjoying the local flavor," C.J. said, standing next

to a stack of metal cages full of crabs clattering to break free.

"Just for a few minutes," Chan said.

"Go on without us," C.J. said. "There's no reason why we can't say our goodbyes now."

"True," he said, "but we've come this far. Let's go as far as the city. Take your time. What's the hurry? Right?"

"Right," C.J. said, "no rush, but I thought you were staying on Paradise Island. We're going to Nassau."

"I want to try to find the passport office first," he said, which sounded like a plausible story for sticking with them. "I may as well stay in Nassau tonight, so I won't have to fight Monday morning traffic."

C.J. shrugged. "Whatever suits you."

Chan appeared mesmerized at the goings-on in the vibrant shantytown beneath the bridge. She had an awestruck look on her face, mouth slightly agape, eyes a little wider than normal.

As he followed her focus, he wondered why everything seemed to be painted in bright colors. Was it to cover the discarded building materials, mainly planks of bowed plywood and sheets of bent corrugated metal? Or did the locals understand the hypnotic beauty of the backdrop; that in order to be noticed, the manmade materials had to be as bright as a peacock?

When Chan and C.J. were finished sightseeing, they continued their trek to the blue shack.

C.J. towered above the crowd like a human periscope. The boy shaded his eyes, then announced, "I think I see the place."

He watched C.J. hoist the backpack over his shoulders and lead the way to a royal blue and white portable building with a crude sign for Ferry Boats nailed above a sliding window.

Vance approached and was greeted by a man with an easy smile and gums for front teeth. "Where to, sir?"

"We're heading to Nassau," Vance said.

"I kin sell you a ticket to de ferry."

"How much and when does the next one leave?"

"Six dollars each and de ferry leaves every 'alf hour."

"How much is a taxi."

"You mean de jitney?"

"Yeah, the jitney."

"'Tis double de price."

C.J. leaned in front of him and interrupted. "I'll take two tickets for the ferry." He removed a wad of cash from his shorts pocket and counted out twelve dollars.

"And one for me," Vance said, handing the man a ten. "Keep the change."

"Thank you," the toothless man said to Vance, tearing three raffle tickets from a roll and handing them out.

They walked toward the ferry landing located at the end of an austere concrete dock. A lone palm tree listed on an angle, yellow and brown-tipped fronds drooping.

Chan said, "If I were you, I'd check into that swanky resort, take a hot shower and a nap and work on sorting out your passport later."

"I think I'm going to look for a place in the city to spend the night."

"Not a bad idea," C.J. said, "you'll be dealing with a bureaucracy. No telling how long it will take to get a replacement passport."

"True," he said, successfully dodging a pair of aggressive street vendors hawking souvenirs and counterfeit merch displayed on a folding table set up behind pitted aluminum barricades. "At this point, all I want is to go home."

The vendors targeted a fortyish tourist dressed like a

cowgirl walking alone behind them. When he turned back to see, they'd corralled her and were holding up 'It's Better in the Bahamas' T-shirts.

Chan and C.J. sat together on a green bench.

Vance stood on the bulkhead watching for the ferry, wondering how close they were to the thirty-minute window. If he was going to find Tonk, he was going to have to figure out how to shadow C.J. and Chan once they got to Nassau.

He saw a man sitting on an upside-down five-gallon bucket at the end of the ferry dock. His makeshift dry dock was constructed from cinder blocks, two-by-four lumber and old tires. He strolled closer to see what he was doing. The man was sanding barnacles from the bottom of a tiny sailboat. By hand. He noticed the name of the boat, *Psalm 91* scrawled in faded white paint on the stern. The man glanced up from his work and nodded slowly at him, then folded the sandpaper in half, turned it over and continued rubbing the hull.

Vance wandered back to the dock and sat on the bench next to Chan and C.J. watching the orange sun begin to dip behind the horizon.

"Those people have been waiting over an hour," C.J. said, pointing to a couple sitting on a log throwing rocks in the water.

"How do you know that?"

"I asked them," C.J. said.

He reached into the pocket of his pants and removed his phone. Shading the cover with his left hand, he typed '*Psalm 91*' into the browser. The screen filled with links. He tapped the one titled '*King James Version*' and began to read:

91 He that dwelleth in the secret place of the most High shall abide under the shadow of the Almighty.

[2] I will say of the Lord, He is my refuge and my fortress: my God; in him will I trust.

[3] Surely he shall deliver thee from the snare of the fowler, and from the noisome pestilence.

Just then a loud flapping sound distracted him. He looked up as dozens of seagulls hovered overhead, jockeying for position, looking for places to roost atop the wooden pylons lining the dock. He continued to read.

[4] He shall cover thee with his feathers, and under his wings shalt thou trust: his truth shall be thy shield and buckler.

An omen?

"Ugh," Chan said. "Have you had a recent rabies shot?"

"What?" he asked, shoving his phone in his pocket.

"Look," C.J. said.

A dilapidated blue and white double-decker boat sailed toward the ferry dock. The second story roof looked hand-made, and it resembled the overloaded boats filled with Cubans and Haitians that washed ashore on the Florida beaches. While the lower deck of the ferry was packed with people, apparently no one was brave nor stupid enough to ride on the rooftop.

"Jesus," C.J. said, "We'll make national news when it capsizes, and we're lost at sea."

The ferry boat pilot slowed, rotated a hundred-and-eighty degrees and backed in perpendicular to the concrete seawall. Three old tractor tires draped from the stern. Mismatched faded rubber bumpers in the shapes of big red balls hung from the starboard side like sad Christmas ornaments. A crew member dressed in brown shorts hanging halfway off his ass bent over to pick up a rope, exposing his plaid boxers.

Two dozen tourists held onto each other and onto a

wooden middle handrail above the two-sided wooden bench running the length of the lower cabin. The deckhand with the low-slung pants hopped onto the dock, tied off to a post, then offered a helping hand to the arrivals.

After the boat was unloaded, they waited for the couple who'd been waiting for more than an hour to board first. He let Chan and C.J. go first, then climbed aboard and sat next to the couple. The woman had short fingernails polished black. He didn't like the look: to him, short black fingernails conjured an image of a woman who'd dug a grave at night with her fingertips. The man accompanying her seemed agitated, drumming his fingers on his blue jeans and staring straight ahead. They sat a little too far apart, as if in the midst of a domestic problem.

At least the ferry wasn't crowded. With five passengers and two crewmen, how bad could the trip be? The boat bobbed in the water and soon his brain began to sway in his skull again.

After ten minutes, he stood and walked to the bow to talk with the boat pilot, a malnourished man with bones for legs. "Is there a problem?"

"What you mean?" he asked, cocking his head at him with a confused look on his face.

"The boat. Why aren't we leaving for Nassau?"

"We don't go 'til we have a full load."

"How long does that take?"

He shrugged at him. "We wait 'til others come."

"What others?"

The pilot shrugged again and when the man's phone rang a Bob Marley tune, he took it from his pocket and answered on the first ring.

"Jesus," he said under his breath, heading back to the group.

"What's up?" C.J. asked.

"They're waiting for more passengers."

"From where?"

"Who knows." He felt his phone vibrate in his pocket. He sat on the paint chipped bench as the idling ferry boat huffed a gray cloud of smoke and rocked in the water. Two text messages from Lauren popped up on his screen. They were several hours old. Even the cell towers around here didn't have their shit together.

Promised to text when I landed. Smooth flight. On my way to get my car. Where are you?

He was about to answer when a new alert dinged on his screen. This one was from American Express notifying him of a recent credit card charge at The Poseidon Club. *Fuck.* The message was two hours old.

How could that be? He removed his wallet from his back pocket and opened it. The only credit card he had on him was the Visa drawn on his Cayman bank. Then he remembered. He'd tucked his AmEx under the sleeve of the black leather folder of his passport when he was packing for the trip. Just in case.

"Is everything alright?" Chan asked.

"Yeah," he said, "here," he pulled two one-hundred-dollar bills from his wallet. "Go offer this to the captain of this hunk of junk. Tell him it's his tip if he leaves now."

He watched Chan walk to the front of the boat and have a chat. A moment later the engines revved, and the boat lurched forward surprising C.J. who stood leaning against a wooden post holding the flimsy rooftop deck.

He opened the alert text from American Express. His index finger hovered over the link to the 800-fraud hotline. He was about to tap it when suddenly he had a much better idea.

22

L auren pressed the remote on the visor and waited for the rolling security gate protecting the six-car condo parking lot she shared with her two neighbors to open. Sunday afternoon traffic on the drive from the private airport in Homestead to Coconut Grove was light, and the roads were still wet from the latest downpour. She'd found a gas station after her low fuel light appeared on the dash and put ten dollars' worth of high octane in the tank with the engine running. She'd also placed a call to her therapist and left a voicemail.

While she waited for the gate, she scanned the public park across the street through the passenger window. The homeless encampment where she used to walk her dog had mushroomed. She and many others had called the police and begged their city council reps for help. But it didn't matter what they wanted. They were told there was nothing anyone could do about it. At night there were fist fights. During the day she heard arguments. There was a woman who yelled at all hours during the day and night at something no one else could see. Not to mention the garbage and needles and foul smell that wafted, preventing her from opening the windows.

Her phone rang on Bluetooth. Dr. Molly Westerly's name lit up on the dash.

"Hi Lauren. I got your message. What's up?"

"I'm sorry to bother you on a Sunday but I'm about to have a panic attack," she said, watching the gate protecting her condo roll open.

"What's going on?" Dr. Westerly asked.

"Peter's been in an accident and he's in the hospital."

Dr. Westerly paused. "Peter?"

"My ex-husband," she said, parking in her reserved spot.

"Are you back together with him?"

"No. The hospital called and said I'm still listed as his durable medical power of attorney."

"Wow," Dr. Westerly said. "Is he incapacitated?"

"It sounds like it, but they wouldn't give me any detail over the phone."

"He didn't update his paperwork?"

"Apparently not. The hospital called and asked me to come."

"Oh, wow. When are you going?"

"That's what I wanted to talk to you about."

"It's Sunday, Lauren."

"I know. I shouldn't have asked you."

"Hold on."

Dr. Westerly's phone went quiet for almost a full minute. "Can you make it in forty-five minutes?"

"Yes."

"It'll have to be a short session. I have plans this evening. I'll leave your name with the guard. You remember the drill."

"I do. If you prefer, I could do a video call."

"I don't do those," Dr. Westerly said.

"Okay. I'll see you in an hour."

Sitting behind the wheel, she closed her eyes and rested her head against the seat back. How weird, she'd worked so hard to put the divorce behind her and now it'd come back to life in the most unexpected way. She parked, mindful to push the button to pop the trunk before killing the engine. She got out, and glaring at the dent and broken taillight, grabbed her roller bag, closed the trunk and dragged her suitcase to the outer gate leading to the narrow walkway to her condo.

Seriously?

The key to the house was on the same ring as the car.

She sat on the edge of brick walkway, fighting the urge to cry, feeling a tear welling.

Then she remembered she'd given a key to her neighbor, Matthew.

She rang the bell and waited, but he didn't answer. After a couple of minutes, she pressed the doorbell again.

"Hey you!"

She looked up to see where the voice was coming from. Matthew stood at the open window on the second floor.

She cupped her hands and tilted her head back. "I locked myself out!"

"Oh, you poor thing," he said. "I just got out of the shower. Give me a minute."

She clasped her hands, held them up for Matthew to see and mouthed, 'thank you.'

She walked back to her car and sat behind the wheel to wait. How would it feel to see Peter in a hospital bed? What if his family was there? She'd called his mother out of desperation during their break-up, but Marge didn't answer, and never returned her call. It was a dumb idea to call. She was *his mother*.

She could count the times she'd fallen off each of her horses. It was a lot like getting dumped by Peter: painful and unpredictable.

Just before you fall there's that nano-second when you know you can't save it, the realization that your center of gravity has tilted too far in one direction and the best thing to do is to just let go. Why had she been unable to apply the same logic when it came to Peter and just let go?

It'd started with the affair. She'd sensed something was wrong but when she asked him what, he denied it. She'd been stunned when he came home one evening, sat down and said, '*We're broken.*'

What did that even mean? She'd been through breakups before. But this one was different. It was sudden.

She cringed at what happened next. A series of desperate attempts to save the marriage. Begging him to go to couples counseling. Wheeling and dealing ready to sell her soul.

But he made it clear he had no interest. He'd already moved on.

She checked the time. Three o'clock in the afternoon. She looked for missed calls or messages from Vance but still nothing.

Scrolling through RECENT CALLS she looked for the number for the woman who'd hit-and-run her car, then changed her mind scrolling past it and redialed the woman who'd called from the hospital. Not expecting an answer on a Sunday, she left a voice message telling Jennifer Watkins she was back in Miami, suggesting they meet at 10 in the morning. Traffic would be a bitch on a Monday and by mid-morning the worst of it should be cleared.

Matthew appeared in shorts and flip-flops, key in hand.

"I thought you weren't coming back until next week?"

"Thank goodness you were home," she said.

"Where're your keys?" he asked, unlocking the gate.

"I don't know."

"I have to go and get beautified. I have a hot date." He shimmied his hips. "Sunday Funday."

"With Josh?" she asked, holding her hand out for the key.

"His name is Jeb." He dropped the key in her hand. "You better get me another copy, girl."

She hugged and thanked him, then unlocked the front door and went inside. Next, she removed the green Post-It note from her purse and redialed the number. It rang five times.

"Hello."

"Hello, this is Lauren Gold and—"

There was a delay before she was cut off by a singsong message. "You've reached Cassie. I'm not available to take your call. Please leave me a message."

Did people who recorded greetings like this think it was funny? She stabbed the red button without leaving a message, riffled through the desk drawer in her home office, grabbed the spare key, got behind the wheel of her car and backed out.

If the homeless people wandering in the park across the street were dogs, the community would be outraged, taking matters into their own hands. They'd raise money, post urgent messages on neighborhood apps, offer to pay for food and vet bills and microchips and whatever. Good Samaritans would rush in to foster the animals until their forever homes could be found. But the homeless humans? People just bitched about them, but no one had any ideas about what to do. The longer the barracks were allowed to grow, the more ominous the problem became. The truth was everyone was afraid.

Ever since she'd been accosted in the condo parking lot by a lost soul, she'd become more vigilant. She wanted to get a dog, but where would she walk it? Vance had bought her a gun; a small snub-nosed revolver and she'd refused to go to the gun range with him. She'd stowed it in the bottom of her dresser drawer. She'd have to rethink that.

She checked her phone again. It'd been hours since she texted Vance. Why hadn't he answered yet?

23

The drive from Lauren's Coconut Grove condo to Dr. Molly Westerly's place in Cocoplum was just under twenty minutes. The weather had turned so crisp and clear she opened the sunroof on the Audi. As she approached the guard shack at Dr. Westerly's community, the uniformed man inside stood with his back to her speaking on his phone. When he noticed her in his periphery he turned and held up a finger. A white Bentley with a gaudy hood ornament and smoky windows passed her on the right and entered through the residents-only gate.

The burly guard emerged holding a clipboard. "I haven't seen you in a while. Are you here to see Dr. Westerly?"

"I am."

"May I see your photo I.D. please?"

It didn't matter how many times she'd been there, he always asked. He used to apologize, but not today. She handed him her driver's license and waited while he made a call on the landline.

"Go ahead," he said.

The gate opened and as she entered the exclusive community, she lowered the visor to cut the sun, mindful of the 15-mile per hour signs posted on both sides of the manicured medians recently mowed, mulched and planted with late spring flowers. Long before the affluent fled the Eastern Seaboard for Florida, Cocoplum was already one of the wealthiest enclaves in Dade County.

Like many places of Miami, its original development had a secret past. The stately homes, many of them waterfront, had been built on higher ground with covered boat slips so smugglers could hide their loads of illegal drugs. Recently, the houses and land values had skyrocketed with most now starting in the millions.

Lauren turned left at the second street and parked curbside in front of a sprawling two-story Mediterranean home with beige stucco, brick archways and a red clay tile roof. She walked the slight incline to the arched front doors and slowed as she approached the stoop. It'd been months, maybe more than a year since she'd last seen Dr. Westerly. Even during daylight hours, the iron porch lights with reproduction bubbly glass burned natural gas. She hesitated, staring at the flickering blue and orange flames like glowing logs in a fireplace.

What was she doing here?

Her finger was poised to press the doorbell, but she didn't do it. Instead, she turned to leave.

Dr. Westerly's voice crackled from a small speaker next to the doorway.

"Lauren? Is that you? Lenore will be right there."

A moment later the door opened, and a familiar face invited her in. "Hello, Miss Gold. It's nice to see you."

While Dr. Westerly usually answered the door, today the housekeeper did.

"Hi, Lenore," she said, entering and glancing up at the sky-high ceilings and faux plaster walls painted in neutral tones.

"Dr. Westerly will be with you in a minute." Lenore gestured to the study to the right of the grand foyer. "Please wait for her there. May I get you something to drink while you wait?"

"No thanks."

She wandered into the room and stopped in front of the fireplace studying the photos on the mantle. What a handsome extended family. Had she been too distraught in the past to notice there was a shiny Steinway piano in the room or was it new?

"Lauren."

She turned. "Oh, hi."

"Come here and give me hug."

Dr. Westerly wrapped her arms around her, then stepped back and looked at her. "You look well."

"Thanks for seeing me, especially on a Sunday."

"It sounds important. Please sit," Dr. Molly Westerly said, gesturing.

There was a ritual about the seating arrangement during sessions. Dr. Westerly always sat on one edge of the blue velvet sofa, and she always chose the oversized mahogany chair with the ornate arms and faux zebra upholstery.

Molly put her readers on, picked up a thick beige folder filled with handwritten notes and thumbed through the top few pages.

Cliff notes about her most intimate secrets, she reckoned.

Molly closed the file and looked up. "I haven't seen you for thirteen months. How have you been?"

"Pretty good."

Dr. Westerly smiled. "I was just thinking about you the other day."

"Funny how that works."

"Tell me what's going on with Peter."

"All I know is that he's been in some sort of accident and he's in the hospital."

"I got that much from our call. Have you been to the hospital to see him yet?"

"No. I was out of the country when I got a call from the hospital asking me to come back to Miami. I just landed a couple of hours ago. I called the hospital and left a message to set up a meeting."

"A meeting with who?"

"Someone from the hospital and his family."

"Have you talked to his family?"

"No."

"Have they tried to contact you?"

"No."

"Remind me. What was your relationship with them like?"

"Not good."

"Why not?"

"I guess they just didn't want to get involved in our divorce."

"There're no children involved which makes it easier to cut ties."

"Easy for them," Lauren said.

"Grandkids complicate things. I know from my patients," Molly said.

"The woman from the hospital said his parents are upset that I'm still his legal representative."

"Excuse me." Lenore stood in the archway. "Your tea."

She set a floral and gold teacup, saucer and spoon on the coffee table in front of Dr. Westerly.

"Thank you," the therapist said, waiting for Lenore to leave.

Dr. Westerly tore open a packet of sugar in the raw and sprinkled the light brown crystals into her teacup. "They have every right to be upset." She picked up a small silver spoon with an intricate handle and stirred the sugar. "But not with you. Their son should've updated his paperwork."

"I'll do whatever they want me to do."

Molly sipped her tea, then asked. "How long have you been divorced?"

"Two years."

"That was plenty of time for him to take care of business. How's your stress level been?"

"I've been feeling a lot of anxiety."

"Are you sleeping?"

"I had some trouble a few months ago and it was getting better. Now this happened."

"Are you taking any prescription sleep meds?"

"After what happened? God no." She placed her hands on her breasts.

"That was a good decision."

"They never liked me."

"Who didn't?" Dr. Westerly asked. "His family?"

"Yes."

"What difference does that make now? Here's what I suggest," Molly said. "Ask the hospital coordinators to find a neutral place to meet and make sure there's someone from the hospital present if you have to interact with his family."

"They never called once to say sorry or goodbye, good riddance, or anything."

"Did you expect them to?"

"No. I guess not."

"How's everything else going? Are you seeing anyone?"

There was a long silence.

Dr. Westerly raised her arched eyebrows. "That's not a no."

Lauren brushed her wispy blond hair behind one ear. "It's not a yes either."

"It's alright if you don't want to talk about it."

"That's not it. I don't know the answer."

"Sometimes we don't have to know."

"I met him accidentally on a dating site."

"I'm too old to imagine how that could happen," Dr. Westerly said. "The stories I've heard about internet dating from my patients." Dr. Westerly shook her head and chuckled at whatever she was remembering. "If I'm ever widowed, I'm not putting myself on the internet."

"We haven't had sex. At least not yet."

Molly tilted her head slightly. "Are you waiting for something?"

"That's just it. I don't know."

"What about him?"

"He's never been married."

"Age?"

"Appropriate."

"Lauren, if he's never been married, then the chances he'll jump off the plank now aren't good. How long have you been dating?"

"We're not dating. We're friends who are attracted to each other."

"That qualifies as dating. Does this person that you have a mutual attraction to have a name?"

"Vance."

Molly jotted a note on her pad and peered over her readers. "It's okay to go slow. The slower the better."

"I remember your advice," she said. "Date them with eyes wide open and marry them with eyes half shut."

"Is Peter remarried or in a relationship?"

"I don't know."

"You said you were out of the country when you got the call. Where were you?"

"We were in The Bahamas."

"You and," she looked at her notes, "Vance?"

"Uh huh."

"Did he come back with you?"

"No."

"Were you disappointed about that?"

"He couldn't come back."

"Why not?"

"He lost his passport."

"How did that happen?"

"I don't know." She paused, to think before she spoke. "He saw my scars."

"Scars?" Dr. Westerly said.

"From when I cut myself."

"Oh," Molly said. "How did he react?"

"It caught him off guard. I think he found it confusing."

"That's seems reasonable. Did you explain what happened?"

"I did, I mean I tried."

"How did he react?"

"He didn't run away."

"That's positive," Molly said, chuckling, making a note in her file.

"I gave him my stepmother's phone number."

"The Bahamian?"

Lauren cocked her head. "You remember?"

Molly smiled. "I do. Why did you give him her number?"

"She has connections. I thought maybe she could help him with his lost passport."

"Ah. Right. Did you make plans to see her?"

"No."

"Why not?"

"I don't know. Sometimes it's easier to put things in the past."

"Do you think we can really ever do that?"

"I don't know. I talked to Vivian over the phone and asked if she could help him."

"How did she react?"

"She was very nice."

"You liked her a lot."

"I did. I still do. There was terrible storm and our plane had to make an emergency landing on an out island."

"That's scary. Is that how your friend lost his passport?"

"I don't know but that's when he discovered it was missing."

"Have you spoken to your father?"

This was a subject she didn't wish to discuss. She shook her head no.

Dr. Westerly prodded more. "Have you tried to contact him?"

"No. I told you before, when he dumped Vivian, it felt like he was dumping me at the same time."

"He's your dad, Lauren. I'm not following that thought process."

The topic was off limits. She uncrossed her legs, leaned forward and rested her chin in her hands, gazing out over the turquoise pool in Dr. Westerly's backyard, the late afternoon sun twinkling on the water. "When we were stranded, we got stuck with two other passengers, young people in their twenties. There was something about them."

"What?"

"I don't know."

She reached into her purse and set the deck of playing cards on the low wooden coffee table separating them and pushed it closer to the therapist.

Dr. Westerly picked it up and looked at the cover. "A pig wearing a graduation cap? Did they give these to you?"

"No. I found them. They're weird. Open them up and look at the cards. They have pictures of people on them. They're all college administrators."

Dr. Westerly tapped the cards from the box and pulled the deck out. Lauren craned her neck to see. The Ace of Spades with the no picture and the name Harold Fuchs was on top. Molly's hand shook and she fumbled the deck. The cards scattered onto the tile floor. Molly leaned over to pick them up.

Lauren knelt to help collect the ones that'd sailed under the furniture. She watched out of the corner of her eye and caught Molly putting the Ace of Spades in the file folder with Lauren's name on it. Why would she do that? She was about to ask when Dr. Westerly spoke first.

"Listen, Lauren. I'm sorry to cut this short, but we're veering way off topic, and I have dinner plans with my family."

"Oh, gosh, I'm sorry," she said, grimacing, tapping the cards she'd collected, making a neat pile and setting them on the coffee table.

Molly stood and slid the paperwork under her left arm. For a woman in her sixties she was as nimble as a cat.

"You're doing what you need to do. You probably didn't have to agree to meet with his family. If you get overwhelmed, you could see if the family is willing to hire a lawyer to act as an intermediary. I don't know if that's possible, but it might be worth asking. If he's incapacitated, it means he could have a serious brain injury and the situation might drag out."

"I know."

"If you do decide to meet them, try to stay detached and look after yourself. If it gets to be too much for you, excuse yourself from the situation. Give me a call if you need to."

"May I use your restroom before I go?"

"Of course. Down the hall, take a right, second door on the left."

Lauren passed the kitchen. Lenore stood in front of the sink drying dishes with a red and white striped linen towel. Lauren hurried, and when she was finished, washed her hands. The cloth towels were embroidered with the Westerly family name and the paper ones in an acrylic box were too fancy to waste. She patted her hands on her jeans. When she opened the bathroom door, she saw the door to the right was three-quarters of the way open. Lauren squeezed past and saw Dr. Westerly standing inside a converted coat closet.

Molly glanced over her shoulder, then hurriedly closed the drawer to a tall filing cabinet and shut the closet door.

Lauren stopped, reached into her purse and removed her checkbook.

"That's okay," Molly said, looking at her wristwatch. "This one was a courtesy."

"Thanks," she said, walking to the front door. "You've been a big help. I feel ready now and I wouldn't have without you."

"Call or text me after you meet with Peter's family."

"I will," Lauren said.

. . .

A MILE from Dr. Westerly's mansion, she checked her phone. Still nothing from Vance and no missed calls from the hospital or from the girl who'd hit-and- run her car. She pulled up RECENT CALLS and redialed Cassie. This time, someone answered. The Bluetooth in her Audi switched the call to speaker and the name Cassandra Braman came up on the dash.

"I'm really sorry about your car," Cassie said.

"Accidents happen. I especially appreciate that you left a note with your number." Lauren meant it.

"When can you get a quote for the repairs?" Cassie asked.

"I don't know. It's the weekend so I was hoping to get your insurance information so I can report it."

"I can't give that to you."

"Why not?"

"Because I don't have any insurance."

What? "Then why did you leave a note?" she asked, clenching the steering wheel.

"I want to pay you cash."

"You don't even know how much it'll be?"

"It can't be more than a couple hundred dollars."

She almost laughed. That wouldn't cover the rental car.

"However much it is, I'll pay it," Cassie said.

"The adjustor will have to look at the damage and give me a written estimate for the repairs."

"You can email pictures to your insurance company, and they can even get an estimate on the same day."

How did she know that if she didn't even have insurance? On the other hand, if she was going to pay cash, she could use the estimate to go directly to the body shop and keep the claim off her insurance. "I'll try to get it quickly and I'll text it to you."

"Good," Cassie said, "you shouldn't have to drive around with a broken taillight. I want to take care of it immediately."

Who could argue with this?

"Thank you," Lauren said, "I'll be in touch."

She tapped the red dot on her phone, ending the call and flipped the visor down to shade her eyes as she headed back to the condo. The light up ahead turned yellow. She slowed, then rolled to a stop. Waiting for the light to turn green, she dictated a text to Vance and watched the words form on the screen: Someone with no insurance hit my car in the parking lot at the airport in Homestead. Can you believe it? Where are you?

She pushed the SEND button and a red UNDELIVER-ABLE message popped up beneath the green bubble. What was up with his phone? She tossed her cell phone on the passenger seat.

Her mind wandered back to her meeting with Dr. Westerly. There was something about the way Dr. Westerly reacted to the name printed on the Ace of Spades. Did her therapist know Harold Fuchs?

24

Molly Westerly returned to the room and sat on the velvet sofa in the study she'd converted into a patient office several years ago after she shuttered her full-time practice. She picked up the Ace of Spades and stared at it.

Her housekeeper stood in the archway. "Are you finished in here?"

"Yes. Thank you, Lenore."

Lenore went about her normal tasks of cleaning up. She picked up Molly's porcelain teacup and side plate where Molly placed the used teabag and silver spoon. "Where do you want these, Dr. W.?" Lenore held up the deck of cards.

"I'll take them," Molly said, reaching for the box then hurrying to the front door hoping to catch Lauren. But her patient had already left. She looked at the weird cartoon pig on the cover again, then opened the flap, tapped the bottom, and pulled the deck out with her thumb and forefinger. She took the Ace of Spades from Lauren's file and placed her hand over her heart as she stared at the name. The food chain didn't get higher than Harold Fuchs. He oversaw the federal government's student loan program. But why was he included in the strange deck of cards? Why was there no picture of him? Just his name.

"Honey, are you alone?" her husband asked, peeking into the room and startling her.

"I am." She kept her back to him as she slipped the Ace of Spades back into the box and put the deck in her pocket.

"Are you ready to go?" He glanced at his wristwatch. "We're running late. I just got a text from the kids and the grandkids are getting fussy."

"Tell them to go ahead and order," Molly said, hurrying to the utility closet near the pantry where she kept her patient files.

"I'll pull the car around front," Mr. Westerly said, hobbling in the direction of the hallway leading to their three-car garage.

She opened the middle drawer labeled 'A – M' and thumbed through the file tabs until she got to the Fs, then pulled a thick blue folder with H. Fuchs' name on it. She opened it and scanned a couple of pages. He'd been a patient, but it had been a long time ago.

The front door opened. Her husband saw her in the hallway.

"The car's out front."

"I'm sorry, I'll be right there." She pushed the file drawer shut with her hip, rushed to the kitchen and tucked the deck of cards in the drawer where Lenore the kept dish towels. She grabbed her purse from the pink granite kitchen island, fished for her phone, made a quick telephone call then rushed to the dark blue Mercedes waiting curbside.

"You seem frazzled. Is this about your patient?" Mr. Westerly asked as she got into the passenger's side seat.

She reached over, grabbed his hand and squeezed it. "I'm fine and my patient will be okay, too."

"I think you do too much for them, honey. It's a Sunday."

"I know," Molly said, trying to hide the uneasy feeling growing inside. "I know."

25

V ance tried focusing on the water sloshing against the sides of the water taxi. The late afternoon sun sparkled off the darkening turquoise waters with a view across the channel dividing the docks and the port at Potters Cay from the mainland. In the distance off to the right he saw the lighthouse at the mouth of Nassau Harbour and the manmade jetties that opened to an endless horizon of blue water. The skinny guy with the knobby knees who had to hold his shorts up with one hand was yakking through a rusty white megaphone that he held flush to his lips.

Man, what a day. He couldn't wait to get his hands around that prick Tonk's neck. Did the greasy underemployed barista with a pipe dream of making it to Hollywood manage to check into the room he'd booked for himself at the Poseidon Club and sleep in the bed reserved for him and Lauren last night? Did he order a bottle of Johnny Walker Blue and purchase a couple of nice Italian suits from the hotel's luxury apparel store he'd seen on the internet?

He considered offering the captain another hundred

bucks to get the tour guide to shut up but the couple that had been waiting at the ferry dock an hour before they'd arrived appeared to be enjoying it.

His fists clenched at the thought of Tonk acting the big shot at his expense. What balls. Using his AmEx had upped the ante and as payback he planned to make it his mission to not only get his gun and passport back, but he was also going to find out what they were up to. He felt his phone vibrate in his pocket. Another credit card alert from AmEx. Tonk made a $25 dollar purchase at a place called *Princes and Princesses* in Nassau. What the hell kind of place was that? The fucker left a $50 dollar tip. Did he find a place to buy a blow job somewhere in downtown? Go ahead, you prick. Charge away. Keep it up. *It'll be how I find your pimply fat ass.*

But for now, he'd attempt to enjoy the short ride across the channel to the city of Nassau. He began listening to the guide squawking through a tinny megaphone.

"Before it was called Nassau, the capital city of New Providence was called Charlestown. In the year 1670 Prince Charles of England granted it to six English noblemen who soon brought in fellow British settlers who erected a fort to protect the city. Soon, as the city began to grow, most of the residents of Charlestown were either pirates or merchants. The stakes were high sailing through this very harbor waiting for cannonballs to strike and pirates to board the ships passing to the New World, killing the captains and plundering their bounty. But in the year 1684 Charlestown experienced a setback from which it could never recover. The Spanish invaded and breached the fort, then burnt Charlestown down to the ground."

Vance leaned forward, now intrigued, straining to hear

every word over the lapping of water against the hull of the old boat as it crept toward the city.

"It was later rebuilt and in the year 1695 was renamed Nassau in honor of Prince William the Third, formerly known as Prince Orange-Nassau. By 1718 the British recaptured the islands and proclaimed The Bahamas as a colony. They appointed Woodes Rogers as its original Governor and the Crown issued him a mandate to rid the island of pirates. Rogers was successful and started the first Assembly which adopted as its motto *Expulsis Piratis, Restituta Commercia.*" The guide paused, then asked, "Who would like to try to translate?"

The man who'd been waiting with the woman when they'd arrived at the ferry dock raised his hand.

"Yes, sir."

He had one of those squeaky rat voices. "Pirates Expelled, Commerce Restored."

"That's correct."

The woman pinched his cheek with her trimmed fingertips painted black, then shrugged and grinned.

No woman had better do that to him. Not even in private.

The guide continued. "During the 1950s and 60s The Bahamas became a very popular tourist destination. Many people came to Cable Beach, so named because it got its first telegram cable in 1907 connecting Nassau to the rest of the world. In 1960 Huntington Hartford, the heir to a large American grocery chain bought Hog Island and changed its name to Paradise Island."

Chan turned in her seat and said, "this is fascinating."

He nodded, then continued to listen.

"Today the heart of Parliament Square is the center of local government and is located in downtown Nassau."

He raised his hand.

"Yes?"

"Do you know where the U.S. Embassy is located?"

"Somewhere downtown," the tour guide said, "but ask when we dock. They'll know for sure. I encourage tourists to visit the buildings built by the Loyalists in the 1800s. The Bahamas Supreme Court is located downtown along with a marble statue of Queen Victoria. Another point of interest is Port Charlotte built in the late 1700s. The moats and dungeons are open to the public.

"Nassau also offers shopping and fine dining. New Providence has several world class golf courses. You can stop at the Ministry of Tourism for more information. We've reached," the guide said, holding his pants up as he jumped from the ferry boat to a sad dock, a cracked concrete slab coated with layers of slimy black and green algae. He'd seen fancier bus stations in rural Florida. The guide tied off to a pylon and hugged a glass jar with a handwritten TIPS label while lending his free arm to passengers disembarking.

"Watch your step."

As far as he was concerned asking him for another penny was tantamount to a shakedown. Old Governor Woodes could never rid the place of pirates, or so it seemed.

Poor C.J. still hauled that monstrosity of a backpack like a mule. The woman with the man dropped a ten-dollar bill in the jar. C.J. fished a couple of bucks from his pocket and donated. Chan shot C.J. a look to kill.

As Chan stepped up onto the concrete dock, the tour guide held out the jar and said, "Nice tattoo."

"Nice try," she said, refusing his help.

He got off the boat last and climbed over the damp seawall, spotting a couple of fruit stands and portable souvenir tables set back beneath a concrete overhang. The walkway was nearly black with grime and splotches of chewing gum.

He stopped at the fruit stand and took a bottle of cold water from a red plastic bucket filled with melted ice. "How much?"

"Three dollar."

Chan reached up on tiptoes and unhooked the thermos from her backpack slung over C.J.'s shoulders. She opened the cap, swigged, then handed it to C.J.

Vance took two more bottles from the ice chest, paid cash, then handed one each to Chan and C.J.

"You didn't have to do that," C.J. said.

"I remember when I didn't have two nickels to spare," Vance said. "It's good to be reminded from time to time."

"Thank you," Chan said, cracking the cap and downing half the bottle in one swig.

"I guess this is it," C.J. said, stuffing the water bottle in the side pocket of his hiking shorts. "Thanks for everything."

"Yeah," Chan said. "I guess this is goodbye."

"I guess so. Keep California from turning into hell."

C.J. half-smiled. "I'm afraid it's too late for that." He turned to the woman running the fruit stand where he'd bought the water. "Do you know how to get to the bus stop?" C.J. asked.

"I take de bus every day," she said, adding "it's a walk to the stop. Look for de blue and yellow bench. Take a right on de corner and walk until you see de shelter. Dere is a blue sign on de pole. Today is a slow one so you 'ave to wait longer. De last one today leaves at six."

He checked the time on his phone. It was almost 5 o'clock.

When they were out of earshot, he asked, "Do you know where I can catch a taxi?"

She pointed to the corner. "Follow dem to Woodes Rogers Street. De cabs have de yellow license plates. Look for dat."

He rearranged the strap on his duffle, slung it over his shoulder, waited a minute, then walked toward Woodes Rogers. Watching traffic, he tried to orient his brain to the British style of left-handed roads and cars. Like horsepower from heaven, a blue Chevy Malibu with a yellow license plate magically arrived. As soon as he raised his hand, the driver acknowledged him, pulling forward. He climbed into the back seat.

"Where to?"

"I'm not sure." He saw the ancient meter with the hand-operated flag attached to the dash. "Start the clock and I'll pay you whatever I owe."

"No negotiations."

"Fine. Where is the closest bus stop?"

"I don't know."

Vance lifted his hip, pulled his wallet from his back pocket and showed the driver a hundred-dollar bill. "There's more to be made if it takes longer than a half hour."

"Dere is a bus stop two blocks from 'ere."

"Go that way."

The driver pulled from the curb and as he rounded the bend, Vance saw C.J. and Chan walking along the empty sidewalk. Poor C.J., the mule with the pack on his back. "You see those people?"

"Yes."

"I want you to find a spot where we can watch until they get on the bus and then I want you to follow it."

"De bus runs now and den. It could be more den a 'alf hour."

"That's fine. I'll pay you two hundred for the first hour and fifty for each hour after that. Does that work?"

"Give me de first 'undred."

He held the money out.

"Dis works," the cab driver said, taking a crisp bill and snapping it with two hands.

"Pull forward a little. I don't want them to see me."

The driver followed orders and turned the taxi around.

C.J. stopped in his tracks like a deer sniffing a predator. He ducked in the back seat and peeked out the window. C.J. looked at the Chevy Malibu for a moment then continued walking toward a blue and yellow shelter with a corrugated metal roof held up with four thin wooden posts. There was an empty bench beneath the shelter.

Chan and C.J. sat at opposite ends of the bus stop bench, in the shade. There were no other people waiting. Vance peeked out the open side car window and watched C.J. lean Chan's backpack against one of the skinny yellow painted wooden posts.

"If you don't want dem to see you, you should stay down. I should drive past and wait ahead. When de bus passes, I will follow."

"Okay," he said, laying low in the back seat as the taxi driver drove past the bus shelter and turned onto a side street.

"You can look now," the driver said.

The street where the cabbie turned had a view to Nassau Harbour. He watched as an enormous cruise ship sailed by, a floating fiberglass Taj Mahal at least twelve stories high. The driver made a U-turn and parked at the corner where they could wait and watch. He noticed the corkscrews of gray hair mixed into his near shaven head. The back of his collar had a ring of sweat. He wondered how old he was and how long he'd been doing this job. But those details didn't really matter. It'd be a short encounter if things went well.

Was it possible that yesterday he'd been at the airport in Homestead getting ready to board Blade's plane? *Jesus.* It seemed like a freaking month ago. "How much longer until the bus arrives? Can you check the app? Or if you give me the name of the bus company and I can check it myself."

The cabbie turned around and looked at Vance with a bewildered look on his face. "Dere's an app for de bus?"

"Never mind." He leaned forward. "Any chance you could roll up the windows and turn on the A/C?"

"I kin roll dem up but de air conditioner is broke. Do you want me to do dat?"

"No. We're good."

Did Tonk have the stones to check into his hotel room? He could call the hotel and tell them what Tonk was doing. He smiled at the thought of that pajama boy with the man bun getting busted by hotel security. It was better to wait, better to trap him.

After another twenty minutes passed, he asked, "How often does the bus run on Sundays?"

"I don't know, Sir. From time to time."

Freaking island time.

It was the same with all of them. Regardless of ocean.

He was betting that Chan and C.J. were heading to the rental they'd booked and planned to share with Tonk. He'd asked them what they were going to do in The Bahamas. That R&R ocean adventure story was bullshit. He felt moisture on his palms. Was it from the heat and humidity? Or the adrenaline rush he felt fantasizing about kicking the shit out of that punk, Tonk.

He checked his phone and searched for Vivian's number, making sure he'd saved it. His screen opened to the AmEx charge for *Princes and Princesses,* whatever the fuck that was? He typed in the name of the place into the browser and opened the link. He felt his fists clench. That little shit for brains went to a barber. Hopefully to wash his greasy hair. Then he had another thought, one that drew bile into his throat.

26

"Dere's de bus, Sir," the cabbie said.

Vance saw a lavender and white van pull up to the front of the yellow and blue shelter where Chan and C.J. sat. It wasn't what he'd expected for municipal transportation. It was smaller, a 32-seater like the ones the hotel chains used to shuttle passengers to and from Miami International. The front left bumper was smashed, and the headlight broken. It had one of those cheap orange and black plastic signs leaning against the windshield that said OPEN. To close for the day the bus driver just had to turn the sign around.

"Hold on a minute," he said, watching Chan and C.J. climb board. As the bus driver pulled from the intersection, he saw there were only a few people on board. "Okay, let's go," he said. "Follow it until I tell you not to."

"Yes sir."

Every time the bus driver accelerated puffs of charcoal smoke belched from the exhaust pipe. Vance hadn't noticed before but now he felt the springs beneath the upholstery digging into his seat bones. The shock absorbers and bushings long worn; the Malibu clunked at every pothole.

The bus driver headed south on East Bay Street stopping in front of the British Colonial Hilton, a multistory stucco building with a burnt orange clay tile roof and thatched palm trees that reminded him of the oldest hotels on Miami Beach. Two young men dressed business casual got off. The cabbie waited for them to cross the street then caught up to the shuttle bus.

"Dat is Port Charlotte on the left," the driver said. "Americans like to visit it."

Two recommendations for the same place in one day. He made a mental note.

The bus stopped next at Junkaroo Beach. He looked up and noticed the road sign had changed from East to West Bay Street. An elderly woman stepped off the bus and tottered along the sidewalk on the seaside of the street. He hoped she didn't have far to go.

As the shuttle pulled back onto the road, his driver followed from a distance that wouldn't raise suspicion.

"Do you know where the passport office is?"

"You're an American?" he asked.

"Yeah."

"You lose it?"

"Yep."

"De U.S. Embassy is at Number Forty-Two Queen Street."

Number Ten Downing Street. Forty-Two Queen Street. The British influence was everywhere.

The shuttle driver made a u-turn at Cable Beach and continued the opposite direction on Bay Street from where they'd come. That was weird. Why hadn't Chan and C.J. gotten off yet if the bus was turning around?

"Did you see them get off?"

"No. De busses zig zag sometimes. You owe me another 'undred."

"Right." He opened his wallet and handed him another C-note.

He checked the time. It was after 6 o'clock in the evening. He owed him more than another hundred. His phone vibrated in his pocket. Lauren's name came up on the screen. He looked at it, then pressed the red dot. He typed a text: Can't talk now. Call you back. Sorry about your car.

His phone rang. It was Lauren again. He felt bad, but he had to let it go to voicemail.

The shuttle bus picked up speed. The dips into the potholes got rougher. He leaned forward and rubbed his back. The taxi driver lowered his visor to cut the shards of sun. He took his sunglasses from the side pouch of his duffle bag and put them on.

The driver pointed out the window on the right-hand side.

"Dat is de Parliament Assembly."

He saw a cluster of old neo-classical buildings painted pastel pink. Trailing Chan and C.J. had turned into an informal tour of the places he'd heard about on the ferry.

The bus slowed and the driver activated the right-hand turn signal.

"Do you know where dey is going?"

"No."

The bus turned right on Nassau Street and they followed it for ten or so blocks south. The neighborhood got dicey fast. The kind of poverty he'd seen at home in Liberty City and Overtown.

"Is this place safe?" he asked.

"My brother lives four blocks from 'ere. Dis is the outer edges of de Over-de-Hill District."

"The what?"

"It's where de slaves lived under de British Colonial rule."

It reminded him of the few remaining slums on Grand Avenue in Coconut Grove near Lauren's place. West Grove, or Black Grove, it'd been called, was founded by Bahamians who'd come in the 1800s to work for Miami's wealthy elite. It was on the verge of extinction as developers outbid each other, tearing down the shacks and aging apartment buildings to build luxury homes.

"Is it safe?" he asked again, feeling the empty pouch of his duffle, the place where he'd stowed his missing Glock.

"It depends," he said, following the shuttle driver who took a left on Meadow Street, passing a Super Value convenience store. He could hardly believe where he was. Rusty tin roofs balanced atop wooden-slatted houses. Some with no windows. Part rural. Part urban dystopia. Skinny winding roads, an overgrown jungle.

"Depends on what?"

The bus driver slowed and stopped on a street called Dumping Ground Corner. The bus door opened.

Chan and C.J. stepped off the bus.

"Do you want me to follow dem?"

"Yes. But don't let them see us."

"Dat'll be easy. They'll be watchin' out for demselves."

From the looks of it, C.J.'s head was on a swivel.

Local boys sat on sagging wooden stoops beneath flickering lights, watching the two American tourists.

When C.J. saw the old Malibu, he picked up the pace, then jogged. He and Chan stopped in front of an apricot stucco two-story crap-box set back on a lot overgrown with weeds. C.J. waited outside a locked chain link gate and made a call on his cell. A moment later a man ran down the concrete stairs and let them in. C.J. and Chan glanced over their shoulders as the Malibu passed but Vance couldn't get a good look at the man who'd let them in. It could've been Tonk, but he couldn't be sure.

He looked for a street number but couldn't find one on the house.

"Where are we?"

"I tole you. De Over-de-Hill district."

"I need the address in case I need to come back."

The cabbie cruised around the corner and stopped.

He opened his phone.

"I drive by again. You mark it on GPS."

"No. Don't do a drive-by. This is good." He woke up his phone and dropped a pin on the location. Then he heard a pop, pop, pop in the distance. "What was that?"

"Fireworks. Maybe a gun. I don't know."

"I thought guns were illegal here?"

"Are you serious, Mon? Guns is everywhere."

"Let's get out of here."

"Where to?"

"Paradise Island. The Poseidon Club."

The driver held his hand out. He greased his palm a third time.

"When crime go up in America, it go up here. You Americans," he laughed and shook his head.

"What about us?"

"I tell you more on the way to P.I. We 'ave da time."

27

Vance looked out the window of the Malibu as it chugged to climb the bridge linking the mainland to touristy Paradise Island. The shantytown below the bridge where he'd sailed in with Captain Morgan and ferried across with the knobby kneed tour guide was still half awake. Dim lights emanated from the docks. The big cruise ships lined the north side of Potters Cay. Even from high up, they looked enormous against the backdrop of freighters and gantry cranes and shipping containers stacked ten high in the distance.

"What's your name?" he asked the driver.

"Blagden."

"You don't hear that one every day."

"It means 'dark alley' in Ole English." Blagden made eye contact with him in the rear view and shrugged. "Did you know they sent Prince Charles 'ere in nineteen-seventy-four to grant us our independence? At least dey didn't sent dat pervert Randy Andy. All de American media going crazy over de Epstein thing. I remember da 'eadlines 'bout 'Randy

Andy' on all de newspapers almost every day. You Americans. Your memory is not so good."

He didn't weigh in on Randy Andy. Blagden was right, the memory of the average American was short.

Blagden stopped on the street in front of the casino. "De valet won't let me drive tru," he said.

"I can walk from here."

"If you need a driver, dis is my number."

He took the card with Blagden's number. "Do you mind hanging here for a minute? I'll pay," he said, getting out.

"Are you staying 'ere?" Blagden asked through the open window.

"I'm not sure. I'm going to check and see if I can get a room. Wait for me."

"I wait."

A couple dressed in evening attire strolled toward the Malibu. Vance paused when the man squatted and looked at the yellow license plate. "Can you give us a lift over the bridge?"

"I'm sorry, but no," Blagden said. "I'm off duty."

When they wandered back to the valet stand, Vance headed for the entrance, instantly annoyed at the pinging and dinging of bells and sound effects meant to emulate the sounds of casino winnings. He snaked his way past the slot machines, saw the check-in desk and stood in the red-roped line reserved for VIPs.

"May I help you sir?" an attractive Black woman with a crew cut and a round face asked.

"I have a reservation. I was supposed to check in last night, but my flight was delayed."

"Name?"

"Courage. Vance Courage."

She tapped the keyboard and squinted at the monitor.

"There must be some sort of mistake."

"What kind of mistake."

"According to our records you checked in this morning."

"Huh," he said.

She scanned him up and down and from her expression, she doubted him. "May I see your reservation and travel documents?"

"My girlfriend booked the room in both our names and unfortunately I lost my passport."

"Where is she?"

He hesitated. "She had a family matter and had to go home."

"Hmm," she said, looking at him suspiciously. She chewed her lower lip, and from the lines in her forehead, vexed, as if she was thinking about what to do next. "I'd better call management," she said, shifting her eyes left and right.

"I don't think that's necessary," he said, "I'm sure it's a simple mix up. Would you check and see if you have any available rooms?"

"We do."

"I'd like to book one."

"Do you want a single, double, king—"

"Do you have any suites?"

"Let me check." She made a phone call on the landline.

A burly man in a gray suit approached. "May I see your I.D.?"

"I was just telling this nice young lady that I lost my passport."

"All foreigners must show a passport in order to check in."

"Never mind," he said.

The suit tailed him as he walked through the casino and

out the front door. He jogged down the driveway and saw Blagden waiting on the street.

He got into the Malibu and called Vivian who answered on the second ring.

"Is this Vivian Jackson?"

"Yes."

He saw Blagden glance at him from the rearview and raise his eyebrows. "My name is Vance Courage."

"Yes, Lauren's friend."

"I think she told you I lost my passport."

"Yes, she did. Where are you?"

"At the Poseidon Club."

"You made it here."

"I did but it seems I can't get a room without my passport."

"Oh dear. That's right. The Ministry of Tourism is quite strict about the casinos. You might have trouble checking in anywhere as a walk-in with no passport. I have an idea. I own an Airbnb that's empty tonight. I keep the key in the flowerpot near the front door. If I text the address, can you find your way there?"

"I can. I met a very nice taxi driver who's chauffeuring me around town."

"Give me a minute," Vivian said.

"This is nice of you."

"Lauren is like family. At least she is to me. Tomorrow I'll see about helping you with a visa to get home. Or to stay. Is she coming back?"

"I don't know yet. I think she told you she had some personal business to take care of in Miami. I really appreciate your help."

"It's not fancy. It's a one-bedroom cottage on the East End. It's nice and quiet."

From what he'd learned from his tour so far, east was better than west. Quiet was a bonus.

"You might want to get a bite to eat on the way. There's water and coffee at the cottage but it's in a residential area and there are no restaurants nearby. Phone me if you have any questions. Otherwise, let's plan to talk tomorrow morning. If you have any trouble finding the place or getting in, let me know."

"Thank you. I'll be in touch." He ended the call.

Nice and quiet. What more could he ask for? That reminded him. He'd better get settled in and call Lauren. He'd put her off and she was probably either worried or mad or some combination of the two.

He copied Vivian's Airbnb information, typed Blagden's number from the business card, pasted the address in a text and sent it. He heard it ping. "That's from me," he said, "directions to the place I'm going. Do you know the neighborhood very well?"

"Not so much. Why?"

"I need some food."

"I know a place where you can git de best conch fritters. I kin take you dere."

"I was thinking about something simple, like a bag of potato chips and a hot dog."

Blagden looked at the address on his phone. "We 'ave to go back over de bridge to get to East Bay Street. Dere are convenience stores on de way."

"Stop at one so I can grab something to eat."

Blagden drove south over the Paradise Island bridge, back toward the mainland of New Providence.

What did that woman at the casino think? His clothes were dirty. His hair was greasy. Was it this morning he'd left Chub Cay and survived a squall aboard the *Mis Mama* or was it all a hallucination? Man did he need a shower and a warm bed.

At Bay Street, Blagden turned in the opposite direction from the way they'd gone before, heading east. "Dere's a Super Value Food Store a little bit out of de way off Mackey Street. Dere's a Mickey Dees, too."

"Mickey Dees?"

"McDonald's."

That sounded like a dream. "Take me to Mickey D's."

It was dark out now and the night brought out the sweetness of the ocean air. As Blagden pulled into the McDonald's drive through and stopped behind a battered minivan, the sweet smell of the ocean was overpowered by something better. The aroma of frying grease. His stomach barked for a Big Mac with a side of salty fries.

When the family ahead of them finished ordering, Blagden pulled forward and stopped in front of the small golden arches on a menu board.

While they waited for the food, Blagden turned around in his seat. "Who are you?"

"No one special."

"You can't be no one. You have de phone number for a Jackson with a seaside cottage on East Bay Street. I am born 'ere and most locals rarely bin to de part of de island where I am taking you. It is where de Loyalists first settled. Not de new money, tis what you Americans call de old money. De families who run things for generations live on dat side of the de island where I am taking you."

"I told you. I'm no one. I'm just some guy looking for a place to stay tonight. I lost my passport and soon as I get a new one, I'm going home."

"You is strange," Bladgen said. "From Over-de-Hill to de East End."

It probably did seem odd. The truth was he'd been terrified earlier, unarmed in the ghetto where Chan and C.J. were staying. Dumpster Street or whatever it was called. Apparently, Blagden overheard his conversation with Vivian Jackson and the name meant something to Blagden. Lauren told him Vivian came from a prominent family but what did that mean? He desperately needed sleep. Soon he would need more than that. He was going to need someone with influence. Someone with a lot of influence. Someone like Lauren's stepmother.

28

L auren headed down the hall to the room where the hospital asked her to meet the patient coordinator on the first floor of Mother of Mercy Hospital. As she turned the corner, she slowed her step. Peter's mother, father and sister had already arrived and sat together in the lobby. She checked her phone. It was 9:30 in the morning. She was a half hour early for the meeting and hadn't planned to run into them. She turned to leave.

"Lauren," his mother said, getting up from the chair quickly, practically ambushing her.

"Crap," she said under her breath.

"Thank you for coming," Peter's mother said.

Marge was a short, stocky, woman who dyed her bobbed haircut Lucille Ball-red. Peter had shared a few mother-son secrets while they were still married. Like the one about how much money she'd spent on plastic surgery. And ice cream. But the one secret he'd kept is that mother and son talked on the phone every day for at least an hour.

"How's he doing?" she asked.

"He's doing better," Marge said. "Much better."

She gripped the strap on her purse, digging her finger-nails into her palms. If he was better, why didn't someone call and let her know?

"But it's a head injury," Marge said, "and his doctors want to monitor him for a few days."

A man approached. He was in his forties, wearing a skinny necktie and clogs. He had a full head of black hair that bounced when he walked. "I see you've found each other." He addressed Peter's mother. "Can you give us a moment?" Marge scoffed, then returned to her husband and daughter waiting in the lobby area. The man said, "You must be Lauren Gold."

"I am."

"I'm John Anderson. I'm the patient coordinator trained to help with these kinds of situations."

"Does this happen often?"

"You'd be surprised. It happens more often than you'd think. I'd like to go up to the second floor and meet in the conference room with the patient's family."

She was outnumbered and her flight instinct kicked-in in a big way. It said run. Instead, she said, "Okay."

John motioned Peter's family to join them. She stuck close to John who carried a brown accordion file into the elevator. The fivesome rode in silence and when they got to the second floor, she followed John into a brightly lit confer-ence room with a long table.

She took a seat close to the head of the table where John sat. Marge sat across from her while Peter's father, an unim-pressive man with a limp and a weak chin, sat next to Peter's sister on the same side as Marge. There was solidarity in their camp, she had to give them that.

John opened the file and removed a document she

recognized as the Durable Power Medical of Attorney she'd signed when she and Peter were still married.

"Did you know he hadn't updated his medical directive and you're his designated D.N.R.?" John asked her.

"D.N.R.?" Marge asked.

"Do not resuscitate," John said.

There was a time when she would've relished pulling the plug on him, but those days were over. "I thought he was doing better."

"He is," Marge said.

"You were out of the country, Lauren?" the patient coordinator asked.

"I was. I was on vacation in The Bahamas."

Peter's father glanced up and gave her a sad look. He'd been her closest ally, trying to run interference between Peter and Marge, once sharing that Marge loved her family 'a little too much.'

"I'm sorry you had to cut your trip short," John said. "He's alert and can make his own decisions."

"He's conscious?" Lauren asked.

"No one told you?" John said.

"No. I don't even know what happened to him."

Peter's sister chimed in. "He was riding his bike and a car making a turn out of a driveway didn't see him."

"Peter has asked to see you," John said, lowering his voice.

"I hate hospitals," she said, wishing to get out of there as quickly as possible. The way she saw it, hospitals were factories that turned live people into dead ones. "I have to go," she said, gathering her things and heading for the hallway.

She stood with two strangers waiting for the elevator and when the doors dinged and whooshed open, she froze at what she saw, her mouth agape.

29

Vance woke to a barber shop quartet of barking and howling dogs coming from the house next door, not remembering where he was. He stared up at the low wooden ceiling and mismatched antique furniture. He looked around the room rubbing his eyes, but his brain hadn't kicked into gear yet. He rolled onto his right side and saw the McDonald's bag wadded up on the nightstand and next to it, the card with Blagden's phone number. That was enough to get yesterday to come roaring back.

Didn't Vivian say the place was quiet? The sun was up, filling the bedroom with natural light. He put a pillow over his face and covered his ears with his palms. He recounted yesterday. What time was it? He rubbed his eyes, tossed the pillow on the chair next to the bed and checked his phone. Almost 9 o'clock in the morning. And it was Monday. The passport office was open today.

He sat up in bed feeling woozy from so many hours on the water yesterday. He lifted his armpit, sniffed and grimaced, removed his shirt and dropped it on the floor. He'd meant to shower; he'd fully intended to but after he'd wolfed down a Big Mac and a large order of fries he'd lain down and dozed off early with his clothes on.

When he'd arrived at Vivian's rental, it was dark out and Blagden had dropped him off a block away, worried about the private security patrolling the street. He'd walked the rest of the way and had shone his cellphone light to find the house number. He'd located a planter adjacent to the front door where Vivian had told him the key was hidden. But the key wasn't there. He'd panicked momentarily, wondering if he was at the wrong house. Or if she'd forgotten that she'd rented it to someone else for the weekend. Then he saw a small flowerpot next to the doormat; the key was hidden beneath it.

He stood grasping the rail of the four-poster bed checking his balance. He let go and took three wobbly steps on the wooden floor leading to the sliding glass door, pulled the sheer curtains to the side and looked out. Wow. A breeze kicked up swirling a thin batch of leaves that had accumulated on the small concrete patio behind the white cottage. He stepped out from beneath the veranda and looked over the concrete seawall. He walked down two stairs to a small white gate. There was a grass yard on either side but no beach below. Just a ten-foot vertical drop down to the shallow turquoise waters and below it, large, jagged rocks covered with algae on the seabed.

Jimmy the bartender had warned him before he'd left Chub Cay that the weather forecast was bad, but this morning—30-some miles southwest of Chub Cay—the weather was perfect; he could see the high-rise casinos and resorts across the harbor. A deep horn wailed in the distance. He looked to the west and saw two enormous cruise ships passing in opposite directions at the mouth of the inlet.

He went back inside and changed into swim trucks, found beach towels stacked on a rattan shelf next to the sliding glass door, grabbed one then walked out to the patio. He padded barefoot down the two stairs to the narrow lattice gate, opened it, then turned and grabbed the metal railing on a set of swimming pool stairs leading from the bulkhead to the water. He climbed down and stuck his toe in. The water was cold, and he felt goosebumps erupt on his whole body. He took another step down, and another until he stood in chilly water up to his waist. He held his hands over his head waiting for his torso to adjust to the temperature. At first the cold water ratcheted up the tension in his body, but as it adjusted to the cold and the sun warmed his neck and shoulders, his muscles relaxed. Standing on a stair rail, he squatted, dipped his head under the salty water, then rolled onto his back and floated with his eyes closed wondering if Lauren had ever been here? Wondering how she was doing in Miami.

He swam out a hundred feet from the seawall, then turned back, unfamiliar with the tides and depths and currents of the harbor. He grabbed onto the rail of the swim stairs suddenly noticing a mega yacht sailing the channel. It was familiar, and as the ship passed, he saw the name visible on the stern.

The Parent Minus.

Hmm. That was weird. What were the chances? On the other hand, maybe not. The out islands were like small towns linked to a big city. Maybe the yacht had been stuck on Chub Cay the way they had been due to bad weather. Maybe she'd sailed early this morning when the conditions improved.

Now shivering, he climbed the stairs and grabbed the beach towel he'd left on the patio chair, dried off, glanced at the yacht sailing to port, then went inside in search of caffeine.

He found a coffee pot above the sink, brewed a pot, poured a cup and walked out onto the porch and sat beneath the veranda with the beach towel draped over his shoulders. He could get used to this. The dogs next door began another round of the non-stop barking that had awakened him. He went back inside then googled 'how to replace lost American passport in the Bahamas,' and pressed SEARCH.

Was the internet connection slow or what? While he waited for the results, a text pinged from Lauren's phone: What's up? R u okay? U promised to let me know. Leaving the hospital.

Doggone it. He had promised. He dialed her number; it went directly to voicemail. He walked outside, snapped a picture from the backyard overlooking the harbor and texted it to her with a note: Took you up on your offer. Stayed at Vivian's last night.

He sipped his coffee and stared at the phone screen for a full minute, but she didn't answer. His search for 'lost passport' had timed out. He typed 'U.S. Embassy Bahamas' and hit the return key. The first link on the page led to the official website for the U.S. Embassy. He found the page for Lost and Stolen passports, tapped the link, and while waiting for it to load, refilled his coffee and took a seat at the breakfast nook overlooking the harbor.

He read the warning about Identity Theft and the importance of promptly reporting a missing passport. He opened the link and reviewed the instructions. He was about to fill out the DS-64 form for a lost passport online when he noticed he'd be required to complete another one, a DS-11, the application for a replacement. He closed the form and scrolled down the page. People who planned to travel internationally within 5 days of losing their passport that were still in the U.S. had to do one thing. Those traveling within 5-7 weeks had to do something else. Americans already in The Bahamas who'd lost their passports and planned to travel within 5 days had to go to the Passport Office in person. Appointments were highly recommended. He walked back to the bedroom and called Blagden's phone from the business card. He let it ring twenty times but apparently the cab driver didn't have voicemail.

He tapped the little microphone at the lower right-hand corner of his phone screen and dictated a message. Hi Black Don. You drove me yesterday. Are you available to pick me up and take me to the US Embassy in about 30 mins? He squinted at the message and pushed send without noticing how voice recognition had translated Blagden's name.

Blagden texted right back. I be there in 30 minutes.

Vance dictated another message. Do you need the address?

His phone dinged. I have it in my phone. Be there in 30.

He undressed and stepped into the warm shower. The water pressure sucked but it had a shoulder high window with an ocean view across the channel. He rinsed off, brushed his teeth then returned to the bedroom and opened his duffel. The book Lauren had left was on top of his clothes. He saw the weird deck of cards partially visible from beneath the book. He took both out and set them on the nightstand. He dressed quickly into a pair of clean jeans and a button-down shirt with short, straight tails, then sat in a chair with a linen white cover and opened the book to the *Table of Contents*. He searched and found the games called *California Jack* and *Tonk*. There were more than one of the weird decks of cards with the pigs wearing graduation caps and two had found their way to the villa where they'd stayed the first night. He opened the box of cards. The Ace of Spades was on top. He set it on the bedspread and fanned through the deck looking for any others without headshots of people but didn't see any. Who was Harold Fuchs?

There was no such thing as a coincidence.

His phone rang. MAYBE VIVIAN JACKSON came up on the screen. He answered it on the second ring. "Good morning," he said.

"Top of the morning to you, too. Did you find the cottage?"

"I did. Thank you."

"I hope the dogs didn't bother you too much. I forgot to mention them. They're the only thing keeping me from earning a five-star rating on the travel sites, but my love of dogs eclipses my need for a perfect rating."

"They didn't bother me at all," he fibbed.

"What are your plans today?" she asked.

"I'm heading to the passport office."

"Do you need a lift?"

"I called a taxi."

"Oh?" Vivian said, sounding surprised.

"I got the number of the cabbie who drove me here last night."

"That was smart. The U.S. Embassy is likely to be a zoo on a Monday morning. A lot of passports go missing over the weekend."

"Meaning what?" he asked.

"Nothing other than you could be facing a long wait."

"I don't have any other plans."

"I'd be happy to meet you there," she said.

"If you don't mind, that would be great. I'll buy you lunch. Or dinner," he joked.

"Text me when you arrive," Vivian said.

"I'll see you there." Another call came up. It was too many numbers to count. He ended the call with Vivian and switched to the incoming call without managing to screw it up. "Hello," he said.

"Is this Vance Courage?"

"It is."

"This is Mr. Green calling from Grand Cayman."

This was very weird. None of the eels from the bank had ever called him before. He'd checked the box not to call when he'd deposited the *funds*. But they required a cell number for emergencies.

"Is there a problem?"

"No, Sir. I'm following up on a request to increase your credit line at the Poseidon Club and Casino and it requires further validation."

"What are you talking about?"

"The bank received a call from the hotel where you are checked in, in The Bahamas."

"When?"

"Less than an hour ago. We called to confirm you're staying there, and we were connected to your room, but there was no answer. Is there a problem?"

"No," he said, "no problem."

"To increase your credit limit," Mr. Green said, "we have certain protocols in place. We need a verbal approval from you."

"You know what," he said, "I've changed my mind. There's no need to increase my limit."

"I'll contact the casino immediately," Mr. Green said.

"That's not necessary," he said, "I'll speak to the hotel myself."

"It's our policy to inform the casino of your request not

to increase your limit. These matters can be quite delicate," Mr. Green said.

He could only imagine the infinite possibilities requiring discretion. "I would appreciate it if you let me handle my own affairs."

"We have protocols, Mr. Courage. If I can be of further assistance, please call day or night."

What a load of shit. He was asking for assistance now and he wasn't getting it.

Mr. Green wasn't done. "If you change your mind and would like to increase your limit, we are happy to help you."

If Mr. Green provided much more unwanted help, he might tip Tonk Braman off.

"I understand."

He ended the call with the man at the bank wondering how long Tonk thought he'd get away with impersonating him.

30

The man who'd stood off to the side in the elevator with his back three-quarters to Lauren was tall and thin wearing a tweed jacket with oval patches at the elbows. That's what her father wore every day to work. Adrenaline rushed as she prepared to face him but when the man turned around, she saw that it wasn't him. The thought of running into her father at the hospital hadn't occurred to her. His office was in the professional building across the breezeway and as a psychotherapist, he rarely made hospital visits. It would take a while for her stomach to recover.

"Ground floor?" the stranger she'd mistaken for her father asked.

She nodded.

As the doors closed and the elevator dropped, her phone chimed in her purse. She unlocked the screen and looked at the text message from Vance, surprised to see a photo of an oceanfront view she didn't recognize. She read the message.

Took you up on your offer. Stayed at Vivian's last night.

She hadn't suggested he stay at her stepmother's place.

How did that happen?

Her phone pinged again. She hoped it was Vance with an explanation ignoring her messages. The text was from the insurance adjustor. Yesterday afternoon she'd taken pictures of the damage to her car and uploaded the photos to the insurance company portal.

The text had an attached written estimate for repairs along with instructions to fill out what looked like an accident report needed to determine which party was at fault for the accident. She downloaded the estimate, not surprised to see it was just over $2,500 dollars. She enlarged the PDF. The bid included replacing the taillight, fixing the dent on the back quarter panel and paint. She scrolled through her phone, found Cassandra Braman's number and texted her. I have the estimate. I'll forward it.

Cassie answered immediately. Great. Followed by: Got it. Where can we meet so I can pay you.

She wasn't going to meet Cassie. Lauren texted: Please send the money with one of the apps.

Her phone pinged with a response from Cassie: I can't do that. I'm paying cash.

What she wanted right now more than anything was a reason to get out of this place. She typed quickly and sent the text. I'm at Mother of Mercy Hospital. Pick a place halfway and I'll meet you now.

Cassie answered: There's a sandwich shop in the shopping center off south dixie hwy near southwest 27th Ave.

She typed: Meet you there in 30-mins. She hurried to the parking garage. Time, she knew, killed deals and it was imperative she meet with Cassie ASAP, striking while the proverbial iron was hot. As she inserted the spare key into the car door, she felt the presence of someone walking up behind her.

31

"Hey Blagden, thanks for picking me up," Vance said opening the door to the Malibu. Beneath the mid-morning sun, the blue paint had a metallic sparkle and as he climbed into the back seat, he noticed Blagden wore a silky black track suit with a pair of thin yellow stripes running from his shoulders down the legs of his pants.

"My pleasure. You is a good customer. How was your evening?"

"I slept like a baby. By the way sorry about butchering your name in that text."

"No problem," Blagden said, "You are 'ardly de first one to do it. De kids called me Black Don on the schoolyard. Even my girlfriend do it now when she mad at me. Anyone who dictate a message have de same ting 'appen. Where to?"

"Can you take me to the U.S. Embassy?"

"You is going to 'ave to wait in line. Tis Monday morning and a lot of tourists are looking for dere lost passports."

"So, I've heard."

Vivian's house was off a main road just past a blind

corner and per Blagden's request, he'd walked a block down the street to meet him. Looking out the window of the Malibu, for a moment imagined he was in Massachusetts. The oak trees and sprawling colonial mansions blocked the view to the harbor. He'd not seen any of this in the darkness last night when he'd arrived.

As Blagden headed toward City Center in Nassau the landscape changed from leafy to tropical and the unobstructed view to the harbor returned. They passed the ferry port where he'd met Blagden yesterday. Grasping the back of the empty front passenger seat, he leaned forward to look out the windshield.

Blagden fish-eyed him. "Same deal as we 'ad yesterday?"

"Yes."

"De U.S. Embassy is only five-minute away. I wait for you. Okay?"

"I shouldn't be long," he said. "My friend is meeting me to try to speed it up."

"Friend?"

"The one who owns the house."

"Miss Vivian Jackson."

"You remember."

"Behind all of de glitz and glamor," Blagden said, "dis is a very small town. All de families know each other. The Jackson's are a 'igh-minded group. Dere family bin 'ere as long as mine."

"I've never met her," he said.

Blagden stopped at 42 Queen Street in front of a boxy beige four-story stucco box that looked more like a budget hotel than an American Embassy.

"We 'ave reached," he said.

The stars and stripes waving from the flagpole outside the building was the only sign that it might be the U.S.

embassy. He took a hundred-dollar bill from his wallet, handed it to Blagden, then called Vivian.

She answered on the first ring. "I think I see you," she said. "Are you arriving by taxi?"

"That's me," he said, getting out of the cab and looking around. He saw a woman walking toward him, along the sidewalk. Blagden backed up, did a 3-point turn and sped away without saying goodbye.

Vivian wasn't what he expected. But what had he expected? She wore an understated floral dress to her calves cinched at the waist with a thin metal belt, topped with a narrow white collar. Her heels were low with closed toes. She had a light tan and full head of blonde hair that gave her a youthful appearance.

He felt her eyes upon him, sizing him up. She had full lips, a wide button nose that fit her face and soft brown eyes. Her smile said everything nice about the world.

"Vance?"

"That's me."

She had a hint of a British accent. "I'm Vivian. It is nice to meet you in person."

"Thanks for meeting me here. Rumor has it, it can take all day to straighten out a lost passport."

"Did you by any chance fill out the D.S.-64 form on the U.S. Department of State website?"

"No," he said.

"Good. It's better if you're not in the system yet. That can slow things down but of course it also makes it easier for someone to steal your identity if you don't report your passport stolen right away. I should also tell you we've run into somewhat of an obstacle," she said. "Do you know a man named Tonk Braman?"

32

L auren waited for the man next to her to unlock and get into his car parked next to hers in the hospital parking garage. She couldn't remember what she'd told Vance about her father, or if she'd mentioned him at all. She hadn't spoken to him for three years and as far as she was concerned, another three years might not be long enough.

She backed out, exited the lot, and took Bayshore Drive South toward the sandwich shop off South Dixie Highway where Cassie wanted to meet. She parked in a spot between two landscapers' trucks and checked the time. It was just after noon. She locked her vehicle and got out, the smell of yeast and grease filled the parking lot. The glass door was grimy and smudged. As she entered, she walked around a pair of yellow cones marking the wet floor and looked around.

She guessed the sloppily dressed men sitting in the booth in the back near the restrooms were the landscapers. There were no women here, other than her and the one working behind the counter. Where was Cassie?

"What can I get you," the woman taking orders behind the register asked.

"I'm still deciding." She grabbed a bag of potato chips from the counter and said, "I'll get these for now. Oh, and this too," she said, setting a bottle of cold water she'd taken from the built-in ice cooler next to the register.

She paid then sat at an open booth facing the parking lot. She checked her phone for messages and saw the old text from Vance. She tapped the PHOTOGRAPHY app and scrolled through the most recent pictures of herself standing in front of the bow of *The Parent Minus*. She enlarged them. In one of them her eyes were closed. The next one was fuzzy. Vance would never make it as a photographer. The last one was the best. Wow, that boat was impressive in every way, especially from the low angle looking up she'd asked him to shoot. She selected it and texted it to him with a note. Miss you too.

A black Toyota RAV4 pulled up. It looked vaguely familiar, but from where? The driver parked at an angle in a spot facing the road, taking up two spaces.

If hell on wheels was a person, the girl who flung the door open might've been it. Her hair was streaked in red, white and blue swathes and she wore cutoff jeans, a 'Therapy Human' tank top with a dog beneath it, and white high-topped sneakers.

She stood. If it was Cassie, the girl would know it was her.

Cassie approached and dropped into the booth opposite her without first speaking.

The girl pulled her long multi-colored hair off to one side and slung it over her front shoulder. "You must be Lauren. You're the only woman in here and that black Audi out there is missing a taillight. I'm Cassie," she said, grabbing Laurens bag of potato chips and tipping the bag into her hand. "Do you mind?" she asked.

A little late for that. She moved her bottle of water out of Cassie's reach, setting it down on the hard plastic booth seat.

"Twenty-five hundred dollars is outrageous for a little dent and some broken plastic."

She should've known. "I know but that's what it costs."

"Can't you just take it to my guy?" Cassie asked, handing her an envelope.

Lauren looked inside at the thin stack of twenty-dollar bills. "This is not the deal we talked about. I told you how much. I texted you the estimate. You said you'd bring the cash."

"I lied. I don't have the cash. I'd tell you I'd make payments, but you know how that would go. You'll go crazy trying to bill-collect me and you'd never see the money because I don't have it and I doubt I'll ever have it."

She hit the pause button in her head disconnecting it from her mouth.

Cassie looked away, then up, making eye contact with the landscapers who were passing their table.

The men slowed to a near stop eyeballing them like prey. Both women glared at them. They got the message and kept on moving.

"Dirtbags," Cassie said, adding, "I hit your car on purpose and I'm betting you have uninsured motorist that'll cover your car repairs."

Lauren felt a chill starting at the back of her neck shooting down her spine. She narrowed her eyes at the girl. She'd seen her before. She was the same woman who dropped Tonk and his friends off at the airport in Homestead.

"I'm worried about my brother."

"Your brother?"

"My dad flew you and your friends to Nassau yesterday."

"Not exactly. He landed on an out island and ditched us."

"Tonk's my brother."

That much she'd figured out. "What do you want?"

"I want you to help me."

Lauren studied the girl's face. How could she possibly help if she didn't know what the problem was. "How?" she asked.

"I've been calling him, and I keep getting a CALL FAILED message."

"Maybe it's because he's out of the country."

"No. He goes with my dad all the time."

That was new information.

Cassie grabbed a hunk of patriotic hair slung over her shoulder, wound it in both hands then piled it on top of her head. "I think something very bad is about to happen."

33

V ance stood on the sidewalk looking around at the pastel colonial style government buildings imagining what the city of Nassau must've looked like back when it was Charlestown, before the Spanish torched the city. Were there any remains from that era? Did the Spanish invasion predate the arrival of Vivian's Loyalist family? He wondered if any of her ancestors were tasked with eradicating the pirates running amok in New Providence. Or if they resented the Americans to whom they'd lost during the Revolutionary War. It must have been interesting times when Blackbeard ruled the capitol city. Vivian had asked him to wait outside while she'd gone inside the Embassy. He people watched while he waited for her.

He saw her exit the front doors and approach. "We need to wait a while before we go back. Ever since they started construction on the new building it seems like the old one runs even slower. Would you like to have a tea or coffee while we wait?"

"A coffee sounds good," he said.

"I know a place a short ride from here," she said.

"My treat," he said following her to her Ford Mustang.

She parked a few blocks away near an open market.

He got out and followed her, as he checked out the shops and restaurants and tourists and locals milling about on the sidewalks. Some sat outside at the sidewalk cafes. Others carried shopping bags.

"How much do I owe you for the house last night?"

"That's not necessary," Vivian said.

"Is it available tonight?"

"I'd have to ask my assistant to see if it's available. Check out time is noon. I suppose I should have mentioned that."

He hadn't thought about another check-in. He'd left his duffle at the cottage, and he hadn't cleaned up after himself.

"I hope the dogs weren't too much of a bother."

"Not at all," he lied a second time. Truth was, he'd slept through most of the noise and the dogs served as a much-needed alarm clock.

"People complain quite a bit," she said, leading the way to a cozy coffee house a block away.

"Is there a hold up at the embassy?" he asked.

"I don't know what Lauren told you, but I'm retired from The Ministry."

"She didn't mention it," he said, which was technically true. Lauren said they were 'connected.' "Ministry of what?" he asked.

"Tourism."

That made sense. It also qualified Vivian as a retired civil servant, or maybe even a politician depending on what position she'd held.

"Did you enjoy it?" he asked.

"Most of the time. My younger brother is the Registrar General. I'm not telling you this to crow. Rather I'm mentioning it because when I phoned his office, I found out from his secretary that he had a dental appointment first thing this morning."

Vance looked at her perplexed.

"I'm fairly certain I'll hear from him very soon and if he makes a call to the U.S. Embassy, which I expect he will, it will make the process of getting your passport straightened out much more efficient."

"I see," he said, suddenly feeling awkward and out of place amid her formal social graces.

They arrived at a small storefront coffee house with an arched red metal awning. He rushed ahead and opened the door for her.

When they entered, everyone knew her. You'd think the Queen of England had just arrived the way the staff tailed her like pilot fish.

"I never could figure out what this fuss is all about," she said to him in a theater whisper as they walked between tables set closely together.

He could. Not only was she connected, but she was also unassuming.

The hostess led them to a small pie crust table in the back where the lighting was dim. He pulled one of the high-backed chairs for her then took a seat across from Vivian.

"Would you like the usual?" the young woman waiting on them asked.

"Yes, Annabelle."

"And for you, Sir?"

"Coffee. Black," he said.

When Annabelle was gone from the table, Vivian asked, "Have you heard from Lauren? She mentioned that she had to return home for an unexpected matter."

"We've texted back and forth a few times, but we haven't had a chance to talk."

"Is she coming back?"

"I don't know."

Annabelle set a matching pot and teacup with a golden handle with a pastel flower motif on the white tablecloth. She placed a matching fine china dish with tiny jar of honey, fresh cut lemons and packets of sugar in front of Vivian. His cup of coffee was served in a thick white mug.

When Annabelle was gone, he said, "Her ex-husband was in an accident and she went back to Miami." ı

"Why?" Vivian asked.

His phone vibrated in his pocket. "Hold that thought," he said, looking at the screen. He held his finger up. "It's Lauren. I'm going to step outside for a moment. Will you please excuse me."

Vivian nodded, lifted the pretty pot of hot water and poured steaming water into the matching cup.

He snaked his way through the narrow aisle between tables and answered before he'd made it to the front door. "Hey," he said. "How are you doing?"

"Good," she said. "You made it to Nassau. I got the picture of the place where you're staying. I assume that's where you are."

"It is. I got the picture of the yacht. Are you clairvoyant?"

"Not that I know of."

"I saw it this morning."

"*The Parent Minus?*"

"Yeah. Isn't that weird? It was sailing through Nassau Harbour. I saw it from Vivian's rental house."

"What were you doing there?"

"I called her like you suggested. It's a long story. I'm having coffee with her right now."

"With Vivian?"

He heard the surprise in her voice.

"Yes. She agreed to meet me at the embassy and we had some time to kill. I'm trying to get my passport straightened out. How did it go at the hospital?"

"He's awake and he's expected to make a full recovery."

"That's good."

There was a lag.

"Right?" he asked.

"Of course. Yes."

"And his family?"

"They're relieved. I'm sure," she added.

"Are you coming back? Vivian just asked me, and I told her I didn't know."

"I'm not sure. How did you get to Nassau?"

"I'll tell you later when I have more time."

"I just had the strangest thing happen."

"What's that?'

"You remember I texted you someone hit and ran my car at the airport in Homestead?"

"Uh huh."

"Turns out the person did it on purpose."

"How did you know that?"

"I just met her, and she told me."

"Who . . . her?"

"Cassandra Braman."

"Should that name mean something to me?"

"She's Tonk's sister. She thinks something very bad is about to go down."

The woozy feeling from this morning returned. "I don't understand. How did she know how to find you?"

"Remember when the SUV dropped Tonk, C.J. and Chan off at the airport, and the woman driver seemed like she was about to get into an altercation with Tonk?"

"Yeah."

"That's her. She hit my car and left a note. She wanted to meet."

"Okay," he said, "something is going on."

"She seems scared."

"Of what?"

"I don't know."

"Use your Nancy Drew superpowers and see what else you can find out."

He waited for her to speak.

"Hello?"

Silence.

"Lauren?"

The CALL FAILED warning lit up on his screen. He redialed but got a beep-beep-beep signal instead. He tried again. Same result. He smacked his phone against his thigh.

Fucking cell phone.

34

T he barber at *Princes and Princesses* had tried to turn Tonk away this morning, explaining he'd never styled a White man's hair before. But as far as he was concerned, the barber had done a damn good job cutting his hair and shaving his goatee and mustache. Good enough to pass as the guy on the stolen passport. What luck to discover that Courage had a big line of credit at the casino. When he checked into the hotel casino, a man in a tailored suit appeared out of nowhere. He hadn't directly asked the casino manager to increase his credit line, rather he'd inquired about how he would go about increasing it if he needed to, hoping to figure out how much credit he had. He regretted it now. The well-dressed man excused himself to make a call.

Sweat broke on his palms while he waited. When the suit returned, he told Tonk he'd talked to the bank and that the casino would handle the transfer, if needed. There was no reason to think he'd raised suspicion. If he had, he'd have been questioned by casino security now. They hired the best. Retired Secret Service, US marshals, DEA, CIA, FBI, NSA, you-name-it agents.

Though he'd already checked into the room and would have liked to stay and bask in luxury, he couldn't risk it. Courage was an ex-cop and by now he suspected—possibly even knew—someone was using his identity. It was best to lay low. Even if Courage suspected something, what could he do about it stuck on an out-island trying to get his passport replaced? That could take days, maybe weeks. He'd probably just want to go home. But still, he needed to be careful.

He planned to stay with C.J. and Chan at the slum rental tonight, just in case. He'd accessed a thousand dollars from Courage's credit line earlier and won ten grand at the high roller poker table. Now he wanted to cash the chips in for American dollars. He waited in line in front of a man who could've passed as a politician with slick silver hair combed back with gel. He imagined the old guy standing buck naked while some poor young lady spray painted his drooping nutsack and sagging butt cheeks.

The cage cashier made eye contact with and gestured to the man behind him, signaling him to cut the line in front of Tonk.

Tonk turned around and said to him, "I was here first."

"Don't be so daft," the man said in a British accent.

Daft? He stared at the man's shoes. No socks. Tan feet. Tassels. What a prick.

"Brilliant film," the Brit said.

"What?"

"*Get Shorty.* One of my all-time faves."

Okay, so the Englishman wasn't a total asshole.

Another man, an older one who looked like might be a high roller, took a place in line behind him.

A cashier opened a new window and gestured to the guy behind him. "I can help you over here."

The second guy cut in front of him and stood at the cage to his left where the woman cashier dressed in a black satin vest spoke from behind shiny brass bars. Tonk fished-eyed him, noticing his longish sideburns and the lavender cashmere sweater draped over the back of his shoulders, tied around loosely in front, the sleeves hanging over his baby blue polo. Was he wearing clear lip gloss? *Jesus.* Tonk would've liked to slug him in his high cheekbones. Just to see if it felt as good as he imagined.

"Welcome, Mr. Fuchs," the VIP cashier said, handing him a stack of poker brown chips worth $5,000 each.

Did she say *Fuchs?* Could it be?

Tonk sidled up to the man. He leaned forward and asked, "Has anyone ever told that you look like George Clooney?"

The man who might be Fuchs turned around. "Are you talking to me?"

"Yeah. My sister's a huge Clooeny fan. Mind if I take a selfie with you?"

He didn't give him a chance to answer. He slid next to him, held the burner in their faces and snapped a selfie.

A beefy guy who'd been standing guard nearby rushed over.

"Sorry Mr. Fuchs," the guard said.

The goon looked like he could strangle Tonk with one hand.

"See the sign, pal. No cell phone usage or pictures in the casino."

"It's alright," Fuchs said.

The cashier reached under the desk and produced an envelope. She slid it beneath the bars. "This is courtesy of management, Mr. Fuchs. In case you get tired or would like to freshen up."

Fuchs looked inside the envelope, set it down and pushed it back under the cage window with one finger. "Thanks," he said, "but I'll be staying on my yacht."

Tonk glanced to where he'd seen security guard posted, but the guy was gone. He moved closer behind Fuchs to eavesdrop.

The cashier spoke in a low voice. "Keep it. In case you meet a young lady and would prefer to spend time here in the hotel."

Fuchs took the envelope, folded it in half and tucked it inside his back pocket, then grabbed the poker chips from the counter. "Good luck," he said as he turned and sauntered across the lobby toward the high roller tables in a back room where Tonk had already won over ten grand using seed money stolen from Courage's credit line.

Good luck to you, too, Mr. Fuchs.

'Freshen up' or 'meet a young lady' meant the hotel had comped him a room.

Good to know.

He changed his mind about cashing in his chips and shadowed Fuchs to the high roller room past the slots near the back of the house. A woman with hair as shiny as a wet seal let him in. Scantily clad women staged at different locations around the poker tables noticed Fuchs as soon as he entered and jockeyed to stalk their prey. Why couldn't geezers like Fuchs shop the blue hair market and leave the younger ladies for the age-appropriate guys?

Tonk left the room and hurried outside. He walked past the valet stand and continued around the corner and stood beneath a thatched palm where he'd have some shade.

He pulled up C.J.'s phone number on the burner and

texted. It's Tonk. Lost my phone. He waited a minute, then dialed the number.

C.J. answered on the first ring. "What the hell?" C.J. said. "Where are you? You said you were going to go for a haircut. We've been calling and texting. Chan's super-pissed off. This place is a dump. Have you seen the bathroom?"

"I think I saw him," Tonk said.

"Saw who?" C.J. asked.

"Harold Fuchs. I'm at the casino. Hang on. I'm texting you." Tonk changed screens, selected the selfie he'd taken of himself with Fuchs and sent it to C.J. "See if you can figure out if it's him," he said, watching the green progress bar inch across his screen.

"Got it," C.J. said.

"Don't call. Text me when you get here. I'm going to shadow him."

Tonk ended the call debating how much he planned to tell C.J. about Courage's credit line. He opened the tracking app he'd downloaded on his burner phone. *The Parent Minus* geolocation had changed. It was now less than a mile from the casino.

Could be my lucky day.

As he headed back to the casino entrance, a man accosted him.

"I have a great deal for you," the scruffy guy said.

"What's that?"

He held up a yellow poker chip. "I'll sell you a thousand-dollar mark for seven-hundred U.S. You see I lost my I.D., and the casino won't let me cash it out. It's a great—"

"Yeah, right," Tonk said, pushing past the con man. He chuckled at a bullshitter trying to bullshit a bullshitter.

As he walked back inside, Tonk nonchalantly eyed the

cameras surveilling the entrance as he strolled to the cashiers' rotunda. He stood in the VIP line and waited.

The cashier who'd ignored him earlier motioned him forward.

"I'm sorry for the delay," he said. "How may I help you?"

"I'd like to draw more from my credit line."

"Of course. How much would you like?"

"Can I get another thousand?"

"May I see your passport and hotel key?"

"Certainly," Tonk said, looking over his shoulder as he presented the items.

The cashier padded the keyboard, then asked, "What denomination would you like?"

Knowing higher denominations attracted extra attention, he said, "I'd like it half in fifties and half in hundreds."

"Of course, Mr. Courage."

"Will there be anything else?" the man in the black silk vest asked as he slid the tray with blue and black chips beneath the brass bars.

"Not now," he said, tucking the room key and passport into his pants pocket.

He headed back to the high roller room and showed his key card to the burly man now working the door. Fuchs sat at round green cloth covered table in the back corner.

"May I join you?" he asked, holding his tray of chips.

"Of course," Fuchs said, eyeing his bank.

Tonk sat two chairs to the left of Fuchs, removed his chips from the tray, stacked them on the green speed cloth, then sat out the first hand, to watch how Fuchs would bet. The man who'd already been playing Fuchs smoked a cigar. He sipped his whiskey from a short glass and placed a thousand-dollar bet on the table. Fuchs pushed a purple chip forward, raising the bet another five hundred.

Tonk reached into his pants pocket and fondled the 10 yellow thousand-dollar chips he'd won off a Japanese tourist.

Fuchs raised the cigar-smoker another five hundred. The croupier placed two cards face down in front of each of them. The smoker peeked at his cards then signaled to the dealer for another hit, then raised his hand, signaling he now wished to hold. Fuchs set his cards face down and drummed his fingertips on the racetrack railing of the card table. Every gambler had his bluff. This was Fuchs'. He was taking his time. Drumming. Squinting. Eyes cast down on the green speed cloth. Fuchs lifted his cards an inch or two, then leaned down to reassess his hand, then he stabbed the table with his index finger. The dealer understood Fuchs wanted another card.

His opponent slurped whiskey then promptly raised Fuchs another thousand and gestured for another card. The smoker looked at the new card and flipped the Jack of Hearts over, tossing the rest of the cards up. They scattered on the green fabric. The smoker champed the stogie, downed the remaining booze and slammed the glass on the edge of the table. The croupier scooped the man's chips and pushed the pot toward Fuchs. The loser staggered to his feet, collected his remaining chips and wandered off.

His phone vibrated. He checked it under the table. The message was from C.J.

The picture is Fuchs

Tonk texted a thumbs up as Fuchs placed a black chip on the table and raised his square chin an inch and arched his brows.

This was good. Fuchs was inviting him to play, starting low. Tonk accepted, moving a 100-dollar chip from his pot and pushing it forward on the green cloth.

Game on, motherfucker.

His personal phone vibrated.

He peeked under the table at the screen.

You have to be fucking kidding.

Another freaking call from Savient, the loan debt collection arm run by none other than the U.S. government. He'd tried to make their daily calls stop. He'd changed his phone number a half dozen times. Sometimes his phone rang every hour from 8 a.m. until 8 p.m. Monday through Saturday. The automated system left long voice messages at the end of every collection call. Bugging him now was a message from the universe that he had every right to make them STOP.

"They're building a new embassy," Vivian said, getting out of the Mustang and walking next to him in her erect and purposeful gait. "Of course, it's behind schedule and over budget. Two hundred million U.S. dollars. Can you imagine?"

Vance could. The U.S. government threw taxpayer dollars into the air like confetti. Beyond that, he rather liked the existing building: an understated, four-story structure the color of vanilla ice cream with a flat roof and bars on the windows.

They'd had a pleasant visit at the coffee house. He'd been careful to avoid topics that might lead to talk of Lauren's father. Vivian couldn't have been much more than ten years older than Lauren and it seemed odd to him that Lauren's dad dumped her: men generally ditched their older wives. But there were also those who discarded women like used dixie cups.

Vivian said, "Your state department was scheduled to have a groundbreaking for the new embassy right after

Hurricane Dorian came ashore. We were afraid they would cancel. Or postpone it."

"That was an unbelievable storm," he said, following her into the building.

"We still don't have an official death toll," she said. "It meant a lot to us when your president reassured us construction would continue as planned. It was very uplifting," she said. "Why don't you wait here while I try to locate the person who will help expedite your travel papers."

Lauren was right. Her father was a fool for not keeping his pants zipped.

Vivian saw someone she knew, and he watched as she met up with a Black man in a brown suit. Vivian huddled with the man then motioned him to join them.

"Do you have your Driver's License with you?" she asked him.

He removed his wallet, took it out and handed it to her. Vivian handed it to the man who disappeared down the hall.

"Is there a problem?" he asked her, sensing something was off.

"You didn't report your passport stolen, correct?"

He nodded.

"There might be a problem. Do you recall the last time you saw it?"

"I showed it at the airport when we were leaving Miami."

"When did you first notice it missing?"

"When we were on Chub Cay."

"Hmm," Vivian said.

"What's going on?"

"It appears that someone is using it."

Adrenaline burned through his system. "How do you know that?"

"When my brother called to inquire about expediting a replacement, your embassy called the Poseidon Club Casino inquiring if yours had been used at the hotel. Your last name is rather unforgettable."

"What did the hotel say?"

"My brother hasn't heard back yet."

"Ask him to stop his inquiry."

She looked at him askance. "Why?"

"You asked me if I knew someone by the name of Tonk Braman. I do, and I gotta go," he said.

"What about filing a report?"

"I'll do it later. I hate to be rude, but I need to get my I.D. back and I have to go." He couldn't tell Vivian about the gun and had to get to Tonk before the hotel tipped him off.

"Wait here and I'll fetch your I.D., but you're not going to get far without your passport. You should report it. Stolen ones end up on the Dark Web."

"I'll explain later," he said.

As soon as she returned his Driver's License, he hurried out of the building. When he was two blocks away, he called Blagden while walking through an upscale neighborhood. In less than ten minutes, the cab driver arrived. He climbed into the backseat of the blue Malibu.

"Did Miss Jackson fix de problem?" Blagden asked.

"Take me back to the Poseidon Club," he said, ignoring the question.

36

The last thing Lauren heard Vance say before she'd lost the cell phone signal was to use her Nancy Drew superpowers. That meant finding out more about the Bramans. She started with Cassie's social media. The girl was a prolific social media poster and it took time to scroll through hundreds of posts to find a picture of her father posing in front of the Beechcraft airplane, and another of Tonk from last Thanksgiving. Her ABOUT page hadn't been filled out and her only CHECK-INs were the Flight Base Operation at Homestead and a trip to the zoo. She had two cats named Paul Mitchell and Vidal Sassoon. Scrolling back to the top of her social media, Lauren noticed it has been two months since her last post.

Neither Blade nor Tonk had been tagged in any of Cassie's posts and when she searched for their profiles, she pulled a blank. Blade didn't seem like the type to have a social media presence and Tonk seemed like the type who'd probably deleted his.

She broadened her search on the internet using Cassie's complete name, Cassandra Braman. Advertisements for the background checks filled the first page. Trying a different approach, she typed Tonk Braman into the search bar. His name came up on dozens of ads for background searches, too. When she clicked the link for PayToSee, a message popped up: *'Tonk Braman May Have a Civil or Criminal Record.'*

She debated signing up for the free trial, squeezing her hands into fists, then opening them like claws. Getting ready. She entered her personal and credit card information into the PayToSee portal to gain access to the 30-day free trial. She typed *'Tonk Braman Miami'* into the search bar and waited as a blue wheel turned while a *'Gathering Data'* flashed on the screen. Another message came up, *'Your Information is Almost Ready.'* Then the page populated.

The first category was POSSIBLE ADDRESSES. She clicked on it and saw there was one address in south Miami. The next category was POSSIBLE RELATIVES. She chose it and scanned the list. Cassandra was on it. So was Robert Braman, a.k.a. Blade Braman. She compared the Miami address for Robert to Tonk's and hit pay dirt. She studied the list of other names and possible relatives. Marilyn Braman lived at the same address. She was born in 1959. She looked at Robert, or Blade's, date of birth. 1956. Marilyn Braman was probably Tonk and Cassandra's mother. She'd recently died. Just over two months ago. Around the same time Cassie stopped posting on social media.

She switched screens and clicked on the yellow bar for CRIMINAL HISTORY. There was nothing there. Had the advertisers no shame? The answer was no. Another option popped up on the screen. *'The person you are searching for may have a judgment against them.'* Money was always a motive. A red JUDGMENTS bar popped on the screen. She selected it: *'The person you are searching has a judgment. You* *can purchase a copy of the Court Filing for only $9.99.'* She ponied up and downloaded the PDF file. It was a civil judgment. The Plaintiff was Sallie Mae. The Defendant, Tonk Braman. The lawsuit was a Breach of Contract for *'underlying debt, fees and costs incurred at a California State University.'*

Holy crap. Uncle Sam was suing Tonk for his unpaid student loan to the tune of $280,000 including the original $180,000 plus interest and penalties. *Jesus.* For film school? She had made a pretty good living at it and had never taken a course in film or video production or even business for that matter. She was an English major who'd stumbled into the industry.

She forwarded the PDF file to Vance's cell phone, sent a copy to her own email then exited out of the site and searched 'Marilyn Braman Obituary.'

The top hit wasn't from a funeral home. It was a story in the *Miami Inquirer.* She read the headline. *'Woman Hires Hit Man to Kill Self to Pay Son's Student Loan.'*

Lauren's heart stopped. She had to warn Vance.

37

The springs in the back seat of the Malibu dug into his seat bones still sore from yesterday's travels. It was nearing the lunch hour and the weather was clear and visibility unlimited as the old Chevy chugged over the Paradise Island bridge. He gazed out the open car window at the sapphire seascape below of cruise ships and boats, of the docks and gantry cranes. It was Monday mid-morning and Potters Cay was a beehive of activity. A sleek yacht sailed out of Nassau Harbour toward open water. It reminded him to do something. He scrolled through his text messages, tapped on the picture of *The Parent Minus* Lauren sent, tapped the arrow below the picture and forwarded it to Sarge.

Instantly his phone rang. "*Oye, Gallego,* she's hot. Both of them."

Retired Fort Lauderdale police sergeant Daniel Ruiz's off-color humor never disappointed.

"I need a favor."

"Since when don't you? It's the only time you call."

Always the martyr. "Listen, I don't have a lot of time. If

you enlarge the picture, you can see the registration number on the bow. I want you to find out who owns it."

"Why? Did the horsey chick get tired of waiting for you to put a ring on it and run off with the owner?"

"No. Nothing like that."

"Where are you?"

"The Bahamas."

"You finally getting laid, *Gallego*?"

"Make a call to see if you can find out who owns it. I'll buy you a beer when I'm home."

"I'm no boat expert but that thing has got to be worth some serious dollars," Sarge said. "So, what's with the name?"

"I don't know."

"Sounds fishy." Sarge laughed. "Get it?"

He could imagine Sarge's grandpa belly doing the jig. He was probably rubbing his brown billiard head and twisting the cubic zirconia post in his earlobe.

"See what you can find out. I'm heading into a casino so don't call, text me."

"Don't lose too much *dinero*. Where's the horsey chick?"

"She was here but had to leave early."

"Not a lovers' quarrel I hope."

Sarge simply couldn't help himself. He had a one-track mind. "No. She had a family emergency."

Sarge turned serious. "It should be straightforward to find out. I'll let you know."

"Thanks." He ended the call.

Blagden slowed as they approached the Poseidon Club.

"Do you want me to wait?" the taxi driver asked.

"Can you?"

Blagden held out his hand. Vance handed him a hundred.

"I wait on de other side of de bridge. I don't want to look suspicious."

"Good idea," he said, getting out and hurrying toward the entrance of the casino. Red rose-colored carpets laid around a serpentine of marble floors. Massive chandeliers as big as tractor tires hung from the ceiling. Men in white jackets with royal blue epaulets and white pin-striped shirts walked the floor.

He cruised the first level getting a lay of the casino. The slot machines were crowded with people pulling levers, pushing buttons and staring at the pay lines, waiting for good fortune to strike. Lights flashed and sirens blared as a mountain of coins dropped. The winner, a young man in a blue T-shirt, scooped the money into a plastic cup and moved to a new machine.

Tonk had played poker in college with C.J. and if he'd accessed his Cayman bank credit line, he guessed the punk would be at the high roller tables. He spotted the cashier station built as an island in the middle of the casino floor and took a wide berth around it. He need not look up to know every inch of the casino was under constant surveillance.

After he mapped the layout and located the high roller room at the end of the hall, he approached the cashier.

"May I help you?"

"Yes. I'd like to buy two thousand dollars-worth of one-hundred-dollar chips."

"How would you like to pay?"

"I'd like to use a cash advance on my Visa."

"May I have your Visa and your I.D."

He didn't know the limit on the card. He presented his Florida driver's license with the credit card.

"Are you a guest at the hotel?"

"No."

"You're going to have to fill out some paperwork," the clerk said.

"How did you arrive in the country?" the man asked.

He felt his heart rate pop. "Does it matter?"

"Yes. Tourists arriving on cruise ships may gamble without a passport."

"Then I guess it's my lucky day," he said. "There's nothing quite like a cruise."

"Sir," the cashier said. "I'm sorry to inform you that I'm going to have to take this card."

"Why?"

"You should call your bank, Sir."

He looked up at all the cameras recording him. He held his tongue between his teeth. He wanted to make a threat. They were shutting down the wrong guy. Tonk was impersonating him and getting away with it.

"Do you have any other credit cards with you?"

"I do not."

"If you believe there's some sort of mistake, I'm happy to call the casino manager if you'd like to speak to him."

He glanced up at the monitor above the cashier's brass cage. Was that Tonk standing behind him in the background? He couldn't tell but the guy appeared to make a beeline for the same cashier. Two people with his name would send security into a full court press.

38

"We're going to get ourselves killed," Chan said, standing in line at the CashDayz payday loan store on East Bay Street near the Paradise Island bridge. They'd caught the bus from the rundown rental where they'd stayed in the Over-the-Hill-District last night.

Every square inch of the exterior glass windows was plastered with handmade 'We Buy Gold' and 'Cash for Goods' signs.

"Hang on a sec," C.J. said, sitting on a metal bench in front of the pawn shop. "I need to do something."

He looked around, leaned over and raised his pantleg.

Chan checked for witnesses. "Hurry up."

"You should carry it in your purse."

"It's not big enough for a gun," she said in a low voice. "I wish Tonk would've taken it with him."

"I wish he hadn't stolen it," C.J. said. "What does he need it for? We should've left it in the room."

"It's in my name. What do you think would happen if Moo found it? He might report it. Anyway, you only need to keep it till we catch up with Tonk. It'll be his problem after that."

The wooden shelves inside the payday loan place were filled with suitcase-sized boom boxes, portable C.D. players, flip phones and dishware—anything and everything someone could sell for a buck.

The stuff on the shelves was covered by a layer of dust. The scratched glass cases were filled with a spread of costume jewelry and semi-precious stones strewn on a worn black velvet cloth. A handwritten sign saying 'We buy conch pearls' was taped to the top of the glass display case.

Catching a reflection of herself in a mottled mirror next to a dented red lawnmower that still smelled of gas, she did a double-take and gasped.

"I look like a whore," she said under her breath to C.J.

"Not really," he said. "Look around. You're not wearing an animal print."

She glared at him. "Is that supposed to be a joke?"

"No."

More people inside the pawn shop stared at C.J. than her. A six-foot eight White guy got more eyeballs than she did in her black wig, tight mini skirt and thick eyeliner, false eyelashes and red lipstick.

"I think you look nice," C.J. said.

"Say that again and I'll knee you in the nuts."

"May I 'elp you?" an older woman in a colorful parrot print muumuu asked. She sat on a barrel with her legs spread, her lady business covered by the bird fabric.

Chan stopped in front of her. "We have something we'd like to sell."

Chan took C.J.'s stack of credit cards and showed them to the shopkeeper, then reached into her small clutch and removed her wad held with a rubber band.

The big woman took the cards, continued to sit and removed the rubber bands from one stack, then thumbed through C.J.'s credit cards.

She harrumphed. "You got I.D. for dese?"

They presented their passports to the woman.

She opened the covers and looked at the pictures. "You 'ave another form of de I.D.?"

They fished for their California driver's licenses and showed them to her.

The woman set the licenses down atop the open passports on her left thigh, eyeing them suspiciously, glancing up and down, comparing the photos on each piece of identification.

Chan was about to tell her where she could shove it and go to the pawn shop across the street when the woman let out a jolly laugh.

"I is kidding," she said, showing a capped gold front tooth with a crescent moon. She gestured her hand up and down like a wave and laughed some more. Then she sobered up. "Where did you get all dese cash and gift cards?"

"We worked for them," C.J. said. "They're good."

"What kinda work?"

Like it was any of her concern.

The universities organized all kinds of events and she and C.J. had attended the ones with perks. They gave out gift cards and pizza just for showing up.

"We go door to door handing out church material at home," Chan lied.

The gift cards came from campus activists and political organizations. She and C.J. had sat through dozens and dozens of meetings, suffering through the bullshit some students were passionate about claiming they were going to change the world. Just for showing up, the organizers assumed she and C.J. were on the bandwagon. The organizers handed out gift cards like Halloween candy. But no one ever checked to see if she and C.J. attended any future rallies, or protests, or whatever, which they didn't.

"I take twenty-five percent off de top," the woman said, fondling a large gold hoop earring hanging from her right ear.

"Fifteen," C.J. said.

"Twenty-five is de final offer."

"Fine," Chan said.

She'd have carried the gun herself if she'd had a way to conceal it. This was Tonk's problem, and he'd stuck them with it. What if the casino had metal detectors? She should never have let C.J. agree to bring it to the casino.

While the woman tallied the credit cards with an old electric adding machine, Chan's phone chimed. She checked it.

A message from Tonk. Where the fuck are you guys?

Seriously? She held her finger over the keypad on her phone, then changed her mind and dropped it into her small purse.

Tonk's dad had offered to fly them for free but then he'd dumped them on a remote island. The mailboat trip hadn't set them back too much but they needed cash.

"How much do we have in credit cards?" she asked C.J.

"Three-thousand four-hundred and fifty dollars. She's going to take eight hundred sixty-two dollars and fifty cents leaving us with two thousand eight hundred eighty-seven dollars and fifty cents."

"That's a big cut."

"It's not too late to shop around," C.J. said, craning his neck, watching the shady characters coming and going.

"I just wish she'd hurry. How far are we from the casino?"

"Less than three miles," C.J. said.

"You know the bus route?" she asked.

"Yeah. We're less than a block from the stop."

"That's good because I can't walk forever in these Wizard of Oz shoes. My feet are killing me." She held onto his shoulder, removed one pink stiletto and rubbed her little toe. "While we're waiting, let's go over the plan one more time," Chan said. "Let's start with how long it's going to take you to hack Fuchs' bank account."

39

Vance ambled out of the casino to the valet area while calling Blagden from his cell. He looked over his shoulder to see if anyone was following him.

" 'allo," Blagden said.

"Can you come get me?"

"I kin. Dat was fast."

"How long until you can get here?"

"Just need to go over de bridge."

"Call me when you're on this side and I'll tell you where I am."

He ended the call then walked along a side street leading to a four-story parking garage behind the casino. Beyond it the land opened to a massive construction site that was in the early stages of foundation work. A man stood outside one of the four beige work trailers elevated on cinder blocks. A crane operator moved piles of white sand and loaded it into awaiting dump trucks. Jalopy cars he assumed belonged to the construction workers were parked in a makeshift dirt lot. He looked past what he estimated to be a cleared area about the size of a city block where the sandy earth was being grazed. A row of concrete barriers acted as a temporary bulkhead. Beyond the barriers he saw towering, palm trees with bright green fronds, and beyond the trees, the cobalt blue water.

This was a good place to wait. His phone buzzed in his pocket. Expecting Blagden, he was surprised to see Sarge's name come up.

"Hey."

"*Hola*, dude. I got something for you. The yacht is registered to an L.L.C. based in Delaware."

Delaware. The legal home of the biggest tax dodging corporations and predatory credit card lenders. There were no limits to the interest rate credit companies domiciled in Delaware could charge. He'd learned that when he was practicing law, representing people trying to get out of debt.

"Any names of the individual shareholders?"

"Nope."

"What's the name of the corporation?"

"Higher Eddy, L.L.C.," Sarge said.

"Hmm."

"I was thinking it might be Divorce Court, Inc. or something like that," Sarge said. "*The Parent Minus*? Minus what? The name is hinky."

As cops they'd seen it all. And he agreed. There was something chilling about the name. "Thanks," he said. "And thanks for not calling me *Gallego*. This might be a first."

"*Adios, Gallego*," Sarge said. "And good luck."

As he ended the call with Sarge, an incoming one appeared on screen. He gambled which button to press and got lucky.

"I am 'ere by de casino. Where are you?" Blagden asked.

"Do you know where they're doing construction up the street from the Poseidon?"

"Yes."

"Meet me there. I'm standing across the street from a yellow dump truck."

A minute later he saw the blue Malibu, paint glinting under the midday sun. He hopped in.

"What is you doing 'ere?" he asked. "Why is you hiding?"

"I'm not hiding. I need to go back to Vivian's house to pack." Which was partially true. He didn't have a plan to deal with Tonk. At least not yet.

As Blagden turned onto the main street in front of The Poseidon Club, Vance did a doubletake. Was that C.J. walking toward valet? If it was, who was with him? "Slow down." He craned his neck, then asked, "You remember that couple we followed yesterday?"

"De giraffe wit de girl at de bus stop?"

"Yeah."

"Do a drive by and tell me if that's the guy. I'm going to lay low while you do. There's more cash for you."

"Okay," Blagden said.

He knelt on the dirty rubber floor mat and peeked out the passenger's side rear window. He'd like to have gotten a closer look but if it was C.J., he couldn't take the risk of being seen. He stayed down out of sight and waited.

"I tell you in a minute," Blagden said, creeping along at less than five miles an hour. A driver behind him honked the horn. Blagden went nuts, hanging out the window, "Mudda Sick!" he screamed, making a fist and punching the sky.

He wanted Blagden to calm down. The ruckus would attract attention. He peeked over the bottom of the car window frame. The action had gotten the attention of the tall man and his companion. The pair stopped and stared at the Malibu as it crept by slowly, then passed. They'd not seen him. Blagden had cooled off as fast as he'd heated up.

"Dat is dem," he said calmly.

"What do you mean, them?"

"It's de girl, too."

"No, it's not." He wanted to look out the car window again, but he couldn't take the chance.

"It is her. I seen dat tattoo on her leg yesterday. She is wearing a wig," Blagden said. "All de P.I. mattresses do dat."

"P.I. mattresses?"

"You know. De ones for sale who cross de bridge to Paradise Island." Blagden activated the turn indicator and hung a right onto the main road.

He wanted clarity. "What do you mean 'for sale'?"

"De prostitutes dress up when dey is turning de tricks."

That was impossible. Or was it? Lauren had shown him the scanty clothes and make-up she'd seen in Chan's backpack.

"Where did they go?"

"Dey went inside de club."

"Stop the car."

Blagden did as told.

He got out and jogged around to the driver's-side. "I need your car."

"What? No."

"Listen to me Blagden. I am a rich man. I could buy you a brand-new car if you play this right. You either take my word for it and get out of the car or I'll find another way."

"And what do you expect me to do?"

"I want you to go into the casino and I want you to keep an eye on them. If I am lying to you, you can report me to the U.S. Embassy. You know my name."

"No, I don't."

"My name is Vance Courage."

Blagden wasted time thinking.

"Tick, tick, tick."

"Okay. I do it."

Blagden got out but shut the engine off and took the keys from the ignition.

"Give me a break, Blagden. Give me the fucking keys. If I don't come back, you can tell them I stole your car."

"You know Miss Jackson. How do I know if I can trust you?" He jabbed his finger on the zipper of his black track suit jacket. "It will be me who will be thrown into de Fox Hill prison. Oh Lord."

"Give me the keys."

He held out two one-hundred-dollar bills.

"You and dat cash," Blagden said, shaking his head and taking the money.

"I won't be long." He pointed to his phone. "Here," he peeled off another hundred. "Play the slots."

"Remember to drive on de left side of de road," he said taking more money.

"Right."

"No. Left."

"Got it."

He watched Blagden dressed in his black track suit with the yellow racing stripes head toward the entrance. What was Chan doing dressed like a 'P.I. Mattress'? Lauren had shown him the picture and he'd specifically remembered the black wig in Chan's bag. A picture was forming in his brain. He had to hurry. First, he had to call Vivian.

40

L auren read the headline on her desktop again and printed the story. *'Woman Hires Hit Man to Kill Self to Pay Son's Student Debt.'* Hands trembling, she took the document from the printer tray and sat on the red and black striped futon in her office and read the story slowly.

'TWO WEEKS AGO, a Miami wife and mother of two was found dead in her vehicle of an apparent drive-by shooting, The Times reported previously. Her body was discovered by an early morning jogger who'd seen a 2011 Honda Prelude stopped near a public park off SW 187th street with the driver's side car door open. Shell casings from a .45 caliber weapon were found at the scene. According to police reports the keys were in the ignition and her purse was found inside the vehicle. There were no signs of a struggle. She'd been shot once in the head and once in the chest.

Sources have told The Times a new investigation has been opened and that evidence reanalyzed from the crime scene suggests that the shooting may not have been random. Marilyn

Braman, aged 66 of Homestead, Florida had been pronounced dead at the scene. "We have reason to believe that Mrs. Braman knew her killer," a police spokesman said. "Forensic investigators have been examining a cell phone found at the scene. It is believed to be a burner phone purchased by Mrs. Braman one week before her death."'

Why were the police releasing new information if they didn't have a suspect?

'A new investigation was opened after an unnamed family member attempted to collect Mrs. Braman's life insurance benefits. The amount of the policy has not been disclosed. Mrs. Braman's husband was brought in for questioning. Robert 'Blade' Braman, is a private pilot with a twin-engine plane based out of the Homestead Regional Airport. He was reportedly in The Bahamas on the night of the shooting. Officials at the airport in Homestead are cooperating with investigators and have released flight plan data from the night of Mrs. Braman's death.

"We have reason to believe that this may have been a murder for hire," the Miami P.D. spokesman said. "And we are working closely with the insurance company to determine the facts of the case."'

Lauren took a deep breath and covered her face with her hands, then continued reading.

'Sources tell The Times investigators believe that Mrs. Braman may have plotted her own murder. Sources claim that Mrs. Braman was distraught over her son's student loan totaling more than $180,000 dollars. She'd told friends that she believed the government-backed loans were a form of predatory lending and that her family stood to lose everything and would never be able to pay it back. The retired schoolteacher withdrew $10,000 from her retirement account from the Miami School District Fund just days before her murder. The investigation is ongoing.

The Times has discovered that the Federal Government had

filed a lawsuit against her son, Robert Braman, Jr., et al. Mrs. Braman and her husband had co-signed for a second loan of more than $125,000 of the total $200,000 in outstanding debt. Many parents have collateralized their children's student loans by using their assets in a government backed program called 'Parent Addition.' The Times contacted the loan originator for comment. A spokesman for the company said, "We do not comment on pending litigation."

Student loans made by third parties are backed by the federal government. Economists estimate that there is $1.75 trillion in outstanding student debt. Loans may be serviced by three, four, five or more agencies making it difficult for borrowers to track down details of their loan agreements. Parents who act as guarantors are liable for the loans. "Asset forfeiture is part of the risk parents take when borrowing the money," a person familiar with the matter said. "The loan originators are predatory. They canvas poor neighborhoods. They outsource third parties to target them using call centers and mail.

"The real problem is the loans are a hundred percent guaranteed by the federal government and the colleges and universities have no incentive to determine whether the student will be able to pay back the money. The 'Parent Addition' program is particularly egregious because less than ten percent of graduates will be able to find jobs paying enough to make their loan payments. This is going to make the mortgage crisis look small by comparison. At least there was actual real estate backing those loans," the source said. "Congress has enacted laws making it impossible for borrowers to dispense of the debt via the bankruptcy courts making borrowers permanently liable."

Mr. Braman was unavailable for comment. Mrs. Braman is survived by her husband of thirty-five years, Robert Braman of Miami, son Robert, Jr. 'Tonk' Braman of Miami and Los Angeles, and a daughter, Cassandra Braman of Miami.'

Oh my God.

If the allegations were true, Marilyn Braman may have hired someone to kill herself to pay off Tonk's student loan. When the insurance company suspected fraud, they launched a new investigation. What a tragedy.

She called Vance. It went directly to voicemail. "Call me as soon as you get this. It's important."

She checked the time. Just after 2 o'clock in the afternoon. Next, she called Vivian. It went to voicemail. "Hi Vivian, thanks for helping Vance. I'm trying to get in touch with him but I'm having trouble with cell service. Give me a call when you get this."

Next, she dug through her purse and suitcase looking for the odd deck of cards. This new information about the Braman family student loan debt might connect Tonk to the college administrators. But how?

Damn it. Where were the cards? She dumped her purse out, then remembered she might have left the deck at Dr. Westerly's office.

She called Dr. Westerly and the housekeeper, Lenore, answered.

"Hi Lenore, it's Lauren Gold."

"Hello Miss Gold. I bet you're calling about that deck of cards you left here yesterday."

"I am. May I pick them up?"

"Dr. Westerly isn't here. She thought you might call to get them."

"May I come by now?"

"Yes, of course. I'll leave your name at the gate."

She loaded her stuff back into her purse, hurried to her car and headed to Westerly's place and was almost immediately trapped in stopped traffic. She tapped the horn at the car in front of her. The driver pulled up a foot giving her enough room to pull into the parking lot of a strip mall. She drove down the back alley past the smell of rotting food in dumpsters and mountains of flattened cardboard boxes stacked behind the back doors. She saw an exit leading to the road running parallel to Dixie Highway and put the Audi in park.

Up ahead two fire trucks blocked all northbound lanes. Great. A major car accident. There was no way around it. She rolled down the window, turned the radio to the A.M. traffic report, killed the engine and listened for an update. She pulled up Dr. Westerly's address from RECENT DESTI-NATIONS on the navigation app on her phone. She should've been 7 minutes away but who knew how long it would be now?

How sad was that? Planning your own murder to collect money to pay your kid's debt, then it possibly being all for not if the insurance company wouldn't pay. Something was going down. That's why Cassie hit her car. She had to warn Vance. She composed another text: Call me. Imp. Then she sent it.

Harold Fuchs had something to do with this. She could feel it in every cell in her body.

41

Vance parked the Malibu across the street from the U.S. Embassy and redialed Vivian. He'd called her three times, and she hadn't answered him. He hand-cranked the windows up and manually locked the doors, got out and stood on the sidewalk waiting for a break in traffic. White clouds hung over the building like a blanket, and he could see a cone of heaving rain forming offshore. He jogged to the other side of the street, passing a cluster of fat-trunked palm trees and entered the embassy. When he'd been there earlier with Vivian, the woman in a uniform had waved them through. This time he waited in the security line. He put the keys to Blagden's car, phone, wallet and change in his pockets in a plastic bowl then passed through the X-ray machine. He glanced around then headed to the INFORMATION desk.

"I was here earlier," he said.

"Take a number," the man at the desk said. "And someone will be with you."

He took a number and walked toward the waiting area. There were dozens of people sitting. Some milled about.

ı

He took his cell phone from his pocket and called Vivian again.

An old man with pale skin sitting next to him lifted his walking stick and pointed it to a NO CELL PHONE USAGE sign posted on the wall.

"How long have you been waiting?" he asked the man.

"Since high school," the old man said. "Just kidding."

He looked at his wristwatch. He didn't have time to wait around. The old man sealed the deal.

"I got here an hour after they opened and there was a line around the building. I spent Friday here, too. It only seems to get worse."

This wasn't going to work. He wadded up the ticket and dropped it in the garbage then jaywalked back to the Malibu. He unlocked the driver's side door. Man, it was muggier than a hothouse. He rolled down the front windows and left the driver's side door open while he texted Blagden.

Any update?

No answer. Maybe Blagden's phone was blocked inside the casino. He stared at the screen and waited another minute. Two texts from Lauren popped up on his phone. He didn't read them. He didn't have time. He started the engine, backed the Malibu out of the lot and headed to the Poseidon where he'd left Blagden as a lookout.

HALFWAY OVER THE Paradise Island bridge the sky opened and buckets of rain fell. Vance cranked up his window then fumbled the dash searching for the wipers and headlights. Feeling the car charger cord, he moved it aside and let it hang from the dash while he craned his neck toward the windshield. He drove slowly, pushing buttons and levers until he found the correct ones and watched as the lights reflected off the red taillights ahead and black rubber blades swept water from the glass.

He parked in the construction lot, wiped rainwater from the passenger's side seat with his hand then rolled up the open window. He checked his phone. Still nothing from Blagden.

The rain abated to a light drizzle. He locked the Malibu and jogged toward the Poseidon Club slowing his gait as he reached the berm where the valets parked cars and bellmen loaded luggage onto rolling carts.

He followed a man in a white uniform with royal blue epaulets into the casino and turned left toward the banks of noisy slot machines. He furtively searched for Blagden. As he approached the stealthy room reserved for high rollers, he spotted Blagden sitting in front of a Wheel of Fortune slot machine, pulling the lever.

Blagden nodded when he saw him.

He approached and sat at the machine next to the driver. "I texted you."

Blagden showed him his phone. "It 'tis no good. De battery is dead."

"Do you know where they are?"

Blagden tossed his head in the direction of the closed door where another man dressed in a white uniform stood guard.

He couldn't get in there without I.D. Or could he?

"Do you still have the money I gave you yesterday?"

"Yes."

"Do you play poker?"

"A bit."

"Gimme your phone."

"I am not doin' dat."

"Here. Take mine."

Blagden eyed it.

"I'm going out to your car to wait. I'll take your phone and charge it. You take mine. "Here," he said, peeling off five one-hundred-dollar bills. "I want you to go inside. If the tall guy is there, I want you take a seat at the table with them."

"Den what?"

"Call me if he leaves. The P.I. Mattress with him is going to lure a man out of that door," he said, gesturing to the high roller room.

"How do you know dat?"

"Just do it."

Blagden traded phones with him.

"I need de passcode."

"Six sevens."

"Dat is easy. De giraffe isn't here," Blagden said.

"What are you talking about?"

"De tall guy. He come as far as de front door and den he keep walking."

"Where to?"

"I don't know. I followed de girl."

"Then go in and take a seat at the table with the girl."

He left the slot machines and detoured to the men's room, took a leak at the urinal, washed his hands then took a three-inch wad of paper towels and filled his pockets and headed outside.

The sun was out, and humidity choked him. He shaded his eyes as he trotted to the Malibu. He opened the doors, rolled down the windows and started the engine. He plugged Blagden's flip phone into the charger and watched the screen come to life. He mopped standing water in the interior with the paper towels he'd nicked from the casino bathroom, then sat on the driver's seat with his feet on the ground.

He checked the time. Almost 3 o'clock in the afternoon. If his hunch was correct, Harold Fuchs was gambling. Fuchs wasn't there to win money. He was there for something else.

42

T onk lifted the corner edges of the two cards the dealer pushed his way. "I raise you a thousand," he said, placing brown chip on top of his pile.

He'd taken a seat at the *No Limit Hold'em* table in the high stakes room at the Poseidon Club, next to the target who'd been taking his money. Tonk had been on an intentional steady losing streak. It was a confidence game. The old guy didn't look at the new cards he'd been dealt yet before matching and raising Tonk another thousand. He scanned the room to see what had distracted him.

Fuchs must not have been on his A-game beyond the card game. On the other hand, it'd even taken him a minute to recognize the hot freckled- faced brunette. He'd been pissed that Chan was late but if this was what it took to get ready, it was worth it. He'd never seen her like this, cruising the rose carpet in a tight black mini-skirt. Shapely bare legs. Pink stiletto heels. Long eyelashes and red lipstick. The telltale tattoo on her upper thigh.

What had taken Fuchs so long?

She'd wandered around the green poker tables, paying attention to all the single men except Fuchs.

"Sir?" the dealer asked Fuchs.

He peeked at his cards. "Hit me," he said absently, focused on Chan.

She pounced. "May I?" Chan asked coyly, leaning against the open chair next to Mr. Fuchs, flashing the cleavage Tonk didn't know existed under her androgenous shirts.

Like most men, Fuchs had a built-in stupid button beneath to the zipper of his pants.

"Certainly," Harold Fuchs said, jumping to his feet and pulling a chair for her.

"I'll take a hit," Tonk said, testing Mr. Fuchs.

Harold picked up his cards and showed them to Chan. "What do you think I should do?"

She set her gold vinyl clutch on the wooden edge of the octagonal table and recrossed her legs. "You should get another," she purred.

The expressionless dealer slid a card to Mr. Fuchs who let Chan look at it first. She cozied up to Fuchs, practically nuzzling his neck as she showed the card to the old man and whispered in the silver fox's ear.

"I'll raise you two thousand," Fuchs dared him.

Time to get serious. He'd been sandbagging so far. During their freshman year at the university, he and C.J. regularly went to the Indian-owned casinos east of Los Angeles to take down the suckers. C.J. called it 'strategic incompetence' and by the end of their freshman year, several casinos had banned them for life.

"I'll hold and raise you another two," Tonk said.

Fuchs turned his cards over. He had two eights and a four.

Tonk showed an Ace and a Queen. Fuchs pushed his pile of chips toward Tonk. He neatly stacked them on his side of the table.

A cocktail waitress appeared. She approached Fuchs. "Would you like a drink, sir?"

"I'll have what she's having," Fuchs said, deferring to Chan.

"I'd like a Chivas, neat," Chan said.

"I'll have what they're having," Tonk said, clueless to what 'neat' meant.

As soon the waitress left the table, Harold asked, "Where're you from, hon? You're not a local."

"I'm from California," Chan said.

"Whereabouts?" Fuchs asked.

"Chico. Ever heard of it?"

"Sure. The home of Chico State the second oldest university in the California State college system."

Chan smiled at Fuchs. "Really? I never heard that," she said.

Harold Fuchs leaned over and whispered in Chan's ear.

She glanced over Harold's shoulder at him and raised her chin and eyebrows in a look that he hoped signaled they'd hooked their big fish.

Chan turned toward Harold Fuchs, smiled, and whispered something in Harold's ear.

Harold stood, collected his chips, thanked and tipped the dealer, then said, "It was a pleasure meeting you, young man."

"The pleasure is all mine," Tonk said, gathering up his chips. He knew where C.J. was but where was Fuchs taking Chan? He'd covered his bases. If Fuchs planned to take Chan to his room, he had an elevator key that would take him to the V.I.P. level on the tenth floor whereby the grace of

Lady Luck, he'd checked into Courage's room. He'd seen the cashier give Fuchs the envelope and overheard the convo about using the room in the event the old man met a 'young lady'—certainly code for a prostitute.

He followed them out of the high roller room and found a spot near the slot machines where he could watch them. Harold Fuchs detoured toward the restrooms. They were close to pulling this thing off but the three of them were now separated and that was not part of the plan. He wanted to check the tracking app on his phone to make sure *The Parent Minus* was still docked less than a mile away from where he'd picked up the signal, but he didn't want to risk being spotted using his cell phone inside the casino.

He noticed a shady character wearing a black track suit with yellow stripes sitting alone at a slot machine. The man wasn't playing. Was he being paranoid or was the man watching him? He needed more sets of eyes. As soon as Fuchs came out of the restrooms, he'd know what to do. If the man headed to the elevator with Chan, he'd follow them. If he went out the front door it meant he was heading to the yacht.

When Fuchs finally emerged from the men's room, he didn't go either direction. Instead, he led Chan to the cashier where Fuchs cashed in his chips. As they walked from the counter, a man dressed in a dark gray suit intercepted them and escorted the pair down a hallway. He followed at a safe distance but by the time he turned the corner, Chan and Fuchs had disappeared.

43

L
auren stopped at the security gate leading to Dr. Westerly's Cocoplum enclave. The man working the gate was new to her.

When the uniformed man saw her, he stepped out of the guard shack. "May I help you?"

"I'm here to see Dr. Molly Westerly."

"Your name?"

"Lauren Gold."

"May I see your I.D.?"

She had it ready. He took her license and made a call from the landline. While she waited she checked her phone for messages. Still nothing from Vance. Was something wrong?

The guard stepped out and handed back her license through her car window.

"Go ahead," he said as the iron gates swung open.

She motored slowly and parked curbside in front of the Westerly estate. This time there was no hesitation. She got out, strode to the front door and rang the doorbell. A moment later Lenore answered.

"Come in," Lenore said. "I've been trying to call Dr. Westerly to find out where she put your lost item but she hasn't called me back yet. I'll try again now."

"May I use the restroom?"

"Of course. You know where it is," Lenore said, "down the hall second door on the left."

While Lenore was tethered to the curly cord attached to the landline telephone hung on the kitchen wall near the garage door, she detoured to the coat closet. Working quickly, she opened the top drawer of the filing cabinet labeled A-Z. She thumbed through the folders until she got to the Fs.

FIELDS

FRENCH

FUCHS

She pulled the file, closed the closet door and entered the bathroom, closing and locking the door. While thumbing through the file, she flushed the toilet and ran the water then slid the file folder under her shirt and tucked it into the waistband of her jeans. She washed her hands then used one of Molly's fancy paper napkins, wadding it into a ball and tossing it into a lined straw basket.

When she opened the door, her heart thumped. Lenore stood there.

"Here," Lenore said, handing her the weird deck of cards. "I'm sorry for the wait. Dr. Westerly would like to speak to you."

"What?"

"She's on the phone in the kitchen."

"Okay."

She followed her into the sprawling kitchen. The curly cord attached to the blue wall phone was stretched almost straight, the receiver hanging over the edge of the granite countertop.

Lenore handed it to her.

"Hello?" she said, fingers trembling.

"Hello, Lauren. I wanted to see how it went with Peter at the hospital?"

"Oh, it went well."

"Really?" Molly said, with doubt in her voice.

"He was awake, and they expect he'll make a full recovery."

"That's wonderful news, Lauren."

"It is, and I really appreciate you seeing me. It helped me to prepare for the worst."

"I'm glad," Molly Westerly said. "I tried to catch you before you left to make sure you got that deck of cards but by the time I looked outside, you'd already left. You had other things on your mind. I have to run," Dr. Westerly said. "I'm glad things worked out."

"Thank you," she said, handing the phone back to Lenore.

"I'll walk you out," Lenore said.

"No, no," she said, hugging her purse with both arms. "That's not necessary. I'll let myself out."

She hurried to her car, did a U-turn at the first break on the grassy median, stopped to remove the folder from beneath her shirt and slid it under the driver's seat. A local patrol vehicle was stopped at the guard shack exit. The driver appeared to be chatting with the man. The gate lifted and she tailgated the car in front of her waving to the watchman as she drove past.

Two blocks away she pulled into a gas station and parked on the side of the building. Who was Harold Fuchs and why was he seeing Molly Westerly?

She opened his file and scanned Dr. Westerly's notes. Her handwriting was sloppy, and her comments were hard to read. The one thing she could decipher was 'Marriage counseling,' and 'infidelity.' As juicy as that might've been, it didn't help. She looked at her phone. No new messages. She called Vance again. It rang but he didn't answer. Hanging up at the voicemail prompt, she redialed Vivian. Same thing.

There was only one option.

Searching Buzzer Air, she found a flight she could make out of the Opa-Locka airport. She booked her ticket on her phone. She didn't have time to stop at the condo to get her bag. Traffic was beginning to jam up. *Please God*, she said aloud, *let me make the flight on time.*

44

Vance sat in the old Malibu running his index finger along the cracked driver's seat upholstery waiting for an update from Blagden. He looked at the odometer. The old Chevy had a tick over 200,000 miles; that was a lot of island driving. The bruise on his right hand where he'd punched Blade in the mouth had turned a light avocado green. He untwisted the phone charger plugged into the cigarette lighter and checked to see that it was juicing Blagden's phone. This was the life for Blagden. Shuttling tourists from airports and cruise ships to the casinos and hotels. He'd seen the neighborhood where he'd grown up. Officials named the streets with the word Dumpster in it. How did something like that even happen? Unless it had a colloquial connotation, it was demeaning.

He watched a guy operating a huge crane scoop sand from the square city block that had been grazed and empty it into an awaiting dump truck. He wondered where they were taking the loads of pearl colored sand. A guy wearing a white hardhat spotted him and made a beeline giving him little time to fabricate a story.

"Can I help you," the guy asked.

The construction worker was an American. "I'm waiting for someone."

"You can't park here. This area is reserved for the workers. I don't need to call security, do I?"

"No," he said, closing the door and starting the engine.

"It's an insurance issue," the contractor said. "Barracuda lawyers."

"I understand."

As he backed out of the makeshift lot filled with beat up cars like Blagden's he heard the flip-phone ring. He opened it and saw his own number come up.

"Hey," he said looking over his shoulder as he reversed the old Chevy, "Where are you?"

"I am in de men's room. I saw de girl is with an older mon. Dere is a mon following her dat I don't recognize. He might be de mon we saw last night at de pink house."

It had to be Tonk. "What does he look like?"

"White. Brown hair, brown eyes. Medium build, like you."

"Did you notice any tattoos?"

"He 'ave one on his arm, 'andwriting I tink, but I dint get close enough to see."

"Where are they now?"

"De girl followed de old mon. He cash out his poker chips."

"And the other guy?"

"I tink he is following dem and I am following him."

"Stay on them and call me when you know which way they're going."

"I tink de girl is a prostitute who is going to turn a trick. I won't be able to follow dem if dey go up to de hotel elevator. I need a room key for dat."

There wasn't time to deal with details. "Hang up," he said, "and follow them."

"Is too late for dat," Blagden said. "De man with the tattoo lost them, too. I don't want no trouble."

"Me neither. Wait there," he said, closing the flip-phone.

He drove back toward the entrance of the Poseidon Club and inched past the casino at street level. C.J. stood leaning against the building near a luggage cart. Why wasn't he inside the club? A minute later a brunette in a mini skirt emerged with a distinguished looking older guy dressed like a yachtsman in his chinos and lavender sweater tied around his neck. The man stopped at the wooden valet stand and spoke to the attendant dressed in black. The woman appeared to be looking around for someone.

A moment later a black Lincoln Town car with smoke-tinted glass pulled up beneath the green portico. The driver got out and opened the passenger rear door. The scantily clad woman got in. Next, the driver opened the opposite passenger's side back door for the older man who climbed in next the woman.

He waited and watched as they exited the horseshoe driveway, then he followed the Lincoln as it headed east on Casino Drive. The left turn indicator blinked, and the Lincoln slowed. As the driver hung a left at Paradise Island Drive, he followed from a safe distance. The Lincoln passed the area marked for casino employees and crawled past the Versailles Gardens and French Cloister with terraced gardens overlooking Nassau Harbour. If his instincts were good, he was almost directly across the channel from Vivian's rental house, remembering he hadn't heard from her.

The Lincoln slowed then continued west on Paradise Island Drive toward a private golf club. A minute later the town car turned right onto Harbour Drive where the super yachts docked at the waterfront marina came into view. He watched as the Lincoln turned into the marina parking lot. He parked the Malibu on the shoulder of the road, out of view, and walked on foot. The Lincoln idled near *The Parent Minus*. The older man got out, walked around the back bumper and opened the door for the woman. In less than a minute, a covered light blue golf cart met them at the Lincoln then drove the man and woman to the dock.

The flip-phone rang.

"I lost de mon and de girl but I am following the giraffe. He know de mon with the tattoo on his arm."

"Where are you?"

"Dey two men are in a cab 'en I am in a cab following dem."

"Where are they heading?"

"West on Paradise Island Drive."

"Head toward the resort and look for your car parked off Harbour Island Drive."

The road where he'd parked the Malibu was on higher ground with a view to a multi-story pale yellow stucco building with a red clay roof. He got out and walked to where there was a view to the palm tree lined harbor. He saw a large kidney-shaped swimming pool the same turquoise as the seawater. Given the size of it he guessed it to be part of the resort. He looked around for landmarks. Three flags flew on tall poles planted into the bulkhead just west of the marina: one American, one Bahamian and one British. They were easily visible from the road.

"When you pass the Versailles Gardens, look for three flags on tall poles. The Malibu is parked at three o'clock."

"What is dis about?"

"Wait for me." He ended the call, left the keys in the ignition and the flip-phone on the seat then headed down a sandy embankment toward the bulkhead. A yellow P.T. Cruiser passed slowly. He hid behind the trunk of a thatched palm tree and watched as the car continued on.

A half block away he saw a tall condominium building with harbor views. He hurried that way and sneaked into the pool area. He knelt behind a four-foot permanent rock wall erected between the pool and the bulkhead with thorny bougainvillea vines with purplish flowers planted in the top, draping down the sides. He moved two steps to the right and caught a glimpse of C.J. and Tonk walking toward the embankment leading to the marina.

He had a good idea where they were going. As C.J. and Tonk advanced from the parking lot west of the golf course and stalked down the paved parking lot toward the water, he stayed low as he crept along the hedges inside the condominium pool area. If he'd left his gun at home, he wouldn't be in this mess. If Tonk had it, it would be traced back to him. He'd let them get to *The Parent Minus* first. An ambush was going to be his best chance to stop whatever was going down. It was his only chance.

45

Lauren followed the passengers down the portable stairs, restraining herself from shoulder-bumping them, wishing they would hurry. The people aboard the 50-passenger Embraer jet were tourists on vacation. Once she reached the tarmac, she cut ahead and strode toward the signs for Immigration and Customs. It was a Monday evening, and the Lynden Pindling International Airport in Nassau wasn't busy. She cleared customs, hurried past the duty-free shop and stores selling souvenirs.

Ten minutes later she was in a taxi taking a wild ride to Paradise Island as her local driver cursed at traffic and drove up on a curb to pass another cabbie loading bags into the back of a minivan.

She called Vivian. This time she answered on the first ring.

"Vivian. I've been trying to call you. Is everything okay?"

"I'm sorry I didn't get back to you. Is everything okay in Miami. Vance said you had some sort of personal emergency?"

"I'm back. I got worried when I couldn't reach either you or Vance."

"Where are you?"

"I'm in a cab leaving the airport heading to Paradise Island."

"You're here?"

"I think something bad is going to happen."

"What do you mean something bad is going to happen? To whom?"

"To Vance."

There was a long pause, but Vivian didn't respond.

"Vance hasn't been answering his phone. Did he get a visa?"

"No. He acted strangely at the embassy. I'd made a call ahead to try to make it smoother. But while we were there, he found out someone might be using his passport. I've called him several times, too, but he isn't answering me either. I went to the cottage and looked for him."

"Was he there?"

"No. His bag was there."

"Then he's coming back."

"He can't. I have guests checking in. We had to get the cottage ready."

"What did you do with his things?"

"I packed his personal effects myself. I wouldn't worry," Vivian said.

Wouldn't worry? It was out of character for him to go off the grid.

"I have a question for you," Vivian said. "I found a book on the bedside table and a deck of cards. It was quite odd. It had a pink pig wearing a graduation cap, a mortarboard. He'd left one of the cards on the bed. It had a man's name on it but no picture. The cards had photos—"

She cut Vivian off. "I know about it. The man's name is Harold Fuchs."

"Do you know him?"

"No. But I have a weird feeling he's the reason Vance is off the grid."

"How far are you from P.I.?" Vivian asked.

"Hang on." She leaned forward in the seat and asked the driver. "Do you know how long before we get to the Poseidon Club?"

"It depends upon de traffic," the cabbie said.

"Estimate?"

"Fifteen minutes."

"I'm going to the Poseidon Club," she said to Vivian. "I'll be there in about fifteen. Can you meet me there?"

"I'm looking out the window at the bridge. It's rush hour traffic. I'm leaving the cottage now."

"I thought you had people checking in?"

"I had to drop off some clean towels."

"I appreciate this," Lauren said. "I'll explain in person."

"It will be good to see you, Lauren."

A shiver ran down her neck. "I'll see you there."

46

"**D**is is as far as I can get you," the taxi driver said as Tonk paid the fare. He and C.J. climbed out of the yellow P.T. Cruiser.

"Let's go," Tonk said, checking the tracking app on his phone. The yellow flashing dot showed the yacht was 953 feet from where they stood on higher ground above the marina.

"I think I see it," C.J. said.

The marina where *The Parent Minus* was docked faced Nassau Harbour and was still under construction with yellow tape cordoning off areas. A golf cart approached from the marina parking lot.

The man behind the wheel wore a gray uniform. "Are you a guest of someone?" he asked.

"No," Tonk said, "We're looking around. Is that okay?"

"No."

"We just want to sightsee," C.J. said.

"This is private property," the man said.

A newer SUV pulled up and parked. The man in the golf cart drove away to meet them.

"Do you have the gun?" he asked.

"Yeah," C.J. said.

"Give it to me."

C.J. hesitated.

"Give me the gun," he repeated.

C.J. slowly raised his pant cuff, took the stolen Glock from his hiking boot and handed it over.

Tonk calculated they had a short window of time to download the files from Fuchs computers, make the wire transfers and disappear.

"I didn't agree to do this," C.J. said. "We were supposed to gamble, not hack his freaking computer. We're on foreign soil. We could be charged with international espionage."

"Don't be such a drama king," he said, taking his phone from the pocket of the chinos he'd bought on Courage's AmEx and setting it to SILENT mode. He removed one of the two thumb drives his father had given him. "Here."

C.J. took the small device, tucked it into his pants pocket then followed suit, muting his cell.

They strolled like tourists, passing the condominiums and clubhouse for the resort next door. There were no witnesses hanging around the kidney shaped swimming pool located to the west of the marina. The chaise lounges and chairs were neatly stacked in rows and the table umbrellas had been lowered and strapped. Not seeing anyone, they took a left and walked along the freshly cemented bulkhead leading to Fuchs' tri-level yacht.

As they approached *The Parent Minus* Tonk looked around for security guards, and not seeing anyone, motioned C.J. to follow. The yacht was backed into a corner slip stern-first with the bulkhead on the port side. A floating dock made of cedar-stained hardwood jutted perpendicular to the bulkhead on the starboard side.

He saw a set of portable fiberglass stairs leading from the floating dock to the gunwales. That was strange. But it was also good. They could board from the side of the ship where there was less chance of being seen by anyone onboard. He hurried toward the stairs, the floating dock swaying slightly beneath his feet. He saw a pair of pink heels on the top stair. C.J. saw them too and hesitated. He grabbed C.J. by the arm wishing he could wipe the wide-eyed look off his face. He shouldn't have brought a pussy to do a man's job.

"This is getting real, bro," C.J. said, stalling. "What if something goes wrong?"

"Something is gonna go wrong if you keep standing there like a deer in the crosshairs."

C.J. shaded his eyes and looked toward the parking lot.

What a dumb motherfucker.

"Hurry the fuck up before someone sees us."

Again C.J. hesitated.

He pointed the 9-millimeter Glock at him.

"Hey, hey, hey," C.J. said holding his hands up.

"Get up, you fucking idiot. Get going," he grunted, jamming the tip of the barrel into the small of C.J.'s back. "Right now, that old man is thinking with his dick, and we need to move."

He pointed the gun again at C.J., forcing him to board first. He followed C.J. up the three stairs and when C.J. saw the pink heels, Tonk reached around and tossed them into the water.

"Go," he growled at C.J., forcing him to climb over the gunwale first. They stood side-by-side with their backs pressed against the white fiberglass bulkhead on the starboard side of the transom, away from the windows. Listening.

"What if others are here?" C.J. whispered. "What if Fuchs has security?"

He pointed the gun at him again. He didn't have time for this bullshit. "He's with Chan. If there was someone watching, they'd be on the flybridge or some shit and they'd have seen us by now."

Jesus. If C.J. moved any slower a snail might pass them. He jabbed him in the lower back hard with the tip of the 9-mil. "Go," he ordered.

They'd find a way inside the cabin, a place where they'd have cover. Fuchs wouldn't be on the main level. He'd be in one of the bedrooms on the lower level.

He prodded C.J. forward, pressing the tip of the gun against his spine, forcing him around the corner, using him like a human shield. He followed as C.J. complied, the duo treading lightly on the slatted teakwood transom leading from the swim deck to the outdoor seating area. The portico over the transom led to tinted sliding glass doors opening to the main deck.

"Hold up," he said in a low snarl, taking a knee and crouching under the covered area near the glass doors. He reached into his pocket and removed a piece of paper, unfolded it and studied the line drawing, refreshing his mind about the layout of the three levels of the ship.

"Where did you get that?" C.J. asked in a soft voice, looking at the diagram spread open on Tonk's knee.

"Online." He pointed to the paper showing C.J. where the master bedroom was located on the lower deck, up front, near the bow.

"You lied. We weren't supposed to follow him here. We were supposed to stay at the casino and beat him at poker."

"In some ways you are the biggest dumb mofo. Fuchs has a multi-million-dollar yacht. The chance of him bringing a prostitute here is better than fifty percent. I thought you were a statistics guy. I'll say this, bro, Chan's got bigger balls than you do. You don't see her going all weak-kneed, excuse the pun." He let out a muffled laugh. "Come on," he said, aiming the gun at his tall friend, "let's do this while we still have the advantage. Fuchs is drunk and the little head is doing all the thinking." He tossed his head toward the sliding glass doors. "Open it," he whispered, "and go slow so we don't rock the boat."

C.J. obeyed, gently sliding one glass door open a couple of inches at first, then a foot, making a gap big enough to peer inside and crane his neck left and right.

"Go in," Tonk ordered.

C.J. pushed the door open far enough for the two of them to slip inside. C.J. went first, ducking as he entered. The main deck opened to a climate- controlled modern living area with sofas and tables and artwork on the walls.

"Go that way," he ordered C.J. "It leads to the lower deck."

"Can you imagine what this thing cost?" C.J. whispered.

"Who cares? You need to focus," he said. He could use someone with more brawn than brains right now but C.J. was the one who'd had access to Fuchs' personal information via the California state computers. Fuchs sat on the board of directors for the teachers' retirement fund. "We need to keep moving. You go first."

He followed C.J., herding him down a narrow stairwell leading to the lower deck. He saw the black and gold directional signs for the ENGINE ROOM. The printed layout was accurate. A narrow baby blue carpeted hallway led to the bedrooms located toward the bow of the boat. He grabbed C.J. by the shoulder and held his fingers to his lips, then reached around C.J. and tried the knob on the first bedroom door located to his left. It was unlocked. He opened it just enough to peek inside. It was clear.

He drove C.J. a few more feet down the hallway toward the bedroom on the starboard side. The door was unlocked. He looked in. The bed was made and the room was empty. That meant Harold Fuchs and Chan had to be in the master stateroom straight ahead.

"You do as I say," he said.

C.J. nodded.

"Here we go." He tried the knob. The door was unlocked. Remaining perfectly quiet he opened it an inch, far enough to see Chan wearing the black wig. Her back was to him, skirt hiked up and she was on her knees straddling Fuchs who was tied to the bed. He heard a noise and whispered to C.J. "Did you hear that?"

C.J. nodded at him.

He gently pulled the door shut and backed away.

47

T rying not to call attention to himself Vance took a shortcut through the condo pool area causing him to lose visual track of Tonk and C.J. He saw an opening in the chest high hedges leading to a concrete walkway ending at a T at the artificial seawall. He stopped and peered to his left, shading his eyes from the setting sun. The masts of sailboats bobbed in their slips surrounded by yachts and smaller cruisers.

The condo pool was set back and opened to his right to the south overlooking a large green space separating the buildings from the marinas and dock spaces. Manicured grass led to the concrete sidewalk running the length of the water's edge. It was like a park with no trees. If he walked out from behind the hedged pool area, he'd be exposed. There was no place to take immediate cover.

He waited and watched, squinting at the sun. He saw two silhouettes moving on the wooden dock. One towered over the other and they appeared to be heading toward the biggest ship, a three-story behemoth docked at nine o'clock from where he stood. It had to be Tonk and C.J. He needed to get closer.

The closest dock running parallel to where he stood was lined with wooden pylons planted into the water at three-foot intervals. Four double-decker sport fishing boats with flybridges and radar systems mounted to the rooflines were tied alongside the seawall with a view across the channel to Nassau. He was on high ground now but if he could make it down to the fishing boats, he could use them for cover. A massive cruise ship blared its horn as it passed heading east toward Potters Cay.

He heard voices. A mother and her two children entered the pool area. The little girl wore a pink floaty duck as she skipped along the decorative concrete. The young boy noticed him standing near the hedges. The mother saw him and grabbed her two children by the hands. He smiled and waved, then sauntered out from between the opening in the hedges then hurried toward the fishing boats.

He made it to the dock without being noticed by security and crouched behind a low-profile navy blue sport-fisher with triple outboard motors. From this vantage point he could see a set of portable stairs positioned alongside the super yacht. He watched as C.J. and Tonk climbed the stairs, boarded the boat, then disappeared.

He moved closer, staying hidden behind the row of fishing boats. The new marina where the yacht was docked was under construction with areas cordoned off with orange cones and yellow tape attached to wooden stakes in the ground. He crept until he reached the last sport-fisher with a direct line of sight to the wooden floating dock and the yacht. His heart pounded. It was *The Parent Minus*. When he'd seen the mega yacht docked at Chub Cay, he'd not been able to see the second flag. Now he recognized it as the yellow and blue flag of The Bahamas.

He'd have to move quickly. The enormous ship was docked stern-first at the end of the bulkhead and would leave him exposed from three angles. He watched and waited. The two silhouettes popped into view, and peered around the fiberglass bulkhead. They moved to the transom. A minute later they entered the cabin through the sliding glass doors. He counted to fifteen, then sprinted toward the yacht taking cover on the dock and kneeling behind the portable three-step stairway.

By his count there were at least four people on board. If Fuchs had security, they'd have seen Tonk and C.J. and stopped them from boarding the vessel. If the pair had been spotted after entering the yacht, it was possible they were being detained. But there was no way to know.

What was his plan? He didn't have one. Couldn't make one. No phone and no weapon. Neither Tonk nor C.J. alone had the muscle to stop him. But as a team they posed a bigger risk. If Fuchs had a crew, they would overpower him.

He climbed the portable stairs and scooted onto the gunwale, then dropped down quietly to the deck. He glanced around the side at the dark- tinted sliding glass doors. He didn't see anyone. He crept toward the doors and slid one side open slowly, counted to ten, then he entered the cabin. He heard nothing, nor saw anyone. He treaded softly across the oak floor past the modern living area toward the bow until he saw a stairwell leading to the lower level where the staterooms were located.

He held the handrail as he padded slowly down the stairs, the hum of the generators growing slightly louder. At the bottom stair, to the right, he saw the door leading to the engine room. He peered to his left, then snapped his neck back when he saw C.J and Tonk shoulder-to-shoulder outside the master stateroom. He held his breath and peeked again. The door to the master was cracked open. Tonk held a black Glock 9-mil against his thigh. As if sensing something, Tonk suddenly swiveled his head in his direction.

Adrenaline flowed. He'd reacted in time and was unseen. He quietly backed up a stair taking cover in the stairwell then stood on the third to the bottom tread and monitored his breathing.

He'd been in this position before. Two primitive beings attuned to their most primal hunting instincts. He bet that Tonk would dismiss his intuition as paranoia. He hoped that was what he'd do. He was some punk film school graduate who couldn't even get a real job. But Tonk had his gun and might even know how to use it.

48

As the cab driver took another sharp turn in traffic heading toward the Harry Belafonte Bridge to Paradise Island, Lauren's stomach did a somersault. She held onto the door frame and stuck her nose out the open back passenger window but the smell of burning diesel and gasoline overpowered any trace of fresh air and salt water. The roads were wet from the recent rain, but it was beginning to dry and the cooler drier air that followed a hard downpour soothed her face. The cabbie noticed her shading her eyes in the rearview mirror and lowered the visor to cut the shards of western sunlight piercing the windshield.

She took her phone from her purse and checked for messages from Vance. The green bubbles showed the messages had been delivered but why wasn't he answering her? She called again. It went directly to voicemail. She pushed the red dot on her phone, then pulled up Vivian's number, changed screens and scrolled through recent links on her browser. She tapped the story about the Marilyn Braman investigation, copied and pasted the link, then sent it to Vivian. She paused, then pulled up Vance's chain of unanswered messages and sent the link to his phone, too.

As the driver began the ascent to the apex of the bridge, the sun cast a pink tint over the clear pale blue water with all sizes of watercraft passing beneath the giant bridge designed to handle cruise ship traffic. Brightly painted jet skis and wave runners and hobie cats with sails the color of candy corn and rainbows looked like tiny toys from up above. Suddenly the driver slowed.

She looked to see but couldn't tell why traffic had stopped. "What's going on?" she asked.

"Dere is a stalled car in de right lane up ahead," he said.

She watched him take his phone from a plastic gadget mounted to the dash and shade the screen with his hand.

"It tis a five-minute delay," he said, looking over his left shoulder, yelling out the window, waving his hands aggressively. He was trying to change lanes to enter the left one that was moving, albeit at a snail's pace. He played chicken with an ancient gold Monte Carlo with an imposing metal grill, but the driver wouldn't back down. "Mudda sick, asshole, mudda sick!" he hollered out the window as the other driver challenged her cabbie, hogging the lane with his fender glued to the bumper of the car ahead of it.

Less nauseated, she poked her head out the window and breathed the fresher air high above the harbor. While the driver argued and gestured obscenities at motorists, she closed her eyes for a moment feeling each beat of her heart. When she opened them, he was lane-dueling with the driver of a panel van, winning the contest, cutting into the left lane then muttering something she couldn't make out.

Her phone vibrated in her hand. It was Vivian. "Hey, I'm stuck in traffic."

"I'm at the casino waiting," Vivian said.

Waiting for what? "Did you see my text?" she asked, referring to the link.

"I did but I can't read it right now. Have you heard from Vance?"

"No," she said. "Have you?"

"No. I have someone here who'd like to talk to you."

"Who?"

"Hold on."

"Lauren?"

"Yeah."

"My name is Blagden. I'm a friend of Vivian's. Your friend is in trouble."

Who was he? "What kind of trouble?"

There was a pause. Vivian got back on the line. "I'll explain it later."

"No. I want you to explain it now."

"I can't. I don't have time. I have a call coming in I have to take. I'll call you back."

Vivian ended the call. She called Vance back, but it went directly to voicemail. Damn it! What the hell was going on?

The driver inched along at two miles per hour. "How far is the casino from here?"

The driver looked at his screen. "We are fifteen minutes away."

She checked the time. *Fucking island time.* It'd been five minute delay for the last twenty. She opened the navigation app on her phone and dropped a pin on their location then typed 'Poseidon Club' into the destination. It was .35 miles.

She leaned forward between the seats. "How much do I owe you?"

"We are not dere yet."

"I'm getting out and walking. How much if I get out here?"

"Forty dollar U.S."

She tossed three twenties on the front passenger seat, opened the back door, got out and snaked her way through traffic, jogging along the pedestrian sidewalk, her flip-flops slapping the concrete.

She called Vivian. It went to voicemail. She left a breathless message. "I'm on foot. Wait for me." She tapped the mic icon and repeated the same message and pressed the send button. People stuck in traffic yelled and honked their horns as she passed, some making vulgar remarks and whistling. A few stuck their cameras out of their car windows and recorded video. Highlights for social media.

Her phone buzzed. It was Vivian.

"Hey," she said, breathing heavily, "I'm almost there."

"We're waiting," she said. "Look for a navy-blue Cadillac Escalade at valet."

"Okay," she huffed into the phone. Another asshole blared a car horn at her. She let it go. She had to.

"Lauren?"

"Yeah."

"How well do you know Vance?"

"Why?"

"I'm just asking. I'll see you in a couple of minutes," Vivian said.

She glanced at her phone. Vivian had ended the call.

She sprinted to the bottom the bridge then crisscrossed through vehicle traffic, banging her hand on the hood of a car yelling, "Hey!" at a driver who didn't see her.

The man behind the wheel slammed the brakes and raised his hands at her in an apology. She saw the big blue sign for the Poseidon Club casino and trotted that way zigzagging between cars stopped at the light at the busy intersection. The club was on higher ground. Mustering more energy, she climbed the driveway and saw the dark blue Escalade with tinted windows. It started to drive away. She ran behind the back bumper while redialing Vivian.

Please answer. It rang two more times. *Come on, come on, Vivian. Pick up. What the hell? She told me to wait!*

49

Vance moved down to the second stair leading to the yacht's lower deck berth at the bow of the boat. He leaned against the wood paneled stairwell. Tonk had sensed something, but the boy hadn't trusted his instincts. He didn't dismiss his own instinct and had taken shelter in the ship's stairwell to keep from being spotted. The light hum of the generators coming from the engine room off to his right cancelled out any whispering he might've have been able to hear. He peeked around the corner. Tonk and C.J. still stood together outside the door.

He took a position like a runner in the starting blocks. An ambush was the best strategy. Take Tonk by surprise. Hit him at full speed, then wrestle him to the ground. C.J. wouldn't be up for the fight and would run. Get the gun. Forget the money. Forget his passport. Blagden was waiting for him. He'd make a clean escape.

The yacht rocked slightly. Probably from the tail end of a wake coming from ship traffic in the channel. He heard voices but couldn't tell from where. He craned his neck forward toward the master stateroom listening, keeping his cover, but that's not where the voices were coming from. He crept up the stairwell two treads at a time and waited. Maybe the movement he'd felt hadn't come from a wake. What if someone else had boarded the ship? He returned to the bottom of the stairwell to wait.

After a minute of quiet, he glanced around the corner. C.J. and Tonk had disappeared from outside the stateroom door. Maybe they'd heard voices, too, and had taken cover in one of the spare sleeping berths located on either side of the narrow hallway. He looked out again. Both guest bedroom doors were closed. He padded to the main level then crabbed with his back against the wood paneling in the opposite direction, toward the engine room located to his right. The engine room door was unlocked. He slipped inside and closed the door.

The generators were loud. Man, if he had his phone, he could make a call from here or send a text. But there wasn't time, and if there was, who would he call? He cracked the door open enough to watch the hallway. Still no sign of the two boys.

He tiptoed out of the engine room then hurried toward the master bedroom door and pressed his ear against it. The door leading to the stateroom was hardened, like a submarine hatch. He tested the knob, twisting it gently while holding his breath. It was unlocked. He counted to five then pushed it open an inch. Though it had a faux finish of wood, it had the fluid feel of a safe, reminding him of the fireproof doors at the precinct where they'd stored tactical rifles and seized cash and drugs. The door would double as a shield. He pushed it open another inch, then waited. Then another. A beam of light passed through the master berth into the hallway. The flash of light instantly impaired his vision.

Why was it so quiet? Maybe it was empty. Maybe Tonk

and C.J. knew that. Maybe *he* was being ambushed. He'd enter quickly and take a position behind the door.

He counted to three then shouldered the door open. A man lay naked on the king-sized bed, his wrists tied to the bed posts, his face blocked by the back of the woman straddling him. The woman wore a black wig. Her skirt was hiked up to her white panties. She rode Fuchs, grinding her pelvis against his groin in long, slow motions.

Chan.

Where were Tonk and C.J.?

He heard voices. He glanced over his shoulder and saw Tonk bolt from the guest room and head toward the master like a ram. He slammed the door shut with his shoulder and twisted the deadbolt noticing the hand wheel above the normal lock.

Harold Fuchs struggled but his hands were tied to the bed. "Who the fuck are you?" he growled. "And what the fuck are you doing here?"

The woman atop him raised her pelvis and he watched as she shimmied her skirt down over the tops of her legs. There was no ring of trees tattooed on her thigh. She tugged at the edge of her skirt. He recognized the black fingernail polish. She turned and faced him.

"You're from the ferry boat," he said.

"That's right," she said.

"Tonk has a gun."

"Who's Tonk?" she asked.

"The guy who's come to kill Fuchs."

"No one's coming to kill me," Fuchs said.

"He's got a gun," he said, "I saw it. He's here."

The woman dismounted Fuchs and leaped down from the bed. She pointed a Sig Sauer automatic weapon at him then patted him down, running her hand up his pant leg, around his abdomen and beneath his arms up to his pits.

Satisfied he was unarmed, she asked, "What are you doing here?"

"Who are you?" he asked.

"That's none of your business."

She moved away from him, close enough to keep an eye, but far enough that he couldn't hear as she made a call on her cell.

He approached the bed. "Where's Tonk?" he asked the man still struggling to cover himself with the bed sheets.

"I told you. I don't know who you're talking about."

"He's on your ship," he said. "There're two of them."

The woman in the wig ended the call and holding her gun on him, backed away and reached up, sealing the door with the hand wheel. "The doors and bulkhead are hardened," she said. "Even a 50-cal couldn't penetrate it. On your knees."

"You got this wrong," he said.

She reached into a black bag on the dresser and tossed a deck of cards at him. They were the same as the ones Lauren had found on Blade's plane.

"Do you know what Personality Identifying Playing Cards are?"

He nodded. "It's a Kill Deck."

"Three of these people are already dead. Do you know what the Ace of Spades represents?"

From his kneeling position, he nodded. "I do. It's the highest value target."

"Do you know why there's no picture of him?"

"No."

"Because of us."

"Us? Who's us?"

"It's our job to make sure our clients have no digital footprint."

"Clients?"

"You're about to be arrested for attempted murder."

"I don't know who you are, but you got this all wrong. I'm trying to stop it from happening. You've been shadowing the wrong guy."

"Really," she said, "you fly to Chub Cay with Robert Braman where Harold Fuchs' yacht was docked. You arm his kid with a 9-millimeter Glock, give him your passport, send your lady friend home, give him access to your hotel room and credit card and through some odd coincidence end up here?" she said, loosening the knots around Fuchs' wrists.

"I know what this looks like."

She laughed in his face. "You've got an unusually high line of credit set up at a casino where you've never played before. You're not a gambler, Mr. Courage. You have no verifiable employment. You're aware of patterns. You send up more red flags than a bullfighter. Considering you're an ex-cop with a better than average understanding of the law, please tell me what part I got wrong."

She sure knew a lot. What could he say? She had a theory, and it was a good one. How could he punch a hole in it? When he told her he'd seen Tonk and C.J. on the ship she didn't believe him. Why should she? If he were in her shoes, he'd think the same thing. "If I'm that clever, why did I walk into this obvious trap unarmed?"

"Because that's your plan."

"What are you talking about?"

"Spare me the innocence speech," she said. "I've never met a criminal who's ever committed a crime."

"Tonk and his friend are on this boat right now."

"You criminals are all the same," she said, "with one exception. Dirty cops. They're the worst."

"Where's the girl that was with them?"

"I have a better question," the woman said. "Why did your significant other show the Kill Deck to her therapist?"

"I have no idea what you're talking about."

"Right," she said. "That's the best you can come up with?"

She had it wrong. All wrong. But how could he prove it?

L auren stood outside the casino near the valet stand overlooking a large fountain with a ten-foot-tall statue of Poseidon atop a plinth holding his three-pronged trident in the air. A man in a blue and white uniform wheeling a brass garment cart headed toward her. "Excuse me," he said.

She stepped aside redialing Vivian a second time. Again, it went directly to voicemail. She stabbed the red button on her phone screen and tapped the REDIAL button. On the third try Vivian picked up.

"I'm sorry," Vivian said. "I was on a call."

"You could've put them on hold." She moved aside to let a young couple pushing a baby stroller pass. "I ran on foot to get here, and I saw you drive away. If you'd answered, you would've seen me. You could've stopped."

A noisy tour bus pulled up beneath the portico and parked in front of the statue of Poseidon. She plugged her free ear with a finger. "I need you to come back and get me. Vance is in trouble, and he needs help." When the bus driver opened the pneumatic door it made an ear-splitting hiss.

"Wait there for me," Vivian said.

"I'm not waiting here. Did you look at that link I sent you?"

"I don't have time."

"Yes, you do."

"Hold on," Vivian said.

A moment later Vivian was back on the phone. "We're coming back to get you. Walk down to the corner and wait by the traffic light. We're a block away."

She hurried on foot down the walkway to the street. By the time she arrived at the intersection the Escalade was approaching. The driver stopped on the street, blocking traffic. Cab drivers yelled and blared their horns as she got in. Vivian slid over making room for her.

"I'm sorry we left you behind. I have to skip the pleasantries. How do you know Harold Fuchs?" Vivian asked.

"I don't. I saw his name on these," she said, taking the deck of cards from her purse. "Did you read the story?"

"I scanned it."

The Escalade driver conducted a deft u-turn cutting across four lanes of traffic.

"The kid in the story, Tonk Braman, he was a passenger on the charter flight we booked to get here. The pilot is his dad. That's how we got mixed up in this thing."

"Vance isn't working for someone?"

She cocked her head. "What?" She shook her head. "No. We came here on vacation. Who would he be working for?"

"Wealthy men like Fuchs are targets."

"Why would Vance target him?" Lauren asked.

Vivian leaned forward and spoke to the driver. "Hurry," she said, then placed a call on her cell.

Lauren listened to one side of the conversation. "No, no, hold off . . . no . . . I know . . . just wait."

"Wait for what?" she asked. "What's going on?"

"We thought Vance was going to kill Harold Fuchs."

"WHAT? WHY?"

"I hoped you could tell me, but then I sensed you didn't know. That's probably why he sent you home."

"He didn't send me home."

"Why did he bring a firearm into the country if he didn't plan to use it? That's a big risk. Why did he give his cash and passport to a stranger? I'm afraid he played you."

What made her the expert suddenly? "He did not *play* me. He didn't do any of those things. Tonk stole his money and passport. How should I know why? I don't know anything about a gun," she lied.

"Are you sure about that," Vivian asked?

"Absolutely." *How did Vivian know about the gun?*

Vivian redialed the last number on her phone, and she listened in but Vivian pressed the phone to her ear and turned away. "I'm going to put you on with his friend. Her name is Lauren. She's also my stepdaughter."

She took the phone from Vivian. "Hello?"

"Hello, Lauren. I know where your friend is."

"Who is this?"

"I've been driving him around. I work for de private security firm."

"What private security firm?" Had Vance lied to her?

"De one dat protects wealthy individuals. Meester Fuchs is one of our clients."

"What's Vance got to do with this?"

"We got a tip dat he might be targeting Meester Fuchs."

"A tip from who?"

"I need to patch you through to de team."

"What team?"

"Hold on."

She heard the man come back on the line. "Go ahead," he said.

"Is this Lauren Gold?"

It was a woman. An American.

"Yes."

I'm going to put you on speaker."

"Okay."

The Escalade driver turned off the main road with a view below to a marina still under construction.

"Lauren?"

She recognized Vance's voice. "Where are you?"

"I'm on *The Parent Minus*. They think I tried to set Tonk up to kill Harold Fuchs."

"Why?"

"I don't know," he said. "Where are you?"

"I'm with Vivian."

There was a pause. "You're in Nassau?"

"I'm at a marina on Paradise Island."

The phone went dead. She smacked the screen.

"How is this even happening?"

"We got a tip from Global Cover," Vivian said.

"A tip? About what? From who?"

"It's an international security firm that provides protection to high-net-worth individuals and Harold Fuchs is one the company's big clients. The company owner, an American, tipped off The Ministry when his sister told him about a suspicious deck of cards a patient left at her house."

"What? How do you know this?"

"You asked me to help Vance and when I tried, I found out his passport had been flagged."

"Flagged by who?"

"The U.S. Embassy. The casino contacted the American Embassy when Vance's bank in Cayman thought there was suspicious activity in his account."

"This is a big misunderstanding."

"Really? When passports are stolen, people usually don't wait to report them missing."

Lauren hesitated. She had to come clean about the gun. "There's more to the story. I lied. He told me he forgot to unpack the gun before we left Miami. He's an ex-cop. Having it is second nature. Then the person who stole his passport took his gun, too. That's why he didn't want to report his passport stolen. He had to get his gun back first. He was afraid of the consequences."

Vivian shook her head slowly. "The deck of cards you left is called a Kill Deck."

"What's that?"

"It's a deck that identifies top people on a target list. Your military and the F.B.I. pass them out to troops and prisoners to help catch high value targets. Do you know the meaning of the Ace of Spades?"

"Just that Fuchs was on it."

"That makes him the highest value target."

"Why would anyone target a bunch of college administrators?"

"That's the question we're all trying to answer."

"I know what this must look like," Lauren said.

"I'm not sure that you do."

It really did look crazy.

"Look," Vivian said. "I believe you didn't have anything to do with this. But I'm having trouble believing your boyfriend."

"He's not my boyfriend."

"All the more reason."

She paused and filled her lungs with air. "You have to believe me. Vance has nothing to do with whatever's going on. We came here on vacation. I had to leave to take care of some personal business."

"Mr. Fuchs has a lot of connections," Vivian said. "He's a personal friend of the P.M."

"The P.M?"

"The Prime Minister."

She covered her eyes with her hands and rubbed her cheekbones with her thumbs. "Where're the others? They can vouch for us."

"The others?" Vivian asked.

"Yeah. If you're so convinced he's targeting Fuchs, then you must know there are three other suspects?"

"You mean the three young people on your charter flight."

"Yes. Where's the girl?"

"She's fine. She's at the hotel. The folks from Global were watching them and intercepted her at the casino where she was trying to bait Mr. Fuchs."

"Bait him how?"

"Prostitution."

Jesus. The sleazy clothing, make-up and wigs in Chan's backpack. "I found the deck of cards on the charter plane."

"Did you leave them with your therapist thinking you'd be able to claim doctor-patient confidentiality?"

"What?" This wasn't the Vivian she remembered. "Seriously?"

Vivian stared at her.

"No, that's not why I went to see her. Harold Fuchs was a patient of hers, but I didn't know that until yesterday. I had no idea her brother was in the security business. I'm the one who found Blade on the 'Net and booked the charter. It was a random internet search. It was MY IDEA to come here on vacation. I booked the room at the casino. I'm the one who agreed to let Chan and C.J. stay with us at the cottage on Chub Cay when Tonk and his dad ditched us. How exactly do you figure Vance could've planned this? They're going after the wrong guy and while your people are interrogating Vance, the kid in the news story I sent you is going to get away with . . . with whatever he has planned."

Lauren pressed her face against the vehicle window and shaded her eyes with her hands.

Her heart pounded. Was that *The Parent Minus* docked at the marina? She grabbed the door handle and pulled. But it was locked from the inside. "You have to believe me, Vivian. Vance isn't involved in whatever this is." She wrestled the door, looking for the interior lock. "Let me out. NOW!"

51

"Let her out," Vivian ordered the driver.

The door lock popped. She jumped out and jogged down the sloped parking lot toward the yacht, flip-flops clacking the asphalt, the sun casting long shadows. The floating wooden dock swayed slightly beneath her feet. Stopping at the stern of the enormous yacht, she shaded her eyes with her hands. It was *The Parent Minus.*

Squatting in the shadow of the super yacht, she called Vance's phone again. She heard the familiar ringtone. A man wearing a black track suit with yellow stripes on the arms and legs startled her. Where did he come from?

The stranger approached, killing the incoming call, holding up the phone. He placed his finger to his lips.

She turned to run but he lunged at her, clamping his hand on her forearm.

"Let go of me." What gave him the right to put his hands on her? "Who are you?" she asked, yanking her arm.

"I'm a friend of Vivian's," he said, loosening his grip, testing her to see if she'd run. His whisper turned forceful "You must be quiet."

She wrenched her arm free. "Where's Vance?"

"He's on de yacht."

"What are you doing with his phone?"

"He ask me to hold it for 'im."

"Why?"

"To stay in touch."

"Why?"

"He is following dem."

"Who?"

"Some kids."

"Where are they?"

"They are on de yacht. Dere is two young men. One is tall and de other has a gun. I tink dey is connected to your friend. I tink they intend to kill Mr. Fuchs."

Good God. "Why?"

She heard voices. Blagden jumped to his feet.

"We go now," Blagden said.

Someone was coming toward them. Vivian's floral dress billowed in the breeze, her blond hair glowing pink in the last of the magenta sunset. She approached Blagden, then stopped and stood very close to him. Vivian reached for Blagden's hand and held it. "My God," she said, "you're okay."

Sirens blared in the distance. "Thank you for coming. We must leave," Blagden repeated.

Vivian led the way, hurrying up the hill in her low heels. The Escalade awaited with its running lights on.

Vivian opened the door on the near side and got in. She followed Blagden, trotting around the back bumper and climbed into the middle. The driver lowered his visor and crept forward toward the west exit. A cavalry of hardened black SUV police vehicles sped toward the scene, amber, red and blue lights spinning against the darkening sky. The

SUVs raced in through the east entrance, down the sloped lot and surrounded the yacht. As the Escalade approached the west exit, a black Ford Interceptor with a menacing front grill cut the Escalade off, stopping an inch off the front bumper of the Cadillac, blocking them.

Who was the man in the track suit sitting next to her?

Headlights revealed an imposing man wearing a dark camouflage uniform getting out of the front passenger's side of the Interceptor. He knocked on the Escalade window. Their driver powered down the window. The cop pointed a long black flashlight into the cockpit of the Escalade. Her heart thumped. It was so bright it blinded her momentarily. Their driver stepped out of the vehicle, walked twenty feet from the Escalade and huddled with the cop dressed in paramilitary gear.

The pair strolled back to the Escalade. The officer stuck his head inside the vehicle, eyed Vivian, then said, "Sorry for de inconvenience, Miss Jackson."

Vivian nodded once.

The strapping Bahamian cop got back into the passenger side of the Interceptor. A moment later the patrol car moved, allowing the Escalade through. She turned around in the middle seat and watched the red taillights on the police cruiser dim as it returned to its spot blocking the entrance to the marina. Vivian's driver pulled forward and turned left onto Harbour Drive heading back toward the casinos.

Headlights and tall streetlamps lit the road. They passed palatial homes and palm trees and yachts and sailboats outlined with artificial light. She wanted to ask where they were going, but in some strange way, she didn't care.

She rode in silence between Vivian and Blagden. The mood inside the Escalade was tense. Her father's ex-wife stared out the side window. The Black man in the track suit did the same.

In the distance neon signs glowed from the towering casinos. Soon they were in the middle of busy vehicle traffic.

"Drop me off," Lauren said, a block away from the Poseidon.

"No. Let us at least take you to valet," Vivian said.

There was no use arguing.

The driver stopped at a red light and at the next block, turned into the casino entrance, drove past the valet stand and parked with the engine idling.

A bellman stood outside Vivian's door.

The driver powered down the front passenger window.

"Welcome to the Poseidon Club. May I help you with the luggage."

"We'll be a minute," the driver said.

Vivian leaned forward and addressed Blagden. "May Lauren and I have a moment alone?"

"Of course," he said. "I'll wait in de lobby."

When Blagden was gone, Vivian lifted her purse from the floorboard and placed it on her lap. She reached inside and handed Vance's passport to her.

She took the passport and opened it.

"There's something else I wish I would have talked to you about before now."

This was not the right time. Or place.

"I was respecting your father's wishes."

"What? What's my dad got to do with this?"

Vivian's chest rose as she inhaled deeply bracing for something uncomfortable. There was another lull before she began to speak.

"Your father didn't leave me. It was the other way around."

Her stomach roiled. "What are you talking about?"

"I'm not sure you'll understand. The world has changed in so many ways."

The pit in her gut morphed into anger. "What are you saying." The scene played back in her head. The little exchange Vivian had with Blagden. A glimpse of intimacy. "Blagden?" she asked. "You left my father for him?"

"I've known him since we were children."

How was this possible? She'd avoided her father at the hospital. Hadn't spoken to him in years.

"I don't expect you to understand," Vivian said.

That was good, because she didn't. Her father had protected Vivian. Or had he protected himself?

As if reading her mind Vivian said, "Your father knew you and I had grown close, and he didn't want to hurt you. He thought it best if he took the blame."

She covered her ears with her hands. "I don't want to hear any more."

Opening the door on the Escalade, she staggered out. Her knees buckled. And what happened next was a blur.

T he master stateroom door was locked. The woman he'd mistaken for Chan covered him with the Sig 9-millimeter Luger. She was a professional.

"Beautiful gun," he said, meaning it.

"Optic-ready, right out of the box, low recoil, improved grip. I'd hate to fire it anywhere but the gun range."

"Who do you work for?"

"Why would I tell you that?" she asked, pulling the black wig from her head, and tossing it on the floor. Thick wavy brown hair fell to her shoulders. Though she was of average height and weight, the short black skirt revealed that she was as fit as a jungle cat. "Men," she said, "are easy to trap if you use the right bait."

"Where's the girl?" he asked.

"Are we done here?" Harold Fuchs asked, tucking in his shirt. "I'm getting cabin fever."

"Not yet, sir," the woman said, "not till I get an all-clear from the team."

"Who are you?" Fuchs asked.

"Just a guy at the wrong place at the wrong time," he said.

"I gotta take a leak," Fuchs said, heading to the john.

When he and the woman were alone, she said, "He has to take a piss every twenty-four minutes like clockwork."

The woman's phone rang.

"Yeah. Okay," she said to whomever was on the other side of the call. "Who did you say you are? . . . I can't put him on but I'm going to put you on speaker." She tapped the screen with a short black fingernail. "Go ahead," she said holding the phone in her palm so he could listen.

"You there *Gallego*?"

Why were they putting Sarge through? "Yeah, I'm here."

"Why weren't you answering your phone?"

"I lost it." He wanted to wrap up the call before Sarge said something stupid.

"Hey, remember that yacht you asked me to look into?"

Stupid had arrived.

He made eye contact with the brunette and said, "It's a moot point."

"To you maybe, but since I went to the trouble of digging deep into the documents, turns out the L.L.C. is a front for a guy named Harold Fuchs."

He reached to poke the red dot on her phone to end the call, but the woman yanked it away letting Sarge continue to yak.

"I got more. It's all public record," Sarge said, "turns out the asshole ran a hedge fund before he hit it big with Uncle Sam."

"I appreciate the intel but it's really not necessary," he said loudly.

The woman holding the phone on speaker pointed the Sig at him and jutted her chin.

"But since you've gone to all that trouble—"

Sarge let it rip.

"Fuchs is one evil piece of shit," the retired police sergeant said.

The woman held her hand up. Fuchs understood the gesture.

"Found out he came up with the Uncle Sam guaranteed student loan program that's turned colleges into fucking credit card companies. The kids dig a *muy grande* hole they'll never get out of. Most of them drop out. Some get four-year degrees in bullshit subjects like the history of Bulgarian folk dancing then can't find jobs. Fuchs came up with a solution to that.

"They pitch the parents instead, convincing them if their kids borrow more money to get a masters or some doctoral shit, they'll earn more. They call it *The Parent Addition.*"

Wow. The Parent Minus. What a cynical piece of crap.

"Mom and dad guarantee the loans. Put their houses up as collateral. What parent doesn't want to do right by their kid? They wonder why kids these days—"

He cut him off. "Do you remember the first time I asked you to look into who owns the yacht?"

"You got dementia or something, *Gallego*?"

"Just answer the question."

"Yeah, I remember. That was yesterday."

"Was it the first time I asked?"

"You hit your head or something? That's what I just said."

"I'll call you later with an update."

"That's it? You get laid yet?"

The woman holding the phone made a sour face then jabbed the red dot with a stubby black fingernail, hanging up on Sarge.

He tossed his head in the direction of the bathroom. "If I was targeting him, don't you think I would've bothered to find out who owned the yacht before yesterday?"

"Who was that?" she asked, grabbing a pair of black slacks slung over a leather chair, gripping the chair back with one hand to balance as she stepped into them one leg at a time.

"Tell me who you are first, then I'll tell you who that was."

"Name's Cecilia," she said, pulling her unisex pants up over her curvy hips, unzipping the waistband of the micro skirt, tugging it down over her thighs and kicking it onto the floor.

"He's an old friend. An ex-cop."

"What's his name?"

"Sergeant Daniel Ruiz. Fort Lauderdale police. Retired."

Cecilia made a call, balancing her phone on her shoulder. He stood a few feet from her trying to listen in but only got bits and pieces.

She dropped the phone in her pants pocket, grabbed a lightweight gray jacket from the chair and reached for the hand wheel on the stateroom door.

"Allow me," he said, stepping in front of her. She held the Sig on him as he grabbed two spokes and twisted the wheel, then shouldered the bulky door open.

Harold emerged from the bathroom.

"Stay here," she said to Fuchs. "Let's go," she said to him. "I had a gut feeling those three were up to something and I said so. No one wanted to listen to me."

"The kid's dad has his own airplane. They're a flight risk. If they make it out of here, you'll lose jurisdiction."

"I'm aware," she said, "let's roll."

"Where's your computer?" Vance asked Fuchs.

"It's in my office."

"Lead the way," he said to Cecelia. "The two men are on this ship right now and one of them is a computer expert. The other one might be armed."

"How do know you that?"

"I saw them."

Cecelia stuck her head back inside the stateroom. "Lock yourself in the bathroom," she instructed Fuchs.

He followed her down the hall. She had both hands wrapped on the grip of the Sig as she led the way up the stairwell to a room on the main deck. It had a window. Cecelia peered around the corner, through the glass, then snapped her head back.

"They're in there," she said. "So's my partner."

Jutting his chin, he motioned her to make room for him to look.

C.J. sat with his back to the window facing a computer screen. Tonk held a gun on a man he recognized as the one on the ferry boat with Cecelia.

"You need put those clothes back on," he said, tossing his head sideways, toward the stairwell leading back to the master stateroom.

"They won't get anything off that computer," she said. "We have the best encryption software on the planet."

No system was failsafe. Cecelia and her partner had already made one tactical error. They'd fallen for Chan as a distraction. He'd use the same bait to catch the boys. Turnabout was always fair.

53

He stood guard outside the stateroom while Cecelia changed into Chan's outfit. A minute later she emerged barefoot, wearing the black wig and the miniskirt. They hurried back to Fuchs' office where they'd seen Cecelia's partner, and Tonk and C.J. trying to hack Fuchs' computers.

"What's your partner's name?"

"Elmer."

They stood less than three feet from the window to Fuchs' office.

"Is Elmer armed?"

"Yes," Cecelia said.

Crouching beneath the window he twisted the door handle. It was locked.

"I got it," she said, squatting out of view, typing six numbers onto the keypad. A green light blinked.

"Gimme your gun."

She looked at him sideways.

"You think I can't handle this?"

"Of course, I do," he said, as he spun and elbowed her in

the ribs. She grunted and dropped to her knees. "Sorry." He picked up her gun, then waited a three-count to see if she would retaliate.

She rubbed her ribcage. "Asshole."

He leaned with his back against the wood paneling and pointed the Sig at her. "I need you to listen to me. The guy behind the computer doesn't want anything bad to happen to the girl he's going to think is you. Neither will the guy with the gun. Elmer has to know I'm friendly."

"How?"

"He's your partner. Figure it out."

"Then what?"

Then he initiated the second surprise. He turned the gun on her.

"I'm going to put my hand over your mouth. As we enter the room, I'm going to hold the gun to your head. Then, when we're inside," he whispered, "I'll take my hand off your face. Your partner will recognize you. I'm going for the kid with the gun. Don't fight me. Make sure your partner knows what side I'm on."

"Do I have choice?"

"Not really. Count of three. One . . . two . . . three."

She shouldered the door open. C.J. spun in his chair and jumped to his feet. Tonk froze. That gave him the chance to ram him hard enough to lift the boy off his feet. He pounced, grappling for the Glock, pinning him face down to the floor, pushing his left kneecap between the Tonk's shoulders. The boy grunted like a pig. "I don't want to hurt you," he whispered with his mouth an inch from the kid's ear. "Because I'd rather kill you." He shoved his right arm beneath Tonk's neck, cutting his air. "You're going to roll over on your right side. Understand?"

Tonk groaned and tried to nod.

The kid rolled onto his side. He reached beneath the punk's soft belly, grabbed his weapon, and tucked it into the waistband of his pants then got to his knees. Tonk lay on the floor. He heard voices. Local cops lined the doorway of the office. Cecelia was glued to her phone. She ended the call and approached him.

"You need to get out of here," Cecelia said. "My partner will give you a lift to wherever you're going."

"Come on," Elmer said, "let's go."

They pushed their way out the door; the local cops eyed him. Elmer and Cecelia nodded at the uniforms; a cop-to-cop dog whistle he knew first-hand.

"Where do you want to go?" Elmer asked, motioning him to hurry.

"I have to take a leak."

"There's a head at the end of the hall, on the right."

He found the bathroom, locked the door, wiped his prints from the gun, released the magazine, opened the toilet tank and dropped the Glock inside. They'd find it one day but, it would be long after he reported it stolen from his place in Miami as soon as he got home.

Elmer waited in the hallway.

"Take me to the Poseidon Club," he said.

It was a circus outside. Patrol units swarmed the marina, the light bars atop their Interceptors flickering blue and red against the black sky. Elmer drove up the incline toward the exit to Harbour Boulevard now blocked off with double rows of cop cars. While Elmer talked his way out, a local news truck arrived. They were going to make an example out of Tonk. He wished they would. But not C.J. He was just collateral damage.

54

LATER THAT NIGHT

Vance ended the call staring out the window fifteen stories up overlooking Nassau Harbour. When he'd checked into the Poseidon Club, the management team showed up trying to explain the cluster-fuck they'd caused by failing to notice Tonk Braman was a fraudster impersonating him. According to the casino receipts, Tonk had drained over fifty thousand dollars from his Cayman account. They seemed to think they could make up for it by comping a corner penthouse suite with a panoramic view of Potters Cay. Funny thing was, they were right.

The half-moon cast a wide ribbon of soft light against the harbor water, now as black and glassy as obsidian. Three massive cruise ships had docked for the night, their rows of square windows lit like black and white gingham.

Beyond the docks the city lights glowed. If it'd been daytime, he was pretty sure he'd have been able to see Vivian's seaside cottage across the channel.

He turned away from the picture window and walked to the full-sized kitchen. He took two bottles of water from the fridge then headed to the bathroom inside the luxurious master bedroom to check on Lauren. She'd scared the hell out of Vivian when she'd fainted outside the casino and Vivian and Blagden had cared for her until she regained consciousness.

He set the waters on the bedside table next to the king-sized bed draped with a plush white comforter and covered with a mountain of blue pillows, not daring to sit for fear he would fall asleep. Instead, he stood outside the bathroom door closed three-quarters of the way and tapped gently.

"Come in," Lauren said.

He pushed the door open and inhaled the scent of lavender. He'd ordered room service for two, and while she'd picked at her meal, he'd wolfed his, then drawn a bath for her. He'd had added a generous pour of bath bubbles from a wicker basket next to the tub.

He walked slowly toward the soaking tub catching a glimpse of himself in the mirror, leaning in for a closer look. He combed his fingers through his hair recalling the harrowing mailboat ride and the ferry where Cecelia had shadowed him, and the swim he'd taken at Vivian's cottage. And Blagden conveniently appearing on Woodes Rogers Street. The sun had done him good, tinting his face a light bronze and highlighting his brown hair with a few streaks of dark blond that hid the fatigue.

"How are you doing in here?" he asked, leaning against the sink, far enough away to respect her privacy.

"I need a towel," she said.

He riffled through the cabinets beneath the sinks and found a pile of plush white ones neatly stacked on the slatted wooden shelves. He squatted and took two bath towels from the shelf. "Do you mind if I come closer?"

"I'm not sure how else I'll get a towel unless you plan on throwing it on the floor and running away."

That was the spirit. "You sound better," he said.

As he approached the aroma of lavender got stronger. A thick blanket of white bath bubbles obscured her naked body, stopping at her neck. Her eyes were shut and beads of perspiration glistened on her forehead. He reached down and using the edge of one towel, dabbed the sweat from her brow. "Lift," he said cupping his hand under her neck, slipping a folded towel beneath it like a cushion. She opened her eyes and gazed up at him.

"You look better," he said, resisting the urge to tell her she looked beautiful.

"I feel better," she said lifting her pale arms over her head and adjusting the towel he'd placed behind her neck. Then she sat up slowly and used her hands to gently sweep the waning bath bubbles from her naked breasts. The thin scars reminded him of what she'd done to herself.

"I don't blame those kids for wanting to get even with Fuchs, that greedy asshole," she said.

He pulled a low chair from beneath a make-up station, placed it near the tub and sat. She slid back down into the water but this time she pinched her nose and submerged her head under water. A moment later she popped up like an otter.

Using one hand to squeeze the water from her hair, she asked, "Don't you agree?"

He shrugged.

"How did you get to Nassau without your passport?"

"You remember the old guy sitting at the bar at the Chub Cay resort?"

"Sort of."

"Turned out he's a mailboat captain who operates a freighter that makes runs between the islands, kind of like an offshore Amazon delivery service. C.J. and Chan set it up and I tagged along. I followed them figuring they'd lead me to Tonk."

"Did they?"

He nodded. "I hailed a cab to follow them. Turns out that was a set up. Your stepmother arranged it. She knows the driver."

She folded her arms tightly across her chest covering her naked breasts. "'Knows' is an interesting choice of words."

"I'm not following you."

"He's her boyfriend, or significant other, or whatever."

"The way your dad treated her, you should be happy for her."

She closed her eyes.

"That deck you found on Blade's airplane is a Kill Deck. The Army printed decks of cards during wartimes and put the identities of the fifty-two most wanted war criminals. The Justice Department—"

"I know. Vivian told me. Blagden said Interpol thinks the deck is being used to target the fifty-two people who got the richest off the student loan program. It looks like they're the ones who are being protected."

She disappeared into the bath again and remained under for almost a minute. He was about to check on her when she rose slowly, then grabbed her hair into a ponytail and squeezed the water out.

"I can see it," she said, "think of the deep resentment and the powerlessness they must feel when they're just starting out in life."

He'd called Vivian while Lauren was in the tub to let her know that Lauren was doing fine. Vivian had enlightened him. "The Bahamian government was warned that Harold Fuchs was at the top of the list. They found a tracking device on the yacht and when they arrested Tonk and C.J. they found a thumb drive on C.J. with all Fuchs personal information, including his bank accounts."

"I couldn't find a single thing out about that man," she said.

"C.J. hacked into the State of California's computer network and stole Fuchs' information from the university system database."

"Jesus," she said.

"C.J. told the cops that Tonk planned everything. He says Tonk forced him to hack Fuchs' computer at gunpoint. He claimed Tonk wanted to steal enough money to pay their student loans. I think Tonk planned to kill Fuchs."

"With your gun?" she said.

He narrowed his eyes at her. "Tonk would've have gotten a gun one way or the other. It just so happens he stole mine."

She sat up and covered her breasts with folded arms. "Where *is* your gun?"

"I got it back."

"And?"

"I got rid of it."

"Wow," she said.

"I looked at the link you sent."

Lauren closed her eyes. "I don't know which one of them

is more evil. Tonk will go to prison and Fuchs will set sail somewhere new on his multi-million-dollar yacht."

"He's worth more than ten billion bucks," he said.

She sighed. "Tonk will pay the price, but Fuchs will skate. Life's not fair."

"No clear-minded person ever said it was." He draped the dry towel over his bent knees.

"What do you think will happen to Chan and C.J.?"

"I don't know. Hopefully, nothing."

She stepped out of the tub naked and shivering. He stood and spread the dry towel, then wrapped it around her torso.

"Thanks," she said, blotting the dampness from her body.

He reached for the plush pink hotel bathrobe hanging on a hook next to the soaking tub. She took it from him, then let it drop to the floor. He tried not to stare at her naked body, but he couldn't stop himself. She squeezed his shoulders and walked backwards pulling him toward the bedroom. She grappled for his belt and unbuckled it, felt for the button on his pants, then the zipper.

"Are you sure about this?" he asked, undressing himself.

"Shhh."

There was a knock on the door. He threw on the pink robe to answer it. "I'll be right back."

It was room service. That was weird. They'd already eaten.

"May I?" the waiter asked.

"Sure, set it on the table," he said, returning with a twenty-dollar tip.

The gourmet gift basket came with a bottle of Perrier Jouet champagne in an ice bucket, courtesy of hotel management.

"This is also for you."

The man from room service handed him an envelope with a hotel logo addressed to his room number. When the man left, he opened it. A Visa gift card was wrapped inside a note printed on copy paper.

Sorry for the trouble. I asked my dad for the money to fix Lauren's car and he gave it to me. The gift card is for $3,500. I hope you believe me when I say I was trying to do the right thing. My dad swears he thought my brother and his friends were going to take advantage of Mr. Fuchs gambling with him at the casino. I don't know what to say other than my brother wasn't always like this. Now he will pay for his mistakes. I wish I knew where he got that deck of cards but I guess I'll never know. There are millions of angry young people who can't pay their loans and I guess any of them could have done it.

Take care, Cassie

WOW. Cassie must've been Tonk's sister, and it sounded like she'd hit Lauren's car on purpose. He put the note and Visa card in the desk drawer, tossed the robe at the foot of the bed, pulled the comforter back and climbed in next to her.

"Who was that?"

"No one," he said, tracing his fingers slowly along the tic-tac-toe scars on her breasts, circling them lightly with his fingertips, softly kissing her neck.

"You're sure about this?" he asked, brushing strands of damp hair from her face.

"Shut up," she said, "before I change my mind."

EPILOGUE

As soon as the seatbelt lights dimmed Vance Courage stood in the aisle and pulled his duffle bag from the overhead. He took his phone off AIRPLANE MODE and watched a message from Lauren bubble up on the screen. Miss you. He'd call her on the drive from the airport in Sacramento to the lawyer's office in Chico.

He wormed his way off the plane past frazzled parents searching through piles of collapsible baby strollers on the jetway. He dodged a uniformed flight attendant pushing an empty wheelchair against foot traffic. Following the signs to RENTAL CARS, the line was short and the white Nissan Altima he'd reserved was easy to find in the airport garage. He settled in behind the wheel, entered George Valiant's address into his phone and headed toward Highway 99 North.

He powered down the window and hung his left elbow out. The scenery was rural and flat with skinny trees interrupted by trailer parks, Ma and Pa liquor stores and small churches. He changed lanes to pass a dark blue pickup with a stained mattress wobbling in the bed of the truck. A pair of two-door beaters faced bumper to front bumper on the shoulder sharing jumper cables.

He exited at the off ramp to Highway 32 and took a left, heading west on East 8th Street past a chain paint store and the Neptune Society of Northern California before turning left onto Bartlett Street.

Locating the address, he parked and walked along the concrete path running parallel to a long L-shaped single story office bungalow with front doors facing the parking lot. He stopped at 401B and rang the buzzer.

A tall, skinny man with sagging jowls and deep-set eyes answered.

"You must be Mr. Courage. Come on in and don't be taken aback by the fanciness of the place."

The office was dark and smelled like fireplace ashes and canned tuna. George Valiant gestured to an empty armchair on the other side of his cluttered desk. Black and white family photos filled the credenza behind him. The good news was he looked like he had a big family and could use the money.

"What brings you all the way from Florida to meet with me?" he said, pushing up the wrinkled sleeves of his shirt revealing old sun damage on his forearms.

"I'd like to retain your services."

"For what?"

"You have a client I'd like to help."

"Help how?"

"I'd like to pay her legal fees."

"Why?"

"Why doesn't matter."

"I don't defend people," Valiant said, "I'm a plaintiff's

attorney. The ones I take have no money. I operate strictly on the Deep Pocket theory."

"She's a plaintiff," he said, setting the envelope he brought with him on an open space on the desk and pushing it toward the old lawyer. "I hope this meeting remains confidential."

"That depends on what you want," Valiant said, opening the envelope and looking at the nine thousand dollars cash.

"You're representing a woman whose fireman-husband died in the Camp Fire. The state of California considers him a missing person."

Valiant tugged the fat knot on his fudge brown necktie, twisting and loosening it.

"What do you want?"

"I want you to set up an account that can't be traced to me. I'll want to deposit enough money to keep you motivated to work on her behalf. There's one condition."

"There's always at least one," Valiant said.

"You got ninety days to convince a judge to declare her husband legally dead so she can start collecting what's owed to her."

"And if I don't?"

"I might file a complaint with the California Bar. You never know where those things go."

"Not much of a threat, Mr. Courage. If I get disbarred, I can fish and build birdhouses full time. I'd have retired by now if I wasn't stuck with the grandkids' college tuition."

"Sorry to hear that," he said, getting up from the chair and handing George Valiant a piece of paper. "Call me when you've made the necessary arrangements and I'll start transferring money."

He was about to let himself out when Valiant struggled up from behind his desk and followed him.

"Fire season's coming up," Valiant said. "It's a shame the state didn't treat that widow fairly."

He nodded. A pity indeed. "This is your chance to do something about it," he said.

"By the way," the old lawyer said, "nice name."

"Ditto," he said, letting himself out this time.

On his way to the rental car parked in the lot, his phone buzzed. What did the retired Fort Lauderdale police sergeant, Daniel Ruiz, want?

"Hey."

"*Oye.*"

"What's up?"

"We need to talk," Sarge said, adding, "in person."

"I'm out of town," he said, unlocking the rental.

"You still have a license to practice law?"

"Yeah, but I'm retired."

"I need a favor."

"Sorry, I'd like to help you but—"

"It's for my daughter," Sarge said.

"Is she in some kind of trouble?"

He leaned against the Nissan driver's side door and gazed at the setting sun turning the sky into a fireball.

"It's her husband."

"I'll be home tomorrow. I'd be happy to give you a referral."

"I don't need a referral," Sarge said, sounding more serious than he'd ever heard him before. "I need *you*. My son-in-law is a lawyer and he's been suspended by the Florida Bar for thirty days. It's a delicate situation."

"How can I help?"

"I told Raphael that you're an attorney. He needs someone to fill in while he's away, doing whatever lawyers do."

There was a lull in the convo.

"You owe me," Sarge said. "You're the one who's always doing the asking and how many times have I said no."

He didn't have a legit argument. It was always him asking Sarge for help and his friend had never said no.

"I'm not making any promises, but I'll talk to him," he said. "Set it up."

He ended the call and headed for the airport hotel. Maybe dipping his toe back in the world of law might be interesting, but he doubted it. But Sarge was right. He had a debt to service.

He flicked on the headlights as the sun dropped to a sliver on the horizon. If nothing went wrong with his flight, he'd be home tomorrow in time to take Lauren to dinner. That reminded him, he'd forgotten to call her back. He took his phone from the center console and redialed her from the text message.

ABOUT THE AUTHOR

Reviews are very much appreciated.

Karen S. Gordon has written several award winning thrillers starting with *The Mutiny Girl*. If you enjoyed *Liable*, she would appreciate it you left a review. *Liable* is the sixth installment of the Gold and Courage Series.

Go to the series link here: https://amzn.to/3qci2k7

The adventures of Vance Courage and Lauren Gold continue with another installment in 2024. Title and publication date to be announced.

Pleas sign up for Karen's newsletter at karensgordon.com

ALSO BY KAREN S. GORDON

The Mutiny Girl

"An outstanding debut thriller that has it all: misdirection, intrigue, murder, and family. Captivating and engrossing." — *The BookLife Prize*

"A taut, thrilling drama told exceptionally well." — *Steve Berry, NYT Bestselling Author*

"An engagingly written series starter with a bounty of plot twists and Miami vices." — *Kirkus Reviews*

Killer Deal

"A ripped-from-the-headlines legal thriller that John Grisham fans will love. Highly recommended." — *Best-Thrillers*

" . . . a fast-paced thriller . . . an intriguing look at the hunger for power, the ego of control, the persistence of greed, and two unlikely heroes whom we can cheer for . . ." — *BookTrib*

Express Intent

"Fast-paced, evocative and urgent from the get-go, Express Intent is the best Gold and Courage series book yet." — *Bestthrillers*

<u>Sick Money</u>

"The Bottom Line: A heart-pounding, adrenaline-spiking medical thriller that takes the series into new territory. Highly recommended." — *Bestthrillers*